"IF THERE'S A BETTER HORROR NOVELIST WORKING TODAY, I DON'T KNOW WHO IT IS."
—*Los Angeles Times*

The Resort

"Little weaves an explicitly repulsive yet surrealistically sad tale of everyday horror."

—*Publishers Weekly*

The Policy

"A chilling tale."   —*Publishers Weekly*

The Return

"Bentley Little is a master of horror on par with Koontz and King. . . . *The Return* is so powerful that readers will keep the lights on day and night."

—*Midwest Book Review*

The Collection

"Memorable . . . bizarre . . . disturbing . . . fascinating . . . a must-have for the author's fans."

—*Publishers Weekly*

"Little's often macabre, always sharp tales are snippets of everyday life given a creepy twist."—*Booklist*

The Association

"With this haunting tale, Little proves he hasn't lost his terrifying touch. . . . Graphic and fantastic . . . will stick with readers for a long time. Little's deftly drawn characters inhabit a suspicious world laced with just enough sex, violence, and Big Brother rhetoric to make this an incredibly credible tale."   —*Publishers Weekly*

continued . . .

DISPATCH

Bentley Little

A SIGNET BOOK

SIGNET
Published by New American Library, a division of
Penguin Group (USA) Inc., 375 Hudson Street,
New York, New York 10014, USA
Penguin Group (Canada), 90 Eglinton Avenue East, Suite 700, Toronto,
Ontario M4P 2Y3, Canada (a division of Pearson Penguin Canada Inc.)
Penguin Books Ltd., 80 Strand, London WC2R 0RL, England
Penguin Ireland, 25 St. Stephen's Green, Dublin 2,
Ireland (a division of Penguin Books Ltd.)
Penguin Group (Australia), 250 Camberwell Road, Camberwell, Victoria 3124,
Australia (a division of Pearson Australia Group Pty. Ltd.)
Penguin Books India Pvt. Ltd., 11 Community Centre, Panchsheel Park,
New Delhi - 110 017, India
Penguin Group (NZ), cnr Airborne and Rosedale Roads, Albany,
Auckland 1310, New Zealand (a division of Pearson New Zealand Ltd.)
Penguin Books (South Africa) (Pty.) Ltd., 24 Sturdee Avenue,
Rosebank, Johannesburg 2196, South Africa

Penguin Books Ltd., Registered Offices:
80 Strand, London WC2R 0RL, England

First published by Signet, an imprint of New American Library,
a division of Penguin Group (USA) Inc.

First Printing, October 2005
10 9 8 7 6 5 4 3 2 1

For Paul Houghtaling, teacher and handyman extraordinaire, who has kept the Little houses working for lo these many years.

One

1

There was a witch in my hometown.

Well, it wasn't really a "town." It was a midsized city in overdeveloped Orange County. And I don't suppose she was really a witch, although she served that function for me and my friends.

I had her removed from the streets when I was in high school.

Things might've turned out differently if I hadn't done that.

2

When I was in fifth grade, I was in love with Miss Nakamoto.

She was the youngest, prettiest teacher at Alexander Hamilton Elementary. She was also the nicest, one of those teachers you usually see only in inspirational movies or bad television shows. I remember her giving everyone in class a goldfish in a little bowl, taking us to the beach to look at the tide pools, letting us make movies with her video camera, doing all sorts of off-curriculum things that I'm sure were not approved by the school's administration.

But most importantly, she liked me.

She was the only teacher who had. My first-grade teacher, Mrs. Sobule, hated my guts. Of course, that year I was a bratty, disruptive know-it-all, so I could see her point. But she seemed to enjoy punishing me far too much. In second grade, Miss Corea hated all boys. Mr. Osterwald, in third, was just an all-around asshole, and with my fourth-grade teacher, Mrs. Boorham, it was guilt by association; she disliked me because I was friends with Steve Simmons, who'd been caught the first day of class doing a wicked imitation of her.

Which was why Miss Nakamoto was so wonderful. Unfailingly polite, unendingly patient, willing to overlook minor faults and transgressions while focusing on and nurturing a student's strong points, she was encouraging and inspiring to all of the kids in her class, the good, the bad and the indifferent. To top it off, she was as beautiful as any actress in movies or on TV. And she was giving me straight A's.

So of course I was in love with her.

I still remember the day (how could I not!) when she started the Pen Pal Program. A lot of students laughed, called it the "Pee-pee Program"—anything using the letters *PP* is a prime target at that age—and I laughed, too, pretended like I didn't care, pretended like it was a girls' thing to do. But secretly I was excited. As Miss Nakamoto described it to us, I doodled on a piece of scratch paper, drew a noose and a knife and a hot-rod car, feigning utter disinterest, all the while listening intently to every word she said. Even now, I'm not quite sure what about the concept of a pen pal appealed to me so, why the idea spoke to me, but it did, and as I sat there behind Tony Jacobson and his dumb buzz-cut head, I knew I wanted to do it.

That was strange. I was not a particularly good

writer, had no real interest in corresponding with anyone—my mom had to *force* me just to write to my grandma in Ohio a couple of times each year—but I suddenly wanted to be involved in this program more than anything.

I wanted to write to a girl in Japan, a girl who looked like Miss Nakamoto.

It was weird, really, because I didn't much like girls my own age, didn't have a whole lot of interest in them, although I liked it when Tammy Ferris spun around on the parallel bars at recess and her dress flipped up and we could see her underwear. But I guess I thought my teacher would like it if I wrote to a girl from Japan. *She* was the one I really wanted to write to, and I imagined her being proud of me for writing to a foreign student and maybe taking an extra interest because the girl was Japanese.

That was the impetus, but that was not all of it. Yes, I wanted to impress Miss Nakamoto. But I also wanted the packet that participants would get, wanted the little card with the name and address of my foreign counterpart, wanted the official instruction booklet, wanted the certificate of participation. I wanted everything. I *needed* to be a part of this program, and I suppose that's when my proclivity or talent or whatever it is first raised its head. The idea of having a pen pal opened a door within me, awakened a desire I didn't realize I possessed, and even as I doodled on my paper I knew that I would brave the ridicule of my friends and classmates if need be, but I *had* to do this.

It was as if Miss Nakamoto understood my predicament, because she didn't post a sign-up sheet on the bulletin board the way she usually did. Instead, she told us that anyone who was interested could come to her desk before school, after school, during recess or during lunch. After school would be a good time, I thought. I was busy with my friends during lunch and recess, but most of my friends didn't live in my neighborhood and walked home from school in the opposite direction. I could stay after and no one would know. I even had a backup story, just in case someone caught me. I was going to say that I was doing it for the extra credit.

Miss Nakamoto wrapped up her spiel, and after that it was a normal Monday. We did math and science, social studies and art, and went out for PE and lunch and recess, but in the back of my mind was the thought that I would soon have a pen pal, and my underlying emotion was one of irrational exuberance. Everything seemed to take much longer than it usually did, time passed too slowly, but finally the school day was over, and I lingered at my desk, gathering up my books and pencils and work sheets. Several girls had already signed up for pen pals during lunch and recess, and Missy Lowry and Charlotte Green hung around after class to sign up, as well. Missy noticed immediately that I was dawdling. "What are *you* waiting for?" she asked disdainfully. "Why don't you go home?"

"Missy," Miss Nakamoto cautioned.

"Jason wants a pen pal!" Missy sang, cutting straight to the chase.

Charlotte took up the chant. "Jason wants a pen pal!"

"I do not!" I said, grabbing my things and storming out the door. I could hear Miss Nakamoto giving the two girls a lecture behind me in her soft patient voice. I was suffused with shame, and the thought that those two blabbermouths would spread the word around—even though they had no proof and no corroboration—filled me with dread. But what was even more unbearable was the fact that I would have to wait another day to sign up for a pen pal. My exultation had turned to dejection. On impulse, I ducked around the corner of the building by the boys' bathroom and paused. I could come back early tomorrow and talk to Miss Nakamoto before school . . .

. . . or I could wait until Missy and Charlotte left and *then* sign up for a pen pal.

The excitement returned, and a few moments later I heard the two girls chattering away as they left the classroom and headed down the corridor in the opposite direction of the bathrooms. I waited until I could no longer hear their voices, then gave them an extra minute or so until I was sure they had rounded the corner by the principal's office. I stepped back into the corridor, then hurried over to Miss Nakamoto's room before she left.

She was still seated behind her desk, going through papers, and she looked up as I entered. She smiled at me. "Jason," she said. "Did you forget something?"

I hesitated, cleared my throat. "I'd, uh, like to sign up for a pen pal," I told her.

"Great!" She didn't say so, but I had the feeling that I was the first boy in class to enroll in the program, and that made me feel self-conscious. Miss Nakamoto immediately put me at ease, however. She told me how happy she was that I was going to participate and how she knew I would have fun as well as learn a lot about another culture in a way that I couldn't just by reading books. "A lot of people," she said, "become pen pals for life."

She presented me with a blue folder (girls got pink ones), and in it were my certificate, an instruction booklet, a sample letter, a new ballpoint pen, pre-stamped envelopes and several sheets of stationery. It seemed very official and very adult, and I felt as though I were joining an exclusive club.

Miss Nakamoto opened up a binder. In it were staggered sleeves on which were written the names of various nations. "You can write to students in over twenty

countries," she began, but before she could say more,
I pointed to the sleeve marked *JAPAN*.

"That one," I said. I was afraid to look up at her,
afraid she would see right through me and immediately ascertain my motives.

She withdrew a foldout containing small cards with
the names and addresses of potential pen pals on
them. The left side said *Girls* and the right said *Boys*.
"You can choose any one you like," she told me.

"That one," I said, pointing to a name on the left,
my voice much smaller than I'd intended.

Kyoko Yoshizumi, the card said.

"Wouldn't you rather write to a boy?" she asked.

"No," I managed to get out, though if she had
pressed further, I probably would have caved. I reddened as I took the card with the Japanese girl's name
and address, and my embarrassment only deepened as
Miss Nakamoto smiled at me. But I was excited at the
same time, and I forced myself to meet her eyes. I
saw only kindness there, only understanding.

Did she know what I was thinking? Maybe she did.
Maybe she liked it.

I felt good as I walked home. The neighborhood
around the school was clear, all of the other kids having hurried home save for a few stragglers outside the
office who were waiting for their parents to pick them
up. I liked it that way. I had the sidewalk to myself,
and I could stroll at my own pace, stop to look at
whatever I wanted, and not have to worry about older
kids or bullies. I kicked a crumpled Coke can across
a side street into the gutter, picked up a Super Ball
lying at the edge of someone's ivy and pocketed it.

I saw the witch on Washington, hobbling past an
apartment building, her knobby cane tapping out a
Morse code message on the sidewalk, and I crossed
the street to avoid her. The witch was a fixture in
Acacia, always walking down one street or another.

No one seemed to know who she was or where she lived or where she was going when she walked, but she was old and creepy and though she never said a word, she had an evil stare. My friends and I were afraid of her—it was Robert who'd first started calling her "the witch"—and I'd seen more than one adult step out of her way as though fearful of contact. Rumor had it that she was responsible for the mysterious death of the hundred-year-old pepper tree in front of Acacia High School as well as the disappearance of all the ducks from the pond in Murdoch Park, and though none of our parents believed it, we all did. I think a lot of other people did, too.

I walked past the witch on the opposite side of the street, looking down at the sidewalk in front of me instead of over at her. After that, I turned onto Lomita and sprinted the rest of the way home, running on lawns, leaping over small bushes, barely able to contain my excitement. As soon as I got home, I would take out my new pen and a sheet of my special pen pal stationery, and write a letter to Kyoko Yoshizumi.

That plan died the second I sped past the Shapiros' oleanders and saw the car parked in our driveway.

My dad was home early.

I stopped running, and almost backtracked behind the oleanders, but for all I knew my parents were in the front room and I'd been spotted through the window. I continued on but at a much slower pace, suddenly in no hurry to get home.

My dad looked like Chuck McCann. You know, the guy in those old deodorant commercials who shared a medicine chest with a neighbor on the other side of an apartment wall and always danced away saying, "One shot keeps me good for the whole day!"

My dad wasn't a friendly, dancing kind of guy, though. He was a mean old bastard, a middle-management guy at Automated Interface who hated his job and took it out on his family, and I always had the feeling that he would have been much happier if I had never been born.

My mom was a purebred bitch. One of those pinched, uptight women who usually spent a lot of time in church. Only my mom never went to church.

I never understood why my parents had gotten married. They certainly didn't love each other. Hell, I don't think they even liked each other. In all the years I lived at home, I don't remember ever seeing them kiss or hug or display even a modicum of affection. Their conversations were little more than recriminations for slights or wrongs done to one by the other.

Most likely he'd knocked her up and that's why they tied the knot.

My brother, Tom, three years older than me, was barely part of my universe. I saw him at breakfast and dinner, and that was about it. If our paths crossed outside of the house, on the street, we ignored each other, pretended we didn't know who the other was—which was fine with both of us.

Although Tom was no great shakes academically, he was a good athlete, a football and basketball star, and to my parents he could do no wrong. I was the fuckup, the loser, the dink. With no real talents or abilities, and no interest in anything other than watching TV and hanging out with my friends, I engendered only disapproval and occasional interest from my parents. Mostly, I tried to stay out of their way.

I walked through the side door into the kitchen like I always did, grabbing a handful of Oreos out of the cookie jar, acting as though I hadn't just passed by the Torino in the driveway.

"How was school?" my mom asked perfunctorily. She was sitting at the table, looking through a catalog.

I gave my usual answer. "Fine."

My dad was nowhere to be seen and that made me nervous. If he wasn't on the couch watching television or sitting at the kitchen table drinking a beer and fighting with my mom, that meant he was in another part of the house, and there lay trouble. I remember one time he decided to snoop through Tom's room. He found Tom's stash of *Playboys* hidden under the bed and by the time Tom came home my dad had completely torn the place apart, searching in vain for more contraband. He lectured Tom behind closed doors for over an hour until my brother was in tears, grounded him for a month and took away stereo and television privileges.

And he *liked* Tom.

"Where's Dad?" I asked casually, finally admitting that I knew he was home.

"Backyard," my mom said, and the fact that she didn't elaborate or editorialize worried me. What would he be doing in the backyard? Tom and I were the ones who mowed the lawn and did all of the yard work. The only time the old man ever went out there was to barbecue, and that was only on weekends. I tried to remember if I'd put my bike away in the garage like I was supposed to or if I'd left it out. My dad could find *something* to complain about if he really wanted to, and I didn't want to be on the receiving end of his wrath.

I went to my room to drop off my books and pen pal folder. I hid the folder in the bottom drawer of my desk, beneath a bunch of notebook paper. If the boys at school thought having a pen pal was a pussy thing to do, I could bet my ass that to my dad and Tom it would seem twenty times worse. And I'd get no help, support or sympathy from my mom. Although less predictable in her likes and dislikes, she was far harsher than either of them once set off. No, this was something I needed to keep a secret.

I looked through my window into the backyard. My dad *was* drinking a beer, but he was standing next to the lemon tree, facing the fence, his back to me. That was weird. My dad was not a guy who did stuff like that. He had come home early from work and now instead of harassing my mom in the kitchen or watching TV, he was standing by himself in the backyard staring at the fence. Something was definitely wrong.

I got out of my room before he turned and saw me, then went down the street to my friend Paul's house. Paul went to Catholic school, so I usually only saw him on weekends, but his school and mine got out at the same time, so we were there for each other on weekday afternoons if we needed to get out of the house. I didn't tell him about my new pen pal—if anyone would have understood, it was Paul, but I wanted to keep that secret to myself for now—although I did tell him about my dad.

"Maybe he got laid off," Paul suggested.

The idea sent a chill through my heart. Unemployed, he would be hanging around the house all day every day. And he'd probably be even meaner. "I hope not," I said.

We worked on Paul's go-cart until my mom called me home. Thankfully, my dad was not still in the backyard. The sun was starting to set, and that would have been too creepy. He was in the bathroom. My mom was in the kitchen making dinner. Tom was in the family room watching a rerun of *Star Trek*.

I sat down on the opposite end of the couch from my brother. The microwave made static lines on the television, and the sound of the oven's fan nearly drowned out the dialogue, but I dared not complain. Drawing any sort of attention to myself would result only in increased scrutiny for the rest of the evening, and that was one thing I couldn't have. Despite the unexplained strangeness of my dad's behavior, my mind was still focused on my new pen pal, and I was just putting in time until I could be alone and write Kyoko Yoshizumi a letter.

My dad showed up and changed the channel without a word. He sat on the couch between me and Tom to watch the news, while the two of us went into the kitchen.

After a dinner of microwaved frozen burritos and Jell-O, I went to my room. I closed the door, sat down at my desk and took out my pen pal folder from its hidden spot in my bottom drawer. I withdrew my new pen and a sheet of stationery. I was supposed to be doing my homework, but instead I tried to write a letter to Kyoko.

Tried being the operative word.

I stared at the blank page before me on the desk. What should I say? I had no idea. I never talked to girls at school, and I'd certainly never written to one before. I sat there for nearly an hour, stumped. The only decision I'd made was that I would be twelve years old instead of ten. American girls liked older guys, and no doubt the same thing was true in Japan. But other than that, I was at a loss. I was unable to decide even how to start the letter. "*Dear* Kyoko" seemed too intimate, too familiar, but I could think of no other way to lead off my missive.

I hadn't even begun my math homework, and when my mom walked in to check on me, she saw the unopened textbook. The sound of the door opening had given me enough time to hide the folder and stationery but not enough time to open the math book and take out my homework so I could pretend to be working on it.

"What are you doing?" she demanded. "You're supposed to be doing your homework. What's going on in here?"

"I just finished it," I lied, standing up.

"Let me see."

I should have known I couldn't fool her, and I hemmed and hawed until she nailed me and got me to admit that I'd been goofing off.

"I'm getting your father," she said, lips thin.

I shoved my pen pal folder back in the bottom drawer the second she left the room, and by the time she returned with my dad, I had the real homework out. I'd answered the first question and was doing my best to appear studious, but that didn't save me. They both started in, telling me I was stupid and lazy and would amount to nothing. I took it, nodding as though I agreed, but inside I was thinking about Miss Naka-moto and the girl in Japan who probably looked just like her.

I did my homework, then took my punishment, going to bed early without any television. But I did not fall asleep. I lay awake in my bed, waiting hour after hour until first Tom and then my parents went to bed. When I was sure they were asleep, I got up, crept over to my desk and composed my letter by the light of my little desk lamp. I knew now what I wanted to say, and the words flowed fast and easily. I told Kyoko I was in seventh grade, that I was a champion surfer, that I was a star basketball player and on the student council, that I'd just broken up with my most recent girlfriend, that I played guitar and was starting a rock band.

In other words, I lied about everything.

Aside from my name and address, nothing I wrote on that page was true.

But I felt exhilarated as I finished, licking the gummed flap of the envelope, and I immediately began planning a follow-up letter, one in which I expanded upon my made-up life. *I* was impressed with myself. How could Kyoko not be?

I hid the envelope in my math book, then went

back to bed. I fell asleep, imagining Kyoko reading my letters, falling in love, growing up to look like Miss Nakamoto, then coming to America to marry me.

3

I received her first letter on a Saturday.

The air was filled with the smells of suburbia: newly cut grass, competing flower fragrances, gasoline exhaust from edgers and mowers, the faint scent of McDonald's and Taco Bell from a few blocks over. I remember it clearly even today. I remember, as well, the way I felt when I pulled the mail out of the box and saw the small pink envelope made with unfamiliar paper and affixed with a foreign stamp.

I knew what it was immediately, and I rushed into the house, into my room, closed the door and tore open the envelope.

The letter didn't say much. It was quite a bit shorter than mine, and I sort of resented Kyoko for that, but I had to remind myself that she was writing in English rather than Japanese. She was taking this opportunity to practice a second language, while I was using my native tongue. I read the letter once, twice, thrice. She wrote that she lived in an apartment instead of a house, that her favorite color was pink, that her favorite school subject was art and that she had a large stuffed-animal collection, which seemed kind of babyish and immature to me. But what I liked about her letter was the fact that she signed off with *Love, Kyoko.* It made it clear that this was a girl—I'd concluded my letter with *Sincerely*—and that was very exciting in a new way that I didn't quite understand.

I'd been half afraid she'd reject me, that she'd tell me she wanted to correspond with a girl rather than a boy, and I was happy that she seemed to want to

be my pen pal just like I wanted to be hers. But I
knew we needed to quickly establish some things we
had in common or this was going to go nowhere.

I wondered what she looked like. In my mind she
was still a miniature Miss Nakamoto, but for all I
knew she could be hideously ugly and grotesquely
overweight.

No, I couldn't think that way.

Eventually, I would ask for a photo, but for now I
would just assume that she was as nice and pretty as
I wanted her to be.

I spent the rest of the afternoon playing with Hot
Wheels in my room and then going over to Paul's to
help him wash windows; his mom promised us two
dollars apiece if we did the whole house. I could have
written a response to Kyoko, but I wanted to save
that experience, wanted to savor it, and my plan was
to once again wait until everyone had gone to bed.

We were eating dinner, Mom, Tom and me, and my
dad was late—which wasn't such a strange occurrence.
He often spent Saturday afternoons and evenings with
his friends, hanging out, watching ball games, and
sometimes he lost track of time. Then the phone rang,
and my mom went to answer it in the kitchen. A second later, she was screaming furiously, and we could
tell from her end of the conversation what had happened: my dad had gone to a bar with his buddies, had
too much to drink and was picked up by the police on
his way home. Tom and I looked at each other in a
rare moment of camaraderie, both of us afraid of what
might come next.

My dad had taken the Torino, so my mom piled us
into the Volkswagen, and we drove to the police station. Tom and I sat on a hard bench in the lobby
while my mom ranted and railed at the hapless men
behind the front desk. She was allowed to go in and
see my dad, disappearing behind a metal door that

was opened by a switch behind the counter. She stayed back there for what seemed like an interminable length of time. We saw a woman come in who complained that her minivan had been broken into and her purse stolen, an old man whose parked car had been smacked by a hit-and-run driver, a woman who wanted to get a restraining order against her husband—and all of them had finished their business and were gone before my mom emerged from behind that security door.

"Come on," she said, lips tight. "Let's go."

I looked at Tom. One of us had to ask it. And he was the oldest. "What about Dad?" he said.

"Your father got himself into this mess. He can get himself out. Come on!"

We followed her out to the car, both of us afraid to speak. I had never seen her this mad before, and I wondered if my parents were going to get a divorce. Back at home, our food was cold and still sitting on the table, but I didn't feel like eating. Not that I could have eaten anyway. My mom immediately started clearing off dishes and dumping food down the garbage disposal in a furious frenzy. Tom went to his room, closing the door, but I stayed in the living room, unsure of what to do with myself, expecting at any moment to hear the shatter of broken dishes from the kitchen. I did hear slamming cupboards, banging silverware, even the unusually loud clink of dishware, but she was not out of control enough to break anything.

Despite all that was going on, my mind was calm, serene, like the eye of a storm, focused in perfect Zen-like fashion on Kyoko's letter and what I would write in my response. After the events of the evening, her simple description of stuffed animals seemed even more immature, but in a way that was nice, a refreshing contrast to my family situation. Besides, I was planning to ask a few questions in my letter this time, force her to talk about less babyish things.

My mom came out of the kitchen, saw me sitting on the couch. "What are you doing here?" she screamed. "Go to your room!"

I didn't have to be told twice. I hurried down the hall to my bedroom, where I shut the door. My bedtime was still two hours away and I was wide-awake— so I had a lot of time to kill. I considered writing my letter, but my mom could walk in on me at any time. I didn't have a TV, so I couldn't watch that. I had a small record player, but the sound might carry, and I didn't want her storming down the hall screaming at me to turn it off.

I wondered what Tom was doing in his room.

Finally, I decided to read a book, a science fiction novel called *Time of the Great Freeze* that I'd checked out of the library twice and must have read four or five times already. I found comfort in the tale of a band of humans who survived the next ice age. It was reassuring to me to once again enter their world, and before I knew it, it was time for bed. My mom didn't come over to tell me—she was still in the front of the house and I had no idea what she was doing—so I got into my pajamas voluntarily, put out the light and crawled under the covers.

It was weird lying in bed knowing that my dad wasn't in the house. But it was also nice in a way, and I realized for the first time that I wouldn't really mind if he was gone for good.

I wouldn't mind if my mom were gone, either.

Or Tom.

Against my will, I fell asleep, my mind overburdened by the stress and excitement of the day. When I awoke, the world was dark and a sliver of moonlight shone through the crack in my drapes. I crept out of bed to look at my clock, holding it close to my face so I could see the numbers.

Two fifteen.

Even my mom had to be asleep by now, but just in case, I turned on my desk lamp and waited several minutes until I was sure it wouldn't draw any attention. The house remained still and quiet, and I opened the bottom drawer, taking my pen pal folder from its hiding place. Once again, I withdrew pen, stationery and prestamped envelope.

I started to write.

TWO

1

Our correspondence began in earnest.

I invented a new family for myself, the family I wanted to have, the family I thought I should have. I told Kyoko my dad was a scientist, that he had worked on the Apollo moon rockets and that he was now engaged in a job so top secret even his family wasn't allowed to know anything about it. My mom was a writer for a famous American magazine, an expert cook and interior decorator. I was the most popular kid in school, liked by girls, admired by boys. I omitted the fact that I had a brother.

Kyoko should feel honored just to be corresponding with someone like that, I thought. And she was. Her next letter was gushing, far longer and more detailed than the first, although a lot of it was in broken English. I didn't mind. In fact, I liked the fact that she was forcing herself to the limits of her language abilities in order to communicate with me. It showed a level of interest that went far beyond what was expected from a pen pal.

That letter arrived on a school day, and it was my mom who got the mail. There was no right of privacy in our house, and it was pure luck that my mom didn't open the letter herself. She did ask me about it, and

I explained in a put-upon manner that my teacher was making everyone in class write to a pen pal in a different country and that this was the girl I'd been assigned. My mom lost interest halfway through my explanation, and I could only hope that meant she wouldn't open any letters in the future.

Still, just to be on the safe side, I took out Kyoko's first correspondence, noted the date and postmark and asked her in the future to send everything on the same day as that one in an effort to have all of her letters arrive on Saturday, when I could intercept the mail.

The next envelope arrived two Saturdays later, and I took it into the bathroom, closing and locking the door so I wouldn't be disturbed. This time, Kyoko sent me a picture of herself, and she asked for a photo of me, as well. She was cute, and though she didn't look much like Miss Nakamoto, that didn't seem to matter to me as much as it had at the beginning. The picture had been taken in some sort of park, with pink flowered trees in the background, and I was reminded of the Japanese Deer Park which I'd gone to on a field trip in first grade. It was gone now, but it had been by the freeway in Buena Park, and it was kind of a petting zoo where people could feed deer with pellets of food purchased from gum ball machines. The surrounding buildings were all Japanese, as were the gardens. What I remembered most from the place was a fish, a koi, that popped its head out of the water to smoke a cigarette held in a metal clip. I'd wondered then and wondered now whether that fish would get cancer. It seemed a cruel thing to do to an unsuspecting animal.

I examined Kyoko's photo more closely. Was this a class picture or a snapshot her parents had taken? It was hard to tell. The setting was informal, but the picture quality was good and the pose looked professional. She was wearing what looked like a sailor outfit—a school uniform, according to her letter—and had two pigtails and a little round face. Her smile was wide and happy and made her eyes turn into barely visible slits. She was cute, and if she wasn't quite in Miss Nakamoto's league, there was definitely the potential for her to grow into it.

Where could I keep the picture, though? If Tom found the photo, I'd never hear the end of it. If my parents found it, there'd be countless questions. I slipped the picture into my pocket, flushed the toilet as though I'd been using it, and retreated to my bedroom. Looking around, I tried to think of a good hiding place, then realized that I already had the perfect spot for it: in the pen pal folder. If anyone found the picture there, I could claim it came with the program information I'd been assigned.

Now the question was, could I find a photo of myself to send her? Or, more to the point, did I *want* to use a photo of myself? Would she believe this face belonged to the boy described in my letters?

In the end, I didn't send one. I invented what I thought was a pretty good excuse, explaining that I'd given all of my school photos away to girls from my class, and my parents wouldn't let me send out any of the family's personal snapshots. But I thanked her for her picture and made up for not giving her one of myself by inventing a story about how I stood up for a Japanese exchange student on the playground, chasing away two bigoted bullies who'd been harassing him. That ought to impress her, I thought.

The next morning, I mailed the letter on my way to school, feeling confident, feeling good.

Feeling even better about it by the time I got home, I sat down and wrote her another letter, once again late at night after everyone had gone to sleep, and in this one I said that because of my defense of the Japanese student, the principal of my school had given me a special award and had made me a crossing guard.

Although she hadn't posted a sign-up sheet, Miss Nakamoto soon had a bulletin board devoted to the Pen Pal Program in an effort to convince more students to get involved. There was a map of the world with strings leading from various continents to envelopes on which were written the names and addresses of children from different countries.

And there was a list of participants.

I was immediately subjected to ridicule.

"Jason's in the Pee-pee Program!" Missy crowed.

Even Robert and Edson laughed, and they were my friends.

"It should be called the Pansy Program," Ken Vernon said.

Indeed, I was the only boy on the list, and my face burned with shame. I glanced over at Miss Nakamoto, wondering why she had betrayed me by not keeping everything in strictest confidence, but she smiled back reassuringly, and that gave me the strength to stand up to them. "I'm doing it for the extra credit," I said in a voice that, through intention and not a little luck, was pitched perfectly, a disdainful lecturing tone that sounded bored and above it all, and at the same time disgusted with their stupid and unfounded innuendos.

"Yeah," Ken snorted. "Right."

"You think I want to do this?" I groused. Participants were required to turn in bimonthly reports in order to qualify for extra credit, and I seized on this. "I have to write a letter a week and then write a report about it? Would I do this if I didn't have to?"

They could see that I had a point. And while Missy, Ken, Charlotte and a few others continued to give me a hard time, everyone else bought my excuse. Not only that, but my participation broke the ice. Other boys started signing up for extra credit. They moaned and complained all the way, but they did it, and I found myself wondering if it was all an act with them, as well, if they secretly enjoyed having a pen pal as much as I did.

Maybe Miss Nakamoto was right to have posted the names.

Robert and Edson soon had pen pals, too, and while that should have brought us closer together, it didn't. In a weird way, it pushed us apart. I mean, we were still friends—and would be all the way through grammar school, junior high and high school—but I could never be as open with them as I had been previously. I continued to pretend with them, as well as everyone else, that I was a pen pal unwillingly and out of necessity. I did not tell them that it had become one of the most important things in my life, that I thought about it constantly, that looking forward to getting Saturday's mail helped get me through the long days at school. I kept them at arm's length on this. For all I know, they were lying to me, as well, downplaying their own interest, and in my mind at least, that made us not as close as we had been before.

Paul was the only one to whom I told everything. I suppose I was closer to him because I'd known him the longest, because we'd been playing together since before we went to school, and because he lived on my street. We saw each other more often than we saw our friends from school, and we knew each other's families—and family secrets. Going to Catholic school, Paul also seemed a little more sissified than regular kids, and I guess I thought he'd understand the allure of having a pen pal more than my other friends would.

He did.

"I wish we had pen pals at my school," he told me glumly. "I guess the nuns probably think we'd be writing sex stuff or something, so they don't want to lead us into temptation."

Paul was always thinking about sex stuff.

He looked at me. "So what *do* you write to her about?"

I reddened. Not because I'd been writing to her about sex but because I hadn't. I told Paul the truth. "Mostly I just tell her about how I'm this really cool, tough, popular kid. All the girls want me and all the boys want to be me."

His eyes widened. "Really?"

"Oh, and I'm a champion surfer."

"That's so great!"

I shrugged, proud of my accomplishment but trying to play it down. "How's she ever going to find out? I could say anything."

"You could be anyone you wanted." Paul seemed amazed by this. Amazed and entranced. "You could invent a new personality for yourself. Or take someone else's personality." He shook his head. "Wow."

I'd never really thought of it that way, and hearing him say that made me realize that maybe Paul wasn't as happy with who he was as he seemed to be. He had a good life, certainly a more stable home life than I did, and generally speaking he was pretty content. But still, there was always room for improvement, and it occurred to me that even with his *Brady Bunch* parents and nice private school, maybe he wanted to be a little less wussy than he was, a little more normal.

Maybe everyone wanted to be someone they weren't.

The thought was sobering. Was it possible that even happy people weren't that happy? That everyone was secretly discontent with their lot in life? If that was the case, was there any hope for me? I thought of my parents and my brother. None of them were satisfied; none of them were living the lives they wanted. Robert or Edson, either. Kyoko seemed happy, but maybe that was because she was lying to me the same way I was lying to her. Maybe the only truly happy people were fictional people, like the Jason Hanford I'd created in my letters.

No. I refused to believe that. Kyoko *was* happy. She

was exactly the same way she seemed in her letters, and I was just overreacting.

"So . . . can I check out her picture?" Paul asked.

This was awkward. I'd told him about Kyoko's photo, but I realized that I didn't want him to see it. I didn't want *anyone* to see it. I wanted to keep that for myself.

"Uh . . . no," I said.

Paul frowned. "I thought you said she was good-looking."

"Oh, she is."

"Well?"

I didn't know how to explain it, didn't really understand it myself, but shook my head. What Kyoko and I had was pure and special, and I wanted to make sure that it remained uncorrupted. Letting someone else see her picture, even a friend like Paul, would break the spell, would bring hard outside reality into our fragile pen pal world.

I was saved from having to defend my decision by Paul's mom, who announced from the porch that it was time for lunch. "Would you like to eat over, Jason?" his mom asked. "I could call your mother."

"No, thanks, Mrs. Germain!" I told her. "I'd better go home!"

I said good-bye to Paul and headed back up the block. Paul hadn't laughed at me, and like me, he seemed to think having a pen pal was cool, but I still regretted opening up to him about it. I wasn't sure why, and I had the strange feeling that if I'd written to him instead of talking to him in person, I wouldn't mind so much. I'd be okay with it.

I thought about that as I walked down the sidewalk to my house and realized that I preferred communicating with people through letters rather than face-to-face. It seemed more real to me somehow, and although until now I'd done nothing but lie to Kyoko,

I felt I could be more honest in my letters than I could in person, more myself. I didn't have to act or play games or worry about reactions to what I said. I could just write down my thoughts and feelings in the privacy of my own room, and the recipients could read and react in the privacy of theirs.

I suddenly wished I could write to everyone instead of talking to them. Even my friends.

"Where've you been?" my mom demanded as I came through the kitchen door.

Even my family.

2

I ran out of envelopes far earlier than scheduled, and though I could have asked Miss Nakamoto for more, I was embarrassed to do so. Instead, I took my allowance money and, on the way home from school one Friday, stopped in at the post office to buy some stamps that would enable me to send letters to Japan. I got away from Robert and Edson by telling them that I had to wait at school for my brother, who was supposed to pick me up. As soon as they were down the street and around the corner, I was off.

In the post office, I saw the witch.

I heard her before I saw her—that *tap-tap-tap* of her cane on the floor—and then she rounded the corner of the alcove housing the P.O. boxes and glared at me. One eye was slightly bigger than the other, and both were encased in a face that would have looked disturbing even if it had not been so horribly wrinkled. I glanced quickly away. At close quarters like this, she seemed even scarier than she did on the street, and in her glare I thought I saw recognition. That both worried and frightened me. I didn't care if I was part of the faceless rabble on which she heaped her scorn, but if she was to single me out . . .

I thought of Acacia High School's dead pepper tree and the missing ducks from the pond in Murdoch Park.

She brushed past, close enough for me to smell the strange sweet herbs on her breath. Her bony shoulder would have bumped my arm had I not stepped aside, but I did and I was glad. I didn't want her to touch me.

Once she was past, I forgot all about her. I stepped up to the counter and bought six stamps with postage enough to send six letters to Japan. Six extra letters! I felt free, filled with possibility, the way an artist must feel when viewing a virgin canvas. I'd broken out of the box, and while I hadn't exactly been playing by the official rules of the Pen Pal Program, now I could really indulge myself and do what I wanted when I wanted.

That night, I wrote my longest and most detailed letter yet, describing a fictional day in my life cobbled together from my own daydreams and the overheard conversations of other kids. As I finished, I heard a noise from down the hall. I quickly shut off my desk lamp and remained unmoving, praying I wouldn't get caught. But the sound grew no closer; it seemed to stay at the opposite end of the hall. In the stillness of night, auditory elements were amplified, and as the noise differentiated itself into individual components, I realized I was listening to my parents having sex.

I was filled with disgust. I knew what sex was, of course, but there was no place in my conception of it for this animalistic grunting, and I felt queasy as I hid my letter inside my school notebook and made my way over to the bed as silently as possible. Hiding my head under the pillow, I tried to think of something else entirely, tried not to hear my mom's rhythmic high-pitched squeals, my dad's low guttural groans.

I think that night was the beginning of my nightmares. I cannot really remember having any nightmares prior to then, but I have suffered from them ever since. Often they are so vivid and realistic that not only can I not get the images out of my mind, but I cannot be sure whether what I remember is a dream or something that really happened.

The one that night was a doozy.

I was in my bed asleep, and the light in my room was switched on. "Get up!" my dad ordered. I blinked against the brightness, threw off the covers and put on my clothes, still feeling groggy. Stumbling down the hallway, I went to the bathroom, combed my hair and then made my way out to the kitchen. It was still dark outside—I could see only blackness beyond the kitchen window—and I wondered why my dad had awakened me so early. There was something not right about it, and my muscles tightened with anxiety. Something was wrong with the kitchen light, too, I noticed. It was dimmer than usual and had a flickering quality, like a candle flame. "Eat your breakfast!" my dad ordered, but though I looked around the room, I couldn't see him. A plate of pancakes was on the table, however, and I sat down in my usual chair, preparing to eat.

Across from me, atop what looked like a dirty cardboard box, was a single chicken foot, embedded claws up in a square of brown Jell-O.

I realized that this was my dad.

"What are you looking at?" my dad demanded, and the claws of the chicken foot opened and closed in time with the words. "Eat your breakfast!"

"No!" I yelled, pushing my chair away from the table.

And the chicken foot flew through the air, claws open, to rip out my throat.

I awoke in a cold sweat, believing for a brief disorienting moment that my dad really was a chicken foot embedded in brown Jell-O. Then I saw the dark outline of my desk, a black shape in the bluish nonlight of night, and I thought of Kyoko, who on the other side of the world might have been writing to me at that very moment in a shaft of sunlight. The reality of existence returned to me. I lay there for a moment, listening, but the house was silent, my parents' exertions over. I waited another minute or so, just in case, then got up, walked over to my desk, switched on my lamp, took out my letter and reread it.

I took out my pen.

P.S., I wrote at the bottom.

And continued on for another three pages.

It was both exciting and gratifying when Kyoko's letters began arriving on a weekly instead of bi- or triweekly basis. She, too, had broken the pen pal rules, declining to write the obligatory monthly missive and opting to respond to each of my letters as it arrived, although she still kept to the Saturday schedule as I'd instructed.

I was getting pretty good at writing letters, if I do say so myself, and I thought of writing one directly to Miss Nakamoto. I didn't know her home address, but I could write to her in care of the school, and she would be sure to get it. I even went so far as to pen the first half. I told her she was a very beautiful woman and that I found her very interesting and intelligent. But when I read it over, I could tell that it had been written by a kid. My intent was to send it anonymously, with the hope that she would think it was from an adult, a secret admirer, and we could begin an epistolary relationship, one that would last years. Gradually, she would fall in love with me, and maybe by that time I would be old enough that it wouldn't seem too ridiculous.

It would be a while before my writing skills were

at that level, however. Feeling depressed, I tore up the letter and immediately wrote another one to Kyoko, giving free reign to my mood by describing in detail the divorce of my parents and how tough it was on me.

How I wished it were true.

My dad was getting drunk more and more often. What used to be an occasional thing became first a weekly, then an almost nightly, occurrence. They fought about it, he and my mom, and the fights grew louder and uglier. One evening after dinner, they were arguing in the kitchen. I was in my bedroom doing homework when I heard a plate smash against the wall. That was followed by my mom's incoherent screech and then the clatter of falling silverware. Another plate hit the wall or the floor and smashed loudly. I poked my head out of my door to see what Tom was doing, to see if he was taking all this in, but the door to his bedroom remained closed. I knew he had to hear what was happening, but he obviously didn't want to get involved, and the two of us were not close enough that he would ever share his thoughts or feelings with me.

For some stupid reason, I decided to go out to the kitchen and see if I could calm them down, get them to stop fighting. I poked my head around the corner of the doorway just as my dad, glassy-eyed and lurching, threw a piece of our best china at the wall. It smashed right next to the refrigerator, pieces skittering across the floor to join others already there. "I hate you!" my mom whispered venemously. "One day you're going to die in an accident and I'll be glad!"

"Bitch!" my dad said in a slurred voice, banging his hand down on the counter.

They both saw me at once.

My dad stared dumbly, his alcohol-fogged brain trying to formulate a response. Scowling, he picked up another plate, ready to whale it at me, but my mom was quicker than he was, and before I could utter a word, she strode across the linoleum and grabbed my arm, her fingernails digging deep enough into my skin to draw blood. "Get in your room!" she shrieked.

"I heard you—"

"Get in your room and stay there!" She shoved me into the hallway, then turned back toward my father.

I ran back the way I'd come, crying not from the pain but the humiliation. How could I have been so stupid and naive to think that I could intercede in their argument? Slamming the door to my room, I thought I could hear the muffled sound of Tom laughing.

The next morning, my dad was back to his normal asshole self, and since I had to talk to somebody, I talked to him. For all I knew, he didn't even remember last night. I steered clear of my mom. She was silent as she made breakfast, and that was always a bad sign. Tom, too, sensed the mood of the room and without a word grabbed a piece of toast and dashed out the door, headed for school. I was younger and obligated to eat, but I did so as quickly as possible and got out of the house myself, heading for Robert's, where I waited for him to finish his breakfast before we met up with Edson and walked to school.

When I got home that afternoon, my desk had been ransacked.

I shouldn't have been surprised. And in a way, I wasn't—I'd been expecting this from the beginning. But it still felt like a gross violation of my privacy, and I was both angry and embarrassed as I put books and papers back in their proper places. Had she read my letters from Kyoko? Had she seen Kyoko's picture? At least two envelopes were out of order and their contents had been replaced haphazardly, so those had probably been read. I quickly opened them up and glanced through them, grateful to find that they were early ones and dealt mostly with generic topics. The photo was still hidden and untouched.

If my mom asked me anything, I decided, I would just explain that it was part of a class assignment.

But she didn't. She didn't say a word. She knew that I knew that she knew about my pen pal, but both of us pretended nothing had happened and we maintained our usual muted hostility.

I knew I had to find a new location to store my letters, but there was no privacy in that house. During the next few days, I went over every inch of my room, even went out to the garage and into the crawl space under the house, but could find no safe place to keep my correspondence. Finally, out of desperation, while my parents were at the grocery store and Tom, who was supposed to be watching me, was over at one of his friends' house, I pulled out the bottom drawer of my desk, got my dad's box cutter from his tool chest and sliced a hole in the carpet beneath the drawer. I slid all of Kyoko's letters under the rug and replaced the drawer.

No one would ever find my letters here, I thought.

And no one ever did.

3

It was hard for me to get a sense of what Kyoko's home life was like. I don't know if it was the language barrier, or simply the fact that she was closed and reserved and didn't share easily. Whatever the reason, there were huge gaps in my knowledge of her, gaps my imagination did its best to fill. In my mind, she lived in a close-knit traditional Japanese family, with a geisha-looking mother and a father who wore a business suit even at home. I imagined their lives to be satisfyingly structured, as clean and clear and uncluttered as their bamboo-matted rooms and white paper walls.

My own family situation was more . . . chaotic. When we weren't at each other's throats, we still lived uneasily with each other. My dad was drunk most evenings and mean even when he wasn't. And there was always the threat of violence with my mom. She never hit me that much—and, truth to tell, it never really hurt—but her moods were so volatile, and her anger was so fierce, that I lived with the constant fear that she would explode, beating me unmercifully. This feeling became worse after my dad's arrest, and I believe it was the same for Tom, though the two of us never spoke of it.

Kyoko's school also seemed a lot more tranquil and less rancorous than mine. I wondered if that was a cultural thing or if she was just one of those people who breezed easily through life, smart and pretty and popular, floating above the problems that plagued lesser mortals.

No.

She was a normal kid, neither exceptional enough to draw attention to herself nor distinctive enough to differentiate herself from the crowd.

It occurred to me that I *liked* the fact that I didn't know a whole lot about Kyoko's life. She was, in a way, a blank slate, and I could project my own needs, wishes and aspirations onto her depending on my mood.

The letters flew back and forth between us. One special Saturday, I even received three of them at once, a harmonic convergence that left me feeling exhilarated for the whole week.

Despite the holes in my picture of her—or perhaps because of them—I grew to care about Kyoko much more than I thought I would, and much more than I

intended. She was still a stand-in for my beloved Miss
Nakamoto . . . but she was also a person in her own
right (or in her own write). I liked her, and strange
as it might seem, she was my best and closest friend.
I could tell her anything without fear of being laughed
at or judged.

I grew bolder in my letters, bolder in my lies. The
president of the United States was my mother's
cousin. I might be making a trip to Japan soon because
my dad had invented a supersecret camera that the
Japanese government was extremely interested in obtaining. I'd just taken first in my age group at the
Huntington Beach surfing championships and would
soon be competing against the top high school finalist
in the state.

But in my real life, things weren't going so great.
Dad got picked up again for drunk driving, and the
precious Tom was caught vandalizing a neighbor's
house with two of his loser friends. You reap what
you sow, my grandmother used to say, and I would
have thought that a prime lesson to be learned here.
But of course all the shit came down on me. It was
somehow my fault that the two of them had screwed
up. I was the whipping boy, and my mom yelled at
me, my dad gave me a completely pointless and hypo-
critical lecture, and I was grounded for a week—
despite the fact that I had done nothing wrong.

I had fantasies of bashing my dad's head in with a
rock, putting rat poison in my mom's food and watching her bloat up before puking her bloody guts out.

At school, I got into my first fight. Or *almost* got
into my first fight. Brick Hayward, a big dumb kid
who'd been held back a year, decided at recess one
day that he was going to kick my ass. I knew Brick
by reputation, but he'd never been in any of my
classes, and the two of us had never had any sort of
contact. But he imagined that I'd looked at him the

wrong way when we'd both happened to be in the
library earlier, and he wanted to extract punishment.
He confronted me on the playground, catching me by
the drinking fountains.

"Right now!" he demanded, clenching his fists.
Robert and Edson carefully backed away from me.

My panicked brain tried to think of some way out.
Brick was a good head taller than me, was stronger
and tougher and would beat me to a pulp. *The best
defense is a good offense,* I thought. I looked at him,
hoping I appeared much cooler than I felt. "Are you
stupid?" I asked. There was a gasp from the assembled onlookers. Everyone knew Brick had been held
back, so this had to hit him where it hurt.

His face reddened as he approached me. "Your ass
is grass," he said through clenched teeth.

I held my ground, though every instinct was urging
me to run. "I'm not going to fight you here," I said,
keeping my voice as calm as possible, pretending I
wasn't afraid. "We'll both get suspended."

"Anytime, anyplace."

"After school," I said. "Four o'clock. After everyone's gone." By four o'clock I would be safely home.

"I'll be there," Brick said, and spit on the ground.
He walked away.

I was safe for today, but what was going to happen
when I arrived at school tomorrow? Everyone would
know I chickened out, and Brick would kick my ass
to boot. Not only would I end up beaten to a pulp,
but my reputation would be ruined.

Maybe not. I had an idea.

The next morning, I walked to school with Edson.
A worried Robert waited for us in front of the office.
His mom had dropped him off on her way to work.
"Brick's looking for you," he said. "You better get
your ass to class fast."

"I'm looking for *him,*" I said loudly.

My friends in tow, acting as unwitting moral support, I strode around the building, past the little kids' playground, to the basketball courts, where I knew Brick would be hanging out. There was an almost visible current that swept through and energized the gathered throng of students as I stepped onto the blacktop. Brick turned slowly toward me, but before he could say a word, I advanced on him, pointing. "Where were you?" I demanded.

He wasn't quick on the uptake, as I'd known, as I'd counted on, and, confused, he tried to think of something to say. He'd obviously and with good reason been planning to ask me the very same thing, and now that I'd stolen his thunder, he didn't know how to react. "I waited for ten minutes," I said.

"Where were *you*?" he finally got out, and the anger in his voice made me step back. I had to play this exactly right or my teeth would soon be on the asphalt. "*I* waited for a half hour!"

"Where?" I asked.

"Right here!"

I nodded my head, letting everyone know that was the problem. "I was over by the bike rack," I said.

"We were gonna fight right here!"

"We never spelled it out, and I guess we both got mixed-up." I glanced around, as though checking to make sure no teachers were around. "Today," I said. "Here. Four o'clock."

"Right here!" Brick angrily pointed to the ground at his feet.

"Right here," I agreed.

"You're dead meat!"

"We'll see," I said.

Robert, Edson and I walked away, and as soon as we got around the corner of the building, we stopped. I leaned against the wall so as not to fall down. My legs were trembling. "That was brilliant!" Edson said.

Robert was grinning. "So what's the plan for to-morrow?"

"I don't know," I admitted, "but I have to come up with something."

There was going to be a big turnout for the fight—a lot of people had heard us—so the next morning, I lied and said that I'd shown, but I'd left because there were too many people hanging around. This was supposed to be between me and him. How could I be sure that someone in the crowd wouldn't narc? He tried to argue, but he wasn't good at it, and finally he ordered the assembled kids not to show up to watch; it was just between the two of us.

We rescheduled the fight, and the next day I was even bolder. I accused him of chickening out, but I did it while there was a teacher nearby so he couldn't attack me then and there. I called him a pansy and told him I was tired of this, I wasn't going to do it anymore, he could go fight someone else instead.

And it worked. Although we attended the same school and would occasionally see each other across the playground at recess, the fight never took place and there were no more confrontations. I had success-fully avoided my first fight.

The celebration was short-lived, however, because Paul moved.

That came completely out of the blue. I'm sure that's not really the way it was; I'm sure his parents had endless discussions with each other over whether they should uproot the family for a career opportunity. But from a child's point of view, it happened all of a sudden. One day we were playing, working on the go-cart, and the next he was having to gather all his stuff together because they'd be leaving in a week.

We didn't know how to react. We were kids, we were boys, and although I'm sure he felt as angry about it as I did, we didn't really talk about it, even when I was helping him pack his toys and collections. All I could think of was that I'd be alone on the street, stuck with my parents. There would be no more weekend days and weekday afternoons spent at Paul's house, getting away from my own troubled home, pretending as though I were part of a happy, well-adjusted family. I felt sick and upset, and I wished they could adopt me and take me with them, too.

They moved on a Saturday, and it was the first Saturday in a month that I didn't get a letter from Kyoko. Just a bad day all around. I went down the street to see Paul off, and he was already in the packed car, his dad getting ready to start the engine and take off. If I'd been three minutes later, I would have missed them altogether.

Paul rolled down his window. He was crying. Not sobs, just a few silent tears. And although I felt kind of like crying, too, it still seemed kind of pussyish for him to do that. "I'll write to you," Paul said, trying to smile. "We can be pen pals."

"Yeah," I said. "We'll write."

But we never did.

And the last time I ever saw him, he was waving at me through the back window of the car as his parents drove away to their new home.

Life went on.

More plates were broken in more drunken nighttime arguments, and my dad beat Tom for something he did, although no one would tell me what it was. "When I'm eighteen, I'm hitting the fucking road and never coming back," Tom said, and that was probably the closest we ever came to brotherly intimacy.

One warm Saturday near the end of March, I stayed overnight at Robert's house, camping in the backyard. My mom had never allowed me to sleep over at a friend's house before, and it was a shock that she agreed to it this time. But Robert's mother called with a formal invitation, and I guess my mom found it hard to say no to another adult. If I'd been the one to ask, I'm sure she would have turned me down flat.

But there I was, small suitcase packed, and my mom grudgingly drove me over to Robert's house, putting on a false face and engaging in some light chitchat with Robert's mom before giving me a big hug and a kiss on the forehead and telling me to have fun.

I could not remember the last time my mom had hugged or kissed me.

Then she was gone, and I was free. Edson arrived a few minutes later, and for a goof, Robert and I hid in the garage behind a box, pretending not to hear Edson's increasingly whiny cries of "Robert! Jason! Where are you guys?" Finally, Robert's mom ordered us to come out and play with Edson, and we emerged from the garage laughing uproariously.

We lounged around Robert's room for the next couple of hours, eating Pringles, drinking Cokes and listening to records. Robert had a real stereo, not just a little record player like Edson and I had, and his dad actually had cool albums that he let Robert borrow. We listened to Yes, Supertramp, Heart and Jethro Tull, feeling like teenagers as we took turns putting on the headphones. That got boring after a while, though, and we went outside to play basketball in the alley. There were no adults around, so instead of "Horse," we played "Fuck," and I was the first one to spell the word. We then played "Ass," but the structure of the game was starting to get to us, and we decided to just shoot randomly and not play anything.

Robert made a granny shot from the fence across the alley. "I don't like my pen pal," he said. "The kid's a dick."

"Mine's just boring," Edson said, throwing a hook that fell short. "When's this stupid program going to end?"

I didn't say anything. Both of my friends knew that my pen pal was a girl. Although I'd led them to believe that she had been assigned to me, I'd never said anything negative to them about Kyoko, and I wasn't about to start now. It was a point of honor.

They looked at me, waiting to hear my complaints. Robert's eyes narrowed with suspicion.

"If you don't like your pen pals," I told them, successfully diverting attention from myself, "then get them to stop writing to you."

"How do we do that?" Edson asked.

"Pretend you're a fag," I said, grinning.

"No *way*," Robert said emphatically.

"You wouldn't *have* to pretend." Edson snickered.

Robert nodded. "Yeah, but *we* couldn't get away with it."

"Then do something else. Write something crazy. Scare them."

Edson's eyes lit up. "I could pretend I killed someone and I'm on the lam and I need a place to hide out! I could ask him if I could stay with his family!"

I grinned. "Now you're thinking."

"Or I could say I'm in an insane asylum!"

Robert shook his head. "My guy'd never believe it."

"Why not?" I asked.

"He knows me too well."

"Knows you too well?" I looked from Robert to Edson and back again. "Have you guys been telling your pen pals the *truth?* What's wrong with you?"

"I have to write something," Robert said defensively.

"Yeah, but it doesn't have to be the *truth*. Look," I explained, "you're never going to meet these guys. They don't know who you are. You could pretend to be . . . Murdoch. Or Brick Hayward. Pick someone. They won't know the difference. And you only tell them things that you *want* them to know. Make yourself up. Be who you want to be. Be smarter, more popular, older, cooler, whatever."

"Is that what you do?" Edson asked admiringly.

I smiled in what I hoped was a mysterious manner. "That's for me to know and you to find out."

"Yeah, but your pen pal's a *girl*," Robert said derisively.

I said nothing, and the meaning of that sank in.

"Do you guys write anything . . . nasty?" Edson asked, and there was a gleam in his eye.

"Me to know, you to find out." I grabbed the basketball from him, made a layup, rebounded my own ball and did it again.

It was weird that evening eating dinner with a functional family, where the parents got along and children were not just an annoyance. At the table, everyone laughed and joked and had a good time, just like people on television did. The angry silences and hostile put-downs that I was used to were nowhere in evidence. After dinner, we all sat down to play Monopoly, even Robert's parents, and it was fun.

This wasn't *The Brady Bunch,* though. Robert was still a regular kid, and after his dad set up the tent and sleeping bags in the backyard, then returned to the house and closed the drapes, the three of us sneaked out to see what was happening in the neighborhood. A little brat named Stevie lived a few doors down, and Robert's idea was to hide in the bushes under the kid's bedroom window, make spooky noises and scare the shit out of him. But a dog started barking the second we stepped onto Stevie's lawn, and we beat a hasty retreat. We ran all the way to the corner. A Mustang full of teenagers sped by and from the open rear window flew a water balloon that smashed on the sidewalk at our feet. "Eat it!" someone yelled.

My eyes followed the car as it roared away, but halfway up the block my attention was grabbed by a smaller figure hobbling down the sidewalk.

The witch.

That old hag was haunting me—I'd run into her at the post office again while dropping off a letter to Kyoko—and seeing her by moonlight sent a chill down my spine. "Check it out," Edson whispered, pointing. He looked from me to Robert. "Think we should follow her? See where she lives?"

In answer, Robert put a finger to his lips and scurried down the sidewalk, keeping to the shadows as much as possible, avoiding the circles of light created by the streetlamps every three houses or so.

We followed her down the street. I thought the sound of our movement would be covered by the loud tapping of her cane, but she heard us, and at the end of the block she stopped next to the mailbox and suddenly whirled around, pointing her walking stick in our direction. The cane made a sweep in the air from left to right, and she said something that sounded like "Don't try." As if on cue, a pigeon dropped from the sky and landed dead on the sidewalk halfway between us. The witch smiled, then turned away and headed down the cross street.

"Let's get out of here!" Robert said, and the three of us ran like hell back up the block and around the corner, not stopping until we were once again safely ensconced in our tent in Robert's backyard.

I couldn't wait to write to Kyoko and tell her about this. As soon as I got home, I would lock myself in the bathroom and write her a long letter about staying overnight at my friend's house and our adventure with the witch.

We got into our sleeping bags, compared notes on what had just happened, made plans for tomorrow and bullshitted for a while until gradually the conversation faded away, overtaken by the night. Robert nodded off, then Edson, but I remained awake and alert, so excited thinking about what I would write that I could not sleep. I suddenly realized that, to me, real life was important only as fodder for my letters. Odd as it was, I cared less about experiencing events than writing about them. I didn't write letters to describe my life—I lived my life to have something to write in my letters.

Or to have a springboard from which to launch my lies.

I stared up at the peaked nylon roof of the tent. To give myself credit, I didn't always lie. If something interesting happened, like our experience with the witch, I would incorporate it into the tapestry of fiction I was creating. It was just that, usually, not enough interesting things occurred to justify the frequency of my correspondence—so I simply pretended they did and made things up.

And Kyoko believed it all.

Was she doing the same? I didn't think so. Her stories were too mundane, the things she wrote about too ordinary. She had no secret-scientist father, she was not related to anyone famous or important, she was not a popular surfing champion, she encountered no witches. But that only made me like her all the more. She was enamored with my fictional self, she genuinely cared about her American pen pal, and that made me care about her.

In the morning, the three of us awoke with the dawn. Robert's mom was already making pancakes in the house. I had a quick breakfast, then asked to be taken home. Robert and Edson begged me to stay, reminding me of all the fun things we had planned for this morning, but all I could think of was that I needed to write to Kyoko, needed to put everything down in letter form before I forgot it and the feeling was lost. I said I was sorry but I had to go somewhere with my family this morning. It was not a lie I could have sold to Paul—he knew me too well—but Robert and Edson were school friends, not neighborhood friends, and I could make them believe that I had the type of family that did things together.

Robert's dad drove me back to my house. I thanked him, said good-bye to Robert and Edson, who'd come along for the ride, grabbed my little suitcase, ran up the driveway to the kitchen door and, with a last wave, went inside.

Where my mom was screaming at Tom in the living room, and my dad sat at the kitchen table staring blearily into a cup of coffee, muttering, "Bastards . . . bastards . . . bastards . . ."

"What are you doing home?" my mom shrieked at me as I tried to sneak past her. "I thought we wouldn't have to put up with you until this afternoon!"

I ignored her and made my way down the hall to my bedroom, where I pushed a pile of dirty clothes against the door to keep anyone from opening it too quickly and then sat down at my desk. It was daytime, it was dangerous, and everyone was awake, but I'd forsaken a day of fun for this and I had to write. I pulled the top off my pen, took a deep breath and let the feeling of joy wash over me.

Dear Kyoko, I wrote. . . .

4

On Easter vacation, I killed my dad.

Not really. But in a letter to Kyoko, I said that my father had died in a tragic automobile accident, killed by a drunk driver. I took a sort of gleeful pleasure in inverting the order of the universe, killing his fictional counterpart with someone quite close to his true self, though of course I professed my deep anguish at the loss of a beloved parent.

I had to kill him off because she kept asking me about my upcoming trip to Japan. She'd even told her parents about it, and the whole family was making plans to meet me. *That* was a narrative thread I should not have started, and while I did not regret lying to

her, I regretted telling that *particular* lie. But all's well
that ends well, and I killed off the fucker and populated his funeral with powerful famous people to boot.

It was the longest letter I'd ever written—and the
most detailed. I found that I enjoyed writing about
my dad's death, and I got a strange sick satisfaction
from describing the details of his demise. The emotions I expressed to Kyoko were far more profound
than any I would know once my dad really died, and
in a way that made the writing a more cathartic experience, since it enabled me to vicariously feel what I
would never have to face in real life.

I had so much fun composing the letter that I immediately followed it with another, equally long. This one
I dated a few days later, and in it I pretended to be
having a difficult time coping with the loss. I could not
eat, refused to go to school and shunned my friends.

Kyoko felt she really knew me by then and took it
hard. The ink on her next letter was stained with tears,
her carefully drawn letters smeared. I felt bad for de-
ceiving her, but even if I wanted to, I couldn't apolo-
gize and take it back. Once a lie of that magnitude
was out there, to admit culpability would amplify its
import. The only thing to do was let it ride.

I was astonished by the eloquence of her commiser-
ation. The shock of sudden death had nullified her
English problems, and though the grammar and syntax
were still not perfect, her words came from the heart
and were more expressive than I ever would have expected. It was as if the curtain of formality that, because of her culture or personality, had always been
between us had been lifted and she was suddenly able
to communicate with me on an open, honest emotional level.

I thought of Paul and how all he ever thought about
was sex stuff. I would be lying if I said I hadn't started
thinking about those things, too, especially since I was

spending so much time writing to and thinking about a girl. A pretty girl. I realized this would be a perfect opportunity to introduce some of that into our relationship.

I told Kyoko I loved her.

I regretted it the second I dropped the letter into the mailbox the next morning, and I was almost tempted to pull some Fred-and-Barney scheme in an effort to get my envelope out again. Embarrassment was my overriding emotion. I spent the next two weeks in an agitated state that took its toll on my concentration and my grades, and made me step on some emotional land mines at home that left me battered and bloody.

To my great relief, she wrote back to tell me that she loved me, too, that she'd loved me for over a month and was so happy that I'd finally said it to her so she could say it to me.

I didn't really love her. And a small part of me even felt guilty for playing her this way, for pretending I had feelings I did not. I *liked* her, of course, but I didn't love her. I realized, though, that I could use her feelings for me to get what I wanted, to push her in a direction I wanted her to go.

And our relationship changed. Just like that. One moment I was in thrall to our epistolary association, a slave to my desire to write and read my pen pal's letters, and the next I was in charge, calling the shots, and those emotions that had held sway were now under my complete control.

I was curious about sex, and I took the opportunity to bring up the subject, playing up my fake relationship experience, lying about things I'd never done and didn't know how to do, writing that I wanted to do them with her. Since we loved each other, I stressed, it wasn't wrong. It was natural, beautiful.

She wrote back the same.

Our letters from then on were nasty.

They weren't pornographic in an adult way. But for two kids our ages with our complete lack of experience, they were pretty down and dirty.

I finally convinced her to send me a picture of herself without any clothes on. She took it herself, standing in front of a mirror in the bathroom. Behind her was a narrow shower stall, to the right a simple silver towel rack attached to a plain white wall. Kyoko herself stood center frame, the camera blocking all of her face save her mouth and forehead. She looked nervous, and she hadn't been brave enough to take off all of her clothes; she'd simply pulled down her dress and underwear, which were bunched around her knees. I could see what I wanted to see, though.

The good parts.

I didn't write back immediately. I'm not sure why. I did look at the picture at night while I rubbed myself in my bed, and I could not stop thinking about it all the next day and Monday at school, but I guess I was a little hurt that she hadn't asked for a similar photo. I probably wouldn't have sent one—but it would have been nice to be asked.

Maybe I also wanted to assert my newfound power a little bit by making her wait for communication from me.

Whatever the reason, I held off for a week, then sat down long after everyone else in the house was asleep, took off my pajamas and underwear and wrote Kyoko my most graphic letter yet. I played with myself afterward, looking at her photo.

The next letter I received was from her father—only it was addressed not to me but to my parents. I recognized the envelope and intercepted it, thinking at first that it *was* for me from Kyoko. But the dark harsh letters of an unfamiliar hand tipped me off that this was something different, and with pounding heart

I brought it to my room, shut the door and carefully opened the envelope, taking out the colorless stationery.

Her father had found and read my letters.

And Kyoko had broken down and confessed all.

The missive was in broken English and hard to understand, but the gist of it was that I had shamed his family and turned his daughter into a whore who would never be able to marry a boy from a good family because she had been ruined by me. Mr. Yoshizumi berated my parents for raising a boy of such low moral character and demanded that they punish me for the unforgivable way I'd corrupted his daughter.

He'd also sent a letter to Miss Nakamoto.

My mouth went dry.

I read the words again to make sure I understood the fractured English. *I write explain to honorable teacher Nakamoto no more pen pal.* There was no mistaking the meaning. My eyes moved up to the middle of the letter. *You punish boy for bad character and moral your duty as parent.*

Well, that was never going to happen. My heart was pounding as I ripped his letter into confetti-sized pieces, then placed the pieces in a Kleenex I took from the box on my desk. I wrapped up the tissue, brought it into the bathroom and flushed it down the toilet. What would happen now? I wondered. Would Miss Nakamoto tell the principal? Would she or the principal call my parents? Would I be suspended from school? Would I be arrested? Anything was possible, and I just hoped that Kyoko's father didn't know Miss Nakamoto's address or the address of the school.

But that was an impossibility. Kyoko's school in Japan had the address of the pen pal company and *they* had the address of my school. No, my only hope was the slim-to-none chance that the post office would lose the letter.

We were not a religious family. We never went to church. But I understood the basic concepts, and for the first time in my life, I folded my hands together, closed my eyes and seriously tried to pray. *Dear God,* I thought, *please don't let Miss Nakamoto get that letter. And don't let my parents find out what happened. Don't let me get into trouble. I'll be good for the rest of my life. I swear it. Amen.*

For good measure, I said the prayer again. And again. And again. Until, finally, I fell asleep.

I arrived at school the next morning nervous and tense. I hung out with Robert and Edson on the playground before class started, but I was distracted and didn't pay attention to the conversation and hardly noticed what we did. The first bell rang, and I followed everyone else off the playground to the classroom.

I sat down at my desk.

Was it my imagination or was Miss Nakamoto avoiding looking at me? It was hard to tell. But she seemed the same as always while she took roll and led us in the pledge, and as she broke us up into reading groups and took group A to the front of the class, I allowed myself to believe that I had at least a day's reprieve.

Then, at recess, she asked me to stay behind.

Her voice was sober, solemn, serious.

I was shaking as I remained in my seat. I knew what was coming. My tongue felt heavy and waxy, my lips dry, and my heart was beating like a tom-tom. She waited until everyone had gone; then she closed and locked the door. From the top drawer of her desk, she withdrew an envelope identical to the one addressed to my parents that I had intercepted.

"I got this letter yesterday," she said slowly. "It is from the father of Kyoko Yoshizumi, your pen pal." She paused. "In it, he says that the two of you have been exchanging . . . uh, inappropriate messages and that you convinced her to send you a photograph of herself without her clothes on. Is this true?"

I hadn't expected Miss Nakamoto to be so blunt and to the point. I was unable to look at her, and I stared down at the top of my desk, feeling hot, my skin burning with shame.

"Jason?" I heard no kindness in her voice, no sympathy.

Still looking down, I nodded silently.

It was painful for both of us, probably as embarrassing for her as it was for me, but that didn't stop her from giving me a long lecture about proper and improper behavior, unacceptable attitudes and unsuitable subjects for discussion by fifth-grade boys. I listened in silence, properly chastised, hoping I appeared contrite enough that this would be the end of it.

Miss Nakamoto folded the letter, put it back in her desk drawer and sighed heavily. "Jason, I am very disappointed in you," she said. "I'm afraid you will no longer be allowed to participate in the Pen Pal Program. Needless to say, you will not be getting any extra credit. Because of what you've done, I will be giving you an F in English and an 'Unsatisfactory' in citizenship. Do you understand why?"

I nodded miserably.

Miss Nakamoto would never love me, I realized. She did not even like me.

"I am very disappointed," she repeated, and her voice was flat, hard.

"Don't tell my parents!" I blurted out. It was the first thing I'd said.

The bell rang. In a few seconds, the other kids would be returning from recess. I looked up at her desperately.

She nodded. "Mr. Yoshizumi told me that he sent a letter to your parents as well as one to me. I'll let them decide how they wish to deal with your actions. I've done all I can from this end."

Thank you, God, I thought.

When I got home, I threw away all of Kyoko's correspondence, even the photos. I tore up my envelopes and stationery, tossed my pens and pencils into the trash.

I did not write another letter for the next six years.

Three

1

Jason Hanford
111 Norfolk Ave.
Acacia, CA 92235

March 13, 1980

Dear Sirs,
I am a longtime customer, and I am very unhappy with your new style of french fries. Your old fries were my very favorite and me and my friends from R. B. Hayes High would have them for lunch several times a week. But your new fries are unedible. Although I used to eat at Buck's Burgers all the time, I just want you to know that from now on I will be taking my business to McDonald's.

Sincerely,
Jason Hanford

I had no intention of taking my business to McDonald's. For one thing, there was no McDonald's next to my school, so I couldn't go there for lunch. For another, I *still* loved Buck's french fries. I was just trying to make a point, hoping that my complaint would spur

the burger stand into bringing back their original
recipe—sliced potatoes fried in sitting grease that were
then hung in a basket and *re*fried when customers
placed their orders. They'd recently switched to some
sort of artificial mashed-potato sticks that came frozen
from some big Eastern warehouse and that were fried
only once. I didn't like them nearly as much.

But the reason I wrote a complaint letter was that
I'd received a typewriter for my birthday. Not a word
processor, not even an electric typewriter, but an old
junky manual typewriter that had been surplused out
at my dad's work. It had been sitting in my room for
almost a month, but the previous weekend I'd cleared
off my desk to make room for it, and I finally decided
it was time to try it out.

To my surprise, I received an apologetic letter from
Buck himself and three coupons good for free full
meals (burger, fries and drink). Buck thanked me for
my opinion and said no final decisions had been made
but that the trial period for the new fries would be
going on for another month or so. He said he hoped
I would come by again and give them another try.

I showed the letter to Robert and Edson at school
the next day, and they were amazed that I got free
food just for complaining. "It's a miracle!" Edson
cried, dropping to his knees and bowing before me.

"Get up," Robert said, looking around as students
passing by turned to stare at us. "You look way too
at home in that position."

Edson stood. "That's funny. Your mama told me
the same thing last night."

I didn't show my parents the letter or tell them
about the free coupons, but on Saturday, my friends
and I made a day of it. We hit the downtown, going
first to the new-wave comic store, where we browsed
without buying anything, then to the Salvation Army
to check out their records. Robert and I had both

become somewhat fanatic record collectors over the past year, and for a buck I picked up an early Todd Rundgren album and the Beatles' *Rubber Soul.*

"Why do you like that *old* music?" Edson sneered. "Even my brother's finally dumped those dinosaurs."

"They're only fifty cents apiece," I pointed out. "I'll pretty much buy anything for fifty cents. Besides, just because it's old doesn't mean it's bad. There's good and bad music everywhere."

Robert grinned at Edson. "I got a Charlie Daniels, a Waylon Jennings and a Hank Junior." He'd recently been on a country-music kick that none of us understood.

Edson just snorted disgustedly and shook his head.

"Video killed the radio star." Robert prodded him.

We walked from the Salvation Army to Buck's Burgers. I handed out the free passes, and we all gorged ourselves on complimentary junk food.

"You have to do this more often," Robert told me.

It was a good idea, and I wrote complaint letters to every fast-food franchise I could think of. McDonald's, Burger King, Jack in the Box, Wendy's. Taco Bell, El Taco, Del Taco, Pup 'n' Taco, Der Wienerschnitzel. I wrote the same thing to each, that I was a longtime customer who had recently had a very unpleasant experience at their eating establishment.

The complimentary passes came rolling in. For the rest of my junior year, my friends and I ate free. We didn't have to buy a single meal. Pizza Hut and Domino's provided us with party pizzas. Baskin-Robbins gave us dessert. I let everyone I knew in on the secret (except my family), and a couple of them attempted to write letters themselves, but for some reason only my efforts were successful. The few people who received replies got only form apologies. I got free food.

"If there's one thing Jason knows how to do," Robert joked, "it's complain."

As a lark—or, more accurately, as an experiment—I wrote a letter to Familyland, pretending to be the president of a campus club who was looking for donations for our fund-raiser. To my complete surprise and utter delight, I received five free passes to the park. I thought of inviting four friends to come along, but then realized that I really had only two *good* friends: Robert and Edson. It would be better just to invite them and then put the other two passes away for later. So that's what I did. I told my parents Edson had won free Familyland tickets in a contest and had invited me to go with him, and on Saturday morning the three of us were on the bus and headed for the amusement park.

We'd taken to riding the bus a lot. All three of us had driver's licenses, but none of us had cars, and we didn't like the restrictions that went with borrowing the family vehicle. Riding the bus kept us free and easy, independent and unencumbered.

I found myself wondering if I wrote a complaint letter to the bus company, whether I could get a free pass.

We got to Familyland early, just as it opened. Our plan was to stay there all day until the place closed at midnight. We wanted to get our money's worth—even though it was free. The first part of the morning was spent racing to the good rides, the thrill rides, so we could get on them before the lines got too big. After that, we tried to pick up chicks in the gift shops and the arcades, asking any female who looked even remotely close to our age if she wanted to go on a ride with us. Finally, two sullen fat girls agreed to accompany Edson and me into the Haunted House, and in the dark of the ride I managed to grab the sweaty hand of the brunette I was with and hold it for a few seconds before she pulled it away. Robert, who hadn't been able to find anyone to go with him, rode alone, which provided a lot of the humor for the day.

Late in the afternoon, we stopped at the Space Bar outside the Rocket Ride to get some Cokes and I heard a familiar voice call out, "Hey, asshole!"

I looked up to see Tom standing in line for the Rocket Ride. My brother was with some skank that he'd been dating for the past few weeks, and he waved at me, grinning. "Thanks for the tickets!"

He'd stolen my other two passes! I wanted to kill him. He'd been snooping in my room, and he had to have been looking pretty deep to find where I'd hidden the tickets. I felt violated. That fucker had invaded my privacy. Thank God I didn't keep a diary or anything. I tried to think of what else he might have run across, what other secrets of mine he might have uncovered.

I hated him at that moment. I didn't like Tom even at the best of times, but at that second I could have easily slit his throat and not lost a moment's sleep.

Laughing, he moved forward in line, and he and the skank disappeared behind the ringed globe of Saturn.

"What was that about?" Edson asked.

But I was too angry to answer. I was trying to think of ways to retaliate. Telling my parents would do no good—they'd just be mad that I kept *them* in the dark about my free tickets—and even though I'd experienced a growth spurt over the past year and was now actually taller than my brother, he could still kick my ass. I thought of the bitch he was dating, and I had an idea.

"Jason?" Robert was waving a hand in front of my face as though trying to awaken me from a trance. It was obvious that he'd been attempting to ask me something.

"Let's get out of this area," I said, grabbing my Coke cup. "My fucking brother's here, and I don't want to see him."

"The Wild West!" Robert announced. He'd been

wanting to go to the cowboy show all morning. Part of his country-western infatuation, I assumed. We'd heard banjo music from behind the wooden fort fence as we'd passed by earlier.

"No way," Edson protested.

But I was the swing vote, and Westernland was far enough away from Spaceland that it sounded good to me. "Let's do it," I said.

"Yee-hah," Edson muttered.

I arrived home that night just after eleven, the three of us having caught the final bus. Tom still wasn't home by midnight, and my parents were fuming about it. Banging his bim in the backseat, I assumed, and I was glad to hear through the walls that my parents were thinking along the same lines. He was going to be in deep shit when he got home.

I was glad.

But that wasn't enough.

I went into Tom's room, found the name and address of the skanky bitch, then went back into my room and took out a sheet of lined notebook paper. *Tom Hanford,* I wrote, carefully disguising my handwriting, *is gay. He is only using you to get back at me because I dumped him. Don't fall for it.* I signed the letter *Phil* and did kind of a flower thing for the dot on the *i.*

I put the letter in an envelope, sealed and stamped it.

I then wrote to the president of Familyland, enclosing my torn ticket stub, and said that I had had a very bad experience at the park and would not be returning.

A week later, I was sent two more free tickets.

And though nothing was ever said, Tom stopped seeing the girl.

Fuck you, Tom, I thought. And smiled.

2

Summertime.

And the living wasn't easy.

Life at home was just as bad as ever. During my junior high years, my dad had become, if not a full-fledged alcoholic, at least a more-than-occasional drunk. But after he'd totaled the car and very nearly killed a woman in a horrific accident that was entirely his fault and resulted in a year's suspension of his driver's license, he'd quit drinking and had even become somewhat religious. Not that there was any discernable difference in his personality or the way he treated me and Tom. He was still as mean and angry as he'd always been, and in some ways more dangerous, since the alcohol had kept him a little less focused and now he was able to concentrate fully on one thing at a time.

Like me.

I was, as he never let me forget, a huge disappointment. Despite the fact that he was a complete asshole at home, my father put on a hearty public face and, like a lot of heavy drinkers, was agreeably gregarious in social settings—even now that he was sober. I, however, was socially awkward and to my dad's dismay had yet to go on my first date, though I'd just turned seventeen. He was also a big sports guy. He was fat now and the most exercise he got was yelling at coaches while he watched ball games on television, but in his day he'd been on the high school football, basketball *and* baseball teams. I was lucky to get a C in PE.

So there were plenty of conflicts to go around.

Luckily, Robert had gotten me a job at Gemco, a discount department store, so at least I had a legitimate reason for getting out of the house at night. Robert had the position I wanted—working in the music

department selling records, tapes and stereos—but I
was desperate to earn some extra cash, and I was
grateful when there was an opening in Toys and he
recommended me to the store's assistant manager.

After a pro forma interview, I was hired to work
twenty hours a week, eight of them on a weekend day,
the other twelve spaced out over weekday evenings.
It was an easy job. The hardest thing I had to do was
clean up after kids who'd taken toys off the shelves,
played with them and left them in the aisles—an occurrence that happened numerous times each shift.
But my supervisor, Ellis Cain, was a complete prick.
The toy department was his domain, and for me to
suggest that it was anything less than a demanding
job that could be handled by only the brightest and
most industrious was belittling to him. He resented
the fact that I, a mere high school student and part-
time employee, found the work simple, boring and
easy to do.

So he took it out on me. He blamed me for anything
that went wrong, he constantly let me know that the
girl who'd had the job before I did had been far better
at it, and if ever a kid puked or pissed his pants or
spilled his Slurpee, he made sure that I, and not a
member of the maintenance crew, cleaned it up.

I grew to hate that son of a bitch.

But I liked getting a paycheck, and I liked the feeling of independence I got from not spending all my
evenings hiding in my room listening to my parents
fight. All in all, it wasn't such a bad deal, and if Cain
could just transfer to another store or even another
department, all would be right with the world.

Robert and I usually spent our breaks together sitting on the low brick wall behind the store. It kept us
from having to sit in the break room with the lifers—
old women who'd been working there since the Stone
Age and who took their jobs *way* too seriously. One

Wednesday evening, Toys was dead—there hadn't
been a sale all night, hadn't even been a browser since
six, when I started my shift—so I decided to take an
early break. I walked over to Music, where a frail old
man in an ugly plaid jacket was arguing with Robert.
"That's not what I wanted, and you know that's not
what I wanted!"

Robert sighed as though he'd repeated his defense
a thousand times. "I *told* you, you wouldn't like it,"
he said. "I warned you."

"That's not the music I wanted! I told you I wanted
the music from *Cosmos*!"

"Yes. And you said the theme from *Cosmos* was
called 'Heaven and Hell.' I told you we had the Black
Sabbath album *Heaven and Hell* but that it probably
wasn't what you were looking for and I was sure you
wouldn't like it. You bought it anyway, and I said that
if it wasn't the right music, you could bring it back.
You did bring it back, and I gave you a refund. I don't
know what else I can do."

"I want the music from *Cosmos*!"

"Well, I'm afraid we don't have it," Robert told
him. "Maybe you should try a record store."

"I am very dissatisfied with the service I've received! Very dissatisfied!"

Robert did not respond.

"Your supervisor will be getting a letter from me!"
the old man promised. "I can assure you of that!"

A letter.

I was like a cartoon character with a lightbulb going
on over his head. I stood there as Robert finished
dealing with the man; then the two of us walked out
the service entrance to the loading dock. We talked
about an upcoming U2 concert we had tickets for, but
my mind was on the exciting idea that I could write
a letter to Gemco complaining about Ellis Cain. I
thought about the quick results I'd gotten from my

letter to Buck's and all of my subsequent missives to fast-food joints and amusement parks.

There was nothing retail businesses feared more than dissatisfied customers.

I went home that night and wrote a letter to the store's manager, another to the president of the company at the corporate headquarters in Delaware. I pretended to be an irate father who'd been trying to buy a new Hot Wheels set but was given the runaround by the incompetent Ellis Cain.

I was off the next week—I'd worked too much over the Fourth of July holiday weekend, covering for the full-timers who were on vacation—but when I returned, Cain was gone. I don't know what went on behind the scenes, whether he was given a lecture and quit in a huff, or whether he'd accumulated other complaints over the years and this was the last straw and Gemco fired him. All I knew was that I suddenly had a new supervisor and Cain was no longer in the picture.

I went home that night feeling elated, powerful.

The feeling lasted until I walked through the kitchen door.

"What are you smiling at?" my dad growled. He was sitting at the kitchen table, and if I hadn't known better, I would have sworn he was drunk. His face was red, the way it used to be when he was drinking, and there was an ugly belligerence in his expression that usually came out only after a hearty consumption of alcohol. But the table was empty of both bottles and cans, and the only thing in front of him was an open Bible.

I shook my head, hoping that would be answer enough to his question, and tried to slip peacefully by, heading toward my bedroom.

"Where do you think you're going?"

"I'm tired," I said.

"Then what were you smiling at?"

"Nothing. I was just thinking of a joke."

"What joke?"

If he'd been drunk, I would have been out of there by now. He would not have been able to sustain this line of questioning. As it was, I might be there for hours. "Where's Mom?" I asked, trying to change the subject.

"Who cares?" he said.

She walked in from the living room at precisely that second, and though she couldn't have heard my question, she heard his answer and deduced backward with that almost supernatural sense of familial logic that mothers possessed. "Get out of my kitchen," she said flatly. Her words were directed at him, but I used the opportunity to escape and hurried down the hallway to my bedroom.

I locked the door behind me, something I'd been doing more and more often. I looked over at my typewriter. I could get my old man fired, I thought. The idea was tempting. My dad had been a ruthless bastard to me for as long as I could remember, and if he hadn't been the family's sole support, if I hadn't needed his money to survive, I would have sat down at that second, written and sent out a letter to Automated Interface and gotten his ass terminated.

Just the thought of squealing on him for some imaginary transgression, getting him hauled before his boss and humiliated, made me feel happy, made me feel good.

My parents went out for dinner that night, a rare occurrence that Tom immediately took advantage of by escaping to hang with his white-trash friends. In his hands was a bong. "You better not say a word!" he warned me as he bailed.

"I don't care what you do," I told him. Tom was a loser. He'd graduated from high school last year but still lived at home because all he had was a part-time job at Builder's Emporium. I think he took one or two classes at Acacia Community College, but he wasn't serious about school, wasn't serious about work and was going nowhere fast. Excellent athlete or not, he hadn't amounted to much, and it did my heart good to hear my parents start in on him with their weekly diatribe, telling him that he'd better shape up or ship out, and as long as he lived under their roof he had to abide by their rules.

On second thought, I decided that I *would* tell them about Tom and his bong.

I had the house and the evening to myself. I was still thinking about that letter, and for fun, I opened my notebook and started writing a complaint to my dad's boss, pretending to be an anonymous coworker who caught him drinking in the bathroom on his break, and harassing an unwilling underage girl in the parking lot, and—

The phone rang.

I jumped, quickly crumpling up my paper. I tossed it into the trash as the phone rang again. I was the only one home, so I hurried out to the living room and picked it up. "Hello?"

"Good afternoon, sir. Are you the man of the house?"

It was someone trying to sell something.

"My balls are on fire!" I yelled, and then slammed down the phone.

I started laughing. I felt strangely invigorated by my exchange with the telemarketer. There was about it the same sort of anonymous power that came with letter writing, although I was reacting instead of acting. I was suddenly in the mood to *really* write that complaint about my dad, and I sat down and wrote a five-page, hugely detailed letter, filled with every criticism and accusation I could come up with, given my imprecise knowledge of his job. I seriously considered sending it off, but then I saw the movement of head-lights through the drapes, and I tore up the pages and flushed them down the toilet before my parents walked into the house.

I had a dream that night that I wrote a letter to myself, and in it I stated, *My dad is a dick.* When I walked out of my bedroom and looked down the hall to my parents' room, I saw my dad sitting on the edge of his bed. His head was a bald dome with a slit on the top of it, he had no arms, and his entire body was cylindrical.

He'd been turned into a penis.

He was a dick.

3

My mom was mad again. Seemed like she was always mad at someone, but this time it was Tom instead of me, so while she stood in the hallway yelling at him through his closed bedroom door, I spent an atypical evening in the family room with my dad. We didn't speak—he read the newspaper while I watched TV—but it was oddly similar to the behavior of a normal family, and the comparison only made me realize how far from the ideal we really were.

"Finally," my dad said, folding the paper, "the city's going to clean up the Eastside."

I knew what he meant by that. There'd been talk of it for years. The east side of the city was poor and primarily Hispanic, and people like my dad wanted to plow down all the homes and put up expensive condos in an effort to kick out the current residents and draw a richer, whiter population—which was apparently what the city council now intended to do. I picked up the newspaper once he put it down, and read the arti-

cle titled REDEVELOPMENT PROJECT APPROVED. It
stated that the neighborhood on the north side of
Eighth Avenue between Murdoch and Grand would
be razed and replaced with a gated community called
the Lakes, featuring two man-made lakes and an
eighteen-hole golf course. The aging mishmash of
small stores, apartment buildings, duplexes and homes
on the south side of Eighth would become a destination shopping/entertainment district with a multiscreen
theater, upscale eateries, boutique stores and a mall
with adjoining parking structure.

I looked at the photo of the Eastside as it was and
at the artist's rendering of the proposed redevelopment.

My friend Frank Hernandez lived in that area, just
past the train tracks near El Nopale market. My favorite taco stand was also there, a little hole-in-the-wall
place where you had to order in Spanish because the
workers didn't understand English.

I'd never been one of those kids who automatically
parroted their parents' beliefs and opinions—not with
my mom and dad—but it was only recently that I'd
begun to seriously question what they said. My dad
was all gung ho for "cleaning up" the east side of the
city, but I liked things the way they were. And the
concept of eminent domain, which we'd just learned
about in our American Government class, seemed ille-
gal and profoundly antidemocratic to me.

So I wrote a letter to the paper about it.

I'm not sure if I actually expected my letter to get
in, but it did. The *Acacia Ledger* was a biweekly
paper, sort of a local complement to the *Orange
County Register* or the *Los Angeles Times*, and the
lead correspondence in the next "Letters to the Editor" was mine.

It was exciting to see my name in print, although
my old man went ballistic. He threw the paper at me

when he arrived home from work. I expected to smell alcohol in his exhalation of breath, but despite his crazed behavior, he appeared to be clean. "How could you humiliate me like that?" he demanded. "What the hell were you thinking?"

He began hitting me.

I was tempted to fight back. He was fat and out of shape, and while I wasn't even remotely athletic, I was younger, thinner and more agile. He could still kick my ass, I knew, but there was an opportunity for me to land one good sucker punch, and if I'd been only a little braver, I would have taken it. Instead, I stood there, blocking as many of his open-palmed slaps as I could, while trying to explain that all I'd done was write a letter and express my opinion, a right protected by the Constitution of the United States.

Tom, in the kitchen doorway, just stood there and laughed, and I realized at that moment just how much I hated my brother. It was my mom who broke things up—though of course she sided with my dad. She made him stop hitting me, but then she started yelling, too, the both of them coming at me in stereo. I took it, but inside I was glad I'd written that letter, and I felt proud of myself for being able to upset them so. My words had power.

In the next issue of the paper, the editorial page was filled with letters denouncing me. One from the mayor, one from the city manager, two from members of the public. The paper itself printed an editorial siding with the city, calling my ideas "inflammatory and counterproductive." I hadn't realized that my opinions would be taken so seriously—I was just a high school kid!—and I'd had no idea that I would hit such a nerve. Of course, racists didn't like to be called racists, and maybe my blunt talk had hit them where it hurt.

I knew I had to defend myself, but that night as I sat at my desk crafting a response, I thought that it would be much more effective if *other* people defended me.

I stopped writing as an idea occurred to me.

I could invent a fake name and fake address, pretend to be someone else, pretend I was just a normal reader who had heard both sides of the argument and thought that Jason Hanford had made a lot of very valid points.

Or I could create a fake organization.

That was even bigger; that was even better. I stared at the blank paper rolled in my typewriter. It had to be something that sounded legitimate but was not the name of an actual group. Hispanic Action Coalition? That sounded good, but I couldn't be sure I hadn't heard that name somewhere else before. Latino Watchdog Association . . . Chicano Rights Watch . . . Mexican American Defense League? The trouble was, they all sounded real.

So what if they were?

That was a legitimate point. Even if a representative from one of those organizations complained about the appropriation of their name and wrote a rebuttal stating that I did not accurately reflect their views, it would be after the fact. I would still get my message out there.

I started writing.

It took me a long time to compose the letter. I worked on it until I started falling asleep, then finished it after school the next day, typing it quickly before my dad came home. I called myself "Carlos Sandoval," after Carlos Santana and Arturo Sandoval, two musicians whose albums I had seen the other day at the Goodwill store, and I claimed to be president of the Hispanic Action Coalition. I stated that the landgrab by the city on behalf of developers, under the guise of eminent domain, was an attempt to legislate away the Mexican population. They were using politics to change the demographics of the city, to make it more white, and it was part of a pattern of discrimination.

To buttress my position, I wrote a quick little letter ostensibly from an outraged citizen. I made her an old lady who'd been born in Acacia and lived here all her life. She said that it was disgusting to see such blatant bigotry finding its way into the policies of our elected officials and driving apart the citizens of the city she loved.

Both letters were printed in the *Ledger* (did they publish *everything* they received?), and the controversy kicked into high gear. Right next to my letters was a dissenting opinion penned by an avowed white supremacist—support that I'm sure city hall could have done without.

The alterna-press jumped into the debate: one of Orange County's two underground newspapers ran a completely erroneous story stating that "Carlos Sandoval" had attended a meeting of local Latino leaders, stealing a quote from my letter; the other published an unsigned staff-written editorial echoing everything that I had said. I was flattered and excited to be at the center of this conflict, but I knew I needed to keep the momentum going, so I wrote a letter to the *Los Angeles Times*, this time pretending to be a businessman from the good part of town outraged by the fact that the city could take away businesses from private owners and essentially give them away to their buddies.

Letters poured in both agreeing and disagreeing with me. I wrote another claiming that this section of the city was a historic landmark and should not be tampered with by petty politicians with ulterior motives. For all of my letters, I invented fake names and addresses, often stealing them from the phone book and tweaking them a little so they were off by one number. Never once was one refused; all of them were published.

My dad commented constantly on the Eastside controversy, voicing his disgust with anyone opposed to redevelopment, but he seemed to have forgotten that I was at the center of it, that my initial letter had kicked it off. He walked in one evening while I was typing an angry anti–city hall polemic once again from President Carlos Sandoval of the Hispanic Action Coalition. I quickly unspooled my letter and casually placed it facedown on the desk, replacing it with another.

"What's wrong with you?" my dad asked, a look of annoyed dissatisfaction on his face. "Hiding in your room, typing letters, when you should be out there trying to pick up girls. When I was your age, I was bagging babes right and left. Like Tom."

"Whoa there," I said. "That doesn't sound very Christian."

He took a belligerent step forward. "Are you making fun of me?"

"No," I lied.

"I'm a Christian, but I'm still a man, goddamn it. Which is more than I can say for you." He glared at me, and I looked away. "How come you don't have a girlfriend, Jason? How come you never date, huh?"

I'd wondered the same thing myself. I'd sort of come to the conclusion that growing up in such a hostile family environment had made me socially inept.

I looked at him. Maybe, I thought, this was one of those bonding opportunities. Maybe if I just reached out, opened up to him, he might meet me halfway and we could forge some sort of ersatz father-son connection. Better late than never, right? I took a deep breath. "I don't really know how to meet girls," I admitted.

"You don't?" He feigned surprise. "I know what you should do," he said, leaning forward. "Get some gonads."

So much for bonding.

He left with a laugh, amused by his own joke, and I sat there feeling embarrassed and humiliated. I'd get no fatherly advice from my dad. The fucker had no interest in being a parent to me. All he cared about was himself. He might not be a drunk anymore, but he was still a selfish asshole.

I locked my bedroom door and finished writing my letter to the editor, putting in specific rebuttals to the arguments that my old man brought up in his daily rants, knowing that it would drive him crazy to read such precise dissections of his reasoning. It felt good to attack him this way, and in a guise of impersonality I came at him viciously, hitting him in his most vulnerable places.

Take that, you prick, I thought.

The next day, I went with Robert, Edson and Frank Hernandez to the little taco place, and it was more crowded than I'd ever seen it. The controversy had been good for business, and Frank suggested that we start a petition to save the homes and businesses on and around Eighth Avenue. I was tempted to tell him what I'd been doing, what I'd been writing, but something kept me from it. I looked up from my carne asada and nodded. "You write one. I'll sign it," I said.

Frank stared morosely out at the street. "They could just take our home, man. You know that? They'd take it and pay us what it's worth—which is shit—and then we'd be fuckin' homeless. Where else could we find a house for that much? We'd end up in an apartment in Santa Ana next to some fuckin' illegals."

"Maybe it won't go through," I offered. "I mean, if everyone got together and—"

"Who you fuckin' kidding?" Frank said. "This place is history." He nodded at my tacos. "Enjoy 'em while you can, man."

Robert and Edson ate in silence. They liked Frank and they liked the little taco place, but I could tell they weren't really comfortable hanging in this part of town, and for all I knew, they agreed with my dad, friend or no friend.

Although I had no personal stake in it, I vowed to fight the redevelopment of this area to the death.

> *Arthur Collingsworth*
> *1243 W. Townley Place*
> *Acacia, CA 92235*
>
> *Dear Sirs,*
>   *As a third-generation Acacian and a successful local businessman, I am appalled at the council's insensitive xenophobic attitude toward redevelopment. I have been following the controversy over the past several weeks and have been distressed and disappointed by the words coming from city hall spokesmen. I'm not a believer in conspiracy theories, but Carlos Sandoval seems to hit pretty close to home in his critique of the city's policies as racist and unbalanced.*
>   *Don't you think that the Hispanic members of our community should have some say over their fate?*
>   *In addition, I would like to state that I am opposed to the government usurpation of private property via eminent domain as a general principle and find your actions in this regard particularly abhorrent. Rest assured, my friends and fellow businessmen will be watching your actions in this matter and will vote accordingly in the next election.*
>
>   *Sincerely,*
>   *Arthur Collingsworth*

The city council met on the third Monday in July. I don't know how many members of the public usually

showed up to such meetings, but this one was packed.
It was kind of funny: most parents would have been
thrilled if their teenagers exhibited such an interest
in civic affairs and local politics that they voluntarily
attended a council meeting, but I was forced to lie to
my parents and tell them I was going to a concert so
they wouldn't bar me from showing up.

None of my friends wanted to go, so I went alone,
sitting in the back, and it was a good thing I got there
early because the chambers were filled by six thirty
even though the meeting didn't begin until seven. I
was the only teenager there, as far as I could tell. It
was mostly all adults, although a few brought their
little kids along. The room was pretty evenly divided
between angry white guys and power-suited developers in favor of razing the area around Eighth Avenue,
and Latino residents, business owners and community
activists opposed. Both sides spoke for what seemed
like an eternity at an open forum, and I had to admit
that the redevelopment supporters were much better
at stating their case. Finally, the time limit for public
comment ran out, and as there were still a lot of people who hadn't had their say and were vocally pro-
testing their shutout, the council voted to continue the
discussion at the next meeting in two weeks.

The mayor scanned the crowd. "May I ask if Carlos
Sandoval is here?"

I stared at the floor, my face hot and flushed, suddenly sure that I would be found out. The entire audience looked around, glancing to the left and right as
though searching for Carlos. It was one thing to write
letters and read them in the newspaper but quite another to see firsthand the effect of those letters. It felt
weird being in the middle of all those people who
thought Carlos was a real person. Half of them had
probably demonized him in their minds, while the
other half viewed him as a potential savior, and even

in my embarrassment I marveled at the fact that the words I'd written in my room and sent out into the world had had such strong reverberations.

The meeting adjourned shortly after tackling a few small unrelated issues. My impression of the evening was that the council was leaning toward approving the redevelopment, especially since the city qualified for some sort of federal grant.

I had to get to work.

The next few weeks were a blur. I didn't dare let my parents see me typing as many letters as I knew needed to be sent—not only to newspapers but to city hall—so I smuggled my typewriter to work so I could write letters on my breaks and lunch periods. I was saving up for a word processor, but for the moment I had only my old manual Royal, and when I wasn't selling toys or picking up after bratty kids, I was impersonating men and women from all nationalities and all walks of life vehemently opposed to redeveloping the Eastside.

I became a better debater with each argument I made, and the people responding to me in print sharpened their attacks, becoming ever more polarized until avowed racists were battling it out with Hispanic radicals, and redevelopment had become a single-issue subject.

I stepped in as the voice of moderation—and opposed the marginalization of an important segment of our community.

Throughout the rest of July and into August, the council dithered, hemming and hawing in the press, unwilling to publicly take a stand. I would have loved to know what was going on behind the closed doors of city hall, what the mayor was saying to the planning commission and the city staff members who had put this whole thing in motion.

Finally, at a special meeting near the end of August

that was attended by residents and reporters and even two Los Angeles TV news crews (who had been alerted to the controversy by "Carlos Sandoval"), the council voted on its plan for Acacia's Eastside and unanimously decided not to use its powers of eminent domain to displace current residents. They left off with a vague assurance that the issue would still continue to be studied and that a happy solution would be found that would result in a revitalized city.

I had saved the Eastside.

It might be overreaching for me to claim that I had single-handedly fought city hall and won, but I had no illusions about the part I had played in all of this. If I had not stepped in and written my letters, the council would have passed the plan way back in July. I had galvanized the community and given words to the speechless, even framing arguments that they could appropriate for their cause.

Frank and I celebrated with tacos.

I took the money I'd saved and bought my word processor.

Four

1

School started again in September.

Senior year.

I had no new cause for which to fight, but I continued writing letters to assorted media outlets, commenting on various issues of the day, making suggestions to television networks about TV shows, and of course I kept up my complaints to restaurants and amusement parks, expanding my horizon to include movie theaters.

Despite my extracurricular successes, things weren't going quite as well at school. I'd never been one to think ahead, but I started planning out my life after graduation, and I decided I wanted to go to college. I wasn't ready for the real world. So for the first time in three years, I paid a visit to my guidance counselor to discuss my options.

Mrs. Zivney was old and humorless and had no real interest in the affairs of students, though that was her job. She listened to me, heard me out, then wearily walked over to a series of file cabinets across the hall and pulled my records. I told her I had no money and my parents certainly weren't the type to pay my way. My older brother, I explained, had not gone to college and was basically a bum, and everyone expected me to follow in his footsteps. "But I want to go to college," I said. "I want to make something of myself. What kind of scholarship do you think I could get?"

I wouldn't get any scholarship, the counselor informed me. My grades weren't good enough. It would take something spectacular on my résumé to make up for the lazy pattern of slightly better-than-average grades in non-advanced-placement classes. Either that or I would have to ace the SATs—which wasn't going to happen.

"She's a treacherous and evil old bitch," I said when I emerged from the meeting. "She should be put down like the mad mongrel that she is." I'd been reading a lot of Hunter Thompson and wanted to try out some of his lingo, but those sorts of words read better on the page than they sounded in person. Like most kids at that age, I was searching for myself, trying on different personae to see if they fit. But whereas most teenagers copped their attitudes from music or movies, I emulated writers. Well, not writers really, but their words. I attempted to make manifest the attitudes espoused in letters, journals and memoirs, though so far it wasn't working out too well for me.

I sighed as I took my lunch from my locker to show Robert and Edson I wasn't serious. "She said I'm not eligible for any scholarships," I told them.

"There are grants," Robert offered. "Other kinds of financial aid."

"Yeah," Edson said. "My sister's on this work-study deal where they got her a job at UC Brea that helps her pay for tuition there."

"Zivney didn't tell me shit," I said. "She didn't mention any of that."

"The point is," Robert said, "there's still hope."

Robert's parents, of course, had started a college fund at the time he was born, and though his grades weren't any better than mine—were a little worse, actually—he could pretty much afford to go anywhere he wanted. Edson was in the same boat I was but didn't seem to care.

I nodded, and the three of us headed off to lunch, but I was already thinking of a plan, another idea that would offset my lackluster academic record and make me a better candidate for scholarships.

Robert and Edson were going to head over to the mall after school. Sheri Pham, a girl from Economics in whom Edson was interested, worked at Clothestime, and they were going to casually walk by the store and try to start up a conversation with her. Besides, Frank worked in the food court and they could probably wrangle some fries or Cokes out of him. I wanted to go, too, but I declined. The mall would always be there.

I had letters to write.

As I'd hoped, Tom was gone and neither of my parents was there when I arrived home. I quickly went back into my bedroom, where I threw my books on the floor and sat down at my desk to write a fake recommendation to the principal. I praised myself for imaginary selflessness, innovation and initiative, pretending that for the past year I had spent my free time not throwing a ball through a hoop or running down a field, but making a real difference in the world by combating alcoholism. My dad had beaten the bottle, and inspired by that, I had researched various support groups, had put them in touch with private and public treatment centers and had coordinated a complicated web of funding and referral services to make sure that people who needed help got it. I'd also written letters to businesses and corporations in an effort to get them to donate money to and/or sponsor these efforts.

I laid it on thick, but as I read over my letter I realized it wasn't enough. The information was there, everything I required to put me over, but I needed bulk, I needed volume. I needed another Carlos Sandoval and his Hispanic Action Coalition, a community service group to tout my accomplishments. I came up with the idea of having a fictitious organization nominate me for a distinguished-service award. Inspired, I wrote six letters of varying length on my word processor, each with a different font, then bundled them together and attached a cover letter from the fictional Sobriety Institute, signed by its president, Hiram Merritt, telling the principal that the school should be very proud to have an ambitious, altruistic young man like myself as part of its student body. The letter stated that I would be the first student from Hayes High—indeed the youngest recipient ever—to be nominated for the Sobriety Institute's Above and Beyond Award.

I sent another packet of letters to the superintendent.

Another to the mayor.

And my life changed overnight.

Well, maybe not overnight. But over a week, as the letters were delivered and the recipients responded, I suddenly went from being a nondescript nonentity to a celebrated humanitarian and inventive, enterprising self-starter who was going to go places in life. The principal, Mr. Poole, sent me a call slip in my homeroom and asked me to meet him in his office, where he shook my hand and congratulated me on my achievements.

I feigned ignorance. "I'm not sure what you're talking about," I said.

"Oh, I'm sorry!" He clapped a hand on my back, laughing. "I got a letter from the Sobriety Institute telling me about all the work you've done with alcoholics. That's quite a feat, young man. And I understand that you were inspired to do this by overcoming your own family tragedy. You are exactly the type of student Rutherford B. Hayes needs, and I'm proud to have you at our school. We all are." He showed me copies of the letters I'd written, and I pretended to be surprised and humbled.

"You're quite a young man."

I nodded, allowing myself a pained smile. "Thank you, sir."

He frowned. "Is there anything wrong?"

I shook my head. "It's just . . ." I trailed off, pretending to think the better of what I'd been about to say. "No. Nothing. Thank you, sir. Everything's fine."

"What is it, Jason? You can tell me."

"Well, I'm proud of what I've accomplished. It's important work, I think. I just wish it didn't take so much time away from school. Mrs. Zivney said I won't be able to get any scholarships, since my grades are good but not spectacular and I'm not involved in any extracurricular activities. And with my dad being . . . well, you know . . . my parents don't have enough money to send me to college."

"This is a travesty!" the principal announced. He led me down the corridor to Mrs. Zivney's office. "There should be plenty of scholarships available for a student with your qualifications. Let's talk to your counselor."

Twenty minutes later, Mrs. Zivney had me taking home an essay question for a full scholarship offered by a private philanthropist's foundation, had given me applications for two private-corporation scholarships and had given me the paperwork for a Pell Grant. In order to boost my profile and make me look better to financial-aid administrators, Principal Poole had appointed me to the school's Student Advisory Committee. "I think you'll be a fine addition to our little group," he said, "and I look forward to getting your unique take on some of the problems confronting our school today. Your input will be invaluable."

I smiled as I walked out of the office. Yesterday,

the principal would not have recognized me if I'd bitten him on the ass. Today I was his bosom buddy. I thought of *Star Trek II: The Wrath of Kahn*. Kobayashi Maru. When in doubt, cheat. If it was good enough for Captain Kirk, it was good enough for me.

Word spread, as I'd hoped it would. Soon all of my teachers knew that I was this great secret do-gooder, and across the board their attitudes toward me changed. They began to read profundity into my silences, began to interpret my vague and general answers in a more positive way. I had no doubt that my grades for this quarter would be greatly improved over the past.

A call to the school from the mayor, extolling my virtues and praising RBH High for turning out such a fine student as myself, did not hurt.

If any of my friends suspected anything, they didn't say. Robert and Edson, in particular, knew that I wasn't involved in any groups that were helping recovering alcoholics. Hell, between school and hanging out and the tight leash my parents kept on me, I didn't have *time* to do anything else. But for some reason we didn't talk about it, pretended I wasn't getting all of this sudden attention. We were best friends, but we weren't being honest with each other and we knew we weren't being honest with each other. There was a barrier between us, and it reminded me of when we were in fifth grade and involved with the Pen Pal Program. I realized for the first time that the three of us would not always be friends, that our friendship might not even survive past high school.

Sandra Fortuna, editor of the *Hayes Report*, our school newspaper, contacted me through Ms. Steinhart, my English teacher, and arranged to interview me about my community work the period after lunch in the cafeteria. I'd admired Sandra from afar for the past three years, ever since she'd been in my freshman PE class. I was a gawky, geeky guy doing my desperate best not to embarrass myself, and she was a poised, self-confident beauty. One time when she bent down to pick up a tennis ball, I caught a flash of panty, and from then on I was hooked. When I found out later that she was not only gorgeous and athletic but at the top of our class academically, I knew that I had no chance in hell with her—not that I would have been brave enough to approach her anyway.

So I intended to milk this interview for all it was worth.

We met at a corner table near the trash cans. She brought along a photographer, a goofy kid from my math class who snapped a few shots and then left, but Sandra remained, pen and notebook in hand, asking me how I'd gotten involved with helping alcoholics, where I'd gotten the idea to solicit donations and contributions from corporations, how I'd hooked up with the Sobriety Institute, why I kept it all so quiet and hid my light under a bushel. I lied extravagantly, building myself up in the humblest way possible, repeating and embellishing upon the biography that Hiram Merritt, the Sobriety Institute's fictional president, had sent to Principal Poole. There was one close call when she wanted me to give her the name and phone number of Merritt or someone else from the institute, but I convinced her that none of them would want to speak on the record because working with alcoholics required a certain degree of anonymity.

After the official interview ended, she hung around, talking. We were both supposed to go back to class, but our passes were good for the whole period, and we remained where we were. I couldn't believe how well we hit it off. I'd had no real experience talking to girls and was by no means good at it, but the conversation flowed naturally. We thought alike, we had similar tastes and similar ideas, and it was as if we'd known each other since kindergarten.

Feeling brave, my self-confidence boosted by my new status, I gathered up the courage to ask Sandra out on a date. I don't know what made me do such a thing, but my standing would never be higher with her than it was at this moment, and I knew I had to act now to take advantage of the momentum. "Would you . . . like to go out sometime?" I asked, trying to make it seem as casual as I could.

"Friday's free," she said.

Her Friday was free? I would have bet that her schedule was booked full a year in advance. Of course, talking to her, I'd discovered that she was not at all what I'd expected. And she'd also decided to be editor of the paper instead of head cheerleader—when she could have been either—so I guess that said something about her.

"Friday would be great," I said before she changed her mind, doing my best to seem pleased but not excited, and definitely not surprised.

That was Tuesday. We ate lunch together the rest of the week, although it wasn't a huddled, lovey-dovey boyfriend-girlfriend thing. It was more casual, more open, and it felt natural—it felt good. We sat, ate, talked and hung out together, and it was as if we'd been friends forever. I usually ate with Robert and Edson, sometimes Frank, but they understood and gave me room. Sandra Fortuna. This was a rare opportunity.

Friday rolled around.

I picked her up at her house just after six. My dad let me borrow his car; he was grateful, I think, for the fact that I was actually going out on a date. Her parents seemed nice but dull—typical parents—but the meeting wasn't *too* painful. And then we were off. I'd made reservations at Salvatore's, a nice Italian restaurant, and while I was a little nervous that my manners weren't up to snuff, that I'd use the wrong fork or wipe my mouth incorrectly on the napkin, things went well.

After that, we went to a movie. I put my arm around her shoulder in the theater but wasn't brave enough to drop it any lower. It was nice, though, and halfway through, Sandra leaned closer and rested her head on my shoulder. We held hands.

In the car, following the film, we talked. We talked for so long that when I finally looked up and glanced out the window, I saw that the parking lot was practically empty. I turned back toward Sandra. We were sitting close, bodies touching. I didn't know where to go from here, wasn't sure if this date was just a one-time thing or if it was the beginning of some type of relationship.

"So what are we?" I asked hesitantly. "Friends?"

"More than friends," she whispered in the dark, and her words thrilled me, sent a shiver of barely contained excitement coursing through my body.

Especially one part of my body.

She couldn't see it, but she felt it, pressing against her thigh, and she reached out a small graceful hand and stroked me through my jeans. We kissed. Tongues. I slipped my hand under her blouse. No bra.

She was fumbling with my belt and unbuckling my pants. Her lips pulled away from mine, and she bent down and took me into her mouth. I'd never even kissed a girl before tonight, and the most I'd been hoping for this evening was maybe a feel, but now her face was in my lap and she was going to town. Her lips moved up and down my stiff organ, and then I exploded in her mouth with the biggest orgasm I'd ever had, pumping what felt like an endless geyser of sperm down her throat. She kept me there until I was spent and then slowly slid her lips off my softening penis, letting out a low satisfied moan. "Mmmmm."

She brushed the hair away from her eyes as she sat up straight, smiling at me. She pulled up my underwear, patting it, and I rebuckled my pants.

"Do you . . . would you . . . want to go out tomorrow night?" I asked.

"I'm sorry," she said. "I can't. Bill West asked me out last week, and I can't back out on this short notice. Not that anything's going to happen," she added quickly, snuggling against my chest and holding me close.

Bill West? If a girl like Sandra Fortuna was willing to go out with a dork like Bill West, I could have asked her out long ago. For once my dad had been right. If I'd only had the balls to act on my impulses, I wouldn't have been such a hopeless dweeb.

It was getting late, and while her parents hadn't said anything about a curfew, mine would go ballistic if I came home after midnight. So I drove her home and dropped her off. She told me to call tomorrow, but I lied and said I was busy. We kissed, and I told her I'd see her at school.

I made a point of looking up Bill West on Monday. We weren't friends by any stretch of the imagination, but as kids who'd gone to the same schools since the first grade, we knew each other. We didn't have any classes together this semester, but I found him during break, sitting on the low brick wall near the band room with a couple of his buddies.

I made as if I just happened to be walking by. "Bill," I said, nodding in greeting.

He glanced over. "Hey."

"I heard you had a date with Sandra Fortuna."

His friends started laughing. "Dude!" one of them said knowingly.

Something hardened within me. I suddenly knew where this was going, and though I didn't want to hear it, I had to. I stepped up to the wall, feigning sympathetic interest, as though we were all part of the brotherhood of guys and I wanted to hear the juicy details.

"She gave me a BJ," Bill said proudly. "On the first date!"

I felt as though I'd been punched in the stomach. I'd expected it, but to actually hear the words was still a shock. My first impulse was to throttle Bill, to grab his pencil neck and choke the life out of him, banging his head against that stupid wall until there was nothing left but a bloody pulp. Instead, I smiled, nodded and stayed to hear the juicy details. My heart grew hard as I heard the details of my own date repeated back to me by someone else.

I saw Sandra at lunch, and she gave me a bright smile from across the cafeteria, and a little girlish free-fingered wave. My face burned. I imagined her bobbing up and down between Bill West's legs, his cock in her mouth. I heard in my mind that satisfied moan she'd let out after swallowing my orgasm. "Mmmmmm."

I wanted to kill her.

Going back to my usual routine, I carried my lunch over to Robert and Edson's table, turning my back on her. She came over anyway, with bright smiles for all, and I sat there seething, saying nothing to anyone, eating my food. I didn't want to talk to her, didn't even want to see her, but when she got up to get a drink, I followed.

I cornered her by the vending machines. "How did your date go with Bill West?" I asked her.

She pushed my shoulder as if I'd said something ridiculous. "What are you talking about? Nothing happened."

"You didn't blow him?"

The words were out of my mouth before I realized I'd said them, and I saw her features darken. "What gives you the right to ask me that?"

"Nothing," I said, turning away.

I felt her hand on my shoulder. "Wait." Her voice was soft and filled with tenderness. She sounded so much like she had Friday night in the car after the movie that it made me feel sad. "I'm sorry," she said. "I didn't mean to bite your head off."

I just stared at her.

"Nothing happened with Bill. I swear to you."

"Nothing?"

"I swear."

Bitch.

I walked away, left my lunch on the table, hid in the boys' bathroom until the bell rang. That afternoon, I wrote a letter to her parents. It was two letters, really. One purporting to be from Mr. Vega, her Spanish teacher, explaining that he had intercepted a series of notes between Sandra and myself, expressing severe disappointment that such an otherwise outstanding student would behave in such a shameful, disgraceful manner. And one from me to Sandra, an example of the graphic correspondence he'd seized. Here I laid it on thick, describing how I'd fucked her hard and taken her up the ass, how she'd been the best I'd ever had, thanking her for taking the initiative to offer such exotic sex, saying, yes, I would recommend her to my friends and, yes, they would be happy to gang bang her if that's what she really wanted.

I dropped the letters in the mailbox.

"Good-bye, Sandra," I said.

2

I saw the witch downtown the following weekend when I hit the thrift stores looking for records.

She was still around and just as creepy as ever, giving me the evil eye as I passed by her in front of Rod's Camera Shop. I remembered that night with Robert and Edson when we were in grammar school and she pointed her cane at us and a pigeon dropped from the sky. She muttered something as I walked by Rod's that sounded like "Doan trite," and then the staccato clicking of her heels and cane were behind me.

I thought I was safe, but a moment later, when I looked back, I saw that she was following me. She'd been heading in the opposite direction, but now she'd turned and was on my tail, and though I was older now, I felt just as frightened as I had as a little kid. A cold shiver surfed down my spine.

Feigning a bravery I did not feel, I stopped and confronted her. "What do you want?" I demanded. My voice, thankfully, sounded very strong.

She held her left hand, palm up, and with her right began making scratching motions on the palm. It looked like she was . . . pretending to write.

My chill deepened.

Don't write. That's what she'd been saying. I was pretty sure it was the 'same thing she'd said to the three of us that night long ago.

She'd been standing by a mailbox, I recalled. And the bird that had fallen from the sky was a pigeon. Carrier pigeons had once been used to deliver messages.

No. This was getting too crazy. I was reading far too much into this, and I turned away from her.

"Don't write!" she screeched at the top of her lungs. Even people in cars turned to stare at her. "They'll find you!"

I had no idea what she was screaming about, and I didn't want to know. The woman was crazy. I hurried quickly away. Maybe she wasn't a real witch, but the truth was that she scared the hell out of me.

I decided to do something about it.

Flush with my success at creating a new college-bound persona for myself, ruining the reputation of Sandra Fortuna and turning back Acacia's tide of re-development, I wrote a series of letters to the mayor, city council and police chief decrying the presence of mentally ill people wandering the streets of our fair city and accosting ordinary citizens. *In particular,* I noted, *there is an old woman commonly referred to as "the Witch of Acacia," who walks throughout the downtown business district scaring away customers from our stores.* I repeated this sentiment in every letter, wording it slightly differently each time, then signed the letters with names that sounded like fine upstanding members of the community, slightly pompous Waspish names like "James R. Worthington" and "Graham Oswald." One I signed with the name of my old buddy Carlos Sandoval, president of the Hispanic Action Coalition, for some flavor and added weight.

Homelessness was now a major national issue, so it was on everyone's mind, but there was no consensus as to how it should be dealt with. The only thing all seemed to agree on was that the mentally ill who were now wandering our streets as a result of budget cuts that had closed outpatient clinics and hospitals should not be where children could come into contact with them—a point I made in my letters.

I told Robert and Edson what I'd done, and they were amazed by my audacity. The witch still creeped them out, too, and Robert said, "You better hope she doesn't find out who wrote those letters."

"Maybe she knows," Edson said.

"Jesus Christ," I told them. "She's not a real witch. There's no such thing."

"Remember the bird?" Edson said.

"Well, if I drop dead or turn into a toad or something, you'll know why. Tell my parents to sue her."

But the truth was that I *was* a little worried. I didn't believe in witches, but the old hag still freaked me out, even at my age, and I planned to make sure that if I ever saw her again, I stayed out of her way.

As it happened, I saw the police pick her up a little

over a week later. I'd mailed my letters over a period
of several days so as to stagger them and not make
them look so suspicious, and I assume the accumula-
tion of complaints caused the police to finally act. The
witch was doing nothing really, simply walking down
the sidewalk the way she usually did, in her weird
birdlike manner, but she was walking in front of the
high school and toward the junior high, and I guess
the proximity to children gave them the pretext they
needed. I was at my locker getting out my sack lunch
and putting away my math textbooks when I looked
out toward the street to see what the commotion was.
I watched two policemen get out of their vehicle, walk
up to her, talk for a few seconds, then lead her to the
backseat of the patrol car.

They drove away.

I couldn't be positive, of course, but I had a pretty
good idea of what had happened, and I immediately
tracked down Robert and Edson to tell them what
I'd seen.

"She's gone," I bragged to my friends. "The streets
are once again safe!"

I wondered what the police were going to do with
her, what they were going to charge her with, how
long it would take until she was back on the street. I
imagined her being photographed and fingerprinted,
wondered whether she'd be scared or angry. This was
all because of me, I thought.

But I didn't have much time to reflect on the day's
events when I got home. The house was in an uproar:
Tom was leaving. My dad was yelling at him from
down the hall and my mom was shrieking crazily in
the kitchen, but Tom emerged calmly from his bedroom, carried a suitcase out to the crappy Dodge Dart
he'd bought, then walked back in to pack more stuff.

"You never could plan ahead!" my dad was shout-
ing. "That's what's wrong with you!"

"Let him go!" my mom yelled. "Let him do whatever the hell he wants! I don't care!"

I didn't even want to get involved, and I walked back to my room and closed the door. I passed Tom in the hallway, but neither of us looked at each other or said a word. Personally, I didn't care what he did. Stay or go, it was all the same to me. I had no contact with him. With him gone, however, there'd be no one else to take the heat off when my parents went on the rampage. I'd bear the full brunt of their anger.

And judging from the screaming outside my door, that was going to start the second he was gone.

I hated my fucking family.

I wondered whatever happened to my friend Paul. I still missed him sometimes. And his family. I wondered, if he had stayed, whether we'd still be friends.

The next week was a living hell. My parents were angry with Tom, but he wasn't there so they took it out on me. My mom, in particular, would chew me out over every little thing, every minor infraction of her ever-shifting household rules. I spent as much time as I could away from home, at school or with my friends. I even lied to my parents and said that someone had called in sick and I had to work two extra nights at Gemco—I spent those evenings at the mall, wandering aimlessly from store to store just so I wouldn't have to be in that house alone with them.

I read in the local paper several days later that the witch had died in jail at the hands of another inmate who claimed to have been "hexed" by the old woman. The witch's name, it turned out, was the prosaic *Nora Wood,* which police discovered from a cache of letters found upon her person. According to the article she was a retired Thompson Industries file clerk whose electrical-engineer husband had died in 1975, leading to a spiraling series of mental problems. The reporter made no mention of the fact that Nora Wood had spent the last decade wandering the streets of Acacia and that a *lot* of people thought she was a witch.

The following afternoon, a Saturday, I received a letter. Luckily I went out to get the mail, because if my parents had done so, they doubtlessly would have thrown the envelope away. It was addressed only to *The Boy,* but everything else was perfect down to the zip code. The envelope's preprinted return address was *Acacia City Police Department,* and the second I saw it, I knew who the letter was from.

The witch.

Instead of making one phone call, she'd asked to write one letter.

I tore open the envelope, but the missive inside was disappointing. And confusing. There was only a sheet of official police stationery and on it the words *Stop now. Don't let them.*

I had no idea what that meant, but I did experience an involuntary shiver of fear as I read the cryptic note, realizing that the witch had been keeping tabs on me, that even if she didn't know my name, she'd known where I lived.

I had nothing to worry about, though.

The old bat was dead.

I went back and reread the article to see if I could find any clues that would help me decipher her message, but other than the reference to her cache of old letters, there was nothing.

I thought for a moment, then tore up both the envelope and her letter, flushing them down the toilet. They belonged in the sewer with the rest of the shit. Instantly, I felt better, as though I'd unburdened myself of some cursed object. Once more, I reread the article. The other inmate may have killed her, I realized, but I was responsible for her death. If I hadn't had her picked up—

Don't write!

—she would still be alive. Curiously, though, I felt no remorse. Instead, I was filled with a strange sense of power, the feeling that I possessed the ability—the *right*—to determine who lived and who died. It was akin to what I imagined doctors felt: the responsibility of deciding how to use a special knowledge or gift, whom to help and whom not.

Robert and Edson did feel remorse. They felt guilty just knowing how and why she'd been arrested in the first place, and for the sake of our friendship, I feigned contrition, pretended to be devastated by the news. But the truth was that I was proud, absurdly energized by this gruesome turn of events. I had slain one of my childhood boogeymen, and I felt good about it.

Again, I thought about writing a letter to my dad's work, getting him fired. The bastard had been on my ass constantly since Tom's departure. I was making almost enough at Gemco to cover my expenses, and I figured that if I did get a scholarship or some sort of financial aid, I could be out of the house and living on my own by September. I wouldn't need shit from that fucker.

So I did it.

I wrote a letter to Automated Interface.

The day he got fired, he came home drunk, the first time in several years, and he threw a water glass at my mom when she started calling him a weak, stupid, selfish prick. She spit on him, then swiveled on her heels and strode out of the kitchen.

I'd been standing by the refrigerator, having come in to get a drink, and I couldn't help twisting the knife.

"What does *God* think about this?" I asked him.

And he hit me.

He hit me in the chest, although I think he was aiming for the stomach, and I backed up, moving away from him. "What does God think about *that*?" I demanded.

"How dare you?" he roared, and came at me. I stepped aside like a bullfighter, and he was so drunk that he tripped over his feet and fell on the floor, bumping his head on the bottom of the stove. I could have hit him or kicked him while he was down—and, believe me, I wanted to—but that would have brought consequences later on. So instead I took the high road. I leaned down and said with as much disgust as I could muster, "You're pathetic."

Turning, I walked down the hall to my room, closing and locking the door behind me.

I lay down on my bed.

And smiled.

Five

1

Principal Poole actually expected me to show up for his SAC meetings and to participate. I found this out when I received a note from the office one Monday reminding me that the advisory committee met that night. Grateful for a legitimate excuse to get out of the house on an evening I wasn't working, I told my parents I had to go to the meeting and walked back to school after dinner. I passed the mailbox where the witch had stopped and pointed her cane at us before the pigeon had dropped from the sky, and I hurried on, shivering. I didn't feel guilty, but I felt responsible, and in that place, in the dark, I was more than a little spooked.

Don't write!

The SAC met in the biology lab. I'm not sure why the principal chose that particular classroom—it seemed kind of weird commandeering student seats and moving them close to the podium, since there were only five of us, and we could have met just as easily in the office conference room—but that's what Mr. Poole wanted, so I made my way down the darkened hallways, past the rows of lockers to the lighted rectangle that was the biology lab door.

The committee consisted of Mr. Poole, me, and

three annoying overachieving students whom I recognized from various assemblies and attendance-
mandatory events but didn't really know.

"We're very informal here," the principal said, and
indeed it was strange to see him in a casual sweater
rather than his usual uniform of suit and tie.

They started out discussing how to better publicize
the school's peer counseling program. They obviously
needed to publicize it better because I'd never even
heard of it. Mr. Poole suggested having the newspaper
do an article on the program. He looked at me, nodded and smiled, as though I'd come up with the idea.
One of the overachievers—Laci, a pretty, blond babe
still wearing her cheerleader outfit from earlier
today—thought we should recruit art students to make
posters.

"Make it a contest!" said Kay, one of those ultraor-
ganized girls who you just knew was going to become
a businesswoman. "Solicit entries from the art classes
and offer a prize for the winning design. We'll have
posters *and* generate buzz!"

I did not want to be here.

The next topic involved the type of surfacing material to be used on the parking lot, which was scheduled
to be repaved over spring break. Admittedly, I wasn't
that familiar with what the Student Advisory Committee was supposed to do, but this seemed way too technical for kids to be deciding. Nevertheless, a heated
discussion ensued, with Laci and Kay arguing vocifer-
ously for some type of coating made from recycled
plastic, while Timothy, the other boy, lobbied for
something cheaper and more traditional.

"What do *you* think?" the principal asked me. All
eyes turned in my direction.

I was clearly out of my depth. I mumbled something
about how this was my first meeting and I wasn't
really qualified to judge, but Kay broke in, "I'm sure
by now you have *some* opinion!"

I didn't really, but just because she irritated me, I said I agreed with Timothy.

The next hour and a half was spent in much the same way, with me being dragged into conversations I neither knew nor cared about, and it seemed to me that the goal soon became to trip me up or make me look stupid. I needed to beef up my résumé for a scholarship, but I wasn't sure if it was worth putting up with this crap. Mr. Poole wasn't any help to me, either. He'd drafted me into this, but now he was looking at me in a strange way I did not like. I was grateful when the meeting ended, and I got off campus as quickly as I could so I wouldn't have to talk to anyone after.

My parents were fighting when I got home, my dad drunk again, and I sneaked past them, coming in the front door rather than the kitchen door, and safely made my way to my bedroom undetected.

Two days later, I was called into the principal's office. I knew it was serious because I was taken out of PE. Call slips came to other rooms from the office quite frequently, but PE always seemed to be exempt—I assume because it was too much trouble to make kids change back into street clothes. I was summoned, however, and not allowed to change but forced to wear my gym shorts. I traipsed across the quad feeling foolish and conspicuous. Amid the over-dressed administrators and secretaries in the office I felt positively naked.

Mr. Poole was waiting for me.

He did not look happy. Leading the way into his office with a minimum of fuss and conversation, the principal closed the door behind me. He moved behind his desk and picked up a folder, not sitting down and not offering me a seat. "I was struck by your behavior at the SAC meeting the other night," he said.

I had a knot in my stomach, dreading what was coming next.

"I thought it odd," he continued, "that someone who was used to meeting with various community groups, who was supposed to have a special facility for getting competing organizations to share resources and communicate with each other, would be so ill prepared and obviously uneasy with the committee setting. So I did a little research." He turned on me. "There *is* no Sobriety Institute. There's no such thing. As for the other organizations listed in the letters we received about you, the two that actually exist have never even heard of you.

"You wrote those letters," the principal said, and the disappointment in his voice made me feel lower than I'd ever felt in my life.

I neither confirmed nor denied it. I simply stood there, exposed and embarrassed, the knot in my stomach tightening.

He stared at me in silence for several moments. "Do you have anything to say for yourself?" he asked finally.

I met his eyes and kept my expression blank, trying to mask the humiliation I felt.

"Go back to your class," he said, and I couldn't tell if that was weariness or disgust I heard in his voice. Both, probably.

I walked through the office in my gym shorts and T-shirt, sprinted back across campus to the boys' locker room and arrived just as everyone else finished showering and was putting on their clothes. "So what was it?" Frank asked. "What happened?" All of the eyes in my row were on me.

I thought of losing my place on the Student Advisory Committee, having my extracurricular activities struck from my record, not getting any grants or scholarships, being stuck in my parents' house. "Nothing," I said.

I went home that afternoon and wrote a letter.

2

Dear Ms. Gutierrez, Mr. Bergman, Mr. McCollum and other Members of the Board,

I don't even know how to tell you what happened to me. I am a freshman at Rutherford B. Hayes High School. XXXXXXXXXXXXXXXX Principal Poole molested me in the girls' bathroom XXXXXXX after school on Friday. He made me XXXXXX do things to him and he had sex with me. I can't tell my parents. I can't tell my friends. I can't tell anyone in the office. I want to kill myself. You're my last hope. It's too late for me, but maybe you can stop him before he does it to anyone else.

3

That was a hard one to write. I was tempted to go into more graphic detail, but I realized this wasn't a *Penthouse Forum* letter, and though my teenage hormones were urging me to insert the description of a hard-core sex scene, my brain was telling me to remain rational and focused. I didn't want to make it sound too cold and formal, though, and I worked hard at getting the tone right while divulging only what was necessary to take that pecker down.

The scratched-out sections were a last-minute addition, an attempt to show the girl's state of mind.

I kept it anonymous so they wouldn't be able to look up names or track down records.

Except it didn't seem to work. I gave the post office a generous three days to deliver it, then added another day for the board to discuss things, but a week passed and then another, and the principal was still in place and at his desk. Of course, there could be turmoil going on behind the scenes—a united front was always

presented to the students—but I needed to make sure
that Poole was ousted as quickly as possible, before
he had time to completely derail my scholarship plans.
I was sure that he'd told Zivney, and no doubt word
had spread among the faculty at Hayes, but I had the
superintendent on my side as well as the mayor. A
few judicious letters, and I could have this whole thing
turned around and working in my favor.

If only I could get rid of Poole.

I wrote another anonymous note. This one from a
secretary. This one to the board *and* the police. In
it, I discussed the principal's inappropriate behavior
toward female students. I pretended that I had been
in the bathroom a week ago and overheard two girls
talking about being forced to give him oral sex. I
wrote that I didn't believe it at first, but today, after
school, he met in his office with a female student who
had been caught smoking marijuana on campus. Instead of the automatic expulsion that should have happened, she'd been let off with a warning, not even a
suspension. And when I heard the noises coming out
of the principal's office, I understood why.

I said that I wished to remain anonymous because
I didn't want to jeopardize my job.

That did the trick.

I have no idea what was said behind closed doors,
but the upshot of it was that Mr. Poole resigned his
position and left the school immediately. *Immediately.*
No two weeks' notice, no farewell speech. I had
mailed my letters on a Tuesday, and by Thursday
morning his office was empty and he was gone. I know
because I entered the administration building for some
contrived reason or other every single day—to check.

I hoped that meant that he hadn't had time to tell
anyone else about his research into the Sobriety Institute, that he now had other, more important things on
his mind that would render that subject insignificant.

I only hoped he didn't put two and two together and realize that both my ascension and his downfall were accomplished by letters. It might make him think.

I should have had him killed.

That was the thought that occurred to me, and it didn't even give me pause. I still felt proud rather than abashed about my part in the witch's death, and I knew that if the need and the opportunity arose, I would not shy away from doing such a thing again.

I gave things a week to settle down, then started asking around, but since it was well into the school year, I was told, one of the vice-principals would become acting principal, and a new full-time replacement for Mr. Poole would not be hired until September. Mrs. Zivney would move up to the position of acting VP for the remainder of the year.

I calculated the angles. I was off the SAC, and Zivney no doubt knew why. But I now had a new counselor, Mr. Tate, and with all of her new added duties, I could probably stay under Zivney's radar. I could still apply for all of the loans and grants I'd originally intended to pursue.

Except that I needed a recommendation from someone impressive, someone higher up, someone farther along the chain than a teacher. Anyone from this administration was out of the question. Alerting one of them to my intentions could derail everything.

The mayor!

Yes. I'd sent him my original packet of letters, too, and I doubted that Poole had had a chance to talk to him about me yet—even if he had, Poole's reputation was now lower than shoe-wiped dog shit.

The mayor would work.

I still had a chance to escape my life.

After school, I told Robert and Edson I couldn't hang out with them, that I had something to do. I caught a ride with Frank, who passed by city hall on

his way home each day, and had him drop me off. I
should have called ahead, but as it happened, the
mayor was in, and he agreed to see me. A secretary
led me to his office, and I put on my Joe Humble act.
"Thank you for seeing me, Mr. Mayor. My name's
Jason Hanford and I'm a student at Rutherford B.
Hayes High—"

As I'd hoped, he remembered my name.

"Jason, of course! Our star humanitarian. How are
you doing?"

Had he been told? It didn't seem so. He appeared
genuinely happy to see me—or at least as happy as a
smarmy local politician could get.

"Oh, I'm okay," I said.

"What brings you by these parts?"

"Well, actually, I'm here to ask you a favor."

He suddenly grew more wary. The "Anything I can
do for you" that I was hoping to hear failed to materi-
alize. Instead, there was only a cautious, "Yes?"

"I need a letter of recommendation," I told him.
"For a scholarship application. I have one from my
English teacher, but I was supposed to get one from
Mr. Poole, too. Now he's gone. I could get one from
one of the vice-principals, but it would carry more
weight if I could get one from somebody higher up.
That's why I thought maybe I could get one from
you."

The recoil was almost physical, but his voice when
he spoke was smooth and calm, inflected slightly with
false regret. "I'm sorry," the mayor said, "but I can't
be seen as playing favorites. I was elected mayor of
the entire city. If I gave you a recommendation and
did not give recommendations to other students at
your school—or students at the other three high
schools in the Acacia district—then I would be saying,
in effect, that you are better or more qualified than
all of the other students."

Yes, I wanted to tell him. *That's the whole point. That's what recommendations are for.*

But I nodded as though I understood his predicament and sympathized.

He must have sensed how he was coming across. "Besides," he said, "I'm really busy right now. I'm not sure I'd have the time to do justice to your achievements. You'd probably be better off getting the superintendent or someone from the district to give you a recommendation. Or, better still, one of the community leaders you work with. It would make you seem more well-rounded."

"I can write it for you if you don't have the time. It won't be too gushing. It won't say I'm better than anyone else. It'll just say that I'm a good student, a valued member of the community, et cetera. All you'd have to do is sign it."

"I can't do that," the mayor informed me with insincere sadness. "It wouldn't be fair."

I nodded, said nothing.

You're going down, motherfucker, I thought.

The word processor was quiet. Not like a typewriter. It was loud when I printed—both the dot matrix and daisy wheel printers I'd purchased were quite noisy—but the actual keystrokes were practically silent. Still, as I wrote my letters to the city council, my dad banged on the door, yelling that it was late at night and I was disturbing his sleep and if I was going to wake up the entire goddamn house with my typing, then by God he was going to come in and smash my—

"You're drunk again," I said through the door, my voice dripping with disgust. "Go back to bed and leave me alone."

"Rick!" my mom yelled at him from down the hall at almost exactly the same time.

Amazingly, he retreated, returned to his room, left

me alone. I knew he'd been feeling guilty about losing his job, and shame over not being able to provide for his family had made him more compliant with my mom's bitchy demands. Even drunk and mean, he was still a shell of his former self, and I felt glad. No one deserved emasculation more.

I continued typing.

I'd been thinking all afternoon and all evening about how to take down the mayor, and I'd finally come up with a plan. I dusted off my old buddy Carlos Sandoval, president of the Hispanic Action Coalition, who had amassed an impressive array of statistics showing that under this mayor, the hiring and promotion of Hispanic employees had dropped to a historic low. There was a consistent pattern of discrimination that tied in with the mayor's aborted push to redevelop the Eastside. What's more, though they refused to come forward for fear of reprisals, several employees admitted privately to having heard the mayor use racial slurs.

I made this up off the top of my head, but I trusted that someone would investigate under the old where-there's-smoke-there's-fire theory and discover whether or not any of it was true. If there did happen to be some sort of hiring discrepancy, everyone would assume bigotry was the cause.

I sent copies of the letter to the *Acacia Ledger,* the *Orange County Register,* the *Los Angeles Times,* the other members of the city council, the city manager and the city attorney. Someone would bite, I knew.

It turned out to be all of them. Carlos Sandoval's diatribe appeared in both the *Times* and the *Register* unedited on exactly the same day—a first, I believe— and when the *Ledger* came out a few days later, it ran an article on the fact that Sandoval had dared to criticize Acacia's wonderful mayor. POISON-PEN LETTER CAUSES CHAOS, read the asinine headline on the front page. The editors were all part of the mayor's circle, cronyism at its most obvious and sickening, and it was with righteous indignation that I fired off a series of letters from various members of the public taking the *Ledger* to task for making more of an effort to discredit Carlos Sandoval than to investigate the charges he made. In my senior government class, we'd just finished talking about the role of the press in a free society, and I was genuinely incensed by the *Ledger*'s actions. My letters were filled with quotes from Thomas Jefferson and other First Amendment heroes, and I assume my passion shone through because all of the letters got in.

That surprised me. I mean, it didn't surprise me that the *Times* and the *Register* printed my letters of support for myself, but the *Ledger* was so actively hostile that I would have thought they'd want to silence all dissent. They printed my letters, too, though, and they even printed a *real* letter from someone who agreed with me, which was both shocking and thrilling.

I felt like I was making a difference.

I *knew* I was making a difference when the mayor resigned.

The resignation of a faceless bureaucrat from one of Southern California's hundreds of cities was not news enough for the *Los Angeles Times,* but the *Register* wrote an article about it and then a follow-up. The *Ledger* devoted its whole damn issue to praising the greatness of Peter Greene, the finest mayor Acacia had ever had, who, for some unspecified reason, had decided to quit his post in midterm in order to "pursue other options" and "spend more time with his family."

I smiled as I read the articles. *Serves you right,* I thought. *Teach you to mess with me.*

But I was back where I started—with no one to write me a recommendation. So I decided that I'd write my own recommendation. I don't know why I didn't think of it before. Why should I beg and grovel for the halfhearted endorsement of someone who barely knew me, when I could write a glowing testimonial to myself and attribute it to a person of truly impressive stature? Hell, the president of the United States could write me a character reference.

No. Public officials wrote on authorized stationery with embossed letterheads. I couldn't use the president or the governor or anyone like that. I needed a civilian, a very illustrious civilian.

I'd have to think about this some more. It deserved some serious consideration.

I had a dream that night, a strange dream in which I was walking along a dusty road in the middle of the desert. Before me was a lone circus tent, its colors faded by the sun, visible tears in the worn fabric. There seemed to be some kind of noise coming from the tent, a low, almost subliminal hum, but the sound was muffled by the heat, by the heavy oppressive air, and it did not increase in volume as I approached.

I reached the tent and walked inside, and there was a single ring made from chipped unpainted concrete. Wandering about in the cool darkness of the tent were children with gray hair and prematurely wrinkled faces, tiny terrors who walked around each other and passed by one another as though they were choreographed extras in a musical. In the center of the ring was the skeleton of what could only be some sort of prehistoric man, an apelike human with thick bones, hunched posture and a flat blunt face with protruding lower jaw. At the air-blasted note from an unseen calliope, the children gathered in a circle outside the ring, holding hands. They began to sing a song of praise, a lilting ditty somewhere between nursery rhyme and hymn, and I realized that this skeleton was their god.

I tried to back up, to make my way out of the tent without being seen. I knew that I would die in the desert, but that seemed infinitely preferable to remaining in here with these aged children and their skeletal deity.

I was almost to the door when the children stopped singing.

And the ape-man's skull swiveled toward me.

I awoke feeling both frightened and despondent, filled with a blackness I had not known before. I had the sense that I had narrowly escaped some horrible fate, that if I had not awakened but peered into the deepset eye sockets of that prehistoric skeleton, I would have been lost forever.

It took me several hours before I finally fell asleep again, and I awoke in the morning feeling tired and ill at ease.

The next day, I received a letter in the mail with no return address, the postmark *Los Angeles*. Inside was a handwritten letter that described my dream exactly, down to the last detail. It was extremely well written because it also captured the *feeling* of the dream, that nightmare sense of foreboding.

It was unsigned.

I read the letter again. And again. But the chill in my bones did not diminish. If anything, it intensified.

Folding the paper carefully, I put it back in its envelope and found for it a safe hiding place. *Who was this from? Why had they sent it? How had they known?* I had questions but no answers, and the more I thought about it, the more it frightened me.

I saved the letter, waiting for another.

But none came.

At least not for a while.

Six

1

Bill Tate
453 Palmera Dr.
Anaheim, CA 92801

Dear General Manager,
  I want you to know that I will no longer be watching KABC news. Your newscast was once my favorite, but I am so annoyed with your weatherman that I can no longer stomach watching the program. The inane chitchat of your anchors is bad enough, but your clownish weatherman is truly offensive to me.
  From now on, I will be watching KNBC.

Sincerely,
Bill Tate

P.S. I have a Nielsen box.

There is no one more self-congratulatory than a Southern Californian. It's as if living here automatically makes people jingoistic jerks. Each night on the local newscasts, comical weathermen act as boosters for the region, gloating about the mild temperatures, rhetorically asking the television audience why anyone would live anywhere else, in a lamebrain attempt to make people feel better about the smog and overcrowding, as though repeating over and over again how great we are, how fortunate we are, might make someone actually believe it. Two days a year, we can see the mountains located right next to us, and invariably the *Los Angeles Times* pastes a big color photograph of the miracle on their front page, along with some caption about how lucky we are to live in such a beautiful environment, apparently unaware of the fact that most of the United States sees such sights daily, not merely when the smog clears after a big storm.

Fuckheads.

Fed up with this mindless boosterism, I wrote letters to all three of the network affiliates complaining about their weather forecasters. I realized they were just weathermen (or a meteorologist, in the case of one), but since they were on a professional newscast, weren't they considered journalists, too? Shouldn't they make an effort to appear impartial? I must have made my point because, lo and behold, they stopped telling me the weather was "nice" or "good" or "beautiful," and just provided me with an objective description of the atmospheric conditions. For a week. Two weeks in the case of NBC. But then they went back to their usual rah-rah buffoonishness like a truck tire returning to a rut in a dirt road.

It became a game. As a linguistics instructor, I informed a male news anchor that the word *junta* was pronounced "hoon-ta," not "jun-ta" as he'd been saying, and was gratified when he caught himself on air and corrected himself. As an offended Japanese American man, I let a white female reporter know that *Hiroshima* was "He-roe-*shee*-ma," not "Hih-*row*-shih-ma," and chuckled to myself when she did a one-eighty on the word.

My dad still hadn't found another job, and sometimes I felt bad about that, but his insistence on re-

maining a complete asshole—hanging around the
house all day drunk, making no effort to look for
work—made it hard to feel sorry for him. He didn't
seem to be all Jesused out anymore—alcohol was once
again his crutch of choice—but he was the same nasty
fat fuck he'd always been, and even my mom had gone
out and gotten a part-time job at the Broadway, as
much to get away from him as to bring in some money
to the household.

I was asked to contribute, too, but steadfastly refused, relying on the old I-didn't-ask-to-be-born line
and letting them know that it was their responsibility
to take care of me.

At least until I could get the hell out of there.

In some ways, I thought, I was becoming like my
dad, which was not a prospect that filled me with great
joy. I was angrier than I used to be, though for no
real reason, and even my friends noticed that I didn't
seem to have much fun anymore. This was my senior
year. I should have been cutting classes and hanging
out and going to parties and picking up babes and
doing the things that everyone did during their last
semester in high school. Instead, I glumly went on
with my life, my only real enjoyment coming from
collecting records and writing letters, two solitary pur-
suits that led me even farther from the mainstream.

I'd decided that my fake recommendation would
come from Paul Newman. He was so famous that everyone would know who he was and be suitably impressed. He also stayed out of the limelight for the
most part, so my lie wouldn't be easy to track down.
To top it off, Newman was a philanthropist, well-
known for his charitable donations and work. His
words would carry weight. I went about creating my
recommendation with a dedication I had never shown
to my actual schoolwork. I could hear my mom's voice
in my head, telling me that if I spent as much time

and effort studying as I did writing fake letters, I might get somewhere in life. That was true, and I knew it was true, but here was where my interests lay. For example, although it was not something I would admit to anyone, I'd taken to reading "Ann Landers" and "Dear Abby" each day. I liked learning about people's personal problems, and finding out about them through their letters seemed particularly appealing. Of course, "Letters to the Editor" was still my favorite part of the newspaper—and not just because my own words were often printed there. This was where reporters didn't tell *us* the news, but we told *them* the news. It was a forum for the public to make clear its opinions and priorities, and I guess what I liked best about it was the fact that it could be so easily manipulated. One or two letters, properly written, could make it appear as though there were a huge groundswell for or against an issue.

Using my employee discount, I bought a papermaking kit from Gemco's arts and crafts section and used it to design a sheet of stationery based on a sample the instruction booklet called "Royalty." At the top, centered, gilt embossed, was Paul Newman's name. I'd considered adding a P.O. box number, but I didn't even know what state he lived in, and something like that could easily trip me up. I decided to keep it simple. The paper itself was expensive looking. Personalized. Off-white, rough and flecked with tiny pieces of olive green that made it appear to have been made from flower stems.

I did this in our backyard, making four identical sheets. My dad saw me working and muttered something under his breath that sounded like "pansy," but he was too drunk to really care what I was doing, and when I ignored him he went away.

It was pretty damned impressive, I had to admit. I dried the paper in my bedroom, and once it was fin-

ished, ran it through my word processor. I had purchased a special daisy wheel for my printer that typed
in cursive script, and I created four identical letters of
recommendation, signing them with a Paul Newman
signature I'd copied from a jar of Newman's Own spa-
ghetti sauce. The signature was the cheesiest part of
my presentation, the weak link that could potentially
give me away, but everything else looked so good that
the total package appeared completely legit.

In May, I found out that I had received the top
scholarship from the Edgar T. Dewbury Foundation,
awarded each year to reward philanthropic achievements by the state's high school seniors. It wouldn't
cover every expense, but it was a big chunk of change
and would enable me to both go to college and get
out of the house. A good thing, too, because I'd lost
out on all of the other scholarships for which I'd
applied.

That same day, a piece of mail was delivered to the
house, addressed to me. My mom had opened it before I came home, carelessly tossing the torn envelope
and crumpled contents on my bed. For all of the letters I sent out—I was buying *rolls* of stamps now,
rather than books—the postal service delivered precious little in return. Even junk mail seemed to avoid
me. It was almost as if there were a shield or force
field surrounding my person, allowing me to send but
not receive. The only letter in recent memory that I'd
been sent was the creepy missive describing my dream.

Which was why I approached this new arrival with
such trepidation.

I picked up the envelope first. There was no return
address and the postmark was so smudged as to be
unreadable. My name and address were on the front,
along with a series of strange, unrecognizable stamps
of low denominations, but . . .

But there was something odd about the writing,

something I could not quite put my finger on. The hand wasn't shaky, the letters and numbers weren't faint, but there was an element of both qualities in the printed address. I picked up the sheet of paper that had come inside the envelope. There was only my name, followed by a comma:

Jason,

It was as if someone had started to write a letter but had given up instantly. I stared at the paper, turning it over in my hands. The unfinished letter was disturbing in a way I could not explain and . . . familiar. Although there was no connection between the two, I associated this piece of mail with the description of my dream. Digging through the bottom drawer of my desk, I found that other letter and compared the handwriting on the two. I saw no similarities, but still the correlation continued in my mind, growing stronger if anything.

No. That wasn't it.

The witch's letter.

Yes! I hadn't saved it, but I never forgot correspondence, never forgot a type font or a signature or a style of handwriting. This one matched the witch's perfectly.

But she couldn't have sent it. She was dead.

I felt suddenly cold.

Although I hadn't wanted to acknowledge it, hadn't wanted to even consider it, I had been aware for some time that there was something . . . *unnatural* about my letter writing. Maybe *unnatural* was the wrong word. *Uncanny,* perhaps. Or *preternatural.* Or *extraordinary.* Even now, I can't quite communicate the subtle sense of heightened or augmented reality that I associated with my letter writing. But it was there—I felt it—and these two missives were of a piece with it, part of the same continuum. What did that mean? I didn't know. I didn't want to know. I didn't even want to think about it.

So I didn't.

2

Prom time approached.

Edson had had a serious steady girlfriend from October through April but had broken up with her over Easter vacation when he took a peek at her diary and found out that she'd been hitting on the UPS guy who delivered to her dad's office on weekends. Now he was scrambling around, trying to find a date. Robert had recently hooked up with Julie Bloom, whom we'd all known since grammar school and who was nice enough, if somewhat bland. Frank had been going steady with Liz Aldaca since they were both fifteen. I'd had a few scattered dates after Sandra Fortuna, but I'd gone through my senior year without getting seriously involved with anyone. My semicelebrity status still ensured that I would never be alone unless I so desired, and I asked out Holly Moch, a girl from my earth sciences class.

Holly was cute, but her nicey nice act had completely disappeared by prom night. She not only expected the usual corsage, expensive restaurant and official prom photos; she wanted a limo and expensive champagne and a whole bunch of outrageous luxuries. As far as she was concerned, this was her one and only high school prom and she was going to make the most of it. I made it clear that none of that was going to happen, and we reached a kind of truce before we got into my parents' station wagon and headed for the pavilion where the dance was being held.

The prom was fun in a ritualized school-sanctioned

way, and afterward we met up with Robert, Edson, their dates and a couple of Holly's friends at a coffee shop for some laughs and late-night discussion. We split up sometime after midnight. I drove back to Holly's neighborhood and parked the car in front of a darkened house a few streets down. There'd been jokes in the coffee shop about making out and back-seat sex, and while I had no plans to see Holly after tonight, there was no reason why we couldn't have a little fun.

She was obviously on the same wavelength because the second I turned off the ignition, she was all over me. She was already out of her dress, her bra came off with a quick snap, and then our mouths were meshed together, tongues working overtime. She pulled away, panting, obviously ready. I was already erect, but I told her to suck it first to make sure it was hard enough. I didn't really want to fuck her—it seemed like too much work—so I just surprised her and came in her mouth. She tried to pull away at the first spurt, but I was ready for that and held her head down until I was finished. Sighing with pleasure, I pulled out, satisfied.

I found myself wondering what Sandra Fortuna was doing right now.

Holly popped up like a jack-in-the-box, all angry and incensed, but I didn't care. I pulled up my pants and then drove her home, leaving her to desperately try to put on her own clothes while we passed down her well-lit street.

I drove back to my house feeling good.

The school year was almost done, and the last few weeks of the semester were a blur. Finals, yearbooks, award ceremonies, rehearsals.

Grad Night was held at Familyland. The amusement park was closed to the general public, and celebrating high school kids from all over Orange County were allowed to run wild within its borders. Prior to that, graduation ceremonies were held in the school's stadium. My grandparents didn't show up, didn't even bother to send congratulation cards, and of course Tom was nowhere to be found, but at least my parents came, and in front of my friends' families they even pretended to be loving and caring and normal.

Robert, Edson, Frank and I spent the night hanging out, along with our various dates. There was a sense of finality about the evening, a feeling that this would be the last time we would all be together like this, that this summer we'd all be moving on . . . and in different directions. The mood was celebratory but sad, and there was an undercurrent of melancholy to the party atmosphere.

Familyland was open for us until dawn, but I was already fading by one, and by two o'clock all I wanted was to find a comfortable place to sleep. I decided to hit the road and said good-bye to all my friends, who urged me to stay. "Take a nap on the train for a few swings," Robert suggested. "You'll get your second wind." But I didn't want my second wind, I wanted to go to sleep, and I told them I'd call them tomorrow. I'd stupidly hooked up with Holly again, but sometime during the evening she'd abandoned me for a jock from Loara High School. I didn't really care, and her defection made it that much easier to leave.

My dad beat the shit out of me when I got home.

I wasn't expecting it, and had no real idea what was behind it. All I knew was that when I walked into my room, it was trashed, the broken remnants of my word processor on the floor, and my dad was seated on my messed-up bed, glaring at me. I had about two seconds to take all that in, and then he was on me, swinging like a lunatic, fists flailing. I did my best to protect myself, but I was tired and caught by surprise, and he was focused and ready. I think he knocked me out, but I'm not sure. All I know is that one minute I was trying to block punches to my head, and the next I was waking up and it was light outside.

I hurt all over, but I forced myself to get out of bed and walk to the kitchen.

"What the hell happened to you?" my mom asked when she saw me. It was midmorning, according to the clock above the oven.

"He came home that way," my dad lied. The old man was sitting at the kitchen table, coffee cup in hand. "I asked him what happened, but he wouldn't tell me. Some type of graduation party fight or something, I guess."

"That's a lie!" I shouted. For one of the very few times in my life, I looked to my mom for comfort and support. "He did this! He attacked me when I came home, and he trashed my room! You can go see it!"

It was obvious she didn't believe me. "Jason." My mom's gaze was hard, her tone of voice disapproving.

"I want charges pressed!" I demanded. "Call the police! Have them take fingerprints!"

"I have never laid a hand on you," my dad said calmly.

I pushed my face an inch from his own. "You're a lying sack of shit."

But he did not take the bait. He turned his head sideways, took another sip of coffee, a small uncharacteristic smile playing about his lips.

I shoved the coffee cup into his face and was gratified to hear his roar of rage and pain as the hot liquid splashed onto his cheeks and chin, dripping down his neck. But I didn't stick around for the retaliation. I fled back to my room, slamming and locking the door, and waited there, trembling, fists clenched, for my dad to come barging in.

But he didn't.

I could hear the murmur of low conversation from

the kitchen, but no footsteps followed me to the back of the house and there were no screaming recriminations from either my mom or my dad.

I looked around my room, filled with a white-hot anger. This was it. This was the last straw. I was going to take my savings and my scholarship money and get out of this house for good.

Only that wasn't enough.

No. I wanted my dad to pay for what he'd done.

I wanted the bastard dead.

And I knew just how to do it.

Excited, I sorted through the jumble of debris on my desk and found a clean sheet of paper and an unbroken pencil. Last weekend, Rosita Aguilar had been killed, struck by a hit-and-run driver while walking across Seventh Avenue. As there were no witnesses, police were relying on friends and family of the murderer to come forward. I knew Rosita. Not well, but enough to speak to if we met outside of school. Her brother and boyfriend were both in gangs, and I knew that they'd rather have a chance at the man who killed Rosita than turn him over to the police.

I wrote to her brother anonymously. Disguising my handwriting should this note ever find its way to the police, making sure I didn't get fingerprints on the paper, I wrote that I'd been a witness to the accident . . . only it had not been an accident. A man had tried to pick up Rosita and she had refused. But the man wouldn't take no for an answer. When she started to run away from him, yelling that she was going to report him, the man put his car into gear and intentionally ran her down before speeding away. I got the license plate number *and* followed the car home.

I gave my dad's license number, our address and a detailed description of my father.

It wasn't the best or most believable story in the

world, but it was all I could come up with, and I wrote the letter with a passion that translated itself to plausibility. Later that day, when my parents were out, I got Roberto Aguilar's address from the phone book and mailed the letter.

The deed was done.

I'm not sure what I felt at that moment. Regret? No, definitely not that. I think I felt satisfied, the way a person would after successfully completing an important job. I walked back home. My parents had returned from wherever they'd gone, and I looked at them as I passed by the living room on my way to my bedroom. I felt nothing. No pity, no sadness, no remorse.

Days passed. A week. But I had no doubts, no worries that Rosita's brother would not take his revenge. I had faith. Faith in Roberto. Faith in my letter more than anything else. I might not be that confident or sure of myself in any other circumstance, but when I was at my desk, paper in front of me, writing, I was king of the world.

The following Thursday night, my dad was late coming home from the store.

It had happened.

I don't know how I knew, but I knew. He'd gone to Vons to buy some booze for himself and tampons for my mom, and he wasn't actually that late. He could have run into traffic, started talking to someone in the checkout line, anything. But the air around me felt charged, electric, and decidedly different.

He'd been killed.

I felt perfectly calm. Calm and a little bit . . . pleased. Strange, I know, but there it was. I looked down at the steadiness of my hands. I was like the godfather, I thought. I could order a hit on someone and it would come to pass—as long as I did it in writing. I sensed very strongly that it was only through letters that my wishes could be made real, that I could effect change. It was my writing that granted me this power, if power was what it was.

I sat there, knowing my dad was dead, and thought about all of the letters I'd written, all I'd accomplished. There seemed, in a way, something magical about it, and while I knew that such a mystical view of a prosaic activity like writing a letter was ridiculous, I couldn't help thinking along those lines. Like songwriters who claimed that they simply channeled music from some higher plane, I felt as though my letter writing tapped into a mysterious force far greater than myself.

The call came an hour later.

My mom had already worked herself into a frenzy, revving up for the fight she intended to instigate the second my dad walked through the door, and it took her a few moments to switch gears. When she did, the entire composition of her face changed. I watched her carefully, intently, as anger changed to sorrow— sorrow for herself. I don't know if she'd ever loved my dad, but at the moment she learned of his death, all of her feelings were centered on herself. I could see her thinking about the new responsibilities she'd have to shoulder, the extra work she'd have to do, the added financial burdens, and I was sickened by her selfishness.

When she spoke to me, though, after hanging up the phone, she was more of a mother than I could ever remember her being before. She came over and hugged me, crying, and when she told me that my dad was dead, the victim of a random drive-by shooting, when she asked if I was okay, she seemed genuinely concerned for my emotional welfare. But in the time it took me to hug her back and reassure her that I was fine, she'd returned to her usual bitchy self.

We separated, awkward with each other once again.

"We should tell Tom," I offered tentatively.

"I don't even know where he is," she said, and the steel was back in her voice. She glanced around the room as though looking for something. "I know he had insurance. I made him get it. I just hope to Christ it's all paid up." She began reciting a litany of my father's financial misadventures, working herself up again, the anger building, and I retreated to my room, pretending I needed some time to myself after receiving such devastating news.

In truth, I *did* need time to myself.

Time to plot my escape.

For there was no way in hell I was going to stay in this house with just my mom here. It was bad enough with both of them, but without another parent to deflect the anger and attention, I could not remain at home. I needed to find a new place to live. I broke out my calculator, added up my bank balance and my scholarship money, tried to figure out how much I would continue to bring in if I kept my Gemco job and took another part-time or even full-time position during the summer.

I needed to leave as soon as possible. Tonight, if I could. I wanted to be out of here before the funeral talk started, before concrete plans had to be made and I got sucked into participating. But what to bring? I would not be coming back, so I had to take everything of importance with me. And it all had to fit in a suitcase and a couple of sacks. That left out my record collection, though. And my stereo. I could live without my desk, bed and other furniture, and since my word processor had been smashed, it was no longer a factor. But I needed my tunes. I'd spent a lot of effort, a lot of time and money, building up my record collection, and I couldn't just abandon it.

I would have to leave tomorrow.

I called Robert and Edson while my mom went to

the coroner's to identify the body. I didn't tell them
about my dad, although they'd find out about that
soon enough. I did tell them I was moving out on my
own and needed their help. They were both impressed
and, I think, a little bit shocked. But they agreed to
come over tomorrow when I called and to help me
take out my stuff.

In the morning I waited, hiding in my bedroom behind a locked door, pretending to be sleeping deeply,
until my mom left to find a funeral home and make
arrangements. The moment she was gone, I called my
friends. I'd spent half the night piling up my records
and packing up my clothes, bagging my important
books and papers, and by the time they arrived in
Robert's dad's Cherokee, I was ready to go.

I could not face my mom directly, so I left her a
hastily written letter that explained I was gone. I had
the money I'd saved from Gemco as well as my scholarship funds, I assured her, so I'd be fine (not that
she really gave a shit). If we'd had a normal family, I
could have called up Tom, moved in with him, but I
didn't even know where he was living. And didn't
care. So Robert drove us around Acacia and Anaheim, Fullerton and Brea, looking for apartments.

We finally found a one-room studio in Orange, a
good ten miles from my mom's house, in an area she
never visited. Robert and Edson waited while I called
the number on the FOR RENT sign from a pay phone.
The owner agreed to meet me at the apartment in a
half hour.

"I still can't believe you're doing this," Edson said,
shaking his head. "Don't you think it's a little
drastic?"

I decided to spring it on them: "My dad was murdered last night."

Silence greeted my revelation. Neither of them knew
what to say or how to react. They knew that my old

man and I did not get along . . . but he was still my
dad. *What would they think if they knew I'd written
the letter that got him killed?* I wondered. I could tell
from the expressions on their faces that they were
even more confused about why I had decided to move
out of my house than they had been before. Abandon-
ing my mom in her hour of need? What kind of son
was I? What kind of *person* was I?

They didn't know what it was like living in that
house, I told myself, but still I knew I had to say
something that would get them back in my corner.

"My mom kicked me out," I lied. "My dad and I
might not have gotten along, but he was the only thing
holding our family together. Now . . ." I shrugged.

"Shit," Robert said sympathetically.

Edson just shook his head.

"So what are you going to do?" Robert asked.

"Hopefully work as much as I can this summer and
then go to college in the fall."

I don't know if my plan sounded naive to them or
merely unrealistic, but it was clear from their skeptical
expressions that they did not think it feasible. No matter. I needed them for the moment to help me trans-
port my belongings, but I was already starting to think
of them as part of my old life. I was starting a new
life now.

The studio apartment was fine, and most importantly, it was cheap. I took it. I showed the owner
proof that I was eighteen, signed the contract and paid
first month's rent, last month's rent and a cleaning
deposit in cash. At the last minute, I'd decided to
bring my mattress, box spring and bed frame, since all
of them would fit into the Cherokee, and I was glad
I had. It was going to be a while before I could afford
any furniture.

Hell, did I even need furniture?

Not really, I decided. As long as I had a place to

sleep, a roof over my head, a stove and a refrigerator, I was set. I also had my stereo, which would help make up for the lack of a television.

It took twenty minutes to unpack, another five or ten to put the bed together. The three of us stood there awkwardly, not sure of what to do or say next. Robert cleared his throat. "We'd better hit the road," he said. "I need to get the car back."

Both of them had homes to go back to, parents who cared. I understood that intellectually, but emotionally I still felt a little jealous. *You'd have a home to go back to if you hadn't had your dad killed,* a small voice within me said, but I ignored it and pushed it aside.

We said our good-byes; then I closed and locked the door, looking around my little one-room apartment.

Home.

This was now my home.

I walked over to the kitchen area in the corner, opening the empty refrigerator, turning on the water in the sink. I didn't even have a glass to drink out of, I realized. I needed plates and silverware, too. I moved to the bathroom, opened the medicine cabinet and the door to the tiny shower stall, took a piss in the toilet. Continuing my tour, I walked along the south wall, looked out the window at the street outside, checked the metal basket hanging beneath the mail slot.

And found a letter.

My fingers closed around the envelope, and I pulled it out.

It was addressed to me.

As late as lunchtime, I'd had no idea where I was going to stay, where I was going to live. I'd decided upon this place only at the last moment.

But there was a letter waiting for me, with a canceled stamp dated yesterday.

A chill passed through me. I wanted to drop the envelope, wanted to throw it away, wanted to leave and find somewhere else to live. But instead I looked at it, opened it.

There was no return address on the envelope, and the letter itself was cryptic. A brief generic *Dear Sir, This is for you.* Enclosed with the letter was a photograph. I saw the back of the photo paper first, the Fuji Film watermark, and for some reason I flashed back to Kyoko Yoshizumi. For a brief fraction of a second, I thought my old pen pal had tracked me down to resume our correspondence and had sent me a current picture of herself.

Then I turned the photo over and saw the circus tent from my dream.

The one with the ancient children and the prehistoric skeleton.

I dropped the picture, staring as it fluttered to the ground.

This is for you.

I didn't know what was going on, but whatever it was, it frightened me. I had a feeling that it had something to do with my dad's death—

killing

—and the letter I'd written to Rosita's brother. I felt like that character in "The Tell-Tale Heart," although it wasn't guilt that plagued me but the fear that I would be caught, that someone knew, that the letter would be retrieved and scientifically tested and it would be proved definitively that I was the writer, that I was responsible for the murder of my own father.

It was a conclusion that made no logical sense but felt true, and I decided to wean myself away from writing. Not for the first time, I was possessed by the distinct belief that composing letters brought me perilously close to the edge of something, a deeper layer or level of reality that most people were never allowed to see. The thought frightened me.

I had to stop, I told myself. I had to stop.

That night, I dreamed of a dark factory where skeletons sat at an assembly line pasting stamps on envelopes that passed by on a conveyor belt.

In the morning, there was an envelope in my mailbox with no return address.

I tore it up without looking inside and dumped the pieces in the garbage can in the alley.

Seven

1

The summer passed quickly, and in the fall I enrolled at UC Brea. It would not have been hard for my mom to track me down had she wanted to do so, but she didn't bother to make the effort and I was glad. I had no desire to see that witch again.

I found a work-study job and was lucky enough to be assigned a cheap dorm room on campus. I bought an old Dodge Dart from a guy on my floor whose dad had bought him a new Jeep.

Edson was at UC Brea, too, but we were in different classes, on different tracks, and we hardly ever saw each other. Robert had gone to UCLA and was living in Westwood. I was not sure what had happened to Frank. As I'd expected, as I'd known, we drifted apart without the glue of public school to hold us together.

But I didn't really care.

I settled easily into college life. I liked it.

2

Cowpunk. Paisley Underground. The music world became littered with the labels of subgenres that didn't stick, and thrift stores piled up with the records of one-hit wonders as the world shifted from vinyl to CD. I made out like a bandit, spending all of my discretionary income on music, expanding my record collection to include everything from ABBA to Zappa.

I briefly dated an unbearably pretentious girl who was into the Cure and Gene Loves Jezebel and who dressed in black emulation of Morticia Addams. "Music is entertainment, not a lifestyle," I told her, but the truth was that I took music far more seriously than she did, and it was *my* inability to disassociate her from her musical taste that eventually drove us apart.

In my spare time, I wrote letters to the *Los Angeles Times* and *Rolling Stone,* even *Pulse!* and *BAM,* two freebie music papers I picked up at Tower Records. I complained about music reviews, took writers to task for their lapses in taste and for having such a herd mentality and made suggestions about which music should be written about, covered and reviewed. Nearly all of my letters got in, even those I wrote under fake names, and to my surprise, my opinions actually seemed to have an effect on the content that appeared in these publications.

I found that I wanted to write only about music. What I'd done to my parents seemed to have left me with an aversion to writing about anything heavier or more serious.

Well, that and the letter I'd received with the photo of the circus tent.

I'd been skirting along a precipice I wanted to be far, far away from, flirting with something I didn't and probably couldn't understand. I had a talent, I realized, an ability to write letters and use them to effect change, to get done what I wanted done. But there was a dark undercurrent present, as well.

I wanted to write letters. I *needed* to write letters.

But I'd made a conscious decision that from here on out the subject matter would remain trivial.

And so I stuck to music.

It was the 1980s, the Reagan decade, and everyone in college seemed to be a business major. I had no major, no idea what I wanted to do with my life. I was tilting toward English because writing seemed to be the only skill I possessed, but my mind was open. I enjoyed the art history class I took, the cultural anthropology course, everything but math and the hard sciences.

In my freshman English class, an overview of modern literature, I learned that in the 1960s, the British playwright Joe Orton had invented two letter-writing personae, one a reader who loved his work and one who hated it. He proceeded to carry on a fake dialogue with himself in the press, alternately condemning his work and praising it in a successful effort to generate controversy and keep his name in the papers.

A man after my own heart.

A letter writer.

That cheered me up for some reason, kept me going.

I went by my old house sometimes, though I wasn't sure why. Nostalgia, perhaps. Or some subconscious desire to rewrite my recent past. My mom lived alone there now, and if my life had been a movie, the thought would have been poignant or melancholy or some damn thing, but the truth was that I felt nothing. I knew my mom. She was tough as steel and twice as cold, and I knew that even though my dad was dead and Tom and I were gone, she was fine, living her life as though nothing had happened.

I saw Tom once, by accident, but he didn't see me. He was at a Mobil station, getting gas, and he looked chubbier than I remembered. I was stopped at a red light, and I watched him emerge from the station office, go up to a car worse than mine and start pumping gas. He was wearing jeans and a T-shirt, and his hair was cut unusually short. I couldn't tell much about him from that brief glimpse, but I hoped he was poor, hoped he was alone, hoped he was unhappy.

It would serve the prick right.

At school, I spent a lot of time in the university library, where I checked out and read all of the Joe Orton plays I could lay my hands on. Walt Whitman, I learned, wrote fake reviews of his work and submitted them by letter to the major newspapers and periodicals of the time.

I read Whitman, too.

And I started writing real letters again.

It was all because of a political science class. The professor, Dr. Emerick, was the sort of wild-eyed Marxist caricatured in bad movies and feared by those who had never attended college. Intensely serious and fiercely intellectual, tall and gaunt with a huge gray beard that hung down to his chest, he was laughed at behind his back by most of his students, but his class was a lot of fun, and I enjoyed it. As part of our midterm, we were each required to write a letter to an elected official or the head of a major corporation, taking him to task for doing something we disagreed with. This was right up my alley, and despite my vow, I knew I could not resist. The temptation was too great. Besides, I rationalized, it was an important part of my grade. I *had* to do it.

So that night, I sat down in front of my IBM Selectric (I could not afford another word processor or a PC at this point) and quickly composed a critique of the governor's recent decision to increase university fees in California. I was taking a position I agreed with but also, more importantly, Dr. Emerick agreed with. The words flowed smoothly, the letter coming so easily that it seemed almost to write itself. I felt

energized as I pulled the paper from the roller and
signed my name at the bottom, more alive than I had
all semester. I wanted to write more. My roommate
was gone for the evening, partying as usual, and by
the time he returned sometime around midnight, I had
created nearly a dozen letters addressed to various
elected officials, newspapers and periodicals. My grade
was secure, I knew, but that wasn't the important
thing. The important thing was that I was writing
again. The dam was broken, and a torrent of words
flowed from my fingertips. Finished with topical
events, I still had a burning need to write, and with my
roommate passed out on his bed, I kept the typewriter
humming, churning out page after page of complaint
letters to all of the restaurants and stores I'd patron-
ized since the beginning of the semester, as adept at
manipulating businesses' fear of public opinion as I'd
ever been.

Within a month, the responses were rolling in.

I was back in the groove, back in the swing of
things. Threads I'd started in Op-Ed letter pages
continued to grow without me, some flowering into
full-fledged controversies with my help. I'd outgrown
McDonald's and Burger King; now it was IHOP and
Don José's and the Black Angus that sent me complimentary passes. My roommate, Don, and I suddenly
became much closer as the freebies arrived, and I soon
had a whole set of new friends with whom I went to
concerts and clubs, bars and meat markets, all thanks
to the medium of complaint letters.

A few well-chosen words of praise for myself in my
work-study job at the student store, a few negative
comments about some of my coworkers, and I moved
up the ranks from stock clerk to floor manager.

It was addicting. And despite what I'd done to my
dad, despite the fact that my previous efforts had
drawn the attention of . . . *something* . . . I kept on,

kept it up. This was who I was, this was what I was supposed to do, and if before I had *liked* college life, now I *loved* it. I was popular, my grades were up, and my soul was satisfied by the intellectual stimulation and emotional satisfaction I gained from writing letters.

All was right with the world.

But I kept an eye on my mailbox.

Just in case.

3

Music has resonance. When I listen to music, I'm taken back in time. Not to the time of the music's origin but to the time it entered my life. Rick Wakeman's *The Six Wives of Henry VIII* doesn't make me think of 1972, the year in which it was released. It makes me think of 1984, the year I found that album at a Garden Grove garage sale.

That was the year I went national.

It was a letter to *Newsweek* taking the president to task for what I saw as inconsistencies in his foreign policy. It was a position I held, but it was also one I knew would impress Dr. Emerick, with whom I now had another class. Mine was the lead letter, the one with a headline, and though the two letters below mine were on approximately the same topic, it was mine that inspired vitriolic responses the following week, including one from a State Department official clarifying what he saw as mistakes and mischaracterizations I'd made.

I lived for this stuff, and I fired off two replies, one under my own name and one under a pseudonym, making all of the readers who disagreed with me sound like uninformed morons, making the State Department official sound like a fascist jerk.

Two days later, I received a special delivery letter in the mail.

It was from the president of the United States.

Not a form letter on official stationery but a handwritten personal note on informal notepad paper signed by Ronald Reagan himself:

> *Dear Jason,*
>
> *I read your* Newsweek *letter critiquing my foreign policy and found it very interesting. Of course, I disagree completely, but I was very impressed by the way you put together your argument and by the way your letter flowed so naturally, so effortlessly, so gracefully. You are indeed a fine correspondent, and I admire your epistolary ability. Your pseudonymous defense of your initial letter was equally inspired, and a rather witty touch. I had a good laugh over that one. . . .*

My heart lurched in my chest. I felt shocked and bone-deep embarrassed, as though I'd been caught masturbating.

He'd recognized my fake letter?

I didn't know how that was possible, but it was true. Reagan had somehow seen through my sham and caught me. From all indications, the man was not the brightest bulb in the pack, yet he'd figured out what none of *Newsweek*'s gatekeepers had been able to notice.

His own letter was not too shabby, either.

I continued reading:

> *. . . I would like to invite you to visit me at the White House. I believe you and I would have a lot to talk about. I cannot of course offer you a ride on* Air Force One *(ha-ha),*

*but I would love to put you up in the Lincoln
Bedroom for a night or two if you could make
your way out to D.C. I think the two of us
would get along swimmingly.*

He signed the letter *Ronnie.*

I read the message again. And again. And again. I
didn't know what to make of it, didn't know what to
do. I thought about the president's offer, considered
it, and discussed it with Don and Dr. Emerick and
some of my newfound friends, all of whom were impressed as hell by the invitation. It was true that spring
break was coming up, and I had coupons for free stays
at a variety of hotel chains, but I still wasn't sure I
wanted to go. The problem (though I refused to admit
it to anyone) was that I couldn't speak as well as I
could write. In letters, I could debate with the best of
them, but in face-to-face conversation with the movers
and shakers of Washington, D.C., I was afraid that I'd
come off as the wiseass punk I really was.

It was Dr. Emerick who convinced me to go. He
stood before me in his office at the top of the Humanities Building, put both hands on the arms of my chair
and, through the tangle of hair that covered his face,
looked into my eyes. "This is your chance to speak
truth to power," he said, voice filled with emotion.
"Don't squander it. You can make a *difference.*"

I looked at him, met his eyes, nodded. "Okay," I
said.

But I didn't do it.

Don wanted to come, but I decided I'd rather travel
alone. So I loaded up the Dodge Dart and headed
east, not planning an itinerary, intending simply to
drive until I got tired and felt like stopping.

I thought it odd that the president would take my

words so seriously. Hell, he was attacked in print every day in newspapers all over the nation. His popularity was sinking, and there seemed to be a lot of people who thought his policies as disastrous as I did. Why would he single me out for a meeting?

But I guess I knew the answer to that already. It was the same reason I received free passes and complimentary tickets when I complained and other people got thank-you-for-your-opinion form letters, the same reason my letters were printed in the newspaper when others weren't, the same reason—

my dad was killed

—I got results when I took on city hall.

Because I had a talent for writing letters.

I got as far as Las Vegas before deciding to turn around.

I couldn't go home. Not yet. Don and Dr. Emerick and everyone were expecting me to bravely and perhaps quixotically take my case—*our* case—to the president, so to maintain the illusion, I would have to be gone at least a week. So, once back in California, I headed north. As before, I had no plan, and as it was starting to get dark when I reached Santa Barbara, I decided to stay there for the night.

The next morning, as I was checking out, the desk clerk said that he had a letter for me. That was impossible. I'd chosen this place at random. No one knew I was here. But he reached under the counter, and sure enough, there was an envelope with my name and room number on it.

"Who gave you this?" I asked, turning it over in my hand. I saw no stamp or postmark; it had obviously been hand delivered.

"It was here when I came on duty this morning," the clerk told me. "I could ask Dane. He was on night shift."

"Could you do that, please?"

The man—Otis, according to his name tag—picked up the phone and dialed a number. After a wait that must have encompassed twenty rings, the call was finally answered, and Otis asked Dane who had dropped off the envelope. Someone he'd never seen before, Dane reported, but he didn't really remember what the guy looked like or how he talked. I thanked the clerk for trying, paid for my stay with a corporate card that still entitled me to three more nights at any Ramada Inn nationwide, then went outside to my car, where I opened up the envelope.

I read the letter. It began, *Dear Jason,* but what followed was a bizarre present-tense second-person description of a sexual encounter with a beautiful woman. (*She is sopping wet, and she spreads her legs wide and pulls your head down to gently kiss her labia. . . .*) What the hell was this? There was no doubt in my mind that it was connected to those other letters I'd received, the ones associated with my dreams. This time, however, the sender had missed the boat. I'd dreamed of nothing even remotely similar, and there was nothing in the strange letter that jogged any part of my memory.

Maybe this was different; maybe it was predicting a dream I would have in the future instead of confirming one I'd had in the past. Of course, now that I'd read it, I might have such a dream because the idea had been placed in my head. So there was no way that would prove anything.

Maybe it was predicting something that would really happen.

No, that was ridiculous. Yes, it was amazing that whoever had written this letter had found me, but this time he'd missed his mark. I tore up the envelope and its contents, tossing them out the window of the car as I hit the highway.

The only thing is . . .

It happened.

Just that way.

I met the woman in San Francisco. She was a waitress at the hotel coffee shop, and something about her reminded me of old Sandra Fortuna from high school. Thinking of Sandra got me thinking about sex, and looking at the waitress, I imagined doing her. It had been a while, and I had to admit the celibate routine was growing old. Something told me I had a chance here. The waitress, Jolene, had no rings on her fingers, and she seemed to hover around me more than any of the other patrons, so I stretched out my dinner, eating slowly, sipping refill after refill of iced tea, ordering a piece of pie for dessert, even though I was full and didn't really like pie all that much. Finally, as I paid my bill, I got up the nerve to ask what time she got off work. "Nine," she said, smiling, and I took her pen and wrote my room number on the bottom of the check.

There was a knock on my door at 9:08.

She was indeed wet down there, and, yes, she pulled my head down to kiss it. I did so hesitantly, tentatively, while she sucked my cock as though her life depended on it. This, too, was predicted in the letter, but at that moment I didn't care, and it was only after I'd finished that I began to reflect on the eerie synchronicity of it all, on the fact that dark elements seemed to have left the page and entered my life.

Indeed, the very next day, I saw a homeless man hit by a pickup truck in fairly heavy traffic. The driver stopped and there were plenty of other people around, but as I passed by, the homeless man, bleeding from his mouth, turned his head to look at me—and smiled. It was spookiest damn smile I'd ever seen, and it remained with me throughout the day, even as I passed by a field littered with the carcasses of dead cows, and saw a pigeon fall out of the sky and land on the table next to me outside a McDonald's.

The witch.

I couldn't help thinking that all of this was letter related, and I did not relax until I finally stopped at a TraveLodge late that afternoon and checked into my room for the night with the admonition to the desk clerk that I was not to receive any messages, that any notes or letters addressed to me were to be immediately thrown away and I was not to be notified.

I was happy to get home, and I made up an elaborate lie about my trip to Washington, D.C., telling everyone how a black town car with a driver picked me up from my hotel and took me straight through the White House gates, where I was led directly to the Oval Office.

I didn't like Nancy, I told them. Her Stepford smile gave me the creeps. But the president was warm and easygoing, and the two of us hit it off. Although he was a good half century older than me, we were comfortable together, and there was none of the awkwardness I sometimes felt while talking to people I considered adults. We'd always thought that Reagan was a nice guy but a little dim, that he'd be a good neighbor, someone you could trust to water your plants and feed your dog while you were on vacation but not exactly the kind of person you'd want running a country. I saw nothing to contradict this preconceived notion. He listened to my arguments but didn't comment or have any visible reaction, and when I was finished, he blithely offered to tour me around the White House.

"Typical," Dr. Emerick muttered.

My story was believed in full, and for a brief period of time, I even became something of a minor celebrity on campus.

The strange thing was, Reagan and I actually began a correspondence.

It started when I wrote a letter apologizing for not

being able to visit him. He wrote back, joking that now he wouldn't be able to change my politics with his breezy charm and Teflon smile. I replied that now I wouldn't be able to change *his*. I added that my initial letter had been a class assignment and my follow-ups had been something of a lark. I told him I'd been wondering why he'd invited me to the White House and semiapologized, saying that if my letters had upset him so much that he'd felt obligated to summon me to Washington, D.C., perhaps he was taking my words a little too seriously.

I'm not upset, Reagan wrote back.

> *But we take all letters seriously. Each letter a person writes represents five thousand people who don't write. Or ten thousand. I forget the numbers and I'm too lazy to look them up. But you can be sure that if one person takes the time to complain about what I said or did, there are a lot of other people who feel the same way but just don't make the effort to do it.*

I thought of that playwright, Joe Orton, writing letters about himself. There must be a lot of us out there writing fake letters, I reasoned, and I found myself wondering how much of the world that was presented to us through politics and the media had been influenced by letter writers. Maybe we spoke for others, maybe we didn't (my guess was that we didn't), but either way, we wielded a disproportionate amount of power.

I realized that I had begun thinking of myself as a Letter Writer—with a capital *L* and a capital *W*. A lot of people wrote letters; a lot of people probably wrote a lot of letters. But most of them did so for fun, for work, to communicate. How many did it because they *had* to? I did, and I found myself wondering if there were others like me, men and women who had this compulsion, this need to write.

I asked Reagan once if there were other constituents with whom he corresponded on a regular basis, but he never answered that question, and though I brought it up again from time to time, I never received a response from him. On some subliminal level, did he know, could he guess, that my letters were different from the others he received? Did he have any clue that he was being manipulated into writing to me, that it was not my personality or my ideas or any ordinary attribute that was compelling him to respond but instead the letters themselves weaving a sort of spell on him?

Gradually, I stopped writing to the president. I'd begun to feel like a fraud. I disagreed politically with Reagan on nearly everything and while we sometimes touched on politics in our correspondence, we stuck primarily to superficial banalities. It didn't seem right to hog his time this way, since neither of us was really getting anything out of it, so I called it off, let it slide.

I missed him, though.

I really did.

Eight

1

Letter Writer.

Just what was that exactly? What the hell did it mean? I spent the rest of my sophomore year trying to figure out who I was, paying only enough attention to my studies to make sure I made the minimum grades to remain in school. I even tried to stop writing, though it was the hardest thing I'd ever done.

I took two jobs in the summer, and it was a relief to be so busy. I was becoming far too introspective. I needed to stop thinking about myself and my problems all the time and just get out and do things, live my life like everyone else was.

But I had too much invested in my letters to stay away from writing. They'd delivered me from my parents' house, they'd vanquished my enemies, they'd brought me money and food, and before the fall semester, I was back before the typewriter and the mojo was working again. I even fell into a Cyrano-like arrangement where I helped Don write letters to a long-distance girlfriend, trying to keep her happy and not suspicious as he fooled around with bimbos that he met in local bars. But I received another one of those unmarked envelopes in the mail the night after I had a terrifying dream about my mom hiring Tom to hunt me down and kill me. I tore it up unopened and flushed it down the toilet, but vowed to write less, to stay off the radar of whoever—

whatever

—was watching me.

Two letters a week, I decided. That would be all. *Moderation in all things.* It seemed a good rule to follow, and it actually seemed to work. My life balanced out a bit. I indulged my desire, fufilled my need, but didn't let it overtake the rest of my life.

My junior and senior years were happy and uneventful.

That's the way I liked it.

That's the way I wanted it.

2

I met Vicki Reed on my first day of grad school. I'd earned my BA in English but was going after an MA in political science, having decided that I would become a high school teacher, and though I'd taken quite a few poli-sci courses, I still had a couple of undergrad makeup classes to finish in order to meet the requirements. Vicki was petitioning for a linguistics course along with me, and for the entire duration of the first session, we both waited in the hallway while the quirky teacher—who obviously had plenty of spaces available—pretended we did not exist.

We chatted while the professor took roll and performed required first-day bookkeeping duties. From another room across the hall, the office of one of the humanities professors, came the sound of music. I leaned back, peered into the open doorway and saw a stocky man with a thick walrus mustache and a graying ponytail. "*Terrapin Station.* The Grateful Dead," I said, identifying the music.

Vicki groaned. "Oh, no. You're not one of those, are you?"

"Those what?"

"Those freaks who know the name of every song on every album by every band."

"I am," I said proudly. "Or at least that's my goal."

"Why?" she asked.

That threw me, and before I could even come up with an answer, she said, "I don't think music should be named. It should just be heard."

"But . . . but then how would you know what to buy?" I asked. "If you hear a song you like on the radio, you have to be able to tell the person at the record store what it is."

"I suppose that's so," she conceded. "But I have nearly a hundred classical albums that were given to me by my dad. I love them all. I don't know the names of any of them, but I love them."

I was incredulous. "But you *have* to know."

"Why? When I'm in the mood, I put one on and listen to it. I don't love it any less because I don't know the name of it. And besides, I've always felt that people memorized music trivia just so they'd be able to impress other people in conversation. What does the name of a piece have to do with anything?"

"Because if you want to hear a *specific* piece of music, you have to be able to select it. Music is not all the same. Sometimes you're in the mood for something fast or slow, or maybe a particular song will go with a particular mood you're in. You can't just grab records at random and put them on."

"I do it all the time."

She was exasperating.

Exasperating but interesting.

And very pretty.

I asked her out on a date.

We both got into the linguistics class, and after everyone else left and we'd been officially added to the roster, we celebrated with coffee at the student center. Sort of a predate date. We talked easily, there were no awkward pauses, and we left each other wanting more. That night, we'd intended to go to a movie—a revival of *Serpico* at the Student Center Theater, with Frank Serpico himself scheduled to speak afterward—but dinner stretched out longer than we'd intended, and we spent another half hour talking in the parking lot before getting into the car, and by that time the movie was half over. Instead, we drove to a nearby park and walked along the trails before settling down on a bench beneath a lamppost to watch the lovers stroll and the joggers jog and the moon rise from behind the nearby condominiums.

Was it love at first sight? Not exactly. But pretty damn close. I'd gone out with a lot of girls in my four years at UC Brea—I'd had sex with a fair number whose names I either never knew or forgot before the end of the evening—but I had never *connected* with anyone like this. It was a cliché to say so, but I really did feel as though we'd known each other all of our lives; the comfort level was that high. It made me sad, too, in a way, made me think of Robert, Edson and Frank, the friends of my childhood whom I'd allowed to just drift out of my life. I'd not been as close to anyone since, and being with Vicki made me realize how much I missed it, how much I hungered to be intimate with someone again.

After that first night, I was sure that she was the person I wanted to be closest to.

She told me she loved me on our third date. I told her I loved her, too.

The semester sped by. I thought about her constantly, we were with each other as much as humanly possible, but surprisingly, our grades did not suffer. If anything, we were good for one another—when we studied together, we actually *studied*—and in the linguistics class we were both headed for easy A's.

Would she like love letters? I sometimes wondered.
Of course. All girls did, pretty much. I desperately
yearned to write to her, knowing that I could express
myself much better in print than I ever could in person. But there was no way to correspond with her that
didn't seem forced and awkward. If one of us were
going on a trip or something, if we were going to be
apart for even a single weekend, I could justify writing
her a letter. But we were both here and we spent all
of our free time together, and it was impossible to do
without it seeming strained.

At my insistence, we took an extended-ed class together for fun: "Music Theory for Non-Music-
Majors," a more in-depth version of the music ap-
preciation course that was one of the general-ed requirements. It was there that I learned about Philip
Glass and John Adams, Steve Reich and Meredith
Monk. But the real discovery was Daniel Lentz. A
West Coast composer who'd taught at USC and UC
Santa Barbara, Lentz wrote music that touched me,
that affected me, that made me think and made me
feel, that just deep down amazed me. I don't know
how or why, but as I listened to the piece the teacher
played, I was stirred in a way I had not been in a
long, long time. The piece was called *the crack in the
bell,* and the text was from an e. e. cummings poem
titled "next to of course god." There were all the trappings of minimalism—repetitive synthesizer lines, clear
operatic female voice—but it came together in such a
way that even sitting there in an uncomfortable desk
in a crowded classroom, I felt excited, as though I'd
discovered something new and entirely original, and
for perhaps the first time in my life I understood how
people became passionate about art. I wanted everyone to hear this music and I wanted them to feel about
it the way I felt.

Vicki reached for my hand. She understood, too! I
squeezed her fingers, met her gaze and smiled, and

after class, I asked the teacher if I could borrow the Lentz album. Although he said no, he promised to make me a cassette tape, which he gave to me at the next session.

Vicki and I both became huge fans, and as much as anything else, it was this shared aesthetic that cemented our bond, that let us know we were meant for each other.

Just as you start seeing vehicles identical to your own once you buy a car, I started finding Daniel Lentz albums in my trips to used-record stores now that I knew who he was. I picked up a CD of *the crack in the bell* at a shop in Anaheim and found two vinyl albums—*Missa Umbrarum* and *On the Leopard Altar*—at Music Market in Costa Mesa. Although she refused to learn the names of any of his compositions, I considered it a personal triumph that Vicki knew the album titles, and between me and the class, I think she started coming around a little to my way of thinking.

We each tried playing Lentz's music for our friends, but even our most musically adventurous acquaintances did not seem to get it. His work spoke to us, though, and the exclusivity of our passion pulled us even closer together.

During intersession, Vicki went home to Phoenix, spending two weeks there with her parents for Christmas, while I remained in my dorm room as usual, pretending the holidays weren't happening. My mom and Tom were somewhere in Orange County, probably still in Acacia, but I made no effort to contact them and they did not contact me. I doubted they'd even spoken to each other since Tom left home. Almost all of my other friends and acquaintances were with their families for the holidays, as well, and the ones who weren't were the ones I couldn't stand being around for very long.

This was my chance to write to Vicki, and I took it.

In the movie *Roxanne*, Steve Martin admits to Daryl Hannah at one point that while she was away on a trip, he wrote her a letter every hour or something equally fanatic. It was a line meant to make the audience laugh, but to me the idea was heaven, and it was what I wanted to do with Vicki.

For some reason, though, I held back. Not in quantity: I wrote her each morning and again each night. And not even in quality: my letters were good, heartfelt, sincere. But I didn't put that extra effort into them, that little bit of alchemy that would have pushed them over the edge and made her beg for more. I told myself it was because doing so would be cheating and I wanted to win her fair and square. Maybe there was a little of that in it, but mostly I didn't want the taint of my letter writing touching our relationship. For there *was* a taint. Letter writing was not some harmless pastime, was not even a blessing or a gift. It wasn't exactly a curse, but that was closer to the truth than anything else. Simply put, I did not want the darkness of my letter writing to infect our life together.

When she returned to Brea, we decided to move in together. The letters I wrote had helped seal that deal, but we'd been talking about it even before she left, and being apart made us realize how much we wanted to be with each other. We wouldn't be allowed to live in a dorm, which meant that I'd lose my work-study discount since I'd be living off campus. Vicki, though, had a friend who was a real estate agent, and that friend found us a great deal on a sublet apartment fairly close to campus.

All was right with the world.

Almost.

The week before classes resumed for the spring semester, Vicki received notice in the mail that she was about to lose her scholarship money because, although her GPA was high, one of the courses she'd taken the previous semester was not eligible for inclusion, according to the award committee. It was a squirrelly scholarship to begin with, I thought, sponsored by Vicki's father's aerospace company, but she needed the money to attend grad school. She had a killer internship lined up, one that could lead to a great job if everything played out as planned, but if she lost the scholarship, she'd have to drop out for this semester— at the very least—and that would cost her the internship and the job.

She cried after reading the letter from the committee, sobbing on my shoulder that she didn't know what to do, that she'd had no idea certain courses were acceptable and others weren't. She'd just assumed that since it was a scholarship based solely on merit, she would receive the money for the entire time she was in graduate school, no matter what. Yes, she had to provide the committee with copies of her transcripts at the end of each semester, but she'd assumed that was a mere formality.

"What's going to happen now?" she asked, her voice catching. "I'm screwed."

"It'll be all right," I said reassuringly.

"How?" she demanded, the tears still streaming down her face. "How will it be all right?"

"I'll take care of it," I promised. "Leave everything to me."

She looked at me hopefully. "Really? Do you think there's something you can do?"

"I have an idea," I told her.

Dr. Edward Lebowitz, PhD

Dear Sirs,
I understand that you are planning to with-draw scholarship support from Vicki Reed, perhaps our most promising student of the past

six years. Without bothering to audit my course or even talk to me about its stringent academic requirements or practical applications vis-à-vis Ms. Reed's intended profession, you have taken it upon yourselves to capriciously decide that Ms. Reed does not deserve to maintain her scholarship because my course does not meet your standards. May I ask what standards those are and who makes the determination as to whether my class meets them?

Vicki Reed will not be able to continue attending UCB without the financial assistance provided by your scholarship and promised her. The university is not willing to lose a student of her caliber without a fight, and rest assured there will be a costly, protracted and very public battle should you decide to withdraw your support of this outstanding student. I, personally, take offense at your casual dismissal of my class and my work. I have been an instructor at this institution for many years and have never before encountered such disrespect for my person or my professional standards. I urge you to reconsider your decision before I bring the president of the university, the Office of Admissions and numerous lawyers into the fray.

Yours truly,
Edmund Lebowitz

3

I kept it from her, my letter writing. Vicki was completely honest with me, telling me of her past mistakes, her little quirks, voluntarily exposing to me her every potential fault, wanting me to know her inside and out: the good, the bad and the ugly. But I withheld this part of myself, the most essential part, who I really was, instead passing myself off as a normal guy who was planning to become a teacher.

Vicki was an inveterate letter writer herself (though not, I might add, a Letter Writer). A political activist heavily involved in the nuclear-freeze movement or what passed for it in suburban Orange County, she was always signing petitions and writing letters to congressmen. I could have helped her. I could have lent an expertise to her causes that I knew no one else had. But I didn't. I got her scholarship back for her, and I was willing to do whatever I needed to do if she was ever personally in trouble, but writing letters for me was like playing with dynamite—sometimes it was effective at clearing rocky trails or blasting tunnels through mountainsides, but it could also blow up unexpectedly, leaving limbless bodies in its wake. I couldn't afford to use it for anything that wasn't absolutely necessary.

Although sometimes I got us tickets to plays in Los Angeles or comped meals at nice restaurants by the beach.

Old habits die hard.

While I'd desperately wanted us to move in together, I'd also felt more than a little trepidation about it. Dating was one thing; living with each other twenty-four hours a day was something else. All right, it wasn't quite twenty-four hours a day. But it was pretty damn close. We were both students at the same university; we had one class together; we'd arranged our other classes and work schedules so we'd be able to spend as much time as possible with each other. It wasn't inconceivable that we might start to get on one another's nerves.

We didn't, though. That was the amazing thing, the wonderful thing. Our lives expanded to include each other, and the more time we spent together, the better we got along and the happier we were.

I started keeping a journal. It was almost like writing letters, and I used the traditional "Dear Diary," in an attempt to quench the burning need within me and satisfy my habit. I liked it, but it wasn't enough, and soon my spare moments were spent scrawling complaint letters to professors and administrators at school, dashing off letters to the school newspaper. I tried to keep my concerns small, my focus local, but it was hard and I did not always succeed.

"Love is all you need," the Beatles sang, but in my case it wasn't true. I *wanted* it to be true. I *wish* I could say that when I was with Vicki she was my everything and I never even thought about writing letters, but the fact was that my girlfriend and my correspondence satisfied two different desires, appealed to two opposing impulses. I needed both.

Then one Thursday, I came home from work and found Vicki sitting on the floor in the middle of our small sitting room, surrounded by scores of opened letters and clipped newspapers. She'd found my archives, my stash of letters—originals, Xeroxes and published versions—and from that, she'd obviously pieced together a picture of what I'd done, what I'd accomplished.

She looked up at me as I entered the room. "You never told me about all this," she said accusingly. "You never let on that you were so politically active." She picked up a Carlos Sandoval letter. "That you fought city hall and won." She threw the letter down, standing amid the pile of papers.

I was angry. My privacy had been violated. But at the same time, I felt guilty and ashamed. I *had* kept this from her. So it was with a sense of relief that I admitted all, that I answered her questions about the chronology of events and how I'd impersonated people from fake organizations.

But still . . .

I held things back.

And lied.

I hadn't saved everything—luckily!—and there was no evidence of some of my more dastardly deeds. For the most part, I'd saved only those letters that had gone public, that I'd submitted for publication. While that was an impressive portfolio in and of itself, it would have paled next to the letters that were left out.

Principal Poole.

The witch.

My dad.

She knew I was a letter writer but not that I was a Letter Writer, and I was content to keep it that way. Nothing good could come of delving too deep. Hell, even I didn't know what I really was or how many others there were who were like me.

We sat together amid my papers as the sky outside grew dark and the room inside grew darker. Neither of us made a move to switch on the lights, as though we both feared that any extra movement on our parts, any attempt to break the spell, would shatter our relationship and leave us alone to pick up the pieces. We were at our most vulnerable point as a couple and things could go either way. So we sat there and talked. Until she was once again reassured that she knew who I was, and I was once again reassured that she hadn't really found out.

We made love after that, but she put away my letters first, returning them to the folders in which she'd found them, and I realized just how lucky I was to have her. She might not know everything, but she understood intuitively how important the letters were to me. It made me love her all the more.

Now, at least, Vicki knew about my letter writing, so there was no longer any need to hide it. I tossed out my namby-pamby reservations, my rationalizations for keeping the two halves of my life separate, and I turned my full attention to writing the letters Vicki wanted me to write.

I got results.

Democrats in Congress grew backbones once again and started passing substantive environmental legislation. Reagan and Gorbachev *both* started negotiating for the elimination of nuclear weapons.

Did Reagan know what I was doing? Like Obi-Wan Kenobi sensing a disturbance in the Force, did he feel me entering the debate, using my letter-writing abilities to push both sides together? I don't know. We'd lost touch. He never wrote to me, and I only wrote to him surreptitiously, under the cover of various pseudonyms and activist groups. I had the feeling that if he *did* know, he wouldn't like it.

Vicki bought me a personal computer.

The Iran-Contra scandal kicked into high gear.

It's amazing what you can accomplish with a letter-head. A simple imprint on a piece of typing paper confers legitimacy on even the most illegitimate ideas and schemes. Who knows who belongs to the myriad ad hoc organizations that spring up to protest controversial issues? I'd had no faith in citizen groups since my fight with the city of Acacia—

and my dad

—over the Eastside, but most people saw the name of an activist organization and their minds conjured up pictures of informed individuals committed to a cause who held regular meetings and appointed officers and consulted lawyers and bargained with elected officials.

I thought of one guy in a room with a PC and a printer.

Like me.

I was far more sophisticated now than I had been in the days of Carlos Sandoval and the Hispanic Action Coalition. I hadn't even noticed at the time, but the acronym for that fictitious organization was *HAC*. And that's what I felt like when I thought back to those days. A hack. I was so far beyond that now.

Still, old Carlos had served his purpose and had gotten a lot done, as had my old buddy Paul Newman, who'd been my entrée into college, where I'd met Vicki.

But I was after bigger fish these days. I was no longer interested in petty deceits like getting myself a free lunch or obtaining a scholarship or even fighting city hall. No, my concerns now were national, and following Vicki's lead, I hit the Reagan administration hard. We signed petitions, wrote letters, made phone calls. Then, to back it up, I brought in the big guns. Unbeknownst to her, I buttressed our positions with words from a whole host of fictitious activist organizations and even experts in the fields of ecological science, environmental law and nuclear physics. Their letters to targeted newspapers and periodicals echoed publicly what our other correspondence said to politicians privately, creating the impression that there was a groundswell of support for our views.

Each letter a person writes represents five thousand people who don't write, Reagan had told me. *Or ten thousand.*

And then . . .

And then we were interviewed.

I had no idea who these men were or where they were from. Vicki and some of her more paranoid friends, particularly those who regretted having missed out on the sixties and feared repressive retaliation for holding politically incorrect views, assumed they were agents of Attorney General Ed "Miranda be damned" Meese out to intimidate us into silence. But I suspected something else even then. Despite their stated intent, they didn't seem to care about the content of the letters as much as the letters themselves. They seemed to me to be trying to find the source of the letters, to determine whether the person or persons who wrote them knew how special, how truly effective, the letters were.

There were four of them, dressed identically in black suits that could have denoted federal agent or rigid corporate dress code. They arrived at night, after nine, on a Sunday, and I think it was the time as much as anything that freaked us out. They stood on our humble welcome mat with stone faces, and the man in front stated blandly that they wanted to speak to Jason Hanford and Vicki Reed.

We let them in—we were afraid not to—and they immediately spread themselves around our tiny living room, two sitting, two standing, leaving only a small spot on the couch for us.

"Have a seat," the one man said as he withdrew a pen and clipboard from a flat briefcase. He was the only one who had yet spoken, but the others were also taking out pens and clipboards.

We sat, not knowing what else to do.

The questions came fast and furious, from first one man and then another, none of them speaking over each other but none allowing even a hint of breathing room between answer and next question.

"How many letters do you estimate you write per year? Per month?"

"Do you write letters every day?"

"Do you send all of the letters you write?"

"Is most of your correspondence personal, professional or political?"

"Do you ever write more than one draft of a letter?"

"Do you ever send the same letter to different organizations or institutions?"

The questions kept coming, all of them in the same vein. I looked from one man to another. *They know,* I thought, and the idea chilled me to the bone. But I did not let on that I was at all suspicious. I simply answered each question as it came, and pretended as though such a Sunday night interrogation was routine.

"May I ask what all this is about?" Vicki asked at one point.

"You may not," came the terse reply.

They left less than half an hour after coming in, giving us no clue as to who they were or why they'd interviewed us. Before walking out the door, the first man to have spoken, the one I assumed was the leader, turned back. "Tell no one we were here," he ordered us. "Or we will return."

I watched them get into a black car with no license plates and drive away. I was frightened but furious. My mind was racing through the letters I would write to the authorities if these guys were from some private company or to the appropriate oversight committee if they were governmental agents of some sort. My letters would rip all four of those fucks new assholes. I would be avenged and heads would roll.

Only I couldn't write any letters because I didn't know who the men were or where they were from.

By the time I closed and locked the door, Vicki was rocking back and forth on the couch, holding her stomach, great sobs wracking her body. "We—" I began.

She jumped off the couch. "We can't tell anyone about this!" she cried desperately. "We'll just drop out and—"

"Hold on a minute," I said. "We can't overreact."

"They know who we are! They know where we live!"

We stayed awake the rest of the night. I talked her down and we talked it out, and we decided that the best thing to do would be to stop writing letters of any kind and just lead normal low-key lives. We told all of our friends the next day. They were outraged, they were incensed, they vowed to follow up on this, but none of them had been visited in the night by strange interviewers, and though they were sympathetic, I'm not sure they really understood how we felt.

We were both shaken, but while my anxiety was only temporary, Vicki's took. She became fearful of expressing any opinions in public, even in classes where debating issues was a requirement, and as a result her grades dropped. She stopped seeing her friends and struggled with her internship.

I had time to consider where I was and to look at myself from a distance. There was, once more, a break in my letter writing. Whether self-imposed or the result of outside circumstances, there seemed to be an ebb and flow to my output, a cycle that might not have been natural but was consistent enough to be almost predictable. Again, I had the sense of forces felt but unseen, hard at work beneath the surface of everyday reality.

Gradually the paranoia receded. In many ways, our life together was better than it ever was. The experience with the interviewers had drawn us closer, and our withdrawal from overt political activism forced us to concentrate on each other and our relationship rather than extraneous issues. They'd done us a favor, I joked. Academically, Vicki regained her footing. As she'd planned, as she'd hoped, she was offered a very good job upon graduation, and on the day of the ceremony, with her parents in attendance, I proposed to her.

She accepted tearfully, laughingly, high on emotion.

We decided on a short engagement, opting to marry in Phoenix in July, close to her family. We'd have a week for a honeymoon before she started work. I'd put out my résumé and been on several promising interviews, but I wouldn't know for sure if I'd gotten hired until sometime in mid-August. Until then, I'd continue at my part-time job. So I was flexible.

Vicki wanted to invite my mom to the wedding. I

tried explaining that even in our best days, when I was a little boy, my mom had not been a real mother to me, that we had never been close. When Vicki kept pressing, I decided to just state it flat out: "My mom's a bitch. I hate her."

Still, she tried to contact my mom, who was living at the old house and as cold as ever. I was not surprised when Vicki, disappointed, said that not only would my mother not attend, but she would not send a gift or a card or acknowledge the day in any way.

Actually, I was glad.

We wanted to keep the wedding small, but we invited some of our friends from college and were touched when all of them responded and said they'd come. With the help of Vicki's parents and aunt and cousin, we found a place to hold the ceremony: an old chapel in a renovated ghost town in the desert just outside the Phoenix metropolitan area. Neither of us was religious, and we found a Unitarian minister who agreed to perform the service.

The wedding took place at twilight, with the rays of the setting sun shining through beautiful stained-glass windows and turning the inside of the pioneer chapel a rainbow of colors. The reception was held in an old nightclub in downtown Scottsdale that had been converted expressly for that purpose. Everyone had a great time and told us what a wonderful ceremony it had been.

We left early from our own party and made it back to the hotel, more than a little drunk from the champagne. In our room, we undressed each other and made our way to the bathroom, where Vicki started filling the tub. It was a ritual that had become almost nightly, and when Vicki—*my wife*—looked at me, I saw what appeared to be a slight touch of sadness or disappointment in her face.

"What is it?" I asked.

"What's what?"

"What's wrong?"

"Nothing."

"Something."

She hesitated.

"Come on," I prompted.

She looked at my partially erect penis. "We've *done* everything," she said. "We should have saved something for the wedding night, something to make it special."

She was right. We needed something to differentiate this night from any other.

"We haven't done *everything*," I reminded her.

"You mean that thing you . . . ?"

I nodded. "Yeah."

"I don't know. . . ."

"It's our *wedding* night," I told her.

She thought for a moment, then kissed me. "Okay, then. Let's try it."

And we did.

Nine

1

The years passed.

Like most people, I suppose, I sort of backed into my life. I never *really* intended to be a teacher. That was a fallback occupation—although I'd never bothered to figure out what I'd rather be doing instead. So I had no choice but to take a job teaching civics at a junior high school in West Covina. I hated it. Hated the work, the kids, the other teachers, the commute. After a year, though, through a series of fortunate circumstances, I got in on the ground floor of a start-up company that was creating a series of customized software packages designed to assist secretaries with writing business letters. Letters! It was my job to test the software and see how it worked from a user's point of view, and to come up with instructions that would be easy for the average high school graduate to comprehend. I was able to work from home, at my own pace, and there were no kids or administrators to deal with.

This should have been the perfect position for me. Letter writing? That was my life! How lucky could I get? Still, I found the job boring, and despite the subject matter and the relative freedom, I disliked my work: the repetitiveness of the endless line of software, the mechanical nature of my labor.

But I was with Vicki, and I was happy. We bought a house in Brea, a fixer-upper in a neighborhood that was just starting to turn around. We made friends with our neighbors, went to neighborhood barbecues, put up spooky decorations for Halloween and festive decorations for Christmas. When our son, Eric, came along, I thought my life was complete.

So, of course, I began writing letters again.

I had not forgotten our visit from those intimidating interviewers, but in my mind at least, the threat had receded. Besides, I had never had any qualms about using my abilities to help my family. And that's the way it started. I made sure Vicki got the promotions she wanted and deserved, made sure Eric got the best education possible.

> *Otis McKinley*
> *643 Teasedale*
> *Anaheim, CA 92801*
>
> *October 17, 1990*
>
> *Dear Sirs,*
>
> *As a customer, I am used to the quality products that your company provides. Your employees are always consistently well trained and able to provide the type of fine service that is so rare these days in our industry.*
>
> *But I have never been so impressed as I was recently.*
>
> *Ordinarily, I'm not one to offer unsolicited praise. If I am dissatisfied, I will not hesitate to complain, but I expect quality service as a matter of course and do not think it necessary to praise people merely because they are doing their job competently. But in my recent encounter with your purchasing agent Vicki Hanford, I was*

enormously impressed by her willingness to go above and beyond. Not only was she extremely knowledgeable in regard to the changes in your new product line, but she was willing to rearrange her schedule in order to accommodate mine, and she exhibited a unique grasp of the intricacies of commercial financing.

You are very lucky to have such an outstanding employee working for you.

> *Sincerely,*
> *Otis McKinley*

Jason Hanford
762 Elm St.
Brea, CA 92821

August 1, 1995

Dear Mr. Rousch,
Let me get this straight. My son has excelled in the city of Brea's finest private preschool and has been accepted at the prestigious Emerson Academy of Music, but you are forcing him to attend Ulysses S. Grant Elementary, the school with the lowest test scores in the district, rather than the exceptional Maple Drive Elementary School, because we live one street over the boundary line?

Your hubristic dismissal of my previous plea for flexibility and understanding, and your unwillingness to even acknowledge the six examples I cited of the district's rule bending on behalf of gifted students, leads me to believe that there is nothing I could say or do that would make you treat my son fairly.

Mr. Rousch, you are completely incompetent

and a disgrace to both the community and your
profession. I will work very vigorously against
you in the next election in an effort to ensure
that your misguided policies and inability to do
your job properly will not adversely affect
Brea's youth in the future. You are the worst
superintendent our district has ever had, and I
hope that you find a job more suited to your
abilities—like fry cook at Burger Chef.

> *Sincerely,*
> *Jason Hanford*

It was good to be writing again, and instead of the
shame and remorse I'd often experienced when indulg-
ing my obsession, I felt proud and honorable. I was using
my gift to help my family, and there was nothing more
noble, no higher calling as far as I was concerned.

But . . .

But politics attracted me, and though I kept it from
Vicki by using pseudonyms cribbed from the credits
of old movies, I started writing letters to the editor
again, letters to elected officials. It was in politics that
I'd had my first taste of success, and I still craved that
rush, that special indescribable feeling I got when my
words, put to paper, echoed through the corridors of
power and caused those in charge to change their
minds.

Clifton Powers
221 Cienaga
La Habra, CA 92854

October 12, 1992

Dear Editor,
   Shame on you for stooping to the level of
tabloid journalism. As a longtime subscriber, I

have always counted on Time *to provide me
with incisive, current and, most importantly,
unbiased news. But your continued focus on
Bill Clinton's personal life and your unwillingness or inability to provide in-depth coverage
of George Bush's numerous policy missteps
have caused me to reevaluate my opinion of
your publication. When S & L failures and
other issues that affect the lives of every voter
and taxpayer in this country receive fewer col-
umn inches than an alleged affair, something
is wrong with your priorities and journalistic
judgment.*

Next time, please let People *cover the personal lives of the candidates and stick to discussions of policy, as I and a majority of your
readers expect.*

*Yours truly,
Clifton Powers*

*Edwin Saldana
439 Broadway
Santa Ana, CA 92654*

November 8, 1994

*Dear President Clinton,
How does it feel to have lost the Congress?
As a lifelong Republican, I have to say that I
relish your each and every failure, from your
tactical errors to your backfiring policies. Like
Carter before you, you will be a one-term president, going out not with a bang but a whim-
per. You will have many long years of
retirement in which you can contemplate how
your presidency was the final death knell of
liberalism.*

> *You are the best thing to happen to the Re-*
> *publican Party since Ronald Reagan.*
> *Thank you.*

> Sincerely,
> Ed Saldana

Just as I had done with my parents, I hid everything from Vicki. I was the one working at home, so I was the one who retrieved the mail each day, making it easy to hide the replies to my suggestions and complaints. Usually, I used fake names and addresses, but some of my beefs were valid, and I didn't want Vicki to see the responses and know that I was writing again.

I saved everything in a compartment hidden under the bottom drawer of a filing cabinet in the spare bedroom that I used as my office.

I sent my letters the old-fashioned way because e-mail didn't seem to work. I had e-mail, of course. I utilized it constantly, mostly as part of my job, and to keep in touch with friends and acquaintances from the past. But there was something about the alchemy of ink on paper, of placing a letter in an envelope and having it delivered by the post office, that granted it a power, a magic, that nothing else could replicate. I even tried using my company's software a couple of times, but a true letter, a real letter, could not be artificially generated by a microchip, could not be a static series of variables overlaid atop a generic template. No, letter writing was an art, a *dark* art in my case, but an art nevertheless, and there was a poetry to it that the trappings of technology could not seem to capture.

My approach was scattershot. I had no goal toward which I was working; there was no focus to my efforts. I reacted spontaneously to events as they occurred, to things I read and heard about, to things I was told. I

made sure George Bush was not reelected. Vicki
would have liked that. But I could not help myself,
and I took down the Clintons' health care program
and installed Newt Gingrich and his contractors in the
Congress. Well, *I* didn't install them. But I used my
abilities to influence people and sway opinions. I
seemed to have this need to take down establishment
authority figures. I'm sure a psychiatrist would have
put it down to some sort of unresolved conflict with
my parents, and indeed that was my theory, too. But
I didn't care. When writing letters, I went with the
flow. My approach was instinctual more than intellectual, and if my gut led me off on wild tangents, then
so be it. *Do I contradict myself? Very well, then I
contradict myself.* If it was good enough for Whitman,
it should be good enough for me.

I fanned the flames of Whitewater.

On the surface, my life was going well. We were
upwardly mobile; our family was happy; we were like
the living embodiment of an insurance ad. Likewise,
my letter writing was extremely successful. But those
were not parallel tracks, and I knew that eventually
they would meet. My letters were not merely harmless
balls that I lobbed out into the world. They were more
like bombs or grenades, with repercussions that would
eventually return to bite me in the ass.

But I didn't care.

And I was going to enjoy the ride for as long as
possible.

In the evenings, the three of us would go for walks
around our neighborhood. We'd smile and wave at
our other neighbors on their porches, stopping to
chat with those we met on the way who were strolling
with their babies or their dogs. One night, we walked
farther than usual, past the edge of gentrification that
bordered our neighborhood, onto a street where the
houses had peeling paint, the yards were enclosed
with chain link fences and overgrown with weeds

T-shirted teenagers with shaved heads congregated around low-riding cars, and every square inch of available wall space was covered with stylized spray-painted messages. Amid the jumble of gang tags, I saw on one wall a graffitied rendering of Bart Simpson. I felt vaguely reassured by the fact that gang members watched the same TV shows I did, and realized just how tenuous were my ties with the real world. It was Vicki and Eric who kept me tethered to society.

If left alone to my own devices, I'd probably spend all day every day sitting in my room, typing letters and sending them out, communicating with the world only through the mail.

I realized how lucky I was to have my family and was almost overcome by a powerful sense of emotion, filled with gratitude for the life I had and didn't deserve.

We arrived home, and after playing with Eric for a while and changing him into his pajamas, Vicki said that she was going to take a long leisurely bath and wash off the dust of a tired day. She asked if I'd put him to bed. She gave me a quick kiss, promised in hushed tones that she'd reward me later and went into the bedroom to get some clean underwear and the oversized T-shirt she used as a nightie.

"Come on, little buddy." I rubbed Eric's head. "Go to the bathroom. Brush your teeth. Do what you're supposed to do."

"Okay, Dad," he promised me in a tone of utmost seriousness.

The feeling was still with me, and I had to smile. "I love you," I told him.

"Me, too!" he called out on his way down the hall.

After he was done, I read my son a book, patted his head, gave him a kiss and tucked him in bed. I checked to make sure Vicki was still taking a bath.

Then I went into my office and, as I did once each

week, sat down and wrote an anonymous letter to my mom.

Dear Mrs. Hanford, I began. *You fucking bitch . . .*

2

I received her first letter on June 6, 1996.

I knew who it was from before I even opened it. I recognized the paper, recognized the stamp, recognized the writing. My hand trembled as I tore open the envelope. How was it possible, though? How had she tracked me down? I'd been very careful to make sure I was not listed in any phone book or directory. I unfolded the letter, checked the address at the top, the signature at the bottom.

Yes. It was her.

Kyoko.

I read the letter, my heart pounding. I'm not sure why I was so nervous, but I was. I felt guilty just reading her words, though there was no reason. It was a casual, generic "Hello, how are you? What are you doing?" letter, the attempt by one old pen pal to find out what had become of another. Her English had gotten better over the years, but there were still some quaint misspellings and odd grammar usages that made me smile. I sensed, though, that there was more to this reconnection than that, that Kyoko didn't want to just say hello, that she had some ulterior motive.

Sure enough, I got another letter exactly a week later.

I realized that she was sending them so that they would arrive on Saturdays—just as I'd instructed her when we were children.

I was lucky enough to have checked the mail before Vicki, and I took the envelope into my office, closing and locking the door before reading the letter inside. It was a good thing I did:

> *Dear Jason,*
> *Hello again! I do not tell you last time because I am too embarrassed, but I never stop thinking of you all these years. Do you remember my photo where I am naked? I do! I will send you one now if you want. Could you send me one, too? I think of that all the time. I am still not married. I am saving myself for you. Do you miss me? Do you still love me? Do you still want me? Write me back and let me know.*
>
> > *Love always and forever,*
> > *Kyoko*

I had not written her back after the first letter and I didn't this time, either. But a week later, another missive arrived, this one even more explicit. In it, she said that her fantasy was to have me tie her up and rape her. Hard. In the ass. She also said that she was planning to move to the United States. She had a job lined up with a multinational corporation, and maybe we could get together?

This time, I did write back. I told her in no uncertain terms that I was married, that I had a son, that I loved my wife and would never cheat on her. We might have been pen pals when we were kids, I said, but we did not know each other now, we both had separate lives, and we should not write to each other anymore. It would be better if our correspondence remained a pleasant memory from childhood.

I sent off the envelope the next day, feeling virtuous, feeling strong, feeling good.

But I saved the letters.

And the ones that came after.
I don't know why.

3

It was summer, and Eric was spending the week at
Vicki's parents' house in Phoenix. Due to our busy
schedules, we didn't get a chance to visit them as often
as Vicki would have liked, and she made sure that
each summer he spent at least some time alone with
his grandparents. We took the opportunity to reinvig-
orate our own relationship, to have the sort of free-
form spontaneous sex we used to have before our son
was born.

And the sex was great.

I missed Eric, though. I was the one who worked
at home, I was the one who took care of him all day,
who watched him while Vicki went to her office, and
it seemed strange not having him around. I'd vowed
that I would be a better husband and father than my
father had been—and I was. Not only did I spend
more time with Eric than my dad had spent with me,
but I *liked* being with him.

Although I occasionally wrote letters in longhand
while he ran around, or typed letters on my computer
while he took a nap, I did most of my work at night
and spent my days with Eric, reading to him, playing
with him, taking him for walks. We got to be a familiar
sight in the used-record stores and thrift shops of Orange County, and he grew up listening not to Walt
Disney or *Sesame Street* albums but the Beatles and
the Pogues and Miles Davis and Meredith Monk and,
of course, Daniel Lentz. We also listened to Hank
Williams Jr. together. Yes, Hank Junior. I had, belat-
edly, caught Robert's country-western bug, and was
rapidly filling in those gaps in my record collection

by picking up Charlie Daniels, Dolly Parton and Moe and Joe albums from Salvation Army and Goodwill stores.

I often wondered what had happened to Robert and Edson. Frank, too. And Paul. I thought about searching the Internet for their wherabouts, then sending them e-mails, but something kept me from it. My past was past, and it was easier somehow to remain in the present.

There is a point, I think, where life starts to seem sad, when a person adopts one of those live-in-the-moment philosophies because looking back on all of the missed opportunities is too painful, and looking forward, there does not seem to be the time to create a new future with a different outcome. I wasn't there yet, but I missed my twenties, missed the sense of freedom and possibility. I loved my family and was happy with my life, but I could see where it was going, the road was mapped out ahead of me, and I didn't like that. Things seemed better when I had no idea what the future had in store. Maybe that's why I continued to read Kyoko's letters.

And then . . .

I got caught.

And it all blew up in my face.

I had to meet in person with a programmer from the software company for one of my infrequent face-to-face demos. So I drove to the corporate office in L.A. and spent the day trying to decipher the techno-jargon that was thrown at me as I made my way through the various screens of the new package. As luck would have it, Vicki was scheduled to work only a half day. Our original plan was to have lunch together at a Cuban restaurant near the Orange antique circle. She'd go to antiques stores; I'd check out the used-record and thrift shops. But when—the day before—I found out about my meeting, I told her to go on without me; I'd meet her there if I could, see her back at home if I couldn't.

The damn demo didn't end until after three, and by then the flextime traffic had created gridlock all the way back to Orange County. So it was nearly six by the time I pulled into the driveway.

Something was wrong.

I could feel it, though there were no visible indications that anything was amiss. I was reminded, for some reason, of the time when Vicki had discovered my stash of old letters back in our little apartment in college, and heart pounding, I hurried into the house.

As before, Vicki was on the floor, surrounded by my letters, reading. I could not tell if she had found my secret compartment and taken them from there or if she had found my special diskette and printed them out herself on the PC. But there was a look of revulsion on her face this time. Something about the letters disgusted her. It might have been the content—at least in some cases—but I had the feeling that this ran deeper. She was objecting not to the subjects of the letters but to the letters themselves, to their very existence. I felt like an exposed Dorian Gray, my terrible secrets on view.

Vicki looked up, saw me and reconfigured her face, involuntary revulsion changing to righteous anger. She stood to confront me. "What is this?" she demanded, shaking the sheaf of papers in her hand. "What are all these?"

"Letters," I said glibly, trying to make a joke out of it.

"What about all this right-wing bullshit, all these anti-Clinton diatribes, all these Gingrich apologies?"

"It's not political," I said.

"Not political?" she yelled. "What you've done here is the exact opposite of everything you've ever said, everything we've fought for!" She threw the papers at me. "I don't even know you!"

She was right. She didn't know me, although I wasn't sure whose fault that was. I felt obligated to defend myself, and I was desperate for her to understand, to know that I didn't really mean any of it. But how could I explain to her that it wasn't the specific policies I cared about. Hell, I didn't even consider them when writing my letters. It was the power, the fact that I could change and influence the nation's movers and shakers, the idea that others were dancing to my tune. It was the act of writing, creating the letters themselves, that got me off.

"I'm still the same person I always was," I told her.

"Who is that?" she shot back.

"Remember my nuclear-freeze letters? My disarmament letters?"

"Then what are these?" She gestured to the scattered pages.

Who the fuck was I kidding? I had no real political convictions. My only loyalty was to my letters, my only obligation to my art. I had started on this path with a single altruistic step, wanting to save Acacia's Eastside from redevelopment, but that was the first and last time that my motives had been pure. For me, letter writing was like a drug, and once I was hooked, I needed a fix—and didn't care how I got one.

"You're a liar. You told me you weren't going to write letters anymore," she said accusingly. "You lied to me."

"How do you think you got those promotions?" I said quietly.

She stared at me.

I looked away, immediately sorry I'd said it.

"No," she whispered.

I wanted to deny it, but I knew it was too late for

that, and I shut my mouth before I said something
else and made things even worse.

That wasn't possible.

She stormed out of the room, stomping on my letters as she did so, grinding papers beneath her heel,
kicking others out of the way. My instinctive reaction
was to save them, to push her aside and gather my
babies to me. But I restrained myself and stood there,
trying to come up with an apology or entreaty that
would make her stay and make everything okay.

Down the hall, the bedroom door slammed shut.

As I gathered up my papers, I reflected on my letter
writing. I'd used it for both good and evil. I was responsible for Principal Poole's losing his job, for the
deaths of my father and the witch of Acacia. But I'd
also helped my wife and son, used my talent to create
a better life for them. Didn't that balance out the
harm I had caused?

No. Because just as I had no real political convictions, I had no moral compass, either. I cared only
about the letters. It didn't matter to me what the result
of my words was—only that there *was* a result. It was
the thrill of the conquest that I lived for, the adrenaline rush I got when one of my letters was published
or received a defensive response or caused a panicked
change of heart in its recipient.

Was that more important to me than Vicki?

Than our marriage?

Than our son?

Of course not. And there was no reason for me to
even be considering such a drastic scenario. I didn't
have to choose one or the other. Vicki might be upset
right now, but she'd be all right by morning, and then
we'd talk it out the way we always did.

I heard loud noises from the other end of the hall:
doors and cupboards slamming. She was mad and
wanted me to know that she was mad, but there was

something more than that in it. I had the feeling that she was going through her dresser and closet, packing.

Her reaction was all out of proportion to the objective content of the letters. It wasn't the politics that bothered her so much. Not really. It wasn't even my lying and sneakiness. It was . . . something else. Could it be the letters themselves? On some gut level, did she understand what they really were? Did she sense the dark power that surged behind them? Or—

I looked down at the letter in my hands.

It was from Kyoko.

—I dream that you mount me from behind. You hurt me when you shove it in, but I like the way it hurts. You grab my breasts with your hands and pinch nipples. I scream and you—

I had no ready response. This was not something I could combat. When Vicki stormed out of the bedroom with her suitcase and told me that she was going to her parents' house, I had no ready reply. I stammered and stuttered and tried to come up with a legitimate reason why she should stay, but my words stumbled over themselves.

"I'm not coming back!" she announced as she opened the car door and threw the suitcase in the backseat.

"Vicki . . ."

"I'm not coming back!" She glared at me with a face full of rage and pain and hate.

And fear.

It wasn't just Kyoko.

"I'm sorry!" I called out lamely.

"I don't know *what* you are! But I don't want to be around you, and I don't want you to be around my son!"

"He's my son, too!" I shouted as she got in the car

and slammed the door. "I'm the one who's with him all day! I'm the one who takes care of him!"

I was still screaming at her as she backed out of the driveway, swung the car around in the street and sped away.

Ten

1

I dreamed of the tent again, the circus tent in the desert. Once more, I was walking alone down the dusty road toward the tent. There was no movement of the hot still air, not even a breeze, but the dirty white-and-red-striped canvas flap flipped open as though propelled by a sentient wind. Within the exposed triangular breach lay darkness.

I reached the tent and did not even pause. I walked straight inside.

There were no white-haired children within the canvas confines, no prehistoric skeleton. In the center of the ring was the crucified Christ, his body dead and stinking on the cross, blood dried and skin turned to leather. From somewhere unseen came the tinny sound of old-time music. Two old men sat in the shadowed bleachers, scribbling on notepads or clipboards.

I awoke.

And I was alone in my bed. I rolled over and buried my face in Vicki's pillow. I could still smell her on it: her perfume, her shampoo, her moisturizer, her soap. "Vicki," I said.

And cried myself to sleep.

In the mail the next day was a letter with no return address. Just in case, I ripped open the envelope:

Dear Jason,
   You are walking down a dusty desert road
toward the red-and-white striped circus tent. It
is hot and you are sweating, but inside you feel
cold—

I tore up the letter and the envelope, threw them away.

2

The end of our marriage was conducted through a series of letters. From her lawyer to me, from my lawyer to her. I tried writing to Vicki directly, pouring my heart and soul into a series of personal entreaties designed to win her back, giving those letters everything I had. She returned every one of them—unopened. Either she knew what I was trying to do, or on some subliminal level, she sensed it.

I don't know what *you are.*

Eric called me on the phone every few days, and each time he was polite but distant. I could tell he was sad, and I wondered what Vicki had told him about me. I didn't want to ask him, and I *couldn't* ask her, because she wouldn't speak to me. I knew from her lawyer that she was asking for full custody and that she wanted to deny me visitation rights, but my lawyer said there was no way that would happen. She'd probably get custody, he admitted—the mother usually did—but I was such an involved father that it was likely I would have a pretty open visitation schedule.

That wouldn't do me much good, though, if they remained in Arizona.

Unless I moved to Arizona.

What would be best for Eric? I wondered. I wasn'

so selfish that I would gratify my own emotional needs at the expense of his, but I found it hard to believe that he'd be better off without a father in his life.

I remembered that when I was a little boy, my friends never liked to come over to my house and I never liked to invite them. My dad was often drunk, and my mom was always mean. So mean that my friends were afraid of her and would rather meet any-place in town other than my house.

Vicki and I had been good parents to Eric—at least until this point—and we needed to continue putting him first. But this was not an ordinary separation. We were playing it as though it were, and that's how it appeared from the outside—the Kyoko letters assured at least that much—but the truth was that Vicki was *afraid* of me. I'd known it that night, and I sensed it even now. She obviously couldn't prove anything—any assertion that I was an unusually successful letter writer would seem like irrelevant lunacy—but we both knew the truth of the situation, and I could understand her point of view. Hell, my letter writing scared *me*. I knew why she wanted to keep Eric away from me.

She was letting him call, though. At least that was something.

Maybe all wasn't lost.

I thought at some point we would have to meet in a room: her and her lawyers, me and mine. But apparently not. The haggling over details continued through faxes and phone calls, through e-mails and couriers and registered letters. I still loved her, and I had an unfounded gut feeling that underneath all of the fear and suspicion and sense of betrayal, she still loved me, too. But all of this . . . process . . . kept us away from each other, pushed us further and further apart until we were little more than cogs in a machine. I did some of my best work writing letters to her lawyers, hitting heights of persuasiveness that I'd never hit before, pushing my abilities to their extremes in a desperate effort to get back my wife and son. If I'd been this on fire when writing about Reagan or Bush or Clinton, world events would have changed; the society we lived in would have shifted direction. But these letters, too, were returned unopened. I was allowed to communicate to Vicki's legal team only through my own attorneys.

I tore the letters up each time they were returned, and whether or not it was my imagination, I thought I sensed their power in my fingertips as I ripped up the paper on which they were printed. It was stupid and superstitious, but just in case, in a primitive home-grown attempt to ward off any repercussions, I dumped some of the torn pieces in the wastepaper basket in my office, dumped some more in the garbage sack under the kitchen sink and flushed the rest down the toilet. The ritual may not have had any real-world effects, but it made me feel better.

The summer dragged on, hot and lonely. I still said hello to my neighbors when I saw them, but I saw them less and less, hid out in my office more and more often, not doing my work, not even writing really, just obsessing over my situation and reading editorial pages, advice columns and epistolary novels. Letters real and fictional. For the first time since we'd moved into the neighborhood, I avoided the Fourth of July block party, not wanting to face my neighbors alone without my family, too embarrassed to answer questions.

I soon came to realize that most of "our" friends were actually Vicki's friends. I didn't really know most of them all that well and didn't really want to know them. My own friends from the past had fallen by the wayside; I'd drifted away from my college buddies just as I had earlier with Robert and Edson and Frank.

Where was I going? I wondered. What was to become of me?

I had no idea.

And the summer continued on.

3

In a portent of the bursting tech bubble to come, my job disappeared along with my stock options, my pension plan and the software company itself. I had no other income and virtually no savings, so I should have been more concerned about it, should have at least cared a *little,* but the truth was that my mind was wrapped up in the pending divorce and custody battle, and I was glad to be shed of the position. I'd hated it anyway, and the assignments that had been piling up had been an albatross around my neck.

As it happened, I was offered a new job almost immediately.

In a most unusual way.

Monday, August 25. A letter arrived in the mail describing in perfect detail the bizarre and terrifying dream I'd had the night before. In the dream, Eric had been at school, and during recess had eaten a small section of the chain link fence that surrounded the playground, then had moved on to the bottom segment of sheet metal on the slide. His teacher had dragged him to the principal's office, and the principal had called us. Both the teacher and the principal were there, and both were obviously afraid of Eric, who sat in a chair in the corner, chastised and worried. He was suspended for a week, and we took him home.

He went back to his bedroom.

"First the nails, now this! What is he?" Vicki demanded.

"Shut up," I told her. "He'll hear you."

"Whatever he is, it comes from you. Nothing like that's ever happened in my family."

"Nothing like this has ever happened in *anyone's* family."

"It's in your genes," she said angrily. "It's your fault."

I stood, suddenly furious. "You want to have a DNA test? Huh? You want to find out once and for all whose *fault* it is?" I grabbed her shoulders and shook her, and at that moment I hated her. "Is that how you think of our son? As someone one of us is at 'fault' for?"

She burst into tears. "I'm sorry!"

We hugged, made up, then walked back to his bedroom to talk to him. He was standing in his underwear before the full-length mirror on his closet door, a screwdriver in his hand. We weren't sure at first what he was looking at or what he was planning to do, but then I noticed that his skin had started to change.

Barely noticeable, it began as a slight discoloration around the ankles. Yet even as we watched, it spread. Vicki gasped as a thin gray tendril moved up his leg and formed a spot on his thigh roughly the size, shape and color of a quarter.

"I'll be metal by morning," he said, and smiled. He lifted the screwdriver to his lips and bit off its tip. "I'm going to eat the car tonight."

The letter quoted every bit of dialogue and described every detail I remembered. As before, the effect sent a chill down my spine.

But this time there was another sheet of paper enclosed with it.

A job application.

I read it over. Once. Twice. Thrice. It was, by far, the simplest and strangest application I had ever seen. My name, address, birth date and Social Security number had already been filled in on the top lines. Below that were two questions I was apparently required to answer: *What qualifies you to be a professional Letter Writer?* and *If hired, how many letters would you be able to write, on average, in an eight-hour period?* At the bottom was a line for my signature.

At the top was the address of the company.

There was no name. That was odd. But at least I now knew where these mysterious letters had been coming from. Apparently, there was a business whose mission was to simply write letters.

And now they wanted me to work for them.

It could be a trap, I reasoned.

No. A person or persons who not only knew where I lived but could see into my mind and know my dreams would have the ability to capture me or take me out at any time. They wanted something else. Perhaps this *was* nothing more than a simple job offer. Perhaps the company was expanding. Or needed additional manpower for some secret project, some big letter-writing campaign that had as its goal the overthrow of the United States government or something equally ambitious. Or . . .

What?

I didn't know.

Whatever the reason, the company had given me its address, if not its name, and obviously wanted me to either write back or show up in person—and that was why I was tempted not to. These letters had been dogging me for years, freaking me out, worrying me, making me second-guess myself, and this was an opportunity for a little payback. The thought of some smug asshole sitting there and stewing in his own juices while waiting for a visit from me that would never come filled me with a kind of cruel joy.

But I could not turn down this opportunity. There

was some type of connection here. Beyond the letters, beyond the dreams, I was linked to these other Letter Writers somehow. I could feel it, an almost tangible bond that made me think of the pseudopsychic attachment that twins were supposed to share. Besides, I knew that if I didn't act now, the company could be gone, relocated to some other building in some other city—and next time there might not be a return address. This could very well be my one and only chance.

Did I want to go? No, not really. To be honest, the thought frightened me. But I *had* to do it, and I locked up the house, got in my car and drove to AAA, where I asked for a street map of Los Angeles.

I parked across the street. Sat there for a few minutes.

It was not a high-rise office building in the downtown area, not a new corporate center in the renovated hinterlands. It was a dingy apartment complex in a fading section of the city, a square two-story structure from the dawn of the space age, with two star-shaped dingbats affixed to the graffitied stucco testifying to its optimistic origin in an earlier innocent time. The name of the complex—*Shangri-La*—was written in stylized letters above a rusted wrought iron gate that provided entrance to what had once been the pool area. This interior courtyard had long since been cemented over, and was now home to what appeared to be a couple of dead potted palms, a few snapped-strap lounge chairs and some broken children's toys.

All this I could see from the driver's window of my car. What I could not see was the door for suite 3. Or, more accurately, apartment number 3.

I remained there, watching, hoping to catch a glimpse of someone going in or coming out, wishing I had a pair of binoculars so I could examine the apartment building more carefully. I was afraid to get out of the car, afraid to draw any closer. I'd been invited here, but just knowing that somewhere within that dingy complex were Letter Writers who were able to see my dreams, who had been dogging me for over a decade, left me practically paralyzed with dread. I kept hoping others would show up. Other Letter Writer applicants. Anyone.

When it became clear that there was only me, I sat there for a little while longer, then got out of the car. A block up the street, a group of kids were racing up and down the sidewalk on their bikes. Closer in, a disheveled man pushed a grocery cart filled with recyclable cans and bottles.

But the apartment building sat there.

No one went in; no one went out.

I was overreacting, reading too much into this. It was the middle of the day. Most people were at work. There were all sorts of reasons why a run-down apartment building was not a hub of social activity at two thirty on a Monday afternoon. And writing letters was a telecommuter's dream. It was the type of business that could easily be done at home, and theoretically, there was no reason its headquarters *couldn't* be in an apartment.

Still . . .

I locked the car door and walked across the street. Next to the curb in front of the complex was a dented and vandalized communal mailbox with small locked cubicles for each individual apartment. I searched in vain for a name, but found only numbers. Across the mailbox someone had spray-painted in stylized letters *Shorty. Chico. Spooky.* A stray line that looked like an arrow led from the word *Spooky* to the mail slot for apartment number 3. That seemed ominous.

Shangri-La.

Nothing seemed to be breaking right today, and the smart, logical part of my mind was telling me to get out of here, run away, abort the mission. It could come to no good end. Still, I pressed forward, walking through the gate into the slummy courtyard. I looked around. A bent screen door hung loosely from broken hinges at apartment number 3. There was no wooden door behind it, and although the apartment inside was open, it was too dark to see anything.

The courtyard was quiet. *Too* quiet. Even noises from the street died before they reached here. I glanced at the other apartments, at the drawn shades and closed doors. I had the feeling that no one else lived here, that all of those apartments were empty, abandoned.

Before me, the doorway to apartment 3 yawned blackly behind the broken screen like the open mouth of a monster.

I gathered what courage I had and strode forward purposefully. Stopping before the door, I knocked on the wooden frame and tried to peer inside. I could see nothing. No outlines of furniture, no sign of people. "Hello!" I called.

Nothing.

Taking a deep breath, I pulled open the broken door and walked over the threshold.

Inside was blackness.

Eleven

1

I awoke in an empty office. Or, rather, came *to*. I had no idea what had happened to me—the last thing I could remember was walking through that doorway into the dark apartment—but it seemed clear that I had been drugged or somehow rendered unconscious and then brought here.

Wherever "here" was.

I was lying on a flat couch, and I sat up straight, looked around. The room in which I found myself had white walls, recessed bars of fluorescent light and a tiled floor buffed so shiny that it reflected the ceiling. It possessed the generic, slightly antiseptic quality of a room in a hospital or law enforcement agency.

I stood, walking over to the closed door at the opposite end of the room.

Suddenly the door swung open. I nearly jumped out of my skin. Two men appeared and immediately positioned themselves to either side of me. Young, wholesome, clean-cut, wearing nondescript clothes that were somewhere between a suit and a uniform, they did not take my arms, but there was still an element of coercion in the way they moved forward, pressuring me to move into the corridor with them.

There was something familiar about the two, and

for a brief befuddled moment my still-dazed mind
could not place what it was.

Then I figured it out.

They reminded me of the men who had interviewed
us about our letter writing back in college.

I said nothing but silently accompanied the men
down the corridor. I realized that I had left my application back in my car, although I was not sure that
made any difference. I did not feel as though I were
being led to a job interview; I felt as though I was a
prisoner being transferred to a new cell. It was a weird
sensation, one I could have doubtlessly dispelled with
a simple question, but I remained silent, not wanting
to speak.

No, that was not true.

I was *afraid* to speak.

Our shoes clicked on the shiny tile with a crisp clar-
ity that was almost martial. We passed closed door
after closed door. Metal frames for nameplates were
affixed to the wall next to each door, but they were
all empty. This building had been either abandoned
or never occupied.

We reached an elevator. The man on my left turned
in front of me, blocking my way, forcing me to stop.
There was no call button, but as if sensing our presence, the doors slid open, and the three of us stepped
inside. The interior of the elevator was burnished
steel, with no buttons or levers or indicator lights, so
I can only assume that we went up, because that's
what it felt like to me.

After a minute or two, the doors slid open once
again, and we stepped out into a corridor nearly identical to the first. *Nearly* because the doors here did
have nameplates—although the only letters engraved
on them were alternating *A*s, *B*s and *C*s. I was led to
one of the *B* doors, and the man on my right
opened it.

I went inside.

They remained outside.

The door closed behind me.

I heard the click of a lock engaging.

I examined the room in which I found myself. It looked like an office, but there was no furniture other than two wooden chairs on either side of a folding table in the center of the gray-carpeted floor. The walls were bare. There was no window.

I'd heard the door lock, but I knew they'd expect me to try the knob and check anyway, so I refused to do it.

I wondered if there was a hidden camera trained on me. Assuming there was, I remained standing, walking casually around the room as though waiting for someone who'd promised to meet me here and was late. If there'd been objects or knicknacks about, I would have picked them up and pretended to examine them. After a while—an hour? two?—my feet started hurting, so I sat down. I did so indifferently, as though not thinking about it, not forgetting for a second that I might be under surveillance.

I crossed my legs, searching for a comfortable position. I had no place to put my arms, so I put them on the table before me, but that felt awkward.

What would happen if I had to go to the bathroom? I was already thirsty and would eventually get hungry, too. Were they expecting me to pound on the door and demand to be let out? Beg for a cup of water?

I wouldn't give them the satisfaction. This was a test. The application had been a ruse to get me in the door. This was the way they were really going to determine whether I would be allowed to write for them.

Allowed?

Yes. This was the major leagues. It would be an

honor and a privilege, a dream come true, to write letters for a living—and I had no doubt that they knew that already. I had no idea what the agenda was here, whether this was part of a private think tank or a clandestine agency within the Department of Defense or the CIA, but I believed—no, I *knew*—that they had found a way to legitimize the letter-writing talent, to harness its potential.

Then why have they been stalking you, invading your dreams? a deep rational part of my brain asked.

I told that part of my brain to shut up.

Time passed.

If it had been late afternoon when I came into this room, which my interior clock had said it was, it now had to be evening. Eight or nine o'clock. I was hungry, and my mouth was so dry that each time I swallowed, I almost gagged, the saliva bunching up in weird configurations on its way down my parched throat. I desperately had to take a piss.

Just when I thought I wouldn't be able to hold it anymore, the door opened and one of the two men who'd accompanied me here—my guards, as I'd come to think of them—said, "Bathroom break." I followed him down the corridor to a knobless door, not speaking, though the guard's words had given me an opening. I adopted the attitude of a prisoner of war.

The man waited outside, while I went in to relieve myself. The small restroom, barely bigger than a large closet, had a urinal and a toilet but no sink. I'd been planning to use the sink in order to get a drink of water, and seeing that there was none made my mouth feel even drier. I used the urinal, then reluctantly walked back out. The man led me back down the corridor to my room.

When I returned, there was a pitcher of water and a glass on the table. I waited until the guard had left, until the door had been closed and locked again, before I nonchalantly reached for the glass and poured myself a drink. I wanted to chug the entire tumbler, but instead took an ordinary sip, trying not to let my face react as the cool soothing liquid slid easily down my dehydrated throat, refusing to let them know how important this was to me, how desperately I needed this. I casually took another small sip, vowing to drink only the one glass.

Who knew how long this pitcher would have to last me.

Until now, I'd been sitting in silence, the only noises in the nearly empty office my own, but suddenly screams issued from the room next door, shrieks of agony so raw that they sounded as though they'd been forcibly ripped from the throat of the man being—

tortured

—interviewed in there.

I knew I was supposed to hear those cries of pain, but I had no idea why. The screams were muffled— my door was shut, his door was shut, and there was a wall between us, after all—but there was no mistaking what they were, just as there was no mistaking the fact that I was meant to hear what was going on.

I had no watch, and there was no clock in the room and no windows, so there was no way for me to gauge the passage of time, but I endured the screams for what felt like the better part of an hour before the door finally opened and a middle-aged man wearing the generic white-collar uniform of a bureaucrat or middle manager stepped inside. He was carrying a black binder, and he sat down in the chair on the opposite side of the table and ruffled through several of the binder's pages before looking up at me. "How are you, Mr. Hanford?" he asked noncommittally.

"Fine," I answered, though I wasn't.

He didn't care, wasn't interested, did not even listen to my answer. "Good," he murmured. "Good." He flipped through several more pages, then stood up. "Anything you'd care to add?" he asked.

From the next room, I heard a piercing screech that did not end but was cut off.

Then, ominously, silence.

"No," I told the man.

"Well, if you do, you'll let us know, won't you?" He didn't pause to wait for a response but walked to the door, tapped on it three times, then opened it and stepped into the outside corridor.

I was alone once again with myself and the silence.

After a while, I poured myself another glass of water and drank it.

After a longer while, I fell asleep.

I awoke hunched over in the chair, my neck muscles stiff and hurting. I'd obviously been in the same position for quite some time. There was food on the table in front of me. Two huge blueberry muffins and a tall glass of orange juice. Breakfast. The muffins were still warm; the juice was still cold. They'd been brought in fairly recently. Still cognizant of the fact that I was probably being watched, I did not dig in the way I wanted to but ate slowly, politely, as though this were an ordinary day and this my ordinary breakfast. I ate both muffins and drank all the juice.

Time passed at an excruciating glacial pace. I had plenty of time to wonder what was happening to me, to think about what the future had in store, but I forced my mind to stay away from those topics. I didn't want to get sucked into that mental spiral, and I purposely occupied my brain by thinking about music, about records I'd recently picked up, records I still wanted to find, records I'd loaned to friends back in high school or college that those friends had never given back. Thinking about old friends made me think about writing them letters, which made me think about writing other kinds of letters, which made me think about why I was here.

I couldn't get away from it.

I really like that Jethro Tull bootleg I bought last week that was recorded on the Passion Play *tour,* I thought. *I just wish I could find one from the* Minstrel in the Gallery *tour.*

After a while, I had to go to the bathroom, and a while after that, the other guard appeared at the door with the same announcement, "Bathroom break." This time, upon my return, I found a pen and a blank piece of paper waiting for me on the table next to a new glass and pitcher of water. When I picked up the paper to see if anything had been written on the other side, I saw a stamped envelope lying on the table underneath the page.

I was expected to write a letter.

But what kind and to whom?

Just as I'd refused to give in and speak to my guards or ask any question of the man who had visited me, I decided that I would not give in to temptation and write. I would continue to do nothing but wait and stare into space.

But as the hours dragged by, that resolution became harder and harder to keep. My mind was racing with ideas, complaints I wanted to make, ideas I wanted to express, questions I wanted to ask.

Still, I refused to write. This was a test.

I wanted to pick up that pen, but I didn't.

I waited.

As before (yesterday?), the bureaucrat returned, carrying his black binder. Once again, he sat down in the chair on the opposite side of the table and looked through the binder's pages. "How are you, Mr. Hanford?"

I didn't answer.

He looked up at me. "You killed your father, did you not?"

I fidgeted nervously, not sure what the right answer was.

"It's a yes-or-no question."

I nodded.

The man smiled. "Very good, very good. And you continued to harass your mother by letter long after you'd severed contact?"

Again I nodded.

"Excellent!"

He closed the binder, standing up. "It's been a pleasure as always, Mr. Hanford." He tapped on the door, it was opened, and he left.

In the silence, in the emptiness, I was forced to look at myself, look within myself, to see myself as I really was, and I did not like what I saw. I was an evil man. Not amoral, as I'd always assumed, as I'd in many ways prided myself on being, but consciously and actively evil. Despite what I'd led Vicki to believe, despite what I'd told myself, I was not a nice guy who'd found himself doing questionable things due to extenuating circumstances. I was a cold-blooded killer, a calculating murderer willing to do anything to make my life easier and more comfortable.

But I could live with that.

The question was, would I do it all again, given the chance? Would I have my dad killed just because he was an asshole?

Yes.

And I'd off the witch and maybe throw in my mom for good measure. And Tom. And Principal Poole. And those interviewers.

It was horrible to admit, but if I was going to be honest with myself, I had to be really honest—no matter how horrible the truth might be. And the truth was that while I didn't *want* to be this way, I was.

Had I always been like this? I wondered. Had I been born this way? Had living with my parents made me into who I was? Or, as I suspected, had the letters done it? Had writing those lies drawn me into a whirl-pool of malignancy that had left me forever cor-rupted? I didn't know, and I'd probably never know. But I saw myself more clearly than I had ever done before.

The minutes crept by. The hours.

I slept.

I dreamed.

I awoke once again in a cramped position in my chair, muscles sore, my fogged brain retaining the resi-due of a nightmare in which I was seated at a child's desk in an old one-room schoolhouse writing a letter, while at the front of the classroom lurked a dark indis-tinct shape that was waiting for me to finish so it could kill me. I could keep it at bay only if I continued to write.

There was movement out of the corner of my eye, white movement near the bottom of the door. Holding my stiff neck, I turned to look and saw that an enve-lope had been slid into the room. I glanced away, knowing without opening it what it contained.

A detailed description of my dream.

My stomach was growling, but I ignored the three granola bars and the glass of grape juice placed next to the pen and paper on the table. I shifted position on the seat, crossing my legs and tensing my buttocks. I really had to take a shit. I waited several minutes, hoping that one or both of my guards would come to escort me to the bathroom, as they had before, but neither of them did and finally, unable to wait any longer, I stood, walked across the room and tried the knob on the door.

As I'd known, it was locked.

My attempt to outlast them already a failure, I

pounded on the door and demanded to be let out. My
commands were ignored, of course. Remembering
how the man with the binder had rapped three times
on the door, I tried that, as well, thinking it was some
kind of code. The door remained locked. I kicked out
in frustration. Fuck them. I started to unbuckle my
pants. I'd take a shit in the corner and let those assholes clean it up.

There must have been some type of surveillance
equipment in the room, because the door suddenly
swung open, and this time both guards stood in the
corridor. "Bathroom break," they said in unison, and
there seemed to be a smirk on the face of the one on
the right.

I hurried down the corridor to the bathroom, in-
wardly cursing them both.

Afterward, I did not flush.

This time I had the smirk, and when I was returned
to my room, I immediately sat down at the table and
picked up the pen:

To Whom It May Concern,
 *I am extremely unhappy with your employ-
ees. They are rude and inconsiderate, and, I
would venture to say, poorly trained. I have
never before encountered men of such stunning
ineptitude. I don't know what kind of operation you are running here, but I must admit I
am not favorably impressed. A problem of this
magnitude cannot be placed solely at the feet
of the individuals directly involved. This is a
management failure, and it is the responsibility
of those at the top of the organizational ladder
to see to it that the entire operation runs
smoothly. You are either unable or unwilling
to do so. I have no respect for you or your*

*authority and will no longer be cooperating
with your grossly incompetent underlings.*

I signed the letter, folded it and placed it in the
envelope. Considering for a moment what to do, I
stood and shoved the envelope under the door. "Deliver this to your boss!" I shouted.

For the next half hour or so, I paced around the
room, wondering if my letter would reach its intended
target, wondering what the reaction would be. I had
a lot of time to think, and I considered the subject of
time itself. How long had I been trapped here in this
office? It felt like three days, but with no clock, no
change in light or atmosphere, no visual cues from the
outside world, my inner rhythm could be totally off. I
could be sleeping for a single hour every six hours, or
I could be sleeping twelve hours every twelve hours.
It was impossible to tell.

Sometime later, the screaming started again. At
first, I thought it might be a tape loop, some type of
psychological warfare tactic used to break prisoners
down. But this screaming was different, and even
though the sound was muffled because of the walls, I
could definitely hear two voices this time, one low and
constant, delivering some type of lecture, the other
high and anguished, crying out in physical pain.

I banged my fist on the wall. "Shut the hell up in
there!" I yelled.

To my surprise, they did shut up. It could have been
a coincidence—the torture session might simply have
ended at exactly that time—but I was pretty sure that
the entire thing had been staged for my benefit.

I ate the granola bars, drank the now warm grape
juice. As I finished the last of the juice, the door
opened and the bureaucrat with the binder walked in.

"Congratulations!" he said cheerfully, hand extended. "You have successfully completed our training

program and are now qualified to work for us and
write letters at the highest level."

Numbly, I shook his hand. "What exactly am I qualified to do?"

"Come on," he said. "There's a party in your honor.
Sort of a get-to-know-you, welcome-aboard mixer."
He led me out into the corridor, walking fast. "You're
really going to like it here."

"Where is *here*?" I asked.

He stopped before a door marked *C*, then rapped
on it with his knuckles three times. The door opened
slowly. "Party's in there," he said. "I have some work
to attend to, but I'll join you shortly. Have fun!" He
pumped my hand. "And, once again, congratulations!"

2

I found myself in what looked like a house. The room
before me, a sitting room of some sort, was decorated
with antiques, making it look like something out of
the 1920s—or the 1960s. I had no idea where I was,
and for a brief disorienting moment, I thought perhaps
I'd gone back in time. But then someone in another
room shouted, "E-mail!" which got a laughing response from the other revelers.

I turned, trying the door that had closed behind me,
but it was locked.

There was a hallucinatory quality to everything that
was happening, but at the same time my surroundings
were very real, very specific, very concrete. Nothing
could be farther from that antiseptic corridor than this
warm, funky room, but I knew that both were here in
the same building.

Where was the building, though? It certainly wasn't
that apartment complex—

Shangri-La

—I had initially entered. Despite all the words of congratulation and the irrational feeling of proud accomplishment I had, the fact remained that I had been drugged or otherwise knocked out and then transferred to this place.

Wherever this was.

For the first time in what felt like several days, I was in a room with a window, and I quickly walked over and looked outside. It was daytime, but the landscape before me was shrouded with fog, allowing only minimal sunlight to penetrate. Curious, I opened the window, pushing the frame up slowly so as not to alert the people in the other room. I stuck my head out, breathing deeply, half expecting to smell the dark dank scent of the grave, or a metallic artificial, machine-made odor, but there was nothing.

I squinted, peering into the thick impenetrable air. I could not see anything, but I *felt* something, a sense that the building in which I stood was fake. I was suddenly grateful for this veil that had been drawn. I didn't want to see what lay behind the mist.

I pulled my head in, closed the window, drew the curtain.

What the hell was I thinking? I supposed I'd been subjected to some sort of behavioral conditioning, like what had happened to Patty Hearst or prisoners of war, which reinforced the idea that this company or agency or whatever it was was affiliated with the DOD or CIA or some other national-security group.

More laughter issued from the other room, and after peering into that void, the sound seemed warm, welcoming. Gathering my courage, I opened the door and stepped out into what looked like the hallway of a midsized home. The conversation was louder here. I could make out individual voices. Men and women. They were talking about—what else?—writing letters.

I walked into the next room.

The cocktail party in progress was like something out of a John Cheever novel. We were in a large upper-middle-class living room. A bearded, barrel-chested man was leaning against the wall next to the fireplace, a drink in his hand, several more lined up on the mantle next to him. On the other side of the fireplace, facing him, confronting him, was a middle-aged woman in a granny skirt with the slightly scattered air of a professional academic. On the couch, crammed together uncomfortably, sat two well-dressed couples who may or may not have known each other. There were seven or eight other people milling about, who ranged in age from early twenties to mid-sixties. One slovenly overweight man wearing willfully eccentric clothes stood by himself against the far wall, staring at his shoes.

It was an eclectic group, and one that seemed to have very little in common save their occupation. I assumed that they were not only writers but Letter Writers.

The woman in the granny dress saw me first. She was facing the stairs, and the movement must have caught her eye. "He's here!" she announced, and all conversation stopped as the gathered throng turned to look at me. I felt embarrassed and didn't know what to say, but the woman came over and took my arm in hers. "Let me introduce you," she said. She nudged me with her elbow. "By the way, what's your name?"

"Jason," I said. "Jason Hanford."

"Mine's Virginia."

I allowed myself to be led into the center of the room. "This is Jason Hanford," Virginia announced. "Our newest Letter Writer." She introduced me to each of the other guests individually. "I'd like you to meet Leo . . . Bill. . . . This is James . . . John . . . Ernest. . . ." I was hugged, nodded to and winked at.

My hand was shaken. We went around the room, then into the kitchen, where two elderly men, one very short and very hunched over, were eating hors d'oeuvres off a silver plate on the breakfast table. ". . . Alexander . . . Thomas . . ." In one of the bedrooms, a fat, florid man was putting the moves on a slim, primly attired young woman. "Charles and Jane."

We all reconvened back in the living room. I glanced around, cleared my throat self-consciously. "I assume you're all Letter Writers here. Like me."

"Don't assume," Virginia said. "It makes—"

"—an ass out of you and me," Leo said tiredly. "I know. We've all seen that episode of *The Odd Couple.*"

It was weird to hear this bearded ascetic talk about an old television show, but it was also reassuring somehow.

"You're *not* all Letter Writers?" I asked.

"Yes," Virginia said. "We are. I was just making a point."

Ernest, still standing by the fireplace, laughed.

"I write editorial letters," Charles offered. "Letters to the editor."

"I write fan letters to actors and authors and musicians," John admitted.

They all began stepping forward.

"I write testimonials." Alexander.

"I write letters to politicians." Thomas.

Every possible use to which a letter could be put was covered.

Bill was writing letters to *Penthouse Forum* and "The Playboy Advisor." "I'm responsible for moving away from anal and into fetishism," he bragged. He leered at Virginia. "Although I know *you're* still into anal."

"You're disgusting," she shot back.

He roared with laughter.

Alexander shook his head. "You debase yourself and those with whom you associate."

Bill turned on him. "Shut the hell up, you crippled old dwarf."

"*You* shut up!" Ernest roared.

Jane laughed, touched my arm. "You caused quite a stir in here, sir." She nodded toward Charles. "Some of his letters weren't getting into newspapers and periodicals because yours were printed instead. It caused quite a little ruckus, let me tell you."

"It's true," Charles admitted. "Our job is to write letters. We're the ones who are supposed to praise and complain and sway opinion. The fact that you were out there horning in on our territory did not go unnoticed."

Ernest laughed loudly, moving away from the fireplace for the first time and swaggering into the center of the room, scotch in hand. " 'Did not go unnoticed?' That's a prissy little euphemism if I ever heard one. The powers that be were livid. Livid!" He gestured expansively, spilling part of his drink. "You were public enemy number one around here. They were having their toadies try to outflank you, sending reams of letters to combat your correspondence."

"But they couldn't do it," Virginia confided, and I thought I heard a secret pleasure in her voice.

James nodded seriously. "You are very powerful."

A chorus of nods and murmured assent greeted his statement. These Letter Writers knew who I was, I realized. They knew my work. They respected me. Hell, some of them had probably been tracking me for years. I looked around at their faces. I had so many questions, I didn't know where to start. "Who are we working for?" I finally asked.

"The company," Ernest said.

"But what company? What's its name?"

"I don't think it has one." James.

"What exactly do we do here?"

Virginia laughed. "Write letters."

"We're like . . . ombudsmen to a certain extent," John explained. "What we do primarily is help people, give voice to those who don't have a voice, write letters on their behalf."

"They don't know we're doing it," Alexander added. "They're not aware that we're helping them. We work behind the scenes, like guardian angels."

"That's a load of shit and you know it," Bill said. "We write letters. That's it. Period. We write them because we're good at it, because we like to do it, because it's who we are. We have no idea of the reasons behind any of it. We have no idea where the letters go or what they're used for."

A small argument broke out between Bill and several other men.

"The point is," Virginia said, "we've been hired to do what we love to do. And what more can you ask from a job?"

I believed her. Sort of.

But . . .

But something was not quite right. I glanced around at the others, and there seemed something false and a little desperate about some of their smiles. I suddenly had the feeling that this was a show being put on for my benefit, that they were not all one big happy family here and that behind the party facade was something darker, a truth I was not meant to see.

There was a knock at the door. Three knocks, actually. And just like that, the party broke up. Several people walked out of the front room into the kitchen. Virginia, ever the polite hostess, opened the door, and as the bureaucrat with the binder stepped into the room, Ernest, Bill and John sneaked around him and

out. It was no longer light outside, I noticed. It was
night. The fog may still have been there, but it was
so dark out that it was impossible to tell.

When had that happened?

And where were we? On the bottom floor of an
office building? In an actual house? It was impossible
to tell. I felt disoriented.

"Enjoying yourself, Mr. Hanford?" the man asked.
He was the same height as me, I noticed for the first
time. And the same build. If I'd been an actor, he
could have been my stunt double. For some reason,
he didn't seem quite as nice or quite as friendly to me
as he'd been when he'd escorted me to the party.

Jane mouthed a good-bye to me and left through
the front door.

Within a minute, maybe two at the most, we were
alone in the room, perhaps in the house.

Was this a house?

"Welcome aboard, Mr. Hanford." The man smiled
broadly. "Rest assured, we appreciate your talent
here, and not only do we want to make use of it, but
we want to cultivate it, nurture it."

"Who's 'we'?" I asked.

He ignored my question. "Salary is negotiable, but
you will be recompensed handsomely, never fear. As
the commute each day from Orange County would be,
shall we say, *impractical,* the company is willing to
provide you with a place to stay free of charge, as
well as with transportation or a vehicle allowance. A
house and a car, basically. As you've already discovered, we have a rich social life here—"

"Here?"

Again he ignored me. "I think you're going to be
very happy in your new position."

There was something intimidating about the man.
Not him personally, but what he represented. He was
the public face of something much larger, and that

was why the other Letter Writers had scattered upon his arrival. They were afraid of this gray little man in his nondescript clothes.

He watched me blandly, awaiting my response.

I didn't give him one.

"It's much more satisfying than writing computer instructions."

Still, I didn't respond.

"Would you like me to take you to your new home?"

"What new home?" I asked.

"The house we're providing you," he said, and I was gratified to hear a tinge of annoyance in his voice.

"I'll stay in my own house," I said.

"But the commute—"

"I'll deal with the commute," I said. "In case this doesn't work out, in case there are layoffs or I'm fired or the company goes bankrupt or I don't pass my probationary period—I assume there's a probationary period—I'm not going to completely uproot myself." Besides, I thought, once I got Eric back, he'd want to be in his own house. And once I got Vicki back . . .

I refused to let go of that fantasy.

"Very well," he said rather stiffly. "But as I'm sure you know, letter writing is not just a vocation. It's an avocation, it's a lifestyle, it's—"

"Right now, it's a new job," I said.

He nodded, and I decided not to push any further. The truth was that he was starting to creep me out a little. I recalled those screams in the next room when he'd visited me in the office, and I shut up.

I had the feeling that he had put the party together for my benefit—not to welcome me, exactly, but to recruit me, to win me over, to convert me. We walked outside. The fog seemed to have lifted, but it was dark; it was night. Halogen streetlamps illuminated a nearly empty parking lot. We had been, not in a house, but in an office building, one of those generic rectangular glass and concrete high-rises that could have been built in 1950, could have been built yesterday. The building was located in what appeared to be Century City, miles and cultures away from the slummy neighborhood in which I'd parked my car and walked into the—

Shangri-La

—apartment complex, but my Toyota was still sitting across the street. Someone had obviously towed it here.

A business card was pressed into my hand. "Report for work tomorrow morning. It's your first day, so you won't be expected to be on time (you'll find we're very flexible here). Just make sure you get plenty of sleep. Then, after you eat breakfast, drive to the office. They'll get you settled in." He offered his hand. "My work's done. It was nice to meet you."

I shook his hand and for some reason felt as though I was sealing an agreement.

He chuckled. "Enjoy."

I wished he'd been more specific. Enjoy what? But that was all he said, and I was as much in the dark now as I had been before he'd shown up. I watched him walk back into the building, then started across the parking lot toward the sidewalk.

I felt tired as I drove back home. I pulled into the driveway and sat for a moment with the headlights off, staring at the dark empty house that until recently I'd shared with Vicki and Eric. I felt sad and depressed, thinking of what I had lost and where I should be in my life.

But *was* that where I should be?

Or should I be where I was now, with other Letter Writers, doing the only thing I knew how to do, the only thing I was good at, the only thing I cared about?

I got out of the car, went inside. Throwing my keys on the coffee table, I did not even bother to turn on the lights but trudged down the hallway to the bedroom. Wanting to escape from everything, not wanting to think about any of it, I kicked off my shoes, took off my pants and shirt and climbed into bed in my underwear.

The bed felt too big with Vicki gone, the room too quiet.

I should write to Vicki and Eric, I thought.

I closed my eyes.

I fell asleep.

Twelve

1

I awoke with the dawn, and as I lay there staring up at the ceiling, I was not sure if I'd dreamed about the events of the past few days or if all of it had really happened. I reached over to the nightstand, picked up the remote control and turned on the TV. The *Today* show was on.

Whether it had happened or not, I felt happier and more energized than I had in a year. I sat up, kicked off my covers and got out of bed. I felt like Scrooge on Christmas morning, and I pulled on a bathrobe, casually glancing at my car through an opening in the curtains.

My car.

My car was supposed to be white.

The one in the driveway was black.

I yanked open the drapes, not trusting my own eyes. Sure enough, there was my jack-in-the-box head on the tip of my antenna, the small round crack in the corner of my windshield where a rock expelled from a gravel truck had hit the glass last year, my license plate with its battered TOYOTA OF ORANGE frame.

All on a black car.

It wasn't possible. It didn't make any sense. I backed away from the window. A sinking feeling in the pit of my stomach, I walked out to the kitchen. On impulse, I opened the cupboards. There was cereal, coffee, jars of salsa, cans of refried beans, all of my usual foodstuffs. And boxes of muffin mix and stacks of granola bars.

Muffins and granola bars?

It *hadn't* been a dream.

The phone rang, and I jumped so hard I nearly slipped on the floor. I stared at the phone, hanging in its cradle next to the broom closet. I was afraid to answer it, unsure of who—

what

—might be on the other end.

It stopped after three rings, and I finally forced myself to move, to walk across the kitchen to the refrigerator. Inside were three new containers of orange juice. Thank God. I was thirsty as hell. I took one of the containers out, found a glass and poured myself a drink. From the cupboard, I took out a package of granola bars. I sat down at the kitchen table and forced myself to eat. In the center of the table was a business card. I didn't remember leaving it there, and the sight of that small white rectangle sent a chill down my spine.

And caused my heart rate to accelerate with anticipation.

For despite all of the weirdness, despite my trepidation, I wanted to write letters. I tried to rationalize it, tried to pretend that this was a great career opportunity, but the truth was that I yearned to write letters. I *hungered* for it. And this job gave me a reason to do so, granted legitimacy and purpose to a clandestine activity I had long felt guilty about.

I picked up the card and for the first time read the words on it. The street address was nearby. In Brea.

But how could that be? Did the company have an Orange County branch office? The man yesterday had

specifically told me that my commute would be long
when he offered to provide me with company housing.

None of this made any sense.

A part of me wanted to crawl back into bed and
sleep until all of this was over. But a much stronger
part of me wanted to see this through, wanted to find
out what came next.

The closet in the bedroom was filled with my
clothes—and quite a few items I had never seen before. I put on a pair of black pants, one of my nicer
shirts and my dress shoes. I found my wallet and the
keys to my—

black

—car and went outside. Locking the house behind
me, I got in the car, backed out of the driveway and
drove slowly down the streets to my new job.

The office to which I was supposed to report was
very close, only a few miles from my house. I saw few
cars along the way, though I took the easiest and most
straightforward route there. True, the rush hour was
past, but the streets were as empty as they should
have been at three in the morning rather than ten.
Still, when I pulled into the lot next to the multistory
building, nearly all of the spaces were taken and I
ended up parking at the far end, next to the sidewalk.

It was the same building I had left yesterday in L.A.

I refused to think about that.

My new supervisor, Henry Schwartz, was waiting in
the lobby by the front desk, and, the second I passed
through the front door, he waved me over, introducing
himself. I liked him instantly, trusted him implicitly.
He was a nice guy, a real guy, and there was a definite
connection between us. I was with my own kind, and
as much as I prided myself on being an individual, a
nonconformist, there was something welcoming,
soothing and comforting about at last finding kindred souls.

"So what have you been told about our work here?" Henry asked.

"I was told I'd be writing letters," I admitted.

He laughed. "That you will. We all do. A lot." He nudged me with an elbow. "And you know how much we love that!"

I felt strangely warmed by this acknowledged kinship.

"Come on," he said. "We'll go up to the fourth floor, where you'll be working."

We took the elevator, but while I studied the small cubicle carefully, it looked nothing like the elevator in which I'd ridden with my two guards. Likewise, the fourth-floor corridor did not look as though it was even in the same building as that other one. Henry led me through two fogged-glass double doors into a large, well-decorated office suite. "Sit down," he offered, motioning toward an overstuffed leather couch.

I declined. "I'd rather stand," I said.

Henry walked over to a small bar set into the wall, pouring himself a glass of orange juice. "Want one?" he asked. "Fresh squeezed."

I shook my head.

"So . . . I suppose you're wondering why you're here and what you'll be doing and all that good stuff, huh?"

I smiled. "It crossed my mind."

"We're an independent organization, not affiliated with any government, corporation or institution. I would say we provide a service, but that would imply that we have customers, that we answer to clients. We do not. We, very simply, write letters. On a whole host of topics to a wide range of recipients. I suppose the company is comparable to a think tank, only our job is not to provide ideas or create theoretical scenarios. Instead, we use our talents and abilities to get real-world results. We're doers."

"But—"

He held up a hand. "You're a Letter Writer. I know you know that term, but I'm not sure you're aware of everything it means and the rich history behind it. We have been watching you for quite some time because your letters are not only well written, they get results. They're also smartly targeted and cover a wide range of issues." He smiled ruefully. "They also trumped a few of our own letters, and that was very impressive indeed.

"You see," he said, "*we* write the letters that matter. Sure, people send notes to lovers, friends and relatives. And a few here and there write to newspapers or politicians to complain about this or that. But we're the ones whose letters get in, whose letters get read, whose letters have import.

"We're part of a long, proud, if largely unknown, tradition. Who do you think wrote the Bible?" he asked. "Letter Writers. The Letter of Paul to the Romans. The First Letter of Paul to the Corinthians. The Letter to the Hebrews. The First Letter of John. Letter Writers have been framing the debate since the beginning. How are biographies written? How is the veracity of historical events determined? By reading letters. Correspondence is the bedrock upon which societies are built." He closed his fist. "And we now have a stranglehold on that. Letters are our business, our industry, our raison d'être. And because of that, we can make history; we can change history; we can determine the course of human events.

"Love doesn't make the world go round. Letters do."

It was horrifying, what he was saying. Maniacally egotistical if untrue, terrifying in its implications if correct. Intellectually, I knew that. But emotionally, I felt like a true believer at a partisan political rally, and a part of me wanted to leap up with raised fist and scream, *"Yeah!"*

Letter writing was like a religion to this guy. To all the people here, probably. I wouldn't have been surprised to learn that they all attended a church where kneeling parishioners sang hymns to and worshipped a gigantic envelope.

And I would have been right there with them.

Henry downed his orange juice with one gulp and put a hand on my shoulder. "We are the lucky ones, the chosen ones. We've been recruited to carry on this noble tradition. We've been entrusted with the responsibility of writing tomorrow's letters."

"But *who* recruited us? Who do we work for?" I gestured at the building surrounding us. "Who owns all this?"

He looked lost for a moment, and I could tell this was a question that he'd asked himself more than once. "I don't know," he said. "No one knows."

"But someone has to—"

"No one knows," he repeated. The way he said it made me think that it was a question I was not supposed to be asking. I thought I heard fear in his voice.

"So who wrote those letters I got, the ones that described my dreams, the ones that led me here?"

He looked surprised. "So that's how you were recruited? Interesting."

"Why? How did *you* get hired?"

"I simply received a letter telling me that my work had been noticed and appreciated. I was asked if I wanted to work full-time writing letters and was instructed to appear at a certain office building at midnight." He smiled. "Midnight, right? I should have known something was up with that.

"Needless to say, there was no one there. The door was open, though, and when I stepped inside"—he gestured around—"here I was. Well, not *here* exactly. But in the building, ready for my interview."

"Were you . . . tortured?" I asked.

"No. Were you?"

"No. But I heard—"

He chuckled. "Don't trust everything you hear. Or see. Only trust what you read."

"I never trust what I read," I told him. "I lie all the time in my letters."

"But they're still true," he said.

I wanted to ask what he meant by that, but Henry was already walking out the door. "Come on!" I followed him across the corridor to a door in the wall on the opposite side. "Here's where you'll be working," he said, opening the door.

I don't know what I was expecting, but it wasn't this. We were standing on the edge of what appeared to be a bedroom from the 1950s. Lying on the bed, writing on a notebook, was a trim, attractive middle-aged woman. It was a cutaway room with only three walls, like the set for a movie or a television show. Henry and I stood on a linoleum walkway that passed by the open fourth wall. On the other side of the walkway, opposite the bedroom, was a high-tech office with large windows that appeared to overlook the New York skyline. A jowly older man sat at the desk, typing furiously on a computer keyboard.

"People write best in environments where they are comfortable," Henry said. He nodded to the man and woman, both of whom ignored him, and we continued down the winding walkway through a seemingly endless maze of dens and living rooms, offices and study carrels. I did not recognize anyone. Virginia and the people from the party no doubt worked on some other floor. This was where the other Letter Writers worked, the grunts, and Henry led me past ten, twenty, thirty of those individualized cutaway rooms where these lower-caste Letter Writers toiled.

I found myself thinking that there was no way this massive rabbit warren of writing spaces could fit on a single floor of the building I had entered, but I did not really question it. Not at the time. My mind was focused on other matters.

Letters.

Finally, we came to my work area. Henry stopped in front of that missing fourth wall. "Here we are!"

It was not a replica of my home office, was not even the bedroom of my teenage years. It was a room I'd never seen before, a cramped, oddly shaped area that looked to me like an office in the back of an independent record store. The walls were papered with overlapping posters from various groups and musicians, and the air smelled vaguely of old incense, which did not quite mask a subtle underlying odor of slightly mildewy cardboard: the scent of old records. I figured at first that a mistake had been made—*Aha!* I thought. *They can make mistakes!*—but I discovered almost instantly that I felt perfectly at home here, more at home than I had in my real house. The posters, I saw, were from my favorite artists, their best albums and best tours, and the ambience was one with which I was not quite familiar but desperately wanted to be.

They hadn't made a mistake.

They knew me better than I did myself.

I glanced back down the crooked winding linoleum walkway that led past all those other rooms. For some reason, I was reminded of Little Red Riding Hood's path through the forest. "I have to come all this way every day?" I asked.

Henry laughed. "Goodness, no! There's a door right here." He walked across the room and opened a door that I'd thought was a closet. It led back into the original corridor—straight across from his office. It was the same door through which we'd come in.

I felt a slight twinge of vertigo, but I didn't bother to ask how that was possible. I didn't care. I simply nodded.

"Bathroom's down the hall," he said. "Second door on your left."

I walked around the beat-up desk, saw an old manual Royal typewriter exactly like the first one I'd owned sandwiched between a pile of music magazines and a box of cartoon figurines. On a small adjacent table was a much newer PC with bubble jet printer. I sat down in the well-worn swivel chair. It bulged and sagged in all the right places and felt like it had been form fitted to my body.

Henry smiled. "Here's where the magic happens."

I looked up at him. "So what exactly am I supposed to do?"

He explained. At first, he said, I would be given assignments, specific letters to write to specific people. These instructions, of course, would be delivered to me by letter, and each day, I would come to my desk, open my mail and follow the directions I was given. After a brief probationary period, I would be let loose, set free to write about general subjects, with no minimums or maximums on the number of letters I produced and only the broadest guidelines to follow.

I nodded.

What if I fail? I wondered. *What if I don't produce the required number of letters? What if my letters are of exceedingly poor quality?* I didn't ask these questions, but I thought them, and it occurred to me that if I screwed up a few assignments and flunked my probationary period, I could be fired.

Or tortured.

I'd be the guy new recruits would hear screaming in the other room.

But I didn't care. I loved writing letters. Writing was my drug of choice, and like any other addiction, it consumed me to the extent that everything else was made irrelevant. Even if I *wanted* to turn down this opportunity, I wouldn't be able to do so. The lure was too strong. And I was too weak. When it was all placed in front of me like this, offered up on a silver platter, I had to cave in.

"It's all very informal," Henry reassured me. "As I'm sure you can tell, this is not regular work. And we are certainly not regular employees." He chuckled. "When I first got here, I thought I'd died and gone to heaven."

"And now?" I looked at him.

He smiled, turned away, but not before I saw an expression that could only be called conflicted pass over his features. "We do important work here," was all he said, and once again I understood that the topic was closed for discussion.

I stood. "So . . . when do I start?"

"Now if you want."

"What are the hours?"

"It's up to you. Morning to midafternoon for most people, but that's not set in stone. At the beginning, you work for however long it takes you to complete your assignments. After that . . ." He shrugged.

"What do I do when I'm not working?"

"Whatever you want." He put a hand on my shoulder, and once again I felt that connection between us. "We're calling this a job, but it's not, really. It's a life, a new life, the life people like us have always dreamed about." Smiling, he handed me an envelope. He must have been holding it the entire time, but I hadn't noticed it and it was as if he'd magically pulled it out of the air. "Here," he said. "Why don't you see what this says?"

I ripped open the envelope, pulling out a piece of typewritten paper and a clipped newspaper article.

My first assignment was to write a letter on behalf of neighbors living next to a recently renovated racetrack. The track had been shut down for the better part of a decade because of lawsuits over night races

and noise pollution. The track owners and the homeowners had recently reached a settlement. According
to the article, though, not all of the homeowners had
agreed to the settlement, particularly the ones whose
houses were closest to the track, and they were complaining bitterly that they'd been screwed over by
their other neighbors.

"Should I do this now?" I asked.

"Sure. I'll be in my office across the hall. Come
over when you've finished."

I read the article again, read the instructions. I liked
the fact that I was given free rein, not told what to
write or how to approach the problem, and I sat back
down in my chair, trying to decide whether to use the
typewriter or the computer. Both were ready and rar-
ing to go. I finally decided on the typewriter. It's what
I started my career with, and it was only fitting that I
use it to kick off this new chapter in my life.

I addressed my letter to the owner of the track:

> *Dear Mr. Muldoon,*
>   *There is nothing more pointless than watch-*
> *ing men drive around in a circle for hours. The*
> *numskulls who find this entertaining live sad*
> *and meaningless lives, and are just putting in*
> *their time while they wait to die. The cynicism*
> *of a man like yourself who takes advantage of*
> *these morons is disgraceful. Even more so*
> *when you use those ill-gotten gains to harass*
> *and intimidate the fine upstanding law-abiding*
> *citizens who are your neighbors.*

I laid it on thick, accusing the old fuck of everything
short of molesting his mama. By the time I was done,
not only was he guilty of the most venal and menda-
cious behavior, but I'd implied that I knew several
dirty secrets about him and was not above releasing

such information to the public—unless of course he agreed to sell this racetrack and use the proceeds from the sale to build another one elsewhere.

I cranked out the letter in five minutes, then read it over. It wouldn't change the guy's mind, but it would give him pause. It was the first salvo in what I planned as a quick and nasty war. While he might not move his racetrack, by the time I was through with him, he'd at least agree to build a soundproofing wall between his property and the neighborhood, and he'd pay for some customized acoustic solutions to the neighbors' problems.

Standing up and opening my door, I walked across the corridor to Henry's office. He called out, "Come in!" at first knock, and I stepped inside.

"I'm done," I said.

"Wonderful!"

I held out the sheet of paper. "Do you want to read it, look it over?"

He waved me away. "No. You're a Letter Writer. You know what you're doing. Just send it off."

I went back and looked through my desk until I found a pen, an envelope and a roll of stamps. I signed the letter with a fake name, addressed the envelope, sealed it and affixed a stamp. Henry was waiting for me in the corridor. I looked around. "Is there a mailbox somewhere?"

He grinned, and there seemed to be a twinkle in his eye. "Out the door, at the end of the hall. Come on, I'll show you." We walked down the wide corridor. "Bathroom," he pointed out as we passed it. At the end of the hallway, he stopped. I hadn't noticed before because I hadn't been paying that close attention, but the wall in front of us looked like nothing so much as a church altarpiece. Though they were the same color as the surrounding walls and ceiling and thus invisible from afar, carvings of quills and scrolls, pens and papers, typewriters and printers adorned the facade before us, forming a virtual arch in the squared space. A trail of carved envelopes led to an opening in the center of the wall, a mail slot rimmed with what appeared to be pure gold.

"Here is where we mail our letters," Henry said reverently. He touched the mail slot with his finger.

I knew exactly how he felt. Oftentimes I, too, had gazed upon a mailbox with awe, either the rounded freestanding blue boxes that stood sentry on street corners, or the small rectangular openings in the wall of the post office that led directly to the sorting bins. These were talismans to our kind, the magic portals through which our handiwork passed on the way to its destination.

I took my envelope, dropped it in the slot. It made no noise when it fell. There wasn't that harsh, inappropriately loud *plunk* that occurred when a piece of mail was the first of the day and landed alone at the bottom of the box. No, my letter had touched down softly on a pillow of previous correspondence.

Henry patted me reassuringly on the shoulder, obviously understanding my feelings. Again, I felt all warm and fuzzy knowing we were kin.

"You're going to like it here," he said. "You'll fit right in."

2

I made new friends.

It took a while, because for the first few weeks I didn't really get a chance to meet anyone else. I'd pass by people in the lobby or in the parking lot, then ride up with them in the elevator, and I always made the effort to smile, nod and say hello, but for the most part I went straight to my office, wrote my letters and

then went straight home after work. I liked Henry
Schwartz, we had a good rapport, and we were both
Letter Writers. I understood that in many ways he was
in the same position I was, the same position we all
were. But we were not, could not be, friends. He was
my supervisor, and there would always be the question
as to where his loyalties lay.

I had him pegged for a company man through and
through.

And I was not.

Don't get me wrong. Professionally, I was happier
than I'd ever been, and if I'd had Vicki and Eric back,
I would have considered my life to be perfect.

But my job was *too* good, if that made any sense.
And as much as I loved it, as much as I needed it, I
had the sense deep down that it was not right. It made
me feel the way I used to feel as a child on the day
after Halloween. All day on November first, I'd eat
candy, the trick-or-treat candy I'd collected the night
before. Mars bars for breakfast, Milky Ways for lunch,
Snickers for dinner, Butterfingers for snack. I was in
hog heaven, but a sober, responsible part of me was
always thinking that I should be eating some bread or
fruit or meat or vegetables—*normal* food—to balance
out all the sugar.

And months later, at my next dental checkup, I
would inevitably find that I had at least one new
cavity.

This reminded me of that.

It was great. I loved it.

But I knew it was wrong.

And others did, too.

Gradually, the malcontents shook themselves out,
made themselves known. There was, I discovered,
something of an employee lunchroom on the third
floor, a restaurant, more haute cuisine than cafeteria,
that catered exclusively to those of us who worked in

the building. It was there that I first met Stan Shapiro.
Stan was older than me and had been here since the
Reagan years, writing crank letters to each successive
president. They were all letters about the space program. He enjoyed what he did and believed in what
he wrote, but somewhere along the line had developed
an unshakable belief that his letters were not reaching
their intended destination, that he was made to *think*
he was writing letters to the president in order to pla-
cate him and keep him from *really* writing letters to
the president.

I learned all this a half hour after meeting him, and
by the end of our lunch nearly an hour later, I felt as
though I'd known him forever. He was cranky, cynical,
angry—and I liked him a lot.

A few days later, Stan introduced me to Ellen Dick-
erson and Fischer Cox. Again, we met in the lunchroom. Both Ellen and Fischer were relatively new
here, having come to work at the company only a few
years prior. The two of them were "involved," had
lived together for the past six months, but before starting their jobs here had been married to other people.
Letter writing had taken its toll on those relationships.
They were together now out of sadness, convenience
and desperation but readily admitted that they'd instantly trade what they had with each other if they
could reunite with their spouses again.

I thought of Vicki, thought of Eric.

"It's weird," Fischer said. "This company was built
for us, created for us, and it's great. It's as though we
designed it ourselves. Everything here revolves around
letter writing, which of course is the focus of our lives.
But . . ." He shook his head. "Sometimes it's not
enough, you know?"

I knew exactly what he meant. We all did. And that
night we got together at Stan's for an all-night bull
session. We ended up drinking too much and talking

too much, but we grew closer much faster than we otherwise would have.

Despite our reservations, though, despite our spoken worries and unspoken fears, we loved our jobs. How could we help it? We had TV and movies from all over the world, and access to every periodical on the planet. We were as plugged-in to the currents of contemporary life as it was possible to get. And from within the company we dictated fashions, trends in music, literature, architecture, art. The scales of the political seesaw were tipped one way and then the other by us, and often we worked at cross-purposes as our letters of instruction told us to write contradictory complaints or suggestions. My friends and I discussed what we wrote, the notes we penned on our own and the messages we were directed to write, but we had no idea what others were doing, certainly not the "freeformers," as Stan called them. I had not seen a person from that initial welcoming party, but I knew they were around somewhere, and often I wondered what *they* were writing, or if their work conflicted or contradicted my own.

You were public enemy number one around here, Ernest had said.

You are very powerful, James had told me.

I felt that when I wrote. And I liked it.

I spent more and more time at work, less and less time at home. What was there for me outside of the company anyway? My calls to Eric had become first occasional, then, at the behest of the lawyers, both mine and Vicki's, nonexistent. My contact with Vicki was thirdhand: she spoke to her lawyers, who spoke to my lawyers, who spoke to me. I had no life, I had no family, and reality seemed less real to me each day. I *preferred* looking at the world through a television screen or reading about it through a reporter's eyes.

And writing letters about it.

In an odd way, I grew to appreciate how hard it was to be an artist, to make a living at a creative endeavor. Most people exercised their creativity by recording humorous messages on their answering machines, or providing amusing commentary on family videotapes, or redecorating their houses. But to be forced to produce day in and day out, week after week, was grueling and took much of the fun out of it. Writing letters not because I wanted to, not because I was inspired to, but because it was my job made me appreciate those prolific authors who throughout history had continuously churned out pages of consistently brilliant material regardless of the harsh and complicated circumstances of their lives.

But still, I did it, too, running on that treadmill. I couldn't stop; I couldn't help myself. Wasn't there some lower-form animal, some hamster or rat that, unless halted by an outside force, would endlessly repeat the same action until it died from exhaustion? I was like that. On a conscious level, I might be wearying of the grind, but on an instinctive level, I *had* to write. More than a Pavlovian reaction, it was an instinct that was hardwired into me—and into all of the others.

And we kept on keeping on.

3

Aside from the office building in which we worked, Brea seemed to have become a strangely depopulated city. We never went shopping—food was simply delivered to our houses when we were not there, our refrigerators restocked like those of a hotel minibar—and sometimes I had the unsettling feeling that if I ever stopped at one of the grocery stores along my work route, no one would be there, that the stores were simply false fronts like those in a movie.

The same went for my neighborhood. I saw cars in driveways, lights in houses at night—I even heard the sound of televisions, stereos and radios from other homes, of lawn mowers and leaf blowers from the next street over—but I never saw another person, and more than once I found myself thinking that there weren't any, that this entire neighborhood was fake, created for my benefit, and mine was the only occupied house in this tract. But I was too afraid to knock on one of my neighbors' doors and find out. Sometimes, I convinced myself that everything was real, everything was normal, but at other times I could not help seeing the skull beneath the skin, and I closed my doors and windows, pulled my drapes and focused on the TV, afraid to look at the houses around me.

The fog I'd seen through the window at the party had never returned, but I wondered if it was still there, surrounding everything at a point far enough away that it could not be seen.

Or maybe I was just going crazy.

The oddest thing was how everyone lived in Orange County in a replica of the neighborhood in which they'd lived before. Stan was from Brooklyn, and his house and street were identical to the community from which he'd come. Ellen and Fischer were from Cleveland and Atlanta, respectively, and though they now lived in Fischer's house together, their original residences were copies of those disparate locales. I'd lived here all my life and never seen anything like it. Orange County seemed to have become an impossible amalgam of dozens of different geographies and from the sky must have looked like the play set of a small child who put pieces together at random.

I actually asked Henry about this one time, and though talking to him always cheered me up and did so this time, as well, he didn't answer any of my questions. Once again, I had the impression that he didn't know the answers.

And even if he did, he would be afraid to give them.

I missed my records.

My collection had disappeared, and though I knew the company was behind it, I did not know why. I knew only that in the room where I kept my albums, there were extra couches and pieces of furniture against the walls where shelves were supposed to be. In place of my stereo was another television set. I had always listened to records. I'd used my CD player, frequently, but I'd also enjoyed my turntable on a daily basis, and not a week had gone by that I did not dig into my backlog and pick out some gems from the past.

Suddenly, though, I was forced to remain continuously in the here and now, denied the history and musical depth that my records provided. There were plenty of books around the house, so I could easily read what had come before, but the only music I listened to was what came over the radio or what was played on the MTV or VH1 stations. I asked Henry about this, too, but he feigned ignorance and outrage and suggested I contact the police and tell them I had been robbed. I was tempted to do just that . . . only I never seemed to be able to find the time. Just as I no longer had time to hit my favorite thift stores and used-record shops the way I used to.

It was part of a plan to keep me focused, I rationalized. Letter Writers needed to be laser sharp at all times, concentrated on the here and now, and if this crossed over the line, if breaking into my house and stealing my belongings constituted a criminal act rather than a helpful assist, well, it was still well-intentioned.

Only something told me that this was more than that. Something told me my records had been taken because they meant so much to me, were so important to me. If getting to write letters was the carrot, this was the stick. And it was clear that I was meant to be aware that I was at the mercy of the company.

I missed my records, and I found myself humming a lot, singing to myself when I was home alone, trying to keep the music alive like those book people at the end of *Fahrenheit 451*.

But more than my records, I missed Vicki; I missed Eric.

I wrote them letters. Every day I wrote them letters, telling them what I was doing, how much I missed them, how much I loved them. I poured my heart and soul into the words I wrote, the sentences I crafted for them, knowing that if they received my messages, they would understand.

If.

For I had no idea whether my lettters were getting to them. I slipped the envelopes addressed to Vicki into the mailbox with my daily workload, but the truth was that I did not, could not, know.

So I simply hoped and wrote.

And received no replies.

My best friend, I suppose, was Stan. Our group had gradually grown, and there was a Letter Writer from San Francisco named Shamus who was really into music and was actually closer to my age, but Stan and I had forged a bond based not on similarities of age or background or the things we had in common but rather on the indefinable connection of kindred spirits.

One afternoon, we were in the lunchroom, still drinking and talking after the rest of our "coven," as we'd jokingly begun calling ourselves, had returned to writing. The night before, I'd dreamed of the circus tent again, with the crucified Christ, and this time it had seemed more real than ever. All morning, I'd been thinking about it.

"Are you religious?" I asked Stan.

"I don't know. I guess I'm spiritual to a certain extent. Or was. I was raised Jewish, but as I grew up I dabbled in Buddhism, Christianity, went to Paramahansa Yogananda's Self-Realization Fellowship Temple, tried on a whole bunch of different religions, trying to find one that fit."

"Did any of the Christian stuff stick with you? Deep down, do you still believe?"

"Why?"

"I had a dream last night where I saw Christ's body," I told him. "Crucified. Rotting. In a circus tent in the desert. I've had it before; it's a recurring dream. Only this time two old men were in bleachers to either side of him, writing letters. And . . ." I shook my head. "It doesn't matter. The point is, I knew who he was when I saw him. I believed he was the Son of God. And I knew that he was dead. I could smell the horrible stench of his corpse." I took a swig of beer. "I could still smell it after I woke up. What do you think that means?"

"I don't know," Stan admitted. He looked at me. "Are you Christian?"

"No, not really. At least, I didn't think I was. But . . . it's kind of freaked me out, I have to admit."

"I had a dream like that, too."

We both looked to our right. A white-bearded old man at the next table over had obviously been eavesdropping on our conversation, and he scooted his chair closer to us. "Socrates was tied to a stone slab, and he'd been picked apart by animals."

"How do you know it was Socrates?" Stan asked.

The old man nodded toward me. "How did *he* know it was Jesus? I just knew. Besides, I'm an antiquities scholar. Was," he corrected himself.

"What does all this mean?" I wondered.

"They didn't write," the old man said.

I glanced over at him.

"It's true. Their work lived on through the writings of others, but they themselves were not writers and certainly not Letter Writers." He paused. "I think they were punished for it."

We were all silent for a moment, letting this sink in.

"It makes sense," Stan agreed. "In a sick fucking way it makes perfect sense."

It did. Letter writing was everything; letter writing was all. We might object to that idea intellectually, but still we bought it, believed it.

I asked the question I'd been wondering since dreaming of that hellish tent: "Is there a God?"

The old man laughed harshly. "If there is, he'd better be a Letter Writer or he's going to end up with his balls in a vise."

What of that? I wondered. We had a talent, a gift, a curse or whatever it was, and it had landed us here in this segregated world of our own. But what was our purpose? Were we the champions of those who couldn't write . . . or their tormentors? Were we here to help or hinder? Whose agenda were we furthering with our words?

I didn't know, and the truth was, I didn't really care. Despite all of my qualms, I was doing what I loved to do, what I was born to do. Some of my letters might be hurting people, ending relationships, causing misery—but I didn't care. I never had before, and I still didn't now. Even the fatigue and boredom that sometimes set in after endless days and weeks of the same routine came and went, ebbing and flowing, alternating with the joy and excitement of writing what I loved. I recalled those periods after intense activity where I would stay away from letter writing entirely, and assumed that the same pattern was reasserting itself here.

I wrote to a woman whose son had been in the army and killed on a peacekeeping mission, and pretended to be a friend from his platoon:

> *Dear Mrs. Simmons,*
> *I was with Josh when he was killed, and I just wanted you to know that he died a painful, horrible death. He died cursing you. I don't know what the official line was or what the brass told you, but the truth is that Josh cried like a pussy and pissed himself, shitting in his pants and yelling that he never wanted to join the military, that it was all your fault he was there. You filled his head with all that gung ho patriotic bullshit. With his dying breath, he said, "Fuck my mom! Fuck that whore! Fuck that bitch!" He hated you at the end.*
> *I just thought you should know.*
> *Josh would want you to know.*

I knew that old Mrs. Simmons would feel guilty for the rest of her life, would live out her remaining days in emotional agony, believing that she was a horrible person and responsible for her son's death, but I liked that. I felt the same rush of power that I had first felt when fighting city hall so many years ago. I realized that for all my introspection and attempts at self-improvement, I was the same dark person I had always been. Letter writing brought out the worst in me, and here not only was I allowed to indulge myself to the fullest extent; such extremism was encouraged.

My letters were either formal and cutting in their complaints, or nasty and angry and full of rage.

It was what I wrote.

It was who I was.

Thirteen

1

I accepted a free condominium from the company.

There was a new housing project roughly adjacent to the office building where we worked, in a previously undeveloped area of Brea, a gated neighborhood owned by the company, and one by one my friends and fellow coworkers had been uprooting themselves and moving there, taking advantage of the offer so generously offered by our employer. I finally succumbed, too, and though I did not sell or rent out my house as did so many others, I did pull up stakes and with the help of Stan, Shamus and Fischer transported all of my belongings to my new, smaller digs.

The condo was nice. Airy, well lit, with high ceilings and an efficiency kitchen suited to my bachelor's cooking skills, it was perfect for me. As with my office, it seemed to have been designed with my needs in mind, specifically tailored for me personally, and I found that a little unnerving.

I took from home only the items that were unequivocally mine. A lot of Eric's things I'd shipped over to him the week after he and Vicki had left, but bed, dresser and remaining possessions I left in place, along with everything of Vicki's and those things we had bought together that I thought might have some sentimental value to her. It was a calculated move on my part, an attempt to play her, and I sent her a letter—or, rather, sent one to her lawyers—explaining that I had vacated the house. If the divorce went through, she would probably get it anyway, and I figured if she knew I was gone and it was available, she might move back in.

That's the real reason I moved.

I wanted her in California. I wanted her and Eric close by.

For two weeks after, I phoned my lawyers every day, trying to find out if Vicki had responded, if there'd been any indication she intended to move back. It was only a matter of time, I reasoned. Her life was here, her friends were here, and her parents had to be getting on her nerves by now. But there was nothing. Stone silence from her end, and finally Lou Stevens, the lawyer handling the bulk of my affairs, told me to stop calling.

I did.

But I didn't stop writing letters. I had no idea if they were getting to her, but I assumed they did, and while Vicki might not be reading them, at least she wasn't sending them back.

I considered that a good sign.

To my surprise and somewhat to my consternation, I enjoyed life in my new gated neighborhood. I liked my little condo, and I liked living near my friends. We were like our own small city, a community of Letter Writers, and as much as I hated to admit it, it felt good; it felt comfortable; it felt right.

Stan, of course, grumbled all the way. He was one of the first to jump at the free housing offer, but as usual he saw conspiracies around every corner, ascribed malicious motives to everything the company did, no matter how seemingly benign or altruistic.

There was one weird thing, though. I had a small

white bookcase, three to four feet high, that I'd bought in college and that had been with me ever since. I kept it in my office next to my computer desk.

Only when I brought it to the condo, when I unpacked it from the U-Haul, it was no longer white but a dark simulated wood. I asked Stan, asked Fischer, asked Shamus, if any of them had seen my white bookcase or if any of them knew where this dark one had come from. None of them had.

I put the bookcase in my new office next to my computer desk, unboxed my books and placed them back in it. As with the color of my car and several other small discrepancies I occasionally came across, I put this occurrence out of my mind, chose not to think about it.

But I remembered it later.

2

I got a letter from Kyoko.

Though she was listed as an element in Vicki's divorce petition, I'd almost forgotten about my former pen pal in the hubbub surrounding my new job and my new home. She hadn't written since Vicki and I had separated—in a strange way, it seemed almost as though that had been her goal, and upon reaching it, she had retired—but now she was asking to get together again. The sex talk was gone; there was only an innocent, chaste inquiry. All she wanted, she said, was to meet me.

But I didn't want to meet her. I didn't even want to write to her. I was too tired. I spent enough time writing during the day. At night, I just wanted to relax and veg out.

No, that wasn't exactly true.

I blamed Kyoko for breaking up my marriage.

Yes. That was the real reason I did not write back, the real reason I threw away her letter.

She wrote back a week later, but I didn't even open that one. I threw it away unread. I guess she got the hint, because that was the end of it; that was the last time I heard from her.

3

I started getting other letters, though.

4

Dear Jason,

I watched you last night as you ate your dinner. Macaroni and cheese. Was it good? You didn't smile much, so I wasn't sure you enjoyed it. You just kind of stared at TV when you watched it, too. I thought that was a good episode of Friends, *but you didn't have much reaction.*

At least you enjoyed beating off, though. You really went to town! What were you thinking about when you were stroking yourself? I noticed that you held your balls with your left hand while you pulled on your penis with your right. Were you pretending it was someone else doing it? Fantasizing about Vicki, perhaps?

Or me?

I'll find out eventually.

> *Love,*
> *Your Secret Admirer*

5

Dear Jason,

Stan and Fischer are so full of shit. And don't even listen to what Shamus or Franco say. Ellen and Beth are the only ones with any sense at all. The rest of you? Who can even tell what you think?

I was listening to you guys talk when you were at Stan's house yesterday. Remember when you looked out the window after you ate that first handful of chips? You were practically staring right at me!

But even though you couldn't see me, I could see you.

You were very cute.

Love,
Your Secret Admirer

6

Dear Jason,

I'll bet you miss listening to your own records, tapes and CDs, don't you? Radio plays such crap these days. Why did they take your music collection, I wonder? They didn't take anything of mine. What about your friends, if they really are your friends? I don't think any of their belongings were excluded. Why are you being picked on? Don't you ever wonder about that?

I do.

I saw you naked again last night. After your shower. You forgot to get a towel and you walked out into the hallway to get one out of *the linen closet. You were hard! Had you been playing with yourself in the shower? Maybe you just washed it and got turned on.*

Looked pretty good to me!

Maybe one day you'll let me wash it for you.

By the way, what was that song you were humming? Was that "It's Different for Girls?" I love Joe Jackson!

> *Love,*
> *Your Secret Admirer*

7

Dear Jason,

Wow! That was quite a dream you had last night! The first part was creepy, with the haunted house and the endless swamp and all. But that second part! When you forced Beth to take it up the ass while Fischer watched? I can tell you, I was certainly aroused. My panties smelled like a trout farm after that one!

I had a dream, too. And you were in it. You were naked, of course, but it wasn't really a sex dream, at least not like the kind I usually have. Instead, you just lived in my house and did chores for me: dishes, laundry, dusting, sweeping, vacuuming. Weird, huh?

When I checked your refrigerator yesterday, I noticed that you were getting low on milk. You really like milk, don't you? A lot of men do. A lot of women don't, though. I think it's because women have tits and milk comes from tits and it's just sort of gross.

One time I had a dream where you milked
me like a cow while you took me from behind.
I bet you'd like that, wouldn't you?
Oh, yeah, you need some butter, too. And
luncheon meat.

Love,
Your Secret Admirer

8

Receiving anonymous letters was just as unsettling as ever, and though they were now coming twice a week on a regular basis, I told no one about them. Not even Stan. It could have been anyone writing them, and until I found out for sure, everyone was a potential suspect.

It certainly appeared to be a female, though.

Could it be Ellen, Beth or our newest disgruntled employee, Kerri? I didn't think so. I had no real idea who it might be, however, not even any educated guesses, and that bothered me.

There was an old movie I saw on TV when I was a kid where two girls, as a joke, randomly called people on the phone and said something like "I saw what you did and I know who you are." It freaked the people out. Eventually, the girls called a guy who'd just murdered someone and he thought they were witnesses to the deed and hunted them down.

I could understand now why the recipients of the calls would get so upset. It didn't have to be anything specifically threatening; just an inappropriately intimate knowledge of everyday behavior was enough to make a person paranoid. At work, at home, everywhere I went, I found myself searching the perimeter of each space for a pair of unfamiliar eyes secretively following my every move. I watched everyone I met, trying to determine whether they were paying a little too close attention to me. I felt alone no matter how big a crowd I was in, and never felt as though I was truly by myself even if there appeared to be no one around.

While I didn't tell him specifically about the letters I'd received, I did ask Henry about the mail in general. I'd never seen a postman in our gated community, but I'd started to receive mail, including answers to complaint letters that I'd sent out.

"Yes," he said, "the postal system is in tip-top condition." He laughed. "It has to be with the paces we put it through, don't you think?"

I nodded, smiled.

"We don't have regular delivery, as you've obviously guessed. The company filters out what's unimportant. There's no junk mail or anything generic. But we do have specialized delivery for responses to queries or complaints and, of course, magazines and periodicals. You won't get mail every day, but each time something comes in for you, it will instantly be delivered to your home."

I opted not to open that day's anonymous letter when I arrived home after work. I recognized the type style on the envelope, and as I used to do in the real world, I tore it up and threw it away unopened. As always, this little act of independence made me feel invigorated, and I walked into the kitchen to heat up my dinner of frozen pizza, happy.

It had been a long day. I'd attempted, through letters, to avenge the killing of a Korean teenager by a Russian shopkeeper, and it had taken a lot out of me. Neither party was particularly proficient in English, and it was difficult to adjust my writing so it read as though it had been written by someone who spoke

English as a second language. Stan had invited me over to check out the new James Bond flick on Showtime, but I was too tired, and I declined and spent the evening watching reruns and reading *Keyboard* magazine.

Before taking a shower that evening to wash away the dust of the day, I checked my bathroom carefully for holes or cracks through which someone could peek. I made sure the window was closed, and even peered around the edges of the inset circular light in the center of the room to ensure that no hidden camera had been placed in there.

Then I took a quick shower, wrapping a towel around me immediately after shutting off the water and then slipping my underwear on beneath the towel.

Goddamn that Letter Writer.

Now I knew what it was like to be on the receiving end of our correspondence.

I slipped into a pair of pajamas and walked into the bedroom. I was about to turn on the TV when I heard a strange noise outside, a warbling off-pitch shriek that could have been human, could have been avian. Pulling aside the curtains, I looked out just in time to see a pigeon fall out of the open sky—

—and land flat at the feet of the witch.

The old crone was standing on my front lawn, staring at me angrily, malevolently. I let out an involuntary cry of fear as I quickly closed the drapes. How the hell did she get here? *Why* was she here?

She was dead.

Gathering my courage, I opened the curtains a crack and peered through the narrow opening. The pigeon was still there, but the witch was gone.

Ding-dong.

My doorbell rang.

I hid under the covers like a small child, knowing she had come for me, knowing she had tracked me down in order to avenge her death.

Ding-dong.

The doorbell again.

Ding-dong, the witch is dead, I thought, and almost laughed. Hysteria was very near my surface, and the fear I felt was of the irrational all-consuming sort that afflicted children.

The bell rang eighteen times before finally stopping.

I'd written the letter that led to the witch's death when I was eighteen years old.

Coincidence? Perhaps. But this was all too close for comfort. I was enveloped with paranoia and spent the rest of the night wide-awake in my bed, staring up at the ceiling, which was tinted a flickering blue by the television, and coming up with increasingly outlandish and Byzantine connections between the witch, me and the company.

In the morning, I went outside, got a shovel from the garage, picked up the body of the dead pigeon and tossed it into the garbage can.

On my way to work that morning, I kept my eyes open for signs of anything unusual. I even drove down different streets than I usually did, streets on which I remembered seeing the witch as a kid or a teenager, but there was no sign of her.

In my office, though, I came face-to-face with a poster for the Pigeons plastered on the wall right above my desk.

I'd never liked the Pigeons.

And hadn't there been a Graham Parker poster there yesterday?

I shivered, though the air in my office was stuffy and humid rather than cold. *This* I told my friends about. I even brought it up to Henry. But though Stan and everyone were sympathetic, none of them had ever experienced anything like it or had any ideas on how to deal with it. Both Stan and Shamus told me I could stay in their guest rooms for a while if I was really spooked—they thought if she showed up there, I'd at least have a witness—but I didn't see how that would help, and besides, it felt too much like giving up, like conceding defeat. Henry just flat out didn't believe that it had happened. Or said he didn't. He offered me only a general sort of support and half jokingly suggested that maybe I'd been working a little too hard or should go to bed earlier and get more sleep.

Everything seemed off that day. I tore down the Pigeons poster and beneath it was a reproduction of the cover for Black Sabbath's self-titled first album—the one with a grainy photograph of a witch. In the lunchroom, the tables were decorated with center-pieces featuring foldout vampires, Frankensteins, wolf men, skeletons and witches. It was almost Halloween. I hadn't realized it until now, since there seemed to be no kids here. I wondered what Eric was going to be this Halloween. I realized that it had been months since I'd heard from him.

I didn't get much writing done, but the one letter I did complete was to the police department of a New Jersey bedroom community, asking that a closer watch be kept on some of the homeless people who were threatening young schoolchildren.

The coincidence seemed a little *too* coincidental.

I took off early, driving home and then sitting out on the patio of my minuscule backyard, drinking can after can of beer.

I missed my wife and son terribly.

But I liked being able to write letters.

Ellen called that evening after dinner to check up on me, make sure I was okay. I was still a little drunk but starting to sober up, and I assured her that everything was fine.

"Have you . . . seen anything?" she asked.

"Nothing," I told her. We chatted for a little while longer, then hung up.

But I'd spoken too soon.

It was a Tuesday night, and after watching *NYPD Blue,* I went into the bathroom to take a shit, leaving the television on loud in the living room so I could hear the eleven o'clock news. I was sitting on the bowl, halfway through doing my duty, when I suddenly realized that the house was completely silent.

The television had been shut off.

I tried to tell myself that it was some sort of problem with the circuit breaker, but the light in the bathroom was on, and I could see from the line under the door that the light in the living room was on, as well.

Only the TV was off.

Maybe the set itself was broken, or maybe—

Tap-tap-tap.

If I lived to be a hundred, I would never forget the sound of the witch's cane tapping on the ground, and that was exactly what I heard as I sat there on the toilet with my pants down. I was in the most vulnerable position humanly possible, a piece of shit half in and half out of my ass. I remembered, a couple of years back, hearing a man say that he'd been caught in the Northridge earthquake while puking his guts out with the flu. He'd been bent over and barfing while the ground started to shake, and while everyone else in his neighborhood was running outside or hiding under furniture to protect themselves, he'd been on his knees and heaving. I had that fucker beat a thousand times over.

Tap-tap-tap.

The thing was, I couldn't tell from which direction the sound was coming. Was it inside the house, down the hall, or was it outside on the patio? I finished going, forcing it out, then quickly pulled up my pants without wiping. I stood, pressed my ear to the door.

Tap-tap-tap.

She was inside. I could hear her cane on the hardwood floor of the living room, moving away from the hallway toward the kitchen. My first impulse was to pull up the shade and try to shove my way through the open bathroom window and escape outside. But there was no way I'd ever fit through that small opening, and besides, if she *was* in the kitchen, she'd be able to see me.

I looked around the bathroom for some sort of weapon, found only a small pair of scissors, a safety razor and a plunger. I opted for the plunger and the scissors. At least the plunger had a wooden handle that I could use to swing at her. And if I ended up entangled, the scissors could do far more quick damage than the shielded razor blades.

I opened the door a crack, peeking out.

The hallway was clear, as was what I could see of the living room.

Squeak.

It was the sound of the kitchen door opening. She was going outside onto the patio. I hurried down the hall, through the living room to the kitchen, where the door remained wide open. Even from here, I could see her by the picnic table, hobbling away from me toward the darkness of the lawn. I was frozen, unsure whether to yell at her or wait silently for her to leave, whether to close the door and take refuge inside or dash out and confront her. I compromised by moving forward slowly, quietly, not wanting to draw attention to myself but ready to slam shut and lock the door should she show any intent to turn around and return.

I reached the open doorway, and she swiveled on

her heels and stared at me. I remembered from my nighttime sojourn with Robert and Edson how she'd swept her cane from left to right and said "Don't write," how a pigeon had dropped from the sky and landed dead on the sidewalk halfway between us, and how she'd smiled.

She smiled that way now, and goose bumps washed over my arms. Even as she stared at me, I could see that her cane was moving on the ground, drawing characters or runes or figures in the hard dirt on the edge of the grass.

Then she turned, hobbling into the darkness of the backyard. I waited several seconds for the sound of the side gate opening and closing, but there was no noise, and finally I reached over and flipped on the switch that controlled the backyard floodlights. The entire lawn area was illuminated, but the witch was nowhere to be seen. She'd disappeared.

I waited a few minutes just to make sure, then tentatively stepped outside. I heard nothing, saw nothing and, gaining courage, followed the route she had taken.

There.

In the dirt where her cane had been moving was drawn a strange spirally symbol, what I could only assume was some sort of curse or hex. It looked familiar, but I couldn't place it, couldn't recall where I had seen it before. I rubbed it with my shoe, kicked at it, trying to erase it, but the carving was deep, and finally I got a trowel out of the garage and dug up the dirt, smoothing it over so all trace of the figure was gone.

I closed all of the windows and locked all of the doors.

Just before falling asleep, I remembered where I had seen the witch's symbol: on the carved fresco surrounding the mailbox on our floor at work.

I dreamed of a pigeon that followed me wherever I went, cooing, "Don't write. . . . Don't write. . . . Don't write. . . ."

In the morning, when I awoke, my mail slot had been sealed shut.

Fourteen

1

"I think they're doing it," Stan said. "The company. The letters, the witch, they're behind all of it. That's why Henry's pleading ignorance."

I'd finally broken down and told him *everything* that had been happening. I couldn't keep it to myself.

"But why?" I wondered. "What would be the point?"

He leaned forward. "It all depends on whether you think you're here writing letters to help in some unknown altruistic goal or whether they've simply saddled you with fake busywork to take you out of commission. You've got your 'The Lord works in mysterious ways' approach or your 'They're fucking with me for some nefarious reason' approach. That's the one I'm betting on, and it's what I've been trying to tell you all along.

"As I see it, you've got two choices: accept the status quo and live out your life as a letter-writing drone or put on your Patrick McGoohan Number Six face and try to find out what the hell is behind all this."

I wasn't quite sure I bought into all of his conspiracy theories . . . but I didn't automatically discount them, either. "How do we do that?"

"I don't know," he admitted.

I slapped him on the back. "Thanks," I said. "You've been a lot of help."

After that, the witch seemed to disappear. I neither
saw nor heard any sign of her, and after a couple of
weeks, I decided that she must have served her purpose. She'd completed her mission, said what she'd
come here to say. Stan was wrong. The powers that
be had not used her, were not behind this. Ghost or
no ghost—and that was something I *definitely* didn't
understand, something that for some reason I never
seemed to even *think* about—she'd been warning me
once again to stop writing.

I had to admit that I was open to this message. I
loved letter writing as much as I always had, but the
novelty of my job had worn off, and once again I'd
begun to be troubled by the darker currents that swam
beneath the sunny fun of my abilities. I could tell myself
that the letters I was assigned to write, the correspondence I sent out, were in service of the little guy, were
giving voice to the voiceless, righting wrongs that would
otherwise remain unremedied, but people were being
hurt along the way. Innocent people. I knew it; I could
feel it.

And I didn't care.

That troubled me, kept me awake at night, made
me think that Stan's theories weren't as far-fetched as
some of the others thought they were.

The witch was right. I *should* stop writing letters.

But I didn't.

I couldn't.

Although the witch was gone, the anonymous letters
kept coming, one a week, then two, and I opened
them, hoping to find clues.

Of course, there were only creepy descriptions of
my everyday activities, combined with blatant sex talk:

Dear Jason,
    I love Blue Velvet, *too! I watched it with
you last night, though you didn't know it.
David Lynch is my favorite director. Did you*

used to watch Twin Peaks? *I was hoping you'd masturbate after the movie, and I was so disappointed that you just went straight to bed. . . .*

And

Dear Jason,
I know you don't like to clean (are you one of those macho guys who consider house-cleaning women's work?), but you really need to sweep sometime. That floor in the kitchen, especially, is getting ridiculous. And change your sheets! If you ever hope to have a woman like me over, you're going to have to have clean sheets. . . .

And more.

I showed these letters to Stan, and the two of us shared them with the others, hoping someone might recognize the writing style or the printing font or some small detail that would give a clue as to the identity of the writer. But they were all equally baffled. No one had ever run into anything like this, and the idea that there was some sort of Letter Writer stalker on the loose put everyone on edge. I might be the immediate target, but anyone could be next, and—who could tell?—there might be more than one of them running around.

Stan, of course, thought the messages were fake, created by the Letter Writer who had originally lured us here, the one who headed the company—the Ultimate Letter Writer, as Stan referred to him—in order to test, try and torment me. He was spooked to the bone by the fact that I was being watched so carefully, my every move monitored so thoroughly, and he was certain that he, too, was under close scrutiny at all times.

Maybe he was and maybe he wasn't. I was beginning to think more and more that I was different, that I was special.

You are very powerful.

I continued to believe that the witch I'd seen really was the witch of Acacia and that she had a personal grudge against me. I continued to believe that the letters being sent to me were from a deranged admirer or someone with a secret enmity toward me. I also believed that Stan was right, that I was under constant surveillance, although I wasn't sure that any of these things were at all connected.

As they sometimes did, my thoughts turned to the dream of that circus tent in the desert and Christ's rotting body. The nightmare resonated with me, spoke to me, and I could not help feeling that it had some hidden metaphoric meaning. Maybe everything was breaking down, coming apart at the seams, I thought. Maybe there was no logic, no order, no reason for anything, only a chaos of letters and random activity that were spiraling madly out of control.

Virginia stopped by to see how I was doing. That was a surprise. I was just about to start on a series of complaint letters from customers of The Store, when I answered a knock on my office door and there she was.

"I've been wondering about you!" Virginia said enthusiastically as she gave me a sincere but restrained hug. "How are you faring?"

"Fine," I said, not wanting to get bogged down in detail.

She flopped into my chair, looking around the office. She chuckled as she saw all the music posters. "This really is you, isn't it?"

I felt suddenly annoyed. How would she know if this was me or not? She'd met me once for a brief period of time. No one could size me up that quickly. I wasn't *that* predictable or uncomplicated.

But I couldn't stay annoyed long. She was out of the chair and pacing around my small quarters. There was something very disarming about her, and I was suddenly glad she'd come.

"Where do *you* work?" I asked her.

"On the tenth floor. Would you like to see?"

"I'd love to," I admitted.

"All right, then."

I'd never played hooky like this in the middle of the day. As Virginia correctly pointed out in the elevator, I was steeped in a middle-class work ethic, and despite the fact that Henry had made clear I was free to come and go as I pleased, to work when and where I wanted, I showed up each day at my office by rote, I took only traditional coffee and lunch breaks, and if I ever slacked off and left early, I made up for it the next day, punishing myself for my transgression by depriving myself of one of my breaks.

"Loosen up," Virginia told me. "Live a little."

The elevator stopped on the tenth floor. The metal doors slid open. I would not have been surprised to see a series of intricately realized customized work spaces like we had on the fourth floor. I would not have been surprised to see a gigantic Victorian library.

But I *was* surprised by the sight that greeted my eyes.

Cubicles.

Under the harsh glare of fluorescent lights, modular workstations were grouped in configurations of four or six in a square corporate-looking room that was not impossibly large or in defiance of the laws of physics but conformed precisely to the dimensions of the building as it appeared from outside.

Virginia took my arm and strolled casually forward. Nearly all of the people from the party, as well as a dozen or so more, were seated in gray ergonomically designed chairs in front of flat, identically generic desks, writing. Ernest had a typewriter, Leo a series of calligraphy pens, James a PC, but aside from the writing materials and a few personalized decorations, the workstations all looked the same.

Virginia's cubicle contained a messy pile of papers, a photograph of a garden, a red rose in a vase and, incongruously, a "Dilbert" comic strip thumbtacked to the gray fabric modular wall. A Styrofoam cup of watered-down iced tea with a slice of lemon in it had made a ringed stain on the papers.

Everyone seemed fairly happy or at least content—composing correspondence is all it takes to keep Letter Writers satisfied—but their circumstances to me seemed unbearably depressing. I looked at Virginia. "This is your desk?"

"Yes, it is."

"But why aren't you . . . why are you . . . how come you're working in a place like this?"

"When you're at our level, you don't need all those bells and whistles, a manufactured habitat like some animal in a zoo." Virginia smiled. "*Our level.* Look who I'm talking to!" She gripped my arm tighter. "The truth is, you could work here, too. You don't need some phony 'environment.' Those are for the novices, the hacks, the Letter Writers who require outside stimulation to do their best work. We don't need such superfluous trifles. Neither do you, I'll wager."

I didn't respond. Maybe I didn't need a "habitat," as she'd called it, in order to write effective letters, but I'd much rather work in my fake record store office than in these sterile surroundings.

"You belong here with us," she said, and looked around as though fearful of being overheard. "We have a vacancy, you know."

I didn't answer.

We stopped for a few moments at the cubicles of some of the people I'd met at the party, and chatted casually as though we really were friends who'd run into each other, but soon Virginia began to get visibly anxious, and I sensed that it was time for me to leave. She needed to get back to work. I was still not sure why she had invited me up here, unless it was to tell me about the vacancy, but I didn't feel secure enough to ask. I liked her, but I still didn't entirely trust her, and I wondered if the bureaucrat who had questioned me, the man who'd broken up the party, had put her up to it. I hadn't seen him since that night, yet I had the distinct impression that he was still around, keeping tabs.

Reporting on me to the big boss, the CEO, the Ultimate Letter Writer.

I definitely bought into that aspect of Stan's theory.

Virginia waved good-bye as I got back on the elevator. The doors remained open for an extended moment, and I looked at all of the numbers between the tenth floor and the fourth. What was on them? Who worked there? On impulse, I stretched out my index finger and pressed all of the buttons in order, my pulse accelerating as the numbers lit up. As the doors closed, she was smiling at me, obviously having seen what I'd done, and I took that as tacit approval. Did she have any official standing? Was she even anywhere near the power structure of this place? Probably not. But Virginia had been here a long time, she had to know the ways of this company, and that granted her a certain stature in my book. Her smile gave me the confidence to go through with what I might have chickened out of otherwise.

The elevator sped by the ninth floor, the eighth, the seventh. As it descended past each, the corresponding light blinked off on the panel of buttons, though the elevator itself never slowed and the doors did not open. I pressed the remaining buttons again but the elevator continued on past the sixth floor before finally stopping on the fifth.

The doors slid open.

For some reason, I had not been allowed to visit those other floors, but this one was open to me, and I stepped into what looked like a fantasist's conception of a newspaper office. In the vast open area in the center stood a large anthropomorphic printing press, a massive black octopus-like machine nearly two stories high with gears and levers that formed a smiling face in the middle. From a series of slots near the bottom of the printing press, typed letters extruded into metal trays. All around the giant machine were inset offices with windows that overlooked this central area. Some of the windows were shuttered or covered with mini-blinds, but through others I could see men and women of various ages and nationalities writing intently.

The office to my right, the one closest to me, was dark, its occupant sick or absent for some reason, and I took the opportunity to place my hands on the glass and peek inside. I saw a large old-fashioned oak desk covered with piles of papers, in the middle of which was a keyboard and monitor. On the back wall, barely visible in the gloom, was a poster of what looked like a red pagoda. Stepping back away from the window, I looked at the nameplate mounted on the closed door.

Kyoko Yoshizumi.

My heart began pounding hard in my chest, and my palms were suddenly sweaty.

Kyoko worked here! They had recruited her, too.

But where was she? The office was dark and empty. Maybe she was sick or absent today. Maybe she was on break. Or maybe it was still being prepared for her and she had not yet started working here.

Kyoko was a Letter Writer.

I should have guessed it sooner.

I remembered, as clearly as though I'd seen it yesterday, the photo Kyoko took of herself with her dress and underwear pulled down and bunched around her knees.

It was a strange coincidence that we were both Letter Writers, but the truth was that despite the broken English, I could remember the text of several of her missives even now. And that sympathy piece she'd penned after I'd told her my father died? Sheer genius. I wondered if we had inspired each other, if our brief connection had ignited within each other some sort of nascent spark that had made us into the Letter Writers we were today. If we'd had other pen pals, would we have turned out differently? It seemed almost impossible to believe that the two of us would both be Letter Writers and both end up here. What were the odds?

What had happened to my fifth-grade teacher, Miss Nakamoto? I wondered. Could she be a Letter Writer, too? No, that was too much to expect. Still, how old was she? What did she look like now?

I didn't like thinking about the past. I'd always been that way and still was, preferring to live in the present and not dwell on what had gone before.

But I seemed to be doing a lot of dwelling lately.

Unbidden, a memory of Eric came into my mind. A good memory: last year, in the summer, the two of us walking through Toys "R" Us, him holding my index finger with his tiny hand, chattering away about Thomas the Tank Engine. *It doesn't get any better than this,* I remembered thinking.

Would I ever see him again?

I suddenly felt like crying.

Then the office next to Kyoko's opened, and a man stepped out. He'd obviously been heading for one of those metal trays at the foot of the printing press, intending to pick up copies of the letters he'd written, but he saw me out of the corner of his eye and turned to face me. "Who are you?" he asked. "And what do you want?"

I was just as much of a Letter Writer as he was, and

I faced him with confidence. "I'm looking for Kyoko Yoshizumi," I told him.

"She's out today, but she'll be back tomorrow." He eyed me suspiciously.

Kyoko *was* here!

My stomach was filled with butterflies. After all these years, I would finally meet her. The prospect made me nervous, and I thanked the man, then headed back to the elevator the way I'd come. I returned to the fourth floor and immediately holed up in my office. I'd been intending to send a complaint letter to NBC for canceling one of my favorite shows, but I no longer felt like writing today. Instead, I sat there and daydreamed, trying to imagine Kyoko's life between then and now.

I thought of all the floors above me. Were there other people I knew sitting in an office or created environment? A lot of people worked in this building. Many more than were indicated by the cars in the parking lot. Where did they all come from? Where did they all live? How come I never saw them?

I left early, driving straight home, feeling antsy and ill at ease, not at all sure finally that I did want to meet Kyoko. What if she was fat and ugly and mean? Despite the tone and sentiments of her recent letters, what if she blamed me for everything bad that had happened in her life and hated my guts?

I'd sleep on it, I decided.

That night, I was lying in bed when I heard a noise from up on my roof. A . . . tapping.

The witch's cane.

I sat up in bed, feeling like a frightened child, trying to resist the impulse to pull the covers over my head and hide. She was up there, walking along the slanted side of the sloping roof. I was scared, but I forced myself to get out of bed and speed down the hallway toward the living room, keeping as quiet as I could.

My plan was to quickly open the front door, run out onto the lawn and confront her. I was wearing nothing but my underwear, but I'd long since given up the fiction that there was anyone in my neighborhood who cared.

Above my head, first on the roof above the hallway, then above the living room, I could hear the witch's cane.

Tap-tap-tap.

She was following my progress.

Since she knew where I was, I no longer had to be quiet, and I made a mad dash for the door, quickly turning the locks and rushing outside.

Surprise, surprise, she wasn't up there. She'd already gone, but she'd left behind what looked like a torn sheet that was attached to the chimney and fluttering in the slight breeze. It was a talisman or fetish of some sort, and when it straightened out for a second I could see what looked like painting or writing on it. Some sort of curse, no doubt, but I wasn't about to go up there in the middle of the night and take it down—who knew where that bitch was hiding?—so I simply gave the yard one last cursory glance, then went back inside, locking the door and double-checking to make sure all of the windows had been shut and latched. I'd go up in the morning and remove it.

But in the morning, it, too, was gone, and when I climbed the ladder to get onto the roof, I saw red runic writing on the shingles above my bedroom that looked like it had been drawn in blood. The hose wouldn't wash it off, and my efforts at scraping it with my shoe were completely useless. I'd have to paint over it, or use sandpaper or something, if I really wanted to make it disappear. Did I think the curse or spell or whatever it was would really work? No. But I resented the fact that that old hag could deface my property at will and get away with it.

"I know what you can do about the witch," Stan told me after I'd explained to him what had happened. "Remember how you said you got rid of her the first time? You wrote a letter to the police about her. Do the same thing again." He leaned forward confidentially. "It's what they want you to do anyway. They're testing you to see if you've still got what it takes."

As crazy as it sounded, I thought he might be right. It certainly couldn't hurt to try. So I wrote to the chief of police and laid out in detail a case of harassment and trespassing against her, describing everything that had happened since I'd first seen her on my front lawn.

I took the envelope to the mailbox and dropped it in.

I felt better. Things seemed to be working out. And I walked back to my office in a much better mood.

2

We were often invited to special movie screenings and sneak previews, since a lot of us wrote letters about popular culture. The company usually arranged to show the films at a multiplex in Brea, a new theater with big screens, state-of-the-art projectors and sound, tiered seating. We saw all of the latest movies, often before the general public, not just the blockbusters but foreign films, art films, independent films. They were almost like parties, like Hollywood premieres. Sometimes I saw other people I knew there; sometimes I made new friends. Once, I was even hit on by an elderly gent, who apologized profusely when he realized that he had made a mistake.

This time I went with Fischer and Ellen to see a subtitled Japanese horror movie that had been getting rave reviews and that Fischer wanted to comment on. Shortly after the film started, I experienced a dry-throat coughing fit and went out to the lobby to get a drink of water.

Where I met Kyoko, hurrying in to catch the movie.

I recognized her instantly, and she me. She was beautiful: slim and sexy and modern-looking in the way of the trendiest Japanese models. She looked younger than me, and if I hadn't known better, I would have pegged her as being between eighteen and twenty-four. We stood there for an awkward moment, staring at each other, and then I said, "Hi." Not the best conversation starter, but the best I could come up with under the circumstances.

"Hello," Kyoko said, smiling shyly, although it really did sound closer to "Herro."

I was at a loss. Even under the best of circumstances I was not good at cold meetings. I invariably hemmed and hawed and embarrassed myself with my inability to speak naturally. And right now I could think of nothing appropriate to say to her. "You're a Letter Writer," I offered lamely.

She nodded, reddening.

I didn't feel anything for her, I realized. No sparks flew. I'd lied to her about my feelings in those letters so long ago, and my feelings hadn't changed. On a purely objective level, she was probably more attractive than Vicki, but there was no way in the world I would trade. I loved Vicki. And only Vicki. Although I'd written a letter that morning urging the governor of Texas *not* to pardon a prisoner who was about to be executed but was completely innocent of the murder for which he'd been convicted, I felt pure and good thinking about my wife. In spite of my dark and guilty heart, there was hope for me yet.

"Do you getting my new letters?" she asked. "You like more better?"

A warning alarm went off in my head. "*New* letters?" I said cautiously.

She nodded a little too excitedly. "Yes! I send you thirteen so far. Secret-admirer letters. That what I write, my specialty. I want to surprise you like now. You not know it's me?"

Whatever connection there was or might have been between us was severed at that instant. Kyoko was the one who had been sending me those creepy messages. She'd been spying on me, stalking me, and apparently she was expecting me to fall madly in love with her so the two of us could live happily ever after.

Had she been obsessing over me all these years?

The goose bumps on my arms had nothing to do with the air-conditioning.

"I'm sorry," I said, backing away. I didn't know what to say, how to get away from her, how to get out of this. She started to say something, but I quickly ducked back into the theater and made my way down the darkened aisle until I found my row. I sat back down next to Fischer.

"You all right?" he asked.

I nodded. What I really wanted to do was get out of there and escape. I was afraid she'd sit down next to me. Or in front of me. Or behind me. I was afraid she'd follow me out after the movie and then follow me home.

Of course, she already knew where I lived.

This was a no-win situation. I slumped in my seat, staring uncomprehendingly at the screen, not bothering to read the subtitles. Fischer and Ellen shared popcorn, munching happily, completely unaware that anything was amiss, but I kept waiting for Kyoko to show up.

She didn't. And that was a good thing. It gave me time to think, gave me time to calm down. Maybe I'd misread the whole situation. Maybe it was just a cultural thing, a difference in perception. Maybe she wasn't going to go *Fatal Attraction* on me. But as I thought back on the explicitness of the letters and the implication that she'd been in my house spying on me, that she'd lurked outside other people's houses watching me, I realized that there was no way to put a benign spin on what had occurred. My first instinct was right. She was a stalker.

So what was my next move? Someone so obsessive would not be deterred by a simple request to knock it off and leave me alone. And working for the company was really like living in a small town. We were bound to run into each other again.

Especially if she wanted us to.

Especially if she kept following me around.

The lights went up after the movie ended. Fischer, as usual, insisted on staying for the credits, though he couldn't read a word of them, and I took the opportunity to surreptitiously look around. I didn't see Kyoko among the people shuffling up the aisles on their way out, and I couldn't see her in any of the seats, waiting with us.

Which meant that she had to be in the lobby.

I hewed close to Fischer and Ellen as we made our way out of the auditorium.

But she wasn't there.

In a way, this disappearing act was worse. If I'd been able to confront her, particularly with a witness, I would at least have had the satisfaction of taking some action. And I would at least have known her whereabouts. But as it was, I was denied the catharsis of confrontation, leaving me charged up yet frustrated inside, and I found myself looking behind every corner, anticipating each movement, wondering when she was going to show.

We made it out to the parking lot.

The three of us said our good-byes, I drove home—

And there was a letter from Kyoko waiting for me in my mailbox.

This time I opened it, read it:

> Dear Jason,
>
> It was wonderful to see you again, and I can't wait to get together! Did I surprise you? I hope so! How do you think I look? My breasts may not be as big as American women's, but I can assure you I know how to use what I've got. I've been saving myself for you. I knew you would come here eventually. You didn't save yourself for me, but I forgive you for that. If I ever catch that bitch Vicki, though . . .
>
> Just kidding! (Not really!)
>
> I know you have letters to write. I do, too. Keep in touch. I'll see you soon.
>
> Love,
> Your Dearest Kyoko

This was impossible. I'd left the theater ten minutes ago, yet Kyoko's letter was here, having been delivered with the rest of my mail earlier in the day. There was even a postmark on the envelope.

Besides, was this really Kyoko? The writing here was flawless, but she spoke broken English, and it was hard to imagine that this letter came from the same person to whom I'd spoken. I knew it did, though. Letter writing was a language to itself, and I had no doubt that there were Letter Writers who were grunting, inarticulate dolts but could compose correspondence that would make a nun drop her drawers. It was an ability or a talent that seemed to exist independently of anything else, and I thought of a story I'd read in high school where a scientist discovered that even the stupidest people had elaborate dreams as complex and fully realized as the smartest philosopher.

I reread the letter several times before going to bed. I had a hard time sleeping.

The next day, she sent me two letters. One was covered with Hello Kitty stickers. The other envelope had a piece of Japanese Fusen gum inside. What were we, ten? The letters themselves were much more adult and were fairly explicit about what she wanted from me, although they were by no means as blunt as the secret-admirer letters.

The next morning, on my way to work, I saw her following me. She remained a car length behind, but I could see her clearly through the wide windshield of her Corvette, and it occurred to me that I'd seen that car before around town, in front of my house.

When I was at lunch, she left a note on my desk describing the graphic details of a sex dream she'd had the night before.

I didn't know what to do.

Maybe I could get her fired.

Yes! That would be perfect.

I had no idea how to go about it, and I considered just making something up, lying in a letter that I sent to her supervisor or even the CEO of the company—

the Ultimate Letter Writer

—but she was an employee here, too, and that might backfire. She worked on a higher floor, and for all I knew, that meant she was more senior and higher in rank than I was.

Virginia would know what to do. She'd be able to help me. She'd been here a long time, she knew everyone who was anyone, and she genuinely seemed to like me. If anybody could help figure out a way to get Kyoko out of here it would be her.

I wasn't sure I'd be allowed to just pop up and visit the tenth floor, so I walked across the corridor, knocked on Henry's door and went into his office. I ended up telling him the whole story, and though he professed to find it unbelievable, he did not doubt that I was telling the truth.

"I have an idea," he said.

"Shoot," I told him. At this point, I was open to any suggestion.

"Kill her."

I blinked, stared at him. He still wore the friendly passive expression that he always had, and even his eyes appeared warm and kind.

"Go ahead and talk to Virginia, if you want. Talk to anybody you think will help. Get as many thoughts and ideas as you can. But looking at it from where I sit, I don't see any other way out. Even if she lost her job, she wouldn't necessarily move. She might be able to continue plaguing you for . . . forever. So if you don't want to get together and she does so desperately, either you're going to have to put up with an eternity of harassment or one of you is going to have to go."

"The company would have one less Letter Writer." I couldn't believe I was playing devil's advocate to his lunatic suggestion. He couldn't be serious.

Could he?

"Sometimes," Henry said slowly, "an ideal is more important than an individual. Do you think all of the Letter Writers throughout history who were martyred or persecuted wanted it to be that way? Do you think those men scribbling away within the Bastille, not knowing whether their words would ever be read, let alone published, desired that existence? No. Letter writing is a cause and a calling that is bigger than ourselves. We did not choose this life, we may have had it thrust on us, but it is our duty to rise to the challenge, to pave the way for the future. To *make* the future."

It was a memorized speech but not delivered by rote. He spoke passionately, with feeling.

"I think killing her's your only choice."

"But isn't that . . . a sin?"

He laughed. "You've done it before. We all have."

He was right. I was already a murderer several times over.

I nodded, pretended to agree and muttered some generic comments as a way of excusing myself. I was frightened by the turn this conversation had taken, and I wanted to go back into my little record store office and look at music posters and hide.

I'd talk to Virginia some other time, I decided as I made my way back across the corridor. For the moment, I'd just avoid Kyoko as much as I could and play her off when I ran into her.

I returned to my office and spent the rest of the day writing nontaxing letters about music to *Rolling Stone* and *Vibe* and *Spin*.

"That's freaky," Stan said, and Shamus nodded in agreement. The three of us were on the sidewalk outside the building, getting ready to trek through the parking lot to find our individual cars.

"Yeah," I said glumly. I'd just finished telling them about Kyoko but hadn't mentioned my conversation with Henry. I found it hard to believe it had even happened.

Shamus looked around at the other departing Letter Writers. "Is she here? Do you see her?"

"I'm not looking," I admitted. "I don't want to accidentally make eye contact. She'd take that as a come-on."

"Could *I* hit on her? Hey, maybe if I distracted her, gave her what she needed, she'd leave you alone."

"Go ahead," I offered. "Be my guest."

"She might be waiting for you at home," Stan said seriously. "Maybe in your bed."

The thought had occurred to me.

"You want me to come to your house? Or you want to crash at mine tonight?"

"Running away just because you're offered a little
'strange? Dude!"

We both looked at Shamus, and he shut up,
embarrassed.

"No," I said, resigned. "It's my problem. I have to
learn to deal with it."

"Well, good luck," Stan said. "You have my number. Call me if you need me."

"Me, too," Shamus declared.

We said good-bye and started off toward our re-
spective cars, me on the lookout for a lurking Kyoko
crouching down behind one of the parked sedans, vans
or SUVs.

"At least it's keeping your mind off the witch!" Stan
shouted, waving.

I held up my middle finger to show him what I
thought of his humor and walked over to my car, un-
locking the door. She wasn't hiding in the backseat,
so that first hurdle was jumped. I quickly got in,
pressed the automatic door lock button and started
the engine.

I saw her on my way home.

She was standing on the corner of Brea Boulevard
and Imperial Highway, in front of a gas station, waving at me as though I were in a parade and she one
of the spectators lining the route. She'd changed her
clothes, and she had on a short tight skirt and a
midriff-revealing top. I was supposed to be turned on,
I guess, and she did look sexy, but it was in a slutty,
trashy way that made me even more determined to
stay as far as possible from her.

I sped home, knowing she would not be able to beat
me there now. I parked the car, ran into the condo,
closed and locked the front door and made sure everything was sealed up tight.

Impossibly, Kyoko was on my television that evening. I had just watched a comedy on HBO in an
attempt to escape from my real life, and when I

switched the channel to watch NBC's local newscast, Kyoko was there. I don't know if she'd somehow gotten someone to intercept the signal or if this intrusion was sanctioned by the powers that be, but her pretty face filled the screen, and though there was no sound, she kept mouthing the words, "I love you. I love you. I love you. . . ."

I switched off the television.

I dreamed that night that I was lying in bed and Kyoko, naked and beautiful, sat on my face. But she smelled of ass rather than pussy, and when I tried to get up, tried to squirm out from under her, I couldn't. I was unable to breathe, I was choking to death, and I tried to push her off me, but my hands kept sinking into her skin as though she were made of clay, and the weight of her body kept increasing, pressing over my mouth and nose, cutting off my supply of air.

I awoke just before I died.

3

The witch was gone. Had I written her out of existence?

Could I write Kyoko away, too?

I thought about it. The idea was worth a try, I decided, and I sat down and penned a series of letters from various points of view to various recipients, working at my highest and most inspired level, concocting reasons why she should be fired from the company, why she needed to be removed from the presence of other Letter Writers. The reasons were real and fake: because she was a psychotic stalker, because she was an incompetent letter writer. I used every arrow in my arsenal, and I sent all of the correspondence off at once, hoping that perhaps sheer bulk would be impressive enough to get my point across.

There she was the next day, standing in front of my office when I arrived, holding an elaborately wrapped present, which she gave to me along with an unwelcome kiss. I refused the present, angrily sent it back with her and watched with a sort of grim satisfaction as she dashed to the elevator in tears.

I wrote more letters.

The following day, she sent me a formal note of apology for the present, then plopped herself down next to me at lunch. None of my friends knew what to do or how to react. All conversation stopped, and Stan suggested tersely that it would be better if she left. Shamus, as promised, tried to hit on her, but she shot him down in cute broken English that charmed even Ellen. Kyoko snuggled next to me, pressing her bare leg against mine under the table, and I stood, leaving the rest of my lunch and excusing myself as I returned to my office. According to Stan, she spent the rest of the hour talking about me.

I wrote *more* letters.

The day after that, I found a long black hair on the soap in my shower. And a pair of women's panties mixed in with the clothes in my hamper when I sorted through everything to do the laundry. In my mailbox was a naked picture of her, a recreation of her original photo that she'd taken by herself in my bathroom.

That was the last straw.

I had to kill the bitch.

I tried to unthink that thought but failed. I recalled my conversation with Henry.

I think killing her's your only choice.

No. I couldn't do that.

Although I'd done it before, through letters, and the truth was that if I could get rid of her that way, I would—without feeling any guilt or remorse. Hell, I'd be overjoyed if she keeled over right this second and never darkened my pathway again. But it was one thing to be morally liable for the death of a person, and it was quite another to perform the actual deed. That was why presidents responsible for the deaths of hundreds of innocent civilians in war actions slept like babies at night, while an individual who had too much to drink and accidentally killed a pedesterian would be wracked with guilt for the rest of his life.

Isn't that a sin? I'd asked Henry about killing another Letter Writer.

A sin. Why had I used that terminology? It certainly wasn't the way I usually spoke or thought.

I thought of my dream of Christ's rotting body.

God was dead. There was no sin.

Yes, I decided. I would murder her.

I read the letter accompanying her photo:

> *Dear Jason,*
> *I wrote a letter to Eric today. I told him all about us. I told him I knew you way before Vicki did and that I not only loved you first, I loved you more. I told him that we were together now and we were going to have our own son, a son you'd love far more than you loved him.*
>
> *It hurts sometimes to tell the truth, but it is always the best way to go. It is better to get the pain over now, quickly, than stretch it out.*
>
> *I had another dream about you last night. I was sitting on the toilet and you were standing in front of me, dangling it in my face. I couldn't resist the temptation, and I opened my mouth and took you all the way in and worked on you until you finished.*
>
> *I always dream about us in the bathroom. I think it is because that is where I took that picture of myself. Do you still have it? I have*

thought of you every day since. I wrote the
letter that killed my father because of it. I drove
my mother away because of it. I am here be-
cause of it.

And now we are together once more. And
Vicki and Eric and the whole world know!
Nothing can come between us ever again!

> *Love always and forever,*
> *Kyoko*

Enraged, I tore the letter into little pieces, flinging
the pieces furiously across the room as hard as I could,
only to watch them fall and flutter hopelessly to the
ground a foot or so away from me. She dared to write
to my son? Filling his head with who knew what lies
and psychotic half-truths? I would have beaten her
head against the wall if I'd had her before me at that
moment. My only consolation was that maybe he
wouldn't receive the letter. I still wrote to my wife
and son every day, and I had yet to hear back from
them, so maybe our personal correspondence wasn't
being delivered. Even if her letter did reach him,
though, Vicki would intercept it first. She'd read it,
and she might very well believe it, but she wouldn't
pass it on to Eric. Of that I was sure. She would keep
that information from him.

I looked at the little scraps of letter on the ground.
At least I'd had the presence of mind not to tear up
the envelope. It had Kyoko's address on it.

I was going to need that.

I drove to her house after dark.

She lived not in our gated community but in a Japanese section of the city. It was a mishmash of various
styles and eras, architectures of East and West coexist-
ing side by side. Despite the pagoda roofs, though,

despite the neon signs in Japanese and the bonsai gardens in front of the low simple homes, everything seemed just a little too meticulously detailed, a little too thoroughly thought out. And of course, the streets were strangely empty. Cars were parked along the sides of the streets but not moving, and it was only the blinking of the lights and the presence of random noise from unseen sources that made it seem populated at all.

I drove past Kyoko's house, then parked two doors up.

I was glad she did not live in an apartment or condo, though I had plans for taking care of her if that were the case, as well. But a house was much easier, would allow me to enter and leave much more quickly, and I remained in my car, slumped in the front seat while I waited to see if anyone else drove by.

The streets were deserted, as were the sidewalks, and finally I opened the car door and stepped out. The air here smelled different, at once smoggier and more fragrant than it did in my neighborhood, as though a fleet of buses were idling next to a field of flowers, and I wondered if her city in Japan smelled like that. I'd probably never find out.

She definitely would not smell it again.

Because tonight she was going to die.

I felt no qualms as I walked up the sidewalk, opened the small gate in front of her house and stepped on the series of inset stones that led across the moss-covered ground to her door. A front window was open, the light on inside, and I could hear noise from within. I paused. She was listening to music. Not music on the radio or TV, but music from a record or CD. And I recognized it instantly.

the crack in the bell. Daniel Lentz.

Daniel Lentz was *our* composer, Vicki's and mine.

Hearing his music issue from Kyoko's stereo was like a slap in the face and in a way seemed more an invasion of my privacy than even breaking into my house had. She was not trespassing upon physical space here; she was stomping on my memories and my intimate life with Vicki.

And why was she allowed to have her own music when I wasn't? Especially since her music *was* my music. *My* CDs and records had been taken from me. It was another layer of insult, and it gave me the strength to pound on the front door. "Kyoko!" I called, feigning friendliness, hoping my anger wasn't evident from my voice. "It's me! Jason!"

The door flew open. "I know you come!" she said in her thickly accented English. She was dressed not as though she'd planned to spend a quiet evening at home but as though she'd planned to go club hopping and was not intending to return alone.

There was no one on the street as far as I knew, but I still felt far too conspicuous standing on her stoop like this, knowing what I intended to do. "Could I come in?" I asked. "I'd like to talk to you."

She seemed disappointed, her face falling, matching the petulant tone of her voice. "Just talk?"

"More," I promised. My palms were sweaty.

She brightened instantly, smiling. "I want more, too. Sex. You want sex?"

This was dragging on interminably! I risked a look backward, saw no one, nothing unusual in the darkness. "Yes," I promised. "Sex."

Kyoko grabbed my hand, pulled me in. Her fingers were soft but firm. She closed the door behind us, then immediately reached for my belt. I slapped her hand away. She looked up at me, surprised and hurt. "You say you want sex."

"I lied," I said.

I grabbed her throat quickly and squeezed as hard

as I could, gratified by the expression of shock on her face. Strangling someone looks so easy in movies, on TV, but the truth is that the human neck is tougher than it appears. Her throat bulged against my hands, seeming to grow as the muscles stiffened in self-preservation. Beneath that, the cartilage protecting her trachea and esophagus felt like hardened cowhide. I pushed her to the ground, doing so gently so as not to lose traction but trying to get her in a position where I could more easily apply pressure.

I wanted to choke that bitch, wanted to see, to hear, to *feel* the life leaving her body.

She thrashed about, but until almost the very end, I think, she thought it was some sort of joke, a type of rough foreplay or kinky fetish game. She twisted around awkwardly, intentionally spreading her legs in my sight line so I could see that under her skirt she wore no panties and was completely shaved.

But that reminded me of those panties she'd left in my hamper, and all I could think about was the fact that she'd trespassed in my home, invading my privacy, as the music—*my and Vicki's music*—continued playing on the stereo like some sick-joke reminder of everything that had gone so horribly off course in my life. I thought of the letter she said she'd sent to my son.

"This . . . is . . . for . . . Eric!" I managed to get out.

And then I killed her; then she died.

She pissed herself first, and her bowels evacuated, and the second I let go of her neck, vomit dribbled out of her mouth. I staggered away, sickened, and threw up myself, puking on an end table, the reliably rational part of my brain thinking that I was leaving damning DNA evidence. But at that point, I didn't even care. Opening the door, I stumbled out of the house into the night, wiping my mouth as I hurried across the short yard, through the front gate, down the sidewalk to my car. I felt queasy but not because I had just murdered someone. No, it was the simple physical smell of her waste that made me gag, a reflexive animal aversion that had nothing to do with the moral overtones of what I'd just done.

Hell, if she hadn't shitted and pissed and puked, I'd be on cloud nine right now.

Because I was glad she was dead. I'd done the right thing, and despite my physical repulsion, I felt as though a great weight had been lifted from my shoulders. Just as I had been when my dad had been gunned down, I was filled with a euphoria that I knew, intellectually, to be evil and wrong but that, emotionally, felt satisfying and very, very right indeed.

I drove home.

And it was all over.

I took a long shower and was still in bed in time to catch a rerun of *ER*.

I went to work the next morning whistling a happy tune. In my office, there were no unwanted envelopes, no surprise visits.

My only fear over the next few weeks was a simple one, the same one that any person would have in my circumstances—the fear of being caught. For the next several days, I diligently watched all local newscasts, read all local newspapers, searching for any information about Kyoko's death, any indication that the police were on my trail. But there was no mention of the killing anywhere, her name did not appear in any obituary, and when I scanned the weekly police log that was printed in Friday's edition of the *Brea Gazette*, her address was not listed and no murders at all were mentioned.

Could it be that her body had not been discovered yet?

Or had the company covered it up?

I was tempted to tell Stan what I'd done. I didn't know if he would understand, but he was my friend and I knew he would not turn me in. He would definitely have some theories about what had happened. But I decided not to involve him. Why widen the circle of guilt? This was my doing and mine alone. It would be wrong to drag anyone else into it.

When another week had passed with no news, I gathered my courage and drove past Kyoko's house. I saw no police tape, no FOR SALE sign, nothing unusual or amiss, nothing that would indicate the owner of the house had been murdered.

I sped home.

But the next day I returned, one of her letters in hand, pretending as though I had come on invitation and wanted to visit. My mouth was dry, my palms were wet, but I managed to walk through the small yard and up to the front door, where I first rang the bell, then knocked. "Hello?" I said loudly, as though calling out to see if anyone were home.

There was no answer, of course.

I glanced up and down the street, saw no pedestrians, no moving cars. "Hello?" I called again, and tried the door.

It was unlocked.

I slipped inside quickly. The entryway was spotless, no sign of any struggle, no shit, no piss, no puke. No body. I walked through the house, checking each and every room, but the house was clean, empty. What's more, there was no indication that anyone lived here, no food in the cupboards, no clothes in the closets, no toiletries in the bathroom.

It was over.

And I'd gotten away with it.

I should've been whistling a happy tune. From my point of view, all was right with the world.

But I felt odd and ill at ease, and I hurried out of the house quickly.

I drove home, troubled.

Fifteen

1

Kyoko was gone and there was no sign of the witch. I was free to hang out with my friends, read magazines, watch TV and write letters to my heart's content. I lived in a world designed for me.

But I was still not entirely happy.

When I'd first arrived, my job had seemed like a gift. But the reality of the situation was that the rhythms of my life had become repetitious. Every day, with minor exceptions, was the same. At least Kyoko and the witch had spiced things up. This new lack of adversity had drained the excitement from existence, and the knowledge that ten, twenty, thirty years from now I would be doing exactly the same thing removed any sense of urgency.

Of course, there was always the Ultimate Letter Writer, or "the Ultimate" as we'd begun to refer to him.

Thoughts of our unseen overlord kept us from going completely stir-crazy, and Stan's endless fount of paranoid theories saved us from complacency.

I must admit that even my friends did not seem quite as dissatisfied as I did. And *they* were the malcontents. The vast majority of Letter Writers we met were overjoyed with their lives, excited and happy to

be working here no matter how long ago they'd
started the real world. As far as I was concerned,
though, those people were just cogs in the machine,
unthinking drones who had found their niche.

You are very powerful.

I was different.

Stan had recently revised his theories about our
work. Our letters *were* reaching their destinations, he
said now, even his long dissertations to the president
about the space program. We were, he'd decided, distractions. We were white noise. We kept members of
the public focused on trivial matters so they would
not notice the profound changes that were shaking
society and bringing civilization close to the point of
utter chaos. This was true not just in the United States
but the world over. Within the company, we'd met
Letter Writers from Hungary and the Sudan, from
China and Iran, and we could read in the papers, see
on the news, what was happening in their countries.

Sure, important points were made through our letters. Political statements ran in the press, reached the
eyes of officials, influenced election outcomes and resulted in revisions to policy. But they were lost in the
sea of chatter, the tide of ephemera, that we produced,
the praising and razing of celebrities, the elevation
of culinary fads, the extension of musical trends. Our
strongest and most talented were not put to work addressing the myriad problems of the world's societies.
They were instead diverted to trifling, inconsequential
subjects. I was reduced to complaining about racetrack
noise. Bill was moving the *Penthouse Forum* away
from anal sex and into fetishism.

"I believe," Stan said, "that there are layers of Letter Writers. We're the top layer, the ones who get the
most press, who talk about the ordinary events of daily
life. We're the ones who complain about New Coke
or sexual innuendo on television, or suggest that video

games and record albums should have ratings. But there's a whole other substratum who we never get to see, never get to meet, and they're doing the real work, carrying out the Ultimate's agenda. They're toppling governments and making sure genocide doesn't get reported and food doesn't reach famine victims. They're rearranging the world one country at a time, playing chess with armies and kings and presidents and religions.

"And they're able to do it unimpeded because we're fanning the public's outrage over radio hosts and drawing attention to political candidates' sex lives."

Virginia, I thought, and her coworkers on the upper floors, the floors to which I had no access.

The idea made a lot of sense, and as I sat in my record shop office and listened to the radio, as I watched the latest movies, as I checked out HBO's newest provocative television show, as I got my daily fix of four newspapers, my weekly fix of six magazines, I found myself getting angry over what little effect I really had on the state of things, how small was my vision.

I thought of quitting. I wanted to go back home. My *real* home. Most of all, I wanted to see Vicki and Eric. Even if I couldn't be with them, even if Vicki would never take me back, I wanted to see them.

I even tried praying. I was a Letter Writer, and what were prayers if not verbal letters to God? "Dear Lord," I would always begin, as though I were writing a letter. But my entreaties fell on deaf ears. I still didn't know if there *was* a God, but I did know that if I had his address and could write to him rather than talk to him, I'd have a much better chance of getting results.

The days went by.

The weeks.

On the one-year anniversary of my hiring, the bureaucrat who'd quizzed me in that empty office after my capture and who'd busted up my welcome party visited me at work. He seemed as boring, functionary and subtly threatening as ever. "Mr. Hanford," he said, and his voice brought flashback memories, sent a chill down my spine. "Long time no see. "I realized as I looked at him that there was something not quite right about his appearance. He wore those same strange clothes that looked like both a uniform and a business suit yet were actually neither, but that wasn't the aspect of him that seemed slightly off. No, it was his physical features. Although he had no facial hair, an ordinary haircut, a purposefully neutral expression, there was something about his face that did not look modern.

I looked at him, trying to imagine him in a toga, in primitive skins, and it was far too easy to do.

Why the hell was I even *thinking* that?

"I have here some letters," he said cheerfully. "Anniversary greetings from well-wishers on the tenth floor. Your old friends!" He passed over a bundle of envelopes.

"Thanks," I said, and threw them on the cluttered desk.

"Aren't you going to open them?" He seemed disappointed.

I was glad. "No," I said. "I'm busy. I'll read them later."

"Very well." He suddenly adopted a more formal tone. "I just wanted to see how you were coming along and to wish you well on your anniversary." He smiled. "There will be many more to come."

I didn't give him the satisfaction of reacting. I waited until he left, then picked up the bundle of letters. *Anniversary greetings?* That was odd. I was tempted not to open any of them, to throw them away sight unseen. They'd obviously been solicited. The au-

thors who worked on the tenth floor had been put up
to this, and it was more than possible that there was
a not so benign intent behind it. Perhaps the messages
within were not strictly congratulatory but were in-
fused with a deeper, sneakier, more malevolent
purpose.

Still, at this point, I'd be grateful for anything out
of the ordinary, anything that would disrupt the inertia
that had taken over my life.

I sorted through the bundle, opened Virginia's
letter:

> *My Dear Jason,*
> *Has it been a year already? It seems much*
> *shorter than that to me though undoubtedly*
> *must feel far longer to you. Here's wishing that*
> *your letter writing brings you as much joy and*
> *secret excitement as those letters you wrote with*
> *your friend Paul all those years ago.*

I frowned. Paul? My old friend from childhood? I
hadn't seen him since he'd moved, since he'd looked
at me through the window, crying, promising to be my
pen pal as his family had driven off. How could she
possibly know about him? And what was she talking
about? What letters did I ever write with Paul? What
secret excitement?

Secret.

It was a message! I realized. Virginia was sending
me a secret message! I suddenly remembered that
Paul and I had once tried to write secret messages to
each other in disappearing ink—lemon juice that
would be invisible until heated, whereupon it would
emerge as a brownish, burned-looking series of lines
on the page. It had been hard and ultimately unre-
warding, and we'd never done it again.

Was Virginia now trying to send me messages the same way? I recalled the slice of lemon in her iced tea.

Maybe I was being watched and monitored at all times; maybe I wasn't. But I was willing to take the chance, and I held the paper over a lightbulb, heating it, watching as first lines, then letters, then words appeared: *STOP WRITING. IT IS DANGEROUS.*

My heart was thumping, and I looked over my shoulder to make sure I wasn't being spied upon. On impulse, I picked out another letter, this one from John. I held it over the lightbulb.

Nothing.

I did this to all of the letters in the bundle, and it was not until I came to Ernest's letter that those familiar brown lines reappeared: *RESIST. DO NOT HELP HIM.*

Him.

Now my heart really was pumping wildly. They were talking about the Ultimate. They'd learned something, and were desperately trying to impart that message to me.

You are very powerful.

Stan was right, I thought. We were being used to reshape the world in a different image. *Correspondence is the bedrock upon which societies are built,* Henry had told me my first day. *And we have a stranglehold on that. Letters are our business, our industry, our raison d'être. And because of that, we can make history; we can change history; we can determine the course of human events.*

We were evil. I'd known that for some time now. There was a quote from Aristophanes that I'd read once in a novel by Phillip Emmons and that I'd never forgotten: "Evil deeds from evil causes spring." *We* were the evil causes, and we were spreading evil deeds all across the land. There was nothing good here, and nothing good could come of what we did. Writing let-

ters made us happy, kept us amused, kept us busy. It
was what we did, what we lived for. But it was an evil
addiction and it led only to disaster and destruction.
No matter what we told ourselves, no matter how light
we tried to keep it, the darkness always came through;
it always won out.

The Ultimate knew this. He had harnessed us for
his own secret mysterious purposes, was using us to
impose his will and carry out his plans, and like unwitting pawns, we played along because we were lem-
mings and it was in our nature.

But it was wrong.

I had no real moral compass. None of us did. But
we could discern the truth if we tried. We could perhaps puzzle our way through to determine what was
right and good.

Virginia had.

Ernest had.

Did that mean the others had not? There was no
way to know, and it was always better to be safe than
sorry. "Assume everyone is your enemy until they
prove otherwise," Stan told me once, and though it
was advice he himself seldom followed, it was a good
suggestion nevertheless.

I looked at the two pieces of paper with their
burned brown writing. What to do next? The first step
was to tear up the letters and dispose of the pieces to
leave no evidence. I did so, flushing everything down
the toilet in the bathroom. But I wasn't sure what to
do after that. I wanted to talk to Virginia and get
some more information, but obviously to do so was
dangerous or she would have come in person to tell
me about it. Should I write her a letter? Probably not.
She and Ernest had written their notes in invisible ink
beneath banal congratulation messages. They clearly
didn't trust the sanctity of the mail.

Could I talk to my friends? Should I? I wasn't sure
yet. I had to know more.

I sat back down at my desk, looking at the paper rolled up in my typewriter, the blank screen beckoning me from my monitor. In my pencil holder, new pens of various colors tempted me.

I couldn't stop writing cold turkey. That would be too suspicious. Besides, I didn't think I would personally be able to see that through. Like an overeater confronted with a mountain of chocolate, I lacked the willpower. But I would make sure that my letters were as benign and inconsequential as I could possibly make them. And I'd write as few of them as possible today.

Hell, maybe I'd just take the day off and go to a movie. I'd done that before. It wouldn't arouse much suspicion, and I could avoid having to write anything until I had more information. I checked the movie schedule. There was a mindless Jerry Bruckheimer action movie playing at the multiplex. Just the thing I needed to take my mind off what was happening.

I walked out of my office and headed down the corridor to the elevator.

The theater was nearly full when I arrived. I took the first empty seat I found, and surprisingly, it was next to Shamus. He was playing hooky, too. I hadn't seen him in a few days and I said hello. He nodded distractedly at me, but did not speak. He seemed nervous, ill at ease, as weighted down by hidden burdens as I was. I wanted to ask if anything was wrong, but I didn't get the chance because just then the movie started.

I found myself looking surreptitiously around during the film's daytime scenes, not watching the action on-screen but scanning the heads of the crowd around me to see if I could spot anyone else I knew, irrationally hoping that perhaps Virginia had tried to arrange a meeting here with me.

No such luck.

I left my seat in the middle of the movie to take a

piss. Shamus followed me out of the theater auditorium and into the bathroom, where he stood nervously with his back against the door, keeping everyone out, while he waited for me to finish. I flushed, zipped up, frowned, turned around. "What is it, dude?"

"Look," he whispered conspiratorially, and opened his jacket. The interior pockets, as well as the waistband of his pants, were lined with letters. At least a dozen of them. "They're from yesterday and this morning. I didn't mail them," he said.

I looked at Shamus and I could not have been prouder of him if he had been my own brother. Against all odds, against reason and his very nature, he had made his way through the complex and ambiguous wilderness of letter writing, and on his own had come to the same realization that I'd had to be hit over the head with in order to recognize.

"They're bad," he said. "They're wrong. I can't let them go out."

I nodded. "I know."

"But if I leave them or throw them away or . . . do anything else with them, I'll get in trouble. I'll be punished." He looked at me imploringly. "Won't I?"

"I think so, yes," I told him.

He was shaking. "I don't know why I did this. It was stupid. I should have left well enough alone—"

"No!" I told him, and strode forward, taking him by the shoulders. "You did the right thing. It's what all of us should be doing." I met his eyes. "You know why I'm here today? You know why I'm watching this piece-of-shit movie that I'm not even paying any attention to? Because I knew I shouldn't be writing any more letters, and I needed an excuse."

His expression lightened. "Really?"

"I'm not writing any tomorrow, either, but I don't know what I'm going to do to hide it."

"Can you?" Shamus asked.

"Hide it?"

"No. Not write." He motioned toward the letters in his jacket and waistband. "That was my plan, too. I wasn't going to write. But I couldn't help myself. So I decided to just write whatever I wanted and then not mail it. Kill two birds with one stone."

"I think that's a good idea," I said.

"Yeah, but look where it leaves me. What should I do now?" he asked.

"I don't know," I admitted. "Why don't we go to Stan's, see if he has any ideas?"

"Sure, if you think that's best."

"They may have someone watching us," I told Shamus. "Both of us. We'll leave here separately, then go back to our seats. It won't do to leave while the movie's still playing. Too suspicious. I'll leave at the beginning of the credits, go back to my office and push papers for the rest of the day, catch up on my reading. You wait until the end of the credits, then figure out a way to stall nonsuspiciously for the afternoon, then go out to your car at your normal time. Whoever's in the parking lot first will wait for the other one. Then we'll both drive to Stan's. We won't say a word to him or anyone else until we're safely at his house."

"You think that'll work?"

I shook my head. "I don't know."

That afternoon was the longest I'd ever spent. I kept waiting for my door to be flung open, for that bureaucrat to burst in with his two guards and for them to take me back to that empty office. Or to the one next to that, the one the screams had come from. But the minutes crept by and then the hours. Our plan *did* work, and shortly after five we found ourselves in Stan's driveway, waiting while he drove in.

He parked on the street and walked up to us. "To what do I owe the honor?"

His attitude changed when he saw the looks on our

faces, and his own expression sobered quickly.
"What's wrong? What's happened?" He met my eyes.
"Do we need to talk inside?"

"I think it would be best," I said.

There's something to be said for paranoia. Stan had
rigged up a walk-in closet as a "safe room." Styrofoam
from packing boxes lined the walls to muffle sound,
and in front of that were sewn bedspreads meant to
shut out any hidden cameras or prying eyes. The ceiling, too, was covered with blankets, as was the floor,
and once we were inside, he flipped on a portable
battery-powered camping light, then sealed up the
edges of the door with duct tape before putting up
another blanket in front. It was like being inside a
cloth cocoon.

"Wow," Shamus said, and allowed himself his first
smile of the day. "I guess you knew we were coming, huh?"

"It helps to be prepared."

I explained what had happened. I told my story first,
describing the messages made with lemon juice that
Virginia and Ernest had sent on my anniversary letters, and Shamus' eyes widened. He hadn't heard this
part before. Then I told Stan Shamus' predicament,
and he opened his coat to reveal the letters. There
were even more now. He'd had a busy afternoon.

"I have a fireplace," Stan said. "We'll burn them
in there."

"That's fine for now," Shamus said. "But what
about tomorrow? And the next day? And the next? I
can't come over here every day to burn my letters.
They'll notice that. Even if I find some other way to
get rid of them, they'll figure it out eventually. What
can I do?"

Stan patted his shoulder. "We'll think of something.
For now, let's just get rid of these." He started to pull
down the blanket over the door. "Don't talk about it

while we're doing it. Just keep the conversation light. After we've burned them all, we'll come back in here and talk. Okay?"

"Okay," Shamus and I agreed.

Stan pulled off the tape, opened the closet.

The house was dark. It was only late afternoon, still an hour or two away from dusk; there was no way the sun could have gone down that fast. We'd been in the "safe room" for five to seven minutes, tops.

I looked through the window. It was foggy outside, the way it had been on the day I was hired. And the fog was thick, close. I could not see the driveway, could not see our cars. I didn't like that. I glanced back at Shamus. He was shaking, his face nearly as white as the fog.

Stan said nothing, walked out of the bedroom toward the living room and the fireplace and, with a silent movement of his hand, motioned that we were to follow.

There was pounding on the front door. Not knocking. *Pounding.* A deep, spooky, echoing sound that reverberated through the house. I thought of *Night of the Living Dead* and those zombies trying to break into the old farm where the heroes had hidden, the way the zombies had just kept coming, an endless army of them, seemingly unstoppable.

I glanced out an open window, looked out at the fog. Behind it was blankness, that same cold absence I had sensed upon seeing it for the first time exactly a year ago today. But *in* it were figures. Shapes and shadows. Dark forms that almost coalesced into recognizable creatures before moving back, fading away. I wanted to close the window but was afraid to get near it, was afraid to mention it.

Stan was kneeling before the fireplace, turning on the gas. He took a long match from a nearby box and with trembling hands lit it. The fake logs in the fireplace burst into flame. "Here," he said, motioning for the letters.

The pounding grew louder.

Then stopped.

Shamus was fumbling for the letters in his waist-band. "Hurry!" he said—

—and was immediately sucked out the window.

It happened so fast that I didn't see it occur and had no idea how he had been taken. I couldn't tell if something had reached in and grabbed him or if he had simply been vacuumed out of the room. I could see him outside, though, and he was screaming.

"H-h-h-e-e-e-l-l-l-l-p-p-p-p!" Shamus yelled, stretching out the word as far as his lungs could carry it. We watched him being sucked into the fog, the whiteness closing around him like a folding blanket as he was pulled backward by invisible force. After that came one short terrible cry.

And then silence.

None of his letters had fallen out of his hand; all of the envelopes had been taken with him. Stan and I looked at one another, waiting for the other shoe to drop, waiting for our turn, but instead the fog outside lessened, lightened, and in a matter of moments was gone, that horrifying whiteness replaced once again by the placid normality of Stan's street. It was like watching time-lapse photography, and as close as we were to it, as tactile and three-dimensional as it was, it still seemed fake. I moved closer to the window, peering outside. I could see my car and Stan's out in front of the house.

Shamus' was gone.

Every trace of him had been erased.

The fire was still blazing in the fireplace, and Stan turned it off, shutting the gas valve. His hand was shaking more than ever, and his face was blanched, lips dry and pale. Neither of us spoke for several minutes. We stood there, waiting, just in case something was coming back for one of us. When it became clear that we were safe, that we were not to suffer Shamus' fate, we each took deep breaths and fell onto opposing chairs.

"Where do you think he is?" I asked. My voice came out higher and far weaker than I'd intended.

"I don't know," Stan admitted. "I have no idea. My mind's a complete blank."

"Mine, too."

We looked at one another.

"What now?" he asked finally.

I could not help glancing at the window through which Shamus had been pulled. "You have any ideas?"

Stan thought for a moment. "We go back to work tomorrow, and we do our jobs," he said grimly. "We shut up and write."

2

Distance brought courage, and the next morning I decided to risk everything and go up to talk to Virginia. But when I pressed the elevator button for the tenth floor, it remained unlit and the elevator did not move. I pressed all of the buttons but the only one that worked was the one for the fourth floor, mine.

They were on to me.

They were going to keep me in line.

Nervous, anxious, practically looking over my shoulder every step of the way, I went to my office. I didn't want to write, knew I shouldn't write, but composing a letter was the only thing that could calm me down, and at that instant I desperately needed something to relax me before my blood vessels burst.

I wrote a letter to country artist Robert Earl Keen,

telling him that I liked his new album but still thought *A Bigger Piece of Sky* was his best work. I wrote a nasty letter to the rock group Rush, telling them to pack it in and hang it up, that it was over.

Music again.

Once more, I thought that if I limited my focus to music, I couldn't do any harm.

I just hoped I was right.

The morning flew by. Twelve letters about various rock bands and singer-songwriters lay in perfect order within stacked envelopes to the side of my PC. I felt calm, cool and collected. It was as though I'd been meditating or medicated. The anxiety had abated. Deep down, nothing had changed. Shamus was still gone, I was sure I was still under surveillance, and I desperately needed to talk to Virginia and her friends, but I could handle it now. I no longer felt overwhelmed and under siege.

In the lunchroom, everyone was subdued, and I understood without being told that Stan had gone around and explained to everyone what had happened. I was grateful to him. Having to relive last night might have shattered my newfound equilibrium, and I wanted to maintain this detachment for as long as possible. If I could just narcotize myself for the rest of my life, that would be fine with me.

We didn't speak of it. We didn't speak of anything important. For all intents and purposes, we could have been temp employees working for an ordinary corporation and exchanging impersonal pleasantries on a mandated break. We were afraid to speak openly, and I realized with glum resignation that we had lost, that the Ultimate had won. Not only had he lured us here, made us his drones; he had now managed to quash and quell the only attempt at dissent within the ranks. We stared at each other across the tables, noting but not mentioning the missing seat where Shamus would have been.

Maybe Virginia and her fellow authors would have better luck than we had, I tried to tell myself.

Who the fuck was I kidding? If they'd really wanted out, if they'd been able to find a *way* out, they would have left long ago. They were as trapped as the rest of us.

I dreamed that night of the tent in the desert, the circus tent, only this time it was empty. Its canvas flaps opened, beckoning me, but inside were only mirrors, hundreds of them placed upright all around me in a circle, and I stood there stupidly staring at myself. I walked back out the way I had come, and it segued into another dream I'd had years ago and almost forgotten, where skeletons sat at an assembly line pasting stamps on envelopes that passed by on a conveyor belt. Instead of the desert, the mail factory was where I found myself, and though the skeletons all appeared identical at first, upon looking closer, I saw that one appeared to be Shamus.

I awoke the next morning looking for an anonymous letter that described my nightmare. I was praying for one of those mysterious messages just to prove to myself that I was still relevant, that the Ultimate still worried enough about me to scare me, to try and keep me in line.

But there was nothing.

I showered and shaved, ate my breakfast and went to work.

Where the witch was waiting for me.

I was late and nearly everyone else had already arrived, but as luck would have it, Stan was late, too, and as we walked together toward the entrance of the building, we saw the witch. She was standing next to the corner of the building, and she looked just as she had all those years ago. There was nothing ghostly or ephemeral about her—she was as solid and real as I was—and I poked Stan in the ribs, my heart thumping crazily in my chest. "It's her," I said, unable to catch my breath. "It's the witch."

He seemed more curious than frightened, and he walked over to the corner of the building. I followed close behind, more scared than I was willing to admit.

Stan just came right out and said it: "Why are you here?"

"Don't write," she said, glancing around as though afraid of being overheard.

"You can do better than that," Stan said derisively, and his attitude gave me strength.

"Why were you at my house?" I demanded. My voice was too high, and I cleared my throat. "Why are you bothering me?"

Again the furtive glance. "I worked here, too. I was one, too. But I escaped. I got out." She fixed me with a cold, hard stare. "Until you sent me back."

"You're—" *Dead,* I was about to say, but then I realized that I'd read that in a newspaper article. More than anyone else, I should have known how the news could be manipulated. Maybe she *hadn't* died. Maybe she'd been turned over to the company.

"Stop writing," she said fiercely. "Now!"

"Hey!" a security guard called. I looked to my left, saw him hurrying from the front entrance toward the corner where we stood. He was saying something into his walkie-talkie.

I turned back—

—and the witch was gone.

"Where did she go?" I asked Stan.

He shook his head. He hadn't seen, either.

"Who was that you were talking to?" the guard demanded, running up. From behind him and from around the corner, other guards came running.

"I don't know," Stan said coolly. "But we're late for work." He turned around, walking back toward the building's entrance. I followed.

"What was that?" I said.

"I don't know," he admitted. "But she tried to warn us. And I think it was a major effort for her. I think she risked a lot. We should listen."

I thought so, too, but I was scared. I remembered what had happened to Shamus. Had the witch been warning me all along? I wondered. Had she known I was a Letter Writer even as a child?

Don't write.

What if I'd listened to her way back then?

I couldn't have listened to her, I realized. I wouldn't have been able to stop writing to save my life.

But I could try now, though.

And I did.

I wrote only two letters that day.

3

Weird things began happening at my house again.

They were small things at first, and for nearly a week I assumed they were residual discoveries of mischief by the witch or Kyoko that might have been done months ago but that I hadn't noticed until now. I found a broken plate at the back of the freezer, an empty vodka bottle underneath the bathroom sink behind the plunger. I discovered what appeared to be an aborted letter between the cushions of the couch, a piece of typing paper folded and crumpled with the words *Dear Jason* hastily scrawled at the top.

But then there were occurrences that were definitely *not* the witch's or Kyoko's leftovers. One day I left home the way I did every morning, shutting off all the lights and the television—and returned that afternoon to find all of the lights on, all three TVs blazing, the radio blasting out rock and roll. In my mailbox a few days later was an envelope addressed to me. The name of the sender in the upper left corner was my son's. I ripped open the envelope and quickly opened the letter inside. It was a full page of single-spaced type, the same three words repeated over and over again: *I hate you. I hate you. I hate you. I hate you. . . .*

Someone was fucking with me.

In my office that afternoon, I was sorting through my usual selection of newspapers and magazines when I came across a letter. From Virginia. I'd neither seen her nor heard from her since that cryptic message written in disappearing ink, and sure enough, this letter said only

> *Dear Jason,*
> *I just wanted to drop you a line to say hello.*
> *Paul says hello, too.*
>
> *Virginia*

Excitedly, I held the paper over a lightbulb, watching as the brown scraggly letters appeared.

Your house. Tonight.

She'd found out something important and had worked out a way to get it to me. I allowed myself to get my hopes up. I folded up her letter and put it in my pocket. I wrote nothing at all for the rest of the morning, spent several hours reading magazines, met Stan in the lunchroom for a quiet meal, then left early and headed home. I knew I'd have to wait for a long time, but I was too anxious to stay at work; I'd rather pace ay my place. Besides, I needed to clean up a bit before anyone came over. I'd really let the house go.

I cleaned the living room, the kitchen, my bedroom, my den, the bathroom. I made macaroni and cheese. I washed the dishes.

I waited.

I watched TV.

I waited.

It was after eleven when the doorbell finally rang.
I unlocked the door and opened it, and there they
stood, Virginia and all of the people from my welcome
party. I bade them come in, and for the first time, I
thought that most of the men and women looked familiar. Not because I'd seen them on the tenth floor
or I'd met them at my welcome party, but because I'd
seen them . . . somewhere else. Before.

Ernest clasped my hand, shook it heartily as he
walked in. He looked especially familiar. He looked
like . . . Ernest Hemingway.

I didn't know why I hadn't noticed that before.

I peered more closely at the other Letter Writers
filing in. Some of them I couldn't place, but I'd been
an English major in college, and quite a few of them
resembled famous literary figures. With his long thick
beard, Leo didn't look like an old hippie; he looked
like . . . Leo Tolstoy. Alexander, the short hump-
backed man? Alexander Pope. James? James Baldwin.
Bill? William Burroughs.

I turned to Virginia. "You're Virginia Woolf," I said.
She nodded in acknowledgment.

"You didn't know?" Burroughs chuckled at my obvious astonishment. "Not as quick as we thought."

"Shut up," Virginia told him.

"Bitch."

My head was reeling. Was there a tactful way to
ask what I wanted to ask? I couldn't think of one, so
I just blurted it out. "What *are* you?" I faced Virginia.
"You're dead. All of you died. Are you . . . ghosts?"

They started laughing.

"No one dies," Tolstoy said in his thickly accented
English.

"Not here," Ambrose Bierce added.

"You disappeared," I told him. "Around 1914. No
one knows what happened to you."

He spread his arms. "Now you do."

I faced Virginia. "You committed suicide." I pointed at Hemingway. "You, too."

"I answered a letter," Virginia said softly.

"I tracked down the bastard who'd been hounding me for twenty years," Hemingway said. "What you'd call a stalker today. But when I tried to meet him face-to-face"—he grimaced—"I ended up here."

"Here?" I repeated stupidly. I was beginning to realize that the city surrounding me might not be the city I thought it was. Maybe the company controlled not just the building where I worked or the gated community where I had my condo. I thought of the way the streets of Brea had started seeming unusually empty after I began working for the company. I remembered my feeling that the houses in my old neighborhood had been empty shells, that I'd been the only living person on the street.

"None of us died," John Cheever explained. "We came here like you, tricked or lured or hired. We read about how we supposedly died, or saw it on television, some of us, but it wasn't true. We don't know who those bodies were or how those deaths were arranged, or how our loved ones were fooled. But the truth is, we're alive and well and living in this . . . place. Someone else, for some reason, concocted the circumstances of our demises."

"But—"

"We're still alive?" Cheever's eyes twinkled. "That's the silver lining. We never age, never change. We remain the same age we were when we entered. As will you. Many of us put pen to paper and wrote our stories with the hope of gaining a piece of immortality. The ironic thing is that now we do seem to be immortal. Because of our writing."

"*Letter* writing," Tolstoy said disdainfully. "The most ephemeral writing of all."

I tried to wrap my mind around this.

Virginia put a hand on my arm. "We're taking a chance just being here," she said. "They know we've come to see you. They'll be watching us even more closely now. They'll be watching you. I wanted to come by myself but—" She shook her head.

"We wanted to be here, too," Ernest said.

"You are very powerful." It was the same thing James Baldwin had said that first day, and he repeated it again.

"You're the only one who can help us," Virginia said. "You're the only one who can put a stop to all this. I thought that the first time I met you, especially after reading your work and seeing all the havoc it caused. They know it, too. That's why they have you doing busywork, why they're not giving you the big assignments."

"Who's 'they'?" I asked.

"The Old Ones," Thomas Mann said.

"And maybe the one behind them."

Stan's Ultimate Letter Writer.

"Fog's rolling in." Jane Austen had been stationed by the open door, and the second she spoke those words, a hush fell over the gathering. I thought of Shamus and shivered, chilled to the bone. The others had a similar reaction. Quietly but quickly, they reversed course and started toward the front door, each stopping for a moment to say hello, say good-bye, say thank you, wish me well, touch me. They'd been here only a few minutes, but I'd learned more in those few minutes than I had in the past year. The implications of what I'd discovered were staggering.

"It's not safe," Virginia said on her way out. "Not here. Not tonight. I'll contact you when I can. We need to set something up. We need to talk."

They disappeared into the darkness before the gathering fog. None of them had driven here, so all of them probably lived within the gates of the neighborhood. I wondered why I'd never seen any of them around before.

I closed the door, locked it.

Where were we? I wondered. What was this place? How long had it been here? Who or what was behind it?

There was too much to think about. My mind was overloaded. I wanted to call Stan, but tonight I was probably even more paranoid than he was. Even if my phone wasn't tapped in the traditional Nixonian sense, someone—

or something

—would be listening.

I assumed I'd be up all night, trying to puzzle out the mysterious history and alternate reality of the Letter Writers, but I fell asleep on the couch in the midst of thinking about what I was going to be thinking about, and I didn't wake up until morning.

I went to work as usual, pretending that everything was normal, nothing was going on, my insides roiling, my stomach cramping from the excess acid. Virginia was waiting for me in my office. She seemed nervous and sleep deprived, she looked the way I felt, and she stood when I entered. "We need to talk," she said again.

"Is it safe?" I asked, looking around.

"No. Your place. I'll be over tonight," she promised. "Alone."

She never showed.

I went home and waited for her, stayed up until after one o'clock, and then finally I fell asleep, too exhausted to maintain my vigil. I hoped I'd be awakened by the ring of the doorbell or a loud knock, hoped at least I'd get a phone call or a letter, but I awoke extremely late, well after nine the next morning, and found no indication that she'd made any effort to contact me.

Something must have happened to her, I thought,
and I went to work, checking in with Henry first to
see if he had any news, keeping my ears open at lunch
and break hoping to hear gossip, but if anything unusual had occurred, no one knew anything about it.

Stan remained in his office, so I ate lunch alone. I
saw Ellen and Fischer on the other side of the lunchroom, they waved at me and I nodded back, but we
made no attempt to eat together. How well did I really
know them? I reasoned. They could be spies.

Everyone was a potential enemy. The walls had ears
and eyes.

I stayed in my office, worried, willing myself not
to write.

The day was interminable.

I was about to leave when Henry dropped by and
asked me to stop by his office before I went home.
My anxiety had not lessened during the day—I was
still as nervous and agitated as ever, worrying about
Virginia—but I told Henry I'd be there and a few
moments later knocked on the frosted-glass door.
"Come in!" he called.

The bureaucrat was seated in a chair waiting for me.

I looked over at Henry, feeling betrayed, though I
knew I shouldn't. He did not meet my eyes.

"Hello, Mr. Hanford," the bureaucrat said cheerfully. "I trust you've had a productive day."

I decided to be cagey. "Can't complain."

"Are you happy here?"

"Why do you ask?"

"There's been talk of moving you to the tenth floor.
We think perhaps you're being underutilized."

"You do?"

"Yes. Besides, a couple of vacancies have opened
up."

"I don't like the cubicles," I said. "I like my office better."

"Arrangements can be made."

This fake conversation went on for some time. Too long. I was tired of it as soon as it started, but there was no way to extricate myself and I had no choice but to play along. The talk was circular, ending back at where it had started, with nothing being decided, nothing being changed, nothing being learned. The entire point seemed to be to waste my time, and when I was finally allowed to leave, I found that it was dark out and the parking lot was practically empty.

I drove home.

Where I found Virginia Woolf drowned in my overflowing bathtub, weighted down with rocks.

Ernest Hemingway was in the kitchen, his brains blown out with the shotgun still gripped in his hands.

I panicked. I didn't know what to do and ran out of my condo to my next-door neighbor's, ringing the bell, banging on the door, yelling for help. But there was no answer, just the glow of cold lights and the muted sound of a television. Where *was* everyone? Dashing into the middle of the street, I stood there, face to the sky, screaming at the top of my lungs.

There was no one to hear my cries, however. My screams of anguish and horror dissipated in the cool evening air. After several frightened chaotic minutes, my throat began to hurt, and I stopped, my screams devolving into a fit of coughing. I heard no sirens coming, no neighbors talking, only the generic babble of interior television sets. I looked back at my house and the door I'd left open. In my mind's eye, I saw Hemingway's blood, Virginia's watery stare, but I knew that I would have to go back in there and call someone if I was going to find anybody to take care of the bodies.

What about James Baldwin? I wondered. Was he still on the loose, was he on the run somewhere in the city . . . or was he lying dead in another part of my house?

The front of my condo suddenly looked like a face to me, the open door a yawning maw, the twin porch lights above it demented eyes. I didn't want to go in there. I was *afraid* to go in there. I had no choice, though. Out of habit, I'd dropped my car keys on the coffee table when I'd first walked in. Even if I wanted to drive elsewhere, to the police station, to Stan's, I'd have to go inside and get the keys. Or else try to walk to my destination.

And I didn't feel comfortable walking anywhere in this made-up city.

My throat hurt from screaming, my breath was coming in short sharp gasps, my heart was like a jackhammer inside my rib cage, but I steeled myself and forced my feet to walk back across the asphalt of the road, up the concrete incline of my driveway and through the front door. There were no bodies in the living room, but there was a telephone, and I quickly sorted through the cards stacked next to the phone that served as my address book.

I called Henry.

Why I don't know. I should have dialed 911. But I was not even sure there *was* a 911. Or a police station. Or a hospital. For all I knew, everything about me was an illusion.

Besides, if anyone would know what to do, I figured, Henry would. He answered on the second ring. I told him what I'd found in my condo, told him about Virginia and Ernest Hemingway. I couldn't tell if he was surprised by my call or not, couldn't tell if he'd already known what had happened and was expecting me to call or if my news came to him out of the blue. I didn't care.

I hung up, grabbed my keys and went outside.

Moments later, an ambulance came. At least I assumed it was an ambulance. It was a vehicle that could have been a hearse, could have been a big station wagon, could have been anything. The four men who manned it wore the same nondescript clothes, half suit and half uniform, as my guards, the ones who had escorted me down that intial corridor to the empty office where I was imprisoned, and they walked with the same militaristic step. All four nodded but did not speak to me as they rolled gurneys into my condo to collect the bodies.

I wondered where the bodies were going, but I was too stunned to ask. The witch . . . Kyoko . . . these suicides . . . It was one thing after another.

But were they really suicides?

Who the fuck was I kidding? I *knew* they weren't.

I guess I expected Henry to show up since I'd called him, but he didn't. No one did. Only the four men from the ambulance, and they were wheeling out unidentifiable lumps on the twin gurneys minutes after they'd gone in. I looked but could not tell who was who under the plastic wrap. I saw no body parts, no blood.

They rolled the gurneys into the vehicle, got in themselves, thanked me and were gone.

I was supposed to clean up the mess myself?

Somehow even the fear had fled. Maybe I was in shock. Numb, I walked into my condo to assess the damage, particularly in the kitchen, and—

It was no longer my condo.

I stood in the open doorway looking around, confused. Instinctively, I backed up, stepped off the porch and looked up at the building's facade. It was two stories instead of one and in a completely different style. But . . .

But there was something familiar about this place.

I stepped onto the porch, went inside. I knew this house. I'd never been here before, but I recognized the stone fireplace, the hardwood floors, the built-in bookcases. Without going into the other rooms, I knew what they looked like, knew what kind of furniture they had and where that furniture had been placed.

How was that possible?

I looked at a framed family photograph above the mantle—Vicki, Eric and myself—and I suddenly understood.

This was our dream house. This was the home Vicki and I had talked about, planned for, saved for, hoped for. This was where we'd wanted to spend our golden years together.

I sat down on the sofa with the fabric Vicki would have picked out, and burst into tears. None of it was ever going to happen; none of it would ever come to pass. There was no one to see me, but I covered my face in my hands anyway, sobbing uncontrollably, and I was still sobbing an hour, two hours, three hours later, my throat scratchy, my eyes stinging, my stomach and lungs in pain. I didn't know my body had such a reserve of tears, and I thought the crying might never end, thought it might go on forever, stopping only when my heart gave out and killed me.

But it did stop sometime in the early morning, and though I was tired and could barely see through my blurry eyes and swollen lids, I did not fall asleep. I remained awake until dawn, when I went into my new kitchen, made myself a cup of coffee and had a pair of store-bought blueberry muffins for breakfast. I took a shower, changed my clothes and, on automatic pilot, drove to work.

Where Stan was waiting for me in the parking lot in front of the building.

"You look like shit," he said. "What the hell happened?"

I shook my head and tried to move away from him, tried to blow him off, my mind comforted by the idea that I would soon be in my office, ensconced behind my crowded desk amid my music memorabilia. I could rest there. I could nap there.

He grabbed my arm.

"Hey!" I said.

But he pulled me toward his car. "Come on," he said. "We're not going in today. I have something to show you." His voice was filled with an excitement I had never heard before, a fervor that made him sound reinvigorated, at once younger and more optimistic.

His passion was infectious, and against my will, I found myself catching some of his eagerness. "What is it?" I asked.

He lowered his voice. "I found something. Get in the car quick. We'll talk on the way."

And talk we did.

Actually, he did all the talking. I had just as much to tell him—if not more—but I was too worn and tired and beaten to even start, and by the time he got into it, I realized that his story and mine were interconnected, were both parts of the same whole.

Stan had gone to town. Adversity didn't beat him down. It energized him, and he'd been playing Hardy Boys since our meeting with the witch, making a concerted effort to discover the truths behind the lies we lived, to finally find and meet the Ultimate. Last night, he'd remained in his office, waiting, after everyone had left. He'd tried this tactic before, but he'd been found and kicked out by a team of two men whose job it was to search the building for stragglers. This time, however, he moved around, ducking and weaving down that crooked on-again, off-again path that Henry had taken me down and that led between our various writing environments. If he thought he heard a noise or imagined he heard a person coming, he ducked behind someone's desk or couch and waited it out. Finally, at midnight according to his watch, Stan had exited the door at the foot of the path and found himself in the usual spot in the corridor, in front of Henry's door.

And he'd seen a mailman.

It was one of those generic bureaucrats, "faceless

fucks," he called them, and the man was walking briskly down the corridor away from him, a full canvas sack slung over his shoulder like Santa. He'd just emptied the mailbox at the opposite end of the hall and was clearly taking it to a company mailroom, where it would be sorted for delivery.

Stan knew that if he tried to follow the mailman, he would be spotted instantly, so he ducked back inside the doorway, waited until he heard the bell for the elevator ding and the elevator doors open and shut, then watched the numbers on the panel above.

The elevator was going up.

It was what he'd been hoping. The man was either collecting mail from the floors above or joining members of his team that were doing the same. Stan watched the number eight light up. And stay lit.

He waited there, alert for any sound, ready at any second to sprint back to his own office and hide, but the number did not change.

Three minutes.

Five minutes.

Seven minutes.

Ten.

Did it really take that long to collect the letters from the eighth floor . . . or was that the location of the mail room?

He took a chance and pressed the call button.

The elevator descended.

Stan remembered that I'd told him the only other floor I could go to was the fifth, but he pressed button number eight anyway.

And the doors closed.

He wished he'd been more prepared, wished he at least had a makeshift weapon of some sort, but of course that wouldn't do any good here.

The doors slid open, and he was looking into a massive open room that resembled nothing so much as a nineteenth-century industrial-age factory. Everything was black and dusty, smelling of burning coal and oil; even the hot, humid air seemed pregnant with soot. Exposed pipes, metal support beams and clanking chains hung from the filthy ceiling, attached at various points to a web of interconnected machines that were running full steam.

In the center of all this chaos, two rows of conveyor belts moved endlessly toward the far end of the factory, each piled high with envelopes. This was where the mailman had dumped his load, and indeed a bin nearby was full of empty canvas sacks. There was no sign of the faceless fuck Stan had followed here, or indeed any other bureaucrat, but the conveyor belts were lined on opposite sides with pale skeletal figures who seemed to be sorting rapidly through the envelopes as they passed; they threw some into large open chutes and put postage stamps on the ones that remained.

Just as in my dream.

Stan saw all this in a matter of seconds, and he ducked back into the right front corner of the elevator, furiously pushing the button for the fourth floor, certain that at any moment he would be seen. The elevator did not respond, though, and after several moments of this, he realized he would have to find another way off this floor, another way out, or risk being caught.

He dashed out of the elevator, ducking behind a pillar, realizing too late that he was in full view of a dozen or so drones at the end of the conveyor belt line.

It didn't matter. They saw him, but they didn't care. They might as well have been machines themselves; so single-minded was their focus.

Stan relaxed a little, experimentally stepped out from behind the pillar, moving slowly into full view of all of the skeletal figures. No one rushed out to grab him or stop him, and he strode carefully around the edge of the factory, ready at any moment to run for his life. He found a door marked EXIT, and he opened it, walking through.

Stan paused in his narration. By this time, the car had reached its destination. We were on a street at the edge of Brea that appeared to be only half formed. There was no fog here, but there might as well have been, for we could see nothing clearly. The buildings were but silhouettes, featureless shapes of houses and stores and offices. The road was solid beneath the car but had no color, no texture. The sky was formless, gray.

Stan parked on the side of what should have been the street.

Where were we? Was this even part of the real world? I thought of Virginia, Ernest and the others, what they'd told me, what they'd said. I remembered when I applied for my job how I'd stepped through the door to apartment number 3—

Shangri-La

—and then awakened in an office in the building. I'd been living all this time in some sort of alternate universe.

Or I was going crazy.

Stan stepped out of the car. I followed. Like the city surrounding us, the air was thin, barely there.

He pointed toward what looked like the outline of a convenience store. "It's in there."

"What?"

"The mail factory . . . everything else."

"I thought you said it was inside the company."

"It is. At least, that's how I got in. But geography's not really geography here. When I came out, this is where I found myself. It's a back door. And I went in and out a few times to make sure I could get in and out anytime I wanted, make sure it worked every time. It's real, it's legit."

An alternate world.

"So what's your plan?"

"I want to show you something. It's going to blow your fucking mind."

I was starting to get scared. He seemed a little too secretive, and I didn't like that. I wanted him to tell me where we were going and what I was going to see before we went there, before I saw it. The thought occurred to me that this wasn't really Stan, that I was being led to my slaughter by a simulacrum.

But this *was* Stan. I knew it, deep down I knew it, and if he wanted to show me instead of tell me, he must have had a good reason.

I followed him over the unformed ground to that indistinct building. In the center of that gray space was a fully detailed door, a real door, and Stan reached for the vertical-bar handle and pulled it open.

We walked inside.

We were in a marble passsageway that could have come straight from the set of some old sword and sandal epic. At the far end was a shadowed vestibule, and Stan strode purposefully toward it, his shoes clicking on the polished floor. We passed into the vestibule, and Stan stopped in front of a large stone door. He pulled it open very slightly until there was a crack through which we could peek, and he motioned me over with a silent swing of his arm.

"Look," he whispered when I was next to him.

I looked. It was a roomful of men and women that, at first glance, looked like an old-fashioned secretarial pool, the kind I'd recently seen on TV in the movie *How to Succeed in Business Without Really Trying.* Only I could see right away that there was something wrong with these people. They sat in front of computer screens, typing ceaselessly, automatically shifting fonts on their individual printers to disguise their identities. But their faces looked strange, slow, almost retarded. I frowned, not certain what to make of them.

Stan filled me in. "Their tongues have been cut out," he said in a voice of hushed horror. "They can't talk. They can only communicate by writing."

In a sick way, it made perfect sense. These were the ideal Letter Writers.

I suddenly realized something else. All of these people were familiar. At least most of them were. Some had been dead for years, others were only recently deceased, and a few of them I was sure were still alive.

They were world leaders.

I recognized George Washington, Abraham Lincoln, Mao Tse-tung, Winston Churchill. Presidents, kings, prime ministers, czars, emperors. Their faces were distorted because their tongues had been cut out, but I could tell who they were, and knowing now what I was looking at, I recognized dozens more: Napoléon Bonaparte, Madame Mao, Dwight Eisenhower, Vladimir Lenin, Adolf Hitler, Thomas Jefferson. . . . Not every president was there, not every dictator or foreign ruler, either. But, like Ronald Reagan, political men, men of power, were often inveterate diarists and letter writers. Some of them, obviously, had been *real* Letter Writers, and those were the ones who were kept here, who now powered the machine that, as Henry said, made the world go round. They created the deep black undercurrent atop which we frivolous Letter Writers floated our fluff. Stan had been right. We *were* just distractions, and I realized how brilliant the Ultimate had been in his structuring of this world and his recruitment throughout history.

Throughout history.

How could we ever hope to go against something that powerful?

You are very powerful, James Baldwin had told me.

You're the only one who can help us, Virginia said. *You're the only one who can put a stop to all this.*

Had the Ultimate made a mistake with me? Had I been misassigned?

Virginia and her literary compatriots had obviously believed that to be the case, and I had the feeling Stan did, as well. All I knew was that when I had been free, in the real world, out in the open, I had inadvertently blocked some of the letters from here; I had managed to subvert the Ultimate's intentions. I was capable of far more than I was doing. My talents and abilities were not being properly used.

The only question was whether that was on purpose.

"I want to show you what else I found." Stan carefully closed the door, then led me down the marble passageway, stopping halfway before what looked like a discolored section of wall. He placed his hand on it—

And the wall slid open.

We were in a library. Only it wasn't a library of books but a library of letters. Stacked floor to ceiling on dark wood shelves were piles of stationery, masses of typing paper, sheets of notebook pages, all arranged alphabetically by the first letters of what I assumed were the authors' last names, which were stenciled onto the end caps of the bookcases. The library was enormous but well laid out, and Stan strode up one aisle and across another, easily finding what he was looking for. He sorted through a stack near the bottom of the bookcase and withdrew a handwritten letter. "The first one I ever wrote," he said.

I looked at the childish scrawl, glanced down at the signature: *Stan Shapiro.*

"Every letter I've ever written is here." He gestured toward the papers on the shelf. "Even the ones that were torn up or thrown away." He took the letter, put it back. "Every letter *anyone* has ever written is here."

The two of us looked around at the endless gargan-
tuan stacks.

I walked up to the nearest cross aisle, then turned
right, looking at the call letters. After I'd passed literally dozens of rows of bookcases, I finally found the
*H*s and quickly sprinted between the shelves until I
saw my own name. My output seemed pretty paltry
when arranged this way, but I quickly flipped through
the top half of my first stack and discovered that Stan
was right. In the stack were all of my secret letters to
Vicki and Eric, even a letter I'd started to write to
Virginia Woolf but discarded before finishing. Everything I'd ever written had been archived here.

I grabbed a letter at random from the shelf above
mine, written to a woman named Eileen from a man
named Frank Hanes: *I'm going to slit you snatch to
gullet, then pull out your innards and let the crows eat
them. . . .* I threw the letter down on the floor, reached
for another by an author named Gillian Handweiler:
*I am quite upset by the tone you used to speak with
me on the phone when I called to ask a simple question.
I am not a petty or vindictive person, but I believe you
should be fired for your poor attitude and communication skills, and I will be telling the doctor to do exactly that. . . .*

My head was spinning. What was the point of all
this? Who was keeping these letters and why? How
had they gotten here?

I moved up the aisle, took another letter at random,
read it:

> *Dear Sir,*
>   *I received your memo and agree completely.
> We do need more. To that end, I have decided
> to create another.*
>   *Stan Shapiro is a forty-something Brooklyn-
> ite with paranoid tendencies who loves conspir-*

acy theories and whose sole focus is the space
program. He is about five ten, balding, and
despite his obsessions is fairly social and inter-
acts easily with others—

I stopped, looked over at Stan, heading toward me.
My mouth was suddenly dry.

"What is it?" he asked, seeing the look on my face.

I couldn't say anything, simply handed him the letter. He read it over, staring at me with stricken eyes.
"What do you think it means?" he asked. His voice
was little more than a whisper.

"I . . . don't know," I said. But I was afraid that I
did. I glanced at the signature on the letter, then
looked up at the return address at the top: *Rhys Han-*
negan. The name meant nothing to me. Grabbing a
handful of this guy's letters, I started quickly sorting
through them. In one, Rhys wrote about creating a
woman named Dolores Hernandez. Dolores was a
Letter Writer who loved Mexican soap operas and was
a passionate opponent of free trade.

I knew her; I'd met her.

"I'm . . . a character," Stan said, dazed. He sat down
hard. There was no chair to catch him and he landed
painfully on the floor, though he didn't seem to notice.
"Another Letter Writer wrote about me and I . . .
became."

"Not necessarily—" I began.

"Stop it."

"Just because it's in writing doesn't mean it's true.
You should know that."

"But it *feels* true," he said, and he was right. As
much as I hated to admit it, it *did* feel true.

"In the beginning was the word," he said.

"Maybe . . . maybe . . ." I trailed off, unable to
think of anything comforting to say.

I looked at the letters in my hand. Who was this
Rhys Hannegan? One of the Old Ones Thomas Mann

had mentioned? The letters were all addressed *Dear Sir,* as though Rhys was an underling reporting to his superior. Had he been writing to the Ultimate Letter Writer?

Stan laughed shortly. "I was created in a letter. Someone wrote about me, and here I am. How's that for irony?"

I was stunned, still having a hard time taking this all in. "What if *I'm* not real?"

"What if?"

"Maybe someone wrote about me and made me up—"

"Maybe they did. So fucking what?" Stan stood, and suddenly he was back to his feisty old self. I admired the way he had adjusted so fast, had so quickly regained his equilibrium, but a part of my brain could not help thinking, *Because he was written that way.* "Look, I'm not going to stop writing, stop fighting, stop being who I am, just because I was brought to life by a Letter Writer. I didn't ask to be born, but now that I'm alive, I'm going to make the best of it."

I didn't ask to be born.

I used to say that to my parents.

"However I got here, I'm real enough now. I have a heart, I have a brain, and I have a will independent enough to let me do whatever I damn well please."

That's good, I almost said, but I realized it sounded patronizing.

"The thing is," Stan continued, "I think you're one of the real ones. A *true* Letter Writer. Writers like you come along once in a generation. And whether the Ultimate realizes it or not, you're the real deal.

"You're our ticket out of here."

I shook my head.

"I'm serious."

"How? You think I can get us back? Get *myself* back?"

"Like the Good Witch said in *The Wizard of Oz,*

you've always had the power. And there's no place like home."

I suddenly thought of something. "But is there a 'back' for you? If you really were created by letter, can you return to . . . my world?"

"It's my world, too. Maybe I was created by a Letter Writer. But I don't think I was created *here*. I was brought here, like you, but I was born in the real world. My memories of it are too vivid. There would be no reason to give me these memories, no reason to recreate my old neighborhood if I hadn't had an old neighborhood, no reason to recall my intial hiring if I'd never been hired."

I wasn't sure I bought that logic. Hell, he and the others could have been created the day I arrived for the sole purpose of keeping me company. But there was no way to tell. These letters didn't have dates on them.

"So what do we do now?" I asked.

"You tell me. You're the one who's real."

I didn't like this. It felt weird, and I wished I hadn't learned about Stan—or, at the very least, didn't believe it. But I had learned it, I did believe it, and now talking to him felt almost like talking to myself. I saw him as more of a cartoon character than a person now, a figment of my imagination rather than a flesh-and-blood human being.

I felt as though I'd been abandoned by the one person I could truly count on.

Virginia and the other authors, I wondered, were they real? Or were they characters created by Letter Writers to populate this place and give themselves an air of legitimacy?

Was anything real?

Was *I* real?

Stan said yes, but he was a made-up character.

Maybe all of this was taking place in the correspondence of an author plotting out a novel and discussing it with a colleague. Maybe I'd never been married, never had a son.

My head hurt. I felt dizzy and wanted to sit down.

What would happen if we torched this library? I wondered. Were all of these letters backed up somewhere, ready to be regenerated if destroyed? Or would this world come tumbling down, wink out of existence, while societies all over the earth were thrown into chaos as their underpinnings collapsed, the letters used to determine their courses disappearing?

I looked at Stan. I know he wanted me to just sit down and write a letter that would solve all of our problems, but I had my doubts as to whether that would work. I'd written letters about a lot of things that hadn't been true and hadn't come to pass, and there was no guarantee that anything would be different this time. I still liked the idea of returning to the factory and following the letters out. That was the one physical, concrete truth in all this: we wrote letters and they were delivered in the real world. If we could just find out how they got through, we could do the same.

We discussed this, the two of us, standing there in the middle of the library, speaking softly, our voices echoing and disappearing in the vast room, but the truth was that it was hard for me to take him seriously. I'd deferred to him before because he was older, but the respect I had for him was gone. I felt like a human adult trying to find a way to make Pinocchio into a real boy. The excitement I'd felt earlier, on the way in, that I'd caught from Stan, had dissolved into something like sadness. Yes, I had a shot at finding a way out of here, but as far as I was concerned, it was still a long shot, and at the moment I felt more alone than I had at any time since arriving.

"You need to start writing," Stan urged.

"We're going to follow the mail," I told him. I'd made my decision.

He hesitated. "I'm not sure it'll work for me."

I understood his point; I wasn't sure, either. But I felt closer to the holy grail than I ever had before, and I knew I had to take this chance now.

We walked back through the aisles, through the door out of the library and down the marble passageway to the vestibule, where we stopped. "They didn't see me last time," Stan said. "Or they didn't care. But things might be different now. We're taking a risk."

"Live free or die," I told him, and pulled open the door.

I was looking out at the corridor of the fourth floor of the building where we worked. Across from me was the elevator. I poked my head in, saw the door to Henry's office several yards to my left. I stepped back, turned around, still holding on to the handle of the open stone door. The vestibule and the marble passageway remained.

"Where is it?" I demanded.

"I think they're on to us." I could hear the fear in Stan's voice. "We'd better get out of here."

Was that really the fourth floor of "the Building" before us? Could I simply walk through the doorway and down the hall to my office? It didn't matter. Stan's car was still outside. He had to drive it back or he'd be without wheels. "You go," he told me, realizing the same thing. "I'll meet you there."

I couldn't leave him. "All for one," I said, and we shut the door and hurried back out into that half-formed neighborhood. We weren't being followed, but we both felt as though we were being watched, and neither of us said a word until we were in the car, on the road and several miles away, back where the streets looked like streets and the buildings like buildings.

"Try to write," he pleaded. "You can get us out of here. I know you can."

"What about Ellen, Fischer and the others?"

"Get us all out. Write us all in."

"Do you think any of them are real?"

"I don't know." He thought for a moment. "Ellen and Fischer maybe. They seem to really miss their old lives, their spouses. They don't have your writing talent, obviously. They're not in your league. But there's something about them . . . Beth and the others, I don't know. I don't think so. I mean, if *I'm* just a made-up character . . ."

He had a point.

"I just hope Shamus wasn't," he said softly.

We were back in our offices before noon. No one was waiting for us—no bureaucratic guards, no Henry—and neither of us found any mysterious letters on our desks. There was no time to waste, though, and I sat down in front of my PC, turned it on and immediately began writing. I didn't know how to go about it, so I tried a couple of approaches:

> *Dear Stan,*
> *Here's hoping this finds you well in California. You can stay at my place for as long as you want. I'll be there soon. . . .*

And

> *Dear Stan,*
> *You are not allowed to live with other Letter Writers anymore. You must return home to your old life, to the real Brooklyn, New York, where you will live out your days happily retired with a full pension. . . .*

And

> *Dear Sir,*
>   *Stan Shapiro is no longer a Letter Writer.*
> *He is an ordinary man. . . .*

He didn't go anywhere.

Neither did I.

After taking up Stan's cause, I must have written twenty letters that afternoon to anyone I could think of who could possibly get *me* out. I tried every way possible, from descriptions to demands, pleas to declarative statements, but no matter what I did, nothing worked. There was no change.

Not that day nor the next nor the next . . .

We remained here in our homes and our habitats, going through the same paces we usually did. It was at first frustrating, then dispiriting and finally despair-inducing.

I'd been depressed before, but always in the back of my mind I'd known that my friends were there for me. Now, though, I felt isolated, alone. As far as I was concerned, my friends were nothing more than holograms, fake people created to keep me company. I felt like I was living in a fucking video game or something, and I looked with suspicion upon everything I saw, heard or did. *Don't trust everything you hear. Or see,* Henry had told me when I first arrived. *Only trust what you read.*

He'd known what he was talking about.

Henry, I was pretty sure, was a real person, a real Letter Writer. Was he as powerful as I was? I didn't think so, but that hardly mattered. He'd been placed in a position of authority by the Ultimate or one of his underlings—

the Old Ones

—and while he might have sympathy for me, his loyalty was to his boss. He was not about to bite the hand that fed him. Even if he was brave enough to do such a thing, I'm not sure he would really want to

So while he was nice to me and I liked him, Henry was my enemy.

Still I kept writing.

One day, I wrote the same letter over and over again, in longhand, then on my typewriter, then on the PC, then in longhand again, all day long, until my brain was numb and my fingers hurt. Perhaps repetition would get the job done. Hell, as any politician knew, if you repeated something often enough, people eventually came to believe that it was true. Letter Writers took advantage of this all the time, particularly when writing to newspapers' editorial pages.

But it didn't work this time. I awoke the next morning in my same house, drove to work in my same black car, nodded to Stan in the parking lot as both of us shuffled dejectedly into the building.

Finally, I decided one day not to get out of bed. What was the point? I lay there beneath the blanket, staring up at the ceiling, thinking of the future, and all I saw before me was an eternity of sleeping, eating, reading, writing, mindless, endless rote and repetition. I might as well just stay here. There wasn't any punishment I could receive that was worse than what I was already experiencing.

I remained there all morning. No one called; no one came to get me; I was all alone. I got up only to take a piss. At first I didn't even want to do that—I'd piss in my fucking bed; who gave a shit?—but then I realized that I couldn't just lie in it forever. I'd have to change the sheets, put new ones on, wash the old ones. . . . Just the thought of it made me tired. So I shuffled into the bathroom, took a leak, returned to the comfort of my mattress.

Sometime in the midafternoon, half in and half out of the near continuous sleep state in which I'd been hovering, I heard a sound from the living room: the clanking of metal on metal.

The mail slot next to my front door.

A letter had just been delivered.

For *that* I got out of bed.

I tried to hurry. I wanted to see what the mailman looked like. But by the time I'd reached the front door, unlocked and opened it, he was gone. I ran outside in my underwear, hoping to see him walking up the block or even driving away in a truck or van, but there was nothing; the street was deserted. It was also silent. The fake noises I heard each evening from the other houses were nowhere to be found, and the usual sounds of a suburb—dog barks, bird cries, car engines driving by, kids playing, babies crying—were not there. Literally, the only noise I heard was my own breathing.

I quickly ducked back in the house.

There was a white envelope lying on the floor beneath the mail slot. I picked it up and immediately recognized the handwriting, though I hadn't seen it in over a year.

It was him.

The Ultimate.

I tore open the envelope. On the sheet of paper inside were three words: *I always win.* Enclosed was a photograph of James Baldwin lying on a bed, his eyes wide open and staring, obviously dead. The cause of his death was not readily apparent, but whether the technical reason was heart attack or pill overdose or strangulation, I knew who'd really killed him.

I always win.

I let the photo fall from my hands, the paper, too. I didn't even have the energy to tear them up. I slumped to the floor. He was right. He did always win. How could I have ever thought otherwise? He'd been able to see my dreams since I was a kid, and he knew everything I did. Like Santa, he saw me when I was sleeping; he knew when I was awake. He'd created this entire alternate universe, luring Letter Writers from all over the world, and he'd been doing it for centuries. God knew how old he was. Who was I to think that I could best him in anything?

I was his plaything. He kept me around for my amusement value.

All of a sudden, I was determined to put a stop to that. Maybe I couldn't go up against the Ultimate in a fair fight, but I could throw a wrench into the monkeyworks and make sure that I was no longer a participant, that I could no longer be used. I thought of what Henry had said when I was looking for a way out of the Kyoko debacle: *One of you is going to have to go.*

I could opt out.

It was a big step, a final step, a nonreversible step, but it was the only act of defiance left to me.

As the afternoon turned to dusk and dusk became night, I sat there on the floor, thinking through the ramifications of what I was considering, trying to figure out not only if I *should* go through with it but if I *could* go through with it. Was I brave enough to act?

In the end, I decided that I had nothing to lose.

I considered calling Stan, telling him of my decision, but I told myself he wasn't real, and though I hated myself for it, though I knew that he *was* real, that he had thoughts and feelings just as valid as my own, that he was as physically solid as I was myself, I could not get past the truth of his origin, could not consider him an actual human being.

I stood, walked through the darkened living room to the kitchen, drank an entire half gallon of orange juice, ate the last piece of leftover frozen pizza.

Then I sat down in my den.

And started on my suicide note.

Sixteen

1

I awoke in a hospital in Anaheim.

I was in a room with two other patients, both of them old men and both of them watching the same *Oprah* show on two different televisions. My mouth was dry, completely parched, and when I opened my lips and tried to speak, I couldn't. My throat felt as though it had been scrubbed with sandpaper. I knew there had to be some sort of button I could press to call for a nurse, and my fingers fumbled around at the edge of the bed until they encountered a small plastic rectangle attached to a piece of cord. In the center of the rectangle was a button, and I pushed it.

Seconds later, two uniformed nurses hurried into the room and over to my bed, followed quickly by a doctor. I motioned to my mouth and my throat, tried to talk again and ended up coughing, gagging, nearly throwing up. One of the nurses, the older one, held out a bottle with a curved sipping straw which she adroitly placed between my lips.

I had never tasted anything finer than that small trickle of cool water.

I wanted to drink the whole bottle, but she pulled the straw away from my mouth after a few seconds. "Not too much," she advised. "You won't be able to keep it down at first."

"Do you know who you are?" the doctor asked, shining a penlight in first one eye and then the other.

"Of course," I told him.

As it turned out, they didn't. I'd been discovered without any identification, lying unconscious on a bus stop bench, and had been brought directly to the hospital. If I'd had a wallet, it had been stolen, and the next course of action was going to be to take my fingerprints and see if the police could use them to identify me.

But now I'd awakened.

"How long was I out?" I asked after giving them my name, address and pertinent personal information.

"You've been here for two days. We estimate that's how long you've been in the coma. A day or two longer, perhaps. At the outside."

"But what's the date?" I asked.

"February twenty-third."

"No, I mean the year."

The doctor frowned but told me.

I'd been gone for a year and a half. I'd half expected to have been gone only a day—or ten years. But of course, the times had to coincide. We'd watched their television, heard their radio, read their daily newspapers.

Theirs?

Ours.

I was back.

But had I really been gone?

I wasn't sure.

It seemed almost like a dream, everything that had happened, and surrounded by doctors and nurses and patients, by the hard facts of everyday existence, the surrealism of that life seemed ever more fantastic. Did I even have any letter-writing ability? Did anyone? Or was that something my brain had made up, the intricate delusions of a mentally ill mind? Perhaps my entire history, everything I thought I recalled was false,

illusory. I could be a New Jersey construction worker
named John Johnson who'd had some type of breakdown and imagined he was a magic Letter Writer from
California named Jason Hanford.

I was subjected to a series of blood tests and CAT
scans. I was left on an IV drip but allowed to eat a
small meal.

I couldn't remember how I'd killed myself. That
seemed a major mental lapse. Did that mean it hadn't
happened? Or had the shock to my body from death
made me forget the last moments of my life? I was
alive, but I wondered if I was alive in this world now
but dead in that other one.

That first day, I was allowed to think only of my
health and my tests and the small steps needed to
bring me back up to full speed. But after a long night
of restless sleep, reality intruded. There was talk of
discharging me, and a well-dressed young woman
came in to ask me questions about my insurance plan.
I knew only that it was Blue Cross, knew nothing
about the specific policy, but she said with my Social
Security number she should be able to look it up. She
returned some time later to say that I had been
dropped from my plan and apparently had no insurance, and I was then forced to fill out a lot of forms
that would qualify me for state and federal assistance.

Did I have any relatives? the woman asked, anyone
who could assume financial responsibilities for my
stay? I gave her Vicki's name, and Vicki's parents'
names, address and phone number, but the line was
out of service and no listing could be found for either.
I gave out *my* address and phone number again in case
Vicki was living back there now, but every attempt at
contact was fruitless.

I tried to call my lawyers, but they seemed to have
disappeared. I couldn't remember the name of the
firm Vicki had used.

I asked for a phone and called the North Orange County courthouse, family court division. I still remembered my case number, and after several transfers I reached a clerk who was able to look it up. I'd wanted only an address and phone number, but I was told that as I had not shown up for my court date and even my own lawyers had not been able to locate me, I had lost the judgment. Vicki had been awarded full custody and I had no visitation rights in regard to Eric. I was never to contact either Vicki or Eric except through their lawyers.

I didn't know what *they'd* written about me, the Letter Writers, but obviously letters had been sent. I'd been made out to be some sort of deadbeat dad, and the consensus seemed to be that I'd skipped out on my court dates and disappeared in order to avoid my responsibilities. The strange thing was that the Letter Writers had made an effort to smear me and assassinate my character, but they hadn't concocted a death for me. I wondered why. Maybe ordinary people like me, the nonfamous, didn't merit a death. Or maybe other plans had been made for me.

Or maybe . . .

Maybe no letters had been written at all. Maybe this is simply what happened to fathers who didn't show up to court and forfeited their rights.

I asked the court clerk for Vicki's current address, but she said she was not allowed to give out that information. She did give me the name of the law firm representing Vicki and a phone number, and I called them, but they said that without Vicki's okay, they could not divulge any personal information.

Ask her, I told them.

They promised to get back to me.

Make it fast, I said.

In books, in movies, on TV, kindly doctors and a friendly hospital staff would have kept me under ob-

servation until they were able to determine what was
wrong with me, until the cause of the coma had been
ascertained and I was provided with treatment that
would ensure it would never happen again. In reality,
however, hospitals were like assembly lines, and the
sooner they could get me out of my bed and onto the
street, the sooner they could have the bed free for
another patient. I was kept for an extra day—to make
sure I didn't have a relapse, I suppose, although no
one told me that specifically—and then was given an
appointment with an outside neurologist for the following afternoon and released.

Having no car and no money, I started walking
home. Anaheim wasn't *that* far from Brea, I reasoned.
But an hour later, still in Fullerton and less than halfway there, drenched with sweat from the unseasonal
humidity of the day, I decided to put up my thumb.
I'd never hitchhiked in my life and common sense told
me it was a dangerous idea, but I figured I'd be able
to pick and choose among the people who stopped
and decide for myself whom to travel with; that should
keep me safe.

No one stopped.

I reached a Target store. I intended to walk inside
to get a drink from the water fountain, but on my way
I encountered a man dressed in white collecting
money for a charity.

I suddenly had a plan.

I went inside, got my drink, then came out and stationed myself next to the door opposite the charity
solicitor, the entrance rather than the exit. "Could you
spare some change?" I asked each person who walked
by me. It was embarrassing and humiliating, but within
twenty minutes I had twenty dollars, enough for a bus
ride with plenty left over for tonight's dinner, and I
bought myself a bottle of Very Cherry Snapple, then
walked to the bus stop, studied the routes and waited.

I was soon back in Brea, let off by the bus on Lambert Road, a five-minute walk from my home. It was strange being back, since everything about me was intimately familiar. I may have been gone, but I'd seen these same sights every single day—only now there was life in them. And that made all the difference. Cars were passing by; birds were in the air; a plane crossed overhead. People were on the street and talking. To the south I heard the *chop-chop-chop* of a police helicopter's blades. I smelled car exhaust and frying hamburgers. The sounds and smells were wonderful and I was overjoyed to be once again in the real world, but though I hadn't realized it until recently, I'd been gone a long time and it was a bit of a culture shock. I felt a trifle uneasy, slightly off-balance.

Still, I was excited, and I hurried up the sidewalk, anxious. I had no idea whether Vicki would be there or not, but at the very least I would be able to wash up, relax and finally experience the welcome comfort of just being home.

Except my house was no longer my house.

I slowed. Stopped.

There was a strange car in the driveway, and when I walked cautiously up to the front door, I saw unfamiliar furniture through the living room window. Even if I had a key, which I didn't, I'm not sure I would have tried to let myself in. It would have felt wrong. I pressed the button, ringing the bell, and a moment later a woman in her mid-twenties, cradling a baby, answered the door. "Hello?" she said.

I was tongue-tied for a moment. I could see that that worried her, could tell that she was backing off, getting ready to close the door on me, so I blurted out, "Is Vicki Hanford here?"

"Uh, no," the woman said a little nervously. "My husband and I live here."

I nodded. "When did you buy—?" I began.

"I've got to go," she said. She closed the door, and I heard a dead bolt being thrown.

My house had been sold out from under me. I was homeless.

This was impossible.

But if I'd learned anything in the past year and a half, it was that *anything* was possible.

Where to go? I had no job, no home, no money. I had no idea where Vicki and Eric were. My entire life had been taken away from me. I glanced around at the neighbors' homes, recognized several of the cars in the driveways. I'd always been on good terms with my neighbors and despite the fact that I'd backed off a bit socially after Vicki and I had separated, a few of them I honestly considered friends. I could probably hit them up for money, maybe even stay for a night or two in the guest room Carl Clarkson across the street had had built into one half of his two-car garage.

Or I could go back home to my mom's house.

No. That was not even an option.

I walked over to Carl's. His wife, Joyce, answered the door, and she seemed surprised and more than a little uneasy about seeing me again.

She'd gotten a letter about me.

I was still trying to convince myself that that was not true, that I'd had some type of breakdown or episode and all of my thoughts and memories of letter writing were just fantasy, but deep down I believed it *was* true, that despite the fact that I had no evidence, everything *had* happened just as I remembered it. . . .

I *did* have evidence, I realized. Vicki. Why had she divorced me and taken Eric and hid from me? Because of the letters. She'd told me so. She'd said she was afraid of me and my abilities.

Unless . . .

Unless my mind had added that, made that up, and

she was really afraid of me because of my increasing mental instability.

"Let me get Carl," Joyce said. Pointedly, she did not invite me in. Indeed, she closed the door on me while she went to get her husband. That wasn't like her.

The door opened again a few moments later. "Hey," Carl said. "Long time no see."

"Yeah, I was in an accident," I lied. "I've been in a coma." That part was true, though it sounded less believable than the accident part.

Carl and Joyce looked at each other.

"I'm looking for Vicki," I said. "I got out of the hospital and I found out that my house was sold and I . . . I don't know where she is." I could tell they didn't believe me, and on impulse I dug through my shirt pocket. "Look," I said, showing them my release papers from the hospital. I pointed to the word *coma* on the line declaring why I'd been admitted. "I'm not lying."

Carl looked slightly less suspicious. "We got . . . a letter about you," he said. "Yesterday. It said . . ." He looked at Joyce. "Well, it said a lot of things about you."

A letter.

I felt a tremendous sense of relief. It was true. I hadn't imagined it. I wasn't crazy.

The knowledge didn't make me feel any better, though. In some ways, it made me feel worse. The relief fled almost instantly, followed by fear and apprehension. They were wasting no time. The machine had been set in motion. I'd escaped, and letters were being methodically sent out to anyone with whom I might possibly come into contact, poisoning the waters against me. I wanted to see that letter Carl and Joyce had been sent, but I knew it would be better if I didn't.

I might recognize the author.

They were still suspicious of me, I could tell, but I didn't blame them. The written word was a powerful thing, much more believable than the spoken word, and though the Clarksons had known me for years and did not know the fictional person or made-up agency who had sent them the false information, they would automatically give the letter more credence.

I would not stay in their garage guest room tonight. I would borrow money from them, though, so I could at least get a motel room for the night, and I was about to ask for fifty bucks or whatever they could spare when I suddenly remembered something.

My bank account!

I still had money in the bank. Close to twenty thousand dollars between savings, checking and CDs, if I remembered correctly. I had no wallet, no driver's license, no ID of any kind, so it might be tough to get any money out, but it was worth a try.

I asked Carl for one favor, a drive to Lincoln Mutual, my bank, and though I could tell he didn't want to take me, guilt won out and he agreed to drop me off on his way to the grocery store. I could only imagine what was in that letter they'd been sent. I'd assumed at first that it had depicted me as a deadbeat dad who'd skipped out on his family and disappeared, but Carl seemed nervous on the drive over, as though at any moment I might attack him, and I surmised that the letter's depiction of me had been much worse than I'd originally thought.

The Letter Writers weren't pulling any punches.

Carl dropped me off at the bank and sped away, praying, I'm sure, that he would never see me again. It suddenly occurred to me that the bank might have gotten a few letters about me, too, or Vicki might have drained the account, but thankfully that did not prove to be the case.

I had no ID, but I knew my Social Security number, my bank account number, my PIN number and my secret password, and when the teller compared signatures and went over everything with her supervisor, I was allowed to withdraw funds. I told the bank that I was a victim of identity theft, that all of my credit cards and my driver's license had been stolen, and I was issued a new passbook and given a new account number. I took out five hundred dollars, which should tide me over for a day or two, and left the rest alone.

I found a cheap hotel just down the street from the bank and decided to stay there, make that my home base. In the morning, I would go to the DMV, tell them that my wallet had been stolen, get a new license or at least a temporary one and then see what I could do about getting my car back. There was no way my Toyota would still be parked across the street from the apartment in Los Angeles where I'd disappeared, but hopefully it had been towed away by the police rather than vandalized or stolen, and if the cops hadn't sold it at auction already, there was a good chance I could get it back.

I made a few phone calls—a *lot* of phone calls, actually—and finally I managed to track down the car. It was in a private lot, held by a towing company with which the city contracted, and all I'd have to do to reclaim it was pay the one-thousand-dollar fine, and show a valid driver's license and one other proof of ID.

In other words, I was screwed.

I might be able to rent a car, I thought, go to Avis or Hertz or something.

But they probably required a major credit card.

I didn't know what to do. I'd figure something out, though. And after I got some wheels and found a way to get around, my first order of business was to find Vicki and Eric, set things straight. I'd been gone for

a year and a half, and it tore me apart inside to think
that they believed I had abandoned them or didn't
care about them, that Vicki was trying to think up
diplomatic answers to Eric's sad questions about why
I'd disappeared.

And that was the best-case scenario.

I'd be willing to bet that they'd received letters
about me telling far more vicious and destructive lies.

I'd hire a private investigator if I had to. I'd spend
all the money I had tracking my wife and son across
the country, but I was determined that I would find
them and reconnect and put my life back together.

I fell asleep on a cheap bed with a springy mattress,
listening to the harsh sounds of the couple in the next
room having sex.

I didn't go to my neurologist's appointment the next
morning. I knew there was nothing wrong with me
and didn't want to waste the time. Instead, I took the
bus to the DMV. I *did* get a temporary license, and
afterward I went to the bank, withdrew ten thousand
dollars and then bought a used Volkswagen for three
thousand dollars from a corner car lot.

At this rate, I'd be broke in no time. Which reminded me that, eventually, I was going to have to
find a job.

But long-term plans were not on my radar right
now. I needed to find Vicki and Eric. That was my
priority. Everything else could sort itself out afterward.

I realized that I had no close friends, no one I could
turn to, no one on whom I could depend. My letter
writing had taken me away from that, and it was amazing that I'd even allowed Vicki in. Before the letter
writing had taken over, I'd had close friends. As a kid,
as a teenager, I'd had—

Robert and Edson.

I stood there for a moment, thinking. Could I?
Should I? Dare I?

I was all alone. I needed help. Why the hell not? I drove back to my crappy hotel room, flipped through the torn white pages I discovered in the dresser drawer, and found Edson's phone number and address. He was living in Newport Beach. Robert either wasn't listed or, more likely, had moved out of Orange County and lived somewhere else.

I called Edson, more nervous than I should have been, my hand slippery with sweat on the plastic of the phone. He wasn't there, an answering machine picked up the call, and I left my name and the phone number of the motel along with the room number. I pretended that I was in town for a few days on a business trip and would like to get together with him and talk about old times.

Afterward, I called Vicki's work. Or what *had* been her work—whether she was still there or not I didn't know.

She wasn't.

She and Eric seemed to have dropped off the face of the planet, and for the first time I found myself really scared. What if something had happened to them? What if they weren't hiding—what if they were dead? There were a lot of possible explanations, I told myself. The most likely was that she'd found a job in Arizona, close to her parents' house.

Maybe she'd remarried.

I didn't want to think about that, refused to think about that. At the hospital, the administrator had tried to call Vicki's parents in Mesa, but just in case, I tried again myself. No luck. The line really was out of service.

I sat there in my cheap motel room, on my springy unmade bed, not knowing what to do next, feeling helpless and powerless and lost.

Edson called shortly after noon. "Hello," he said at first in a formal adult voice that I never would have recognized. "May I speak to Jason Hanford?"

"This is Jason," I said.

"Dude!" The voice was deeper than it had been, but the inflections were the same, and I recognized my old friend immediately.

There were tears in my eyes, and I struggled to keep the emotion out of my voice. "Dude."

"I was checking my voice mail at lunch, and I came across your message. How the hell've you been?"

"It's a long story," I told him.

"Well, I want to hear it! We have to get together while you're in town. What are your plans for tonight?"

I glanced over at the blurry television. "Nothing. I was hoping we could talk."

"You want to meet somewhere? You want to come over here . . . ?"

"Your place would be great," I said. "I'd like to see it."

He gave me directions and told me to be there at six. He'd take off work early and be home by then. We spent a few more minutes catching up. He'd been married but was divorced, was an investment banker, had no kids.

"What about Robert?" I asked. "Ever see him?"

"No, man. I don't know what ever happened to him." He paused, and when he spoke again he sounded more subdued. "I miss you guys, you know? I was just thinking about all of us a few days ago, thinking we should have kept in touch."

"And now I called."

"And now you called."

A beep sounded on the line. "I gotta go," Edson said. "A client. I'll see you tonight, though, huh?"

"I'll be there," I told him.

I stood, looked at myself in the mirror. I'd been wearing the same clothes for days. These were the ones they'd found me in, and they hadn't washed them at the hospital before giving them back to me. I needed to buy some new duds before tonight.

I drove to Mervyn's, went to the clearance rack, found a decent long-sleeved shirt and a pretty good short-sleeved shirt, then picked up a pair of jeans. What was I going to tell Edson? How much was I going to reveal?

I didn't know yet. I'd have to play it by ear.

Edson's house was not what I'd expected.

Newport Beach . . . investment banker . . . I'd anticipated driving up to a Mediterranean-style home with peach walls and a red tile roof and a hilltop view of the ocean. Instead, Edson lived on a funky side street on the flat Balboa Peninsula in a gray clapboard house two blocks from the beach. I could see his personality in the house, in its casual patio, and its haphazard landscaping, and that buoyed my spirits. It was reassuring to know that some things never changed and that Edson was one of them.

Sure enough, he was as easygoing as ever. Slightly balder, slightly chunkier, but still definitely the same person he had always been.

"It's all I have left," he announced, gesturing around him. "She got my house in Big Bear and my Hummer." He grinned. "So how goes it with you?"

We went inside to talk. The interior was far more upscale than the exterior, and I had the feeling his ex-wife had been the guiding light behind the decorating. I was not surprised when he ignored the chairs and couch and sat down on the floor next to a compact stereo unit half hidden behind an antique table, and turned on the radio. I was also not surprised that it was tuned to a station that referred to twenty-year-old new-wave songs as "modern rock."

He asked why I was in town and where I lived now, and I immediately set him straight. I explained that I

lived in Brea and my wife had recently left me, but
did not elaborate, saying that it was still too painful
to talk about. "It wasn't anything bad," I assured him.
"There was no abuse or anything—"

"I know that," he told me. "I wouldn't have even
thought it."

For the first time in I couldn't remember how long,
I felt at ease, at home. Edson and I had drifted apart,
we hadn't seen each other for two decades, but the
reconnection was immediate. We'd known each other
as kids, and that meant we each knew the real person
beneath our false adult appearances. There was a
shorthand we had together, a comfort level that only
real intimacy could bring.

I thought of the kinship I'd felt with the other Letter Writers, how excited I'd been at first to meet others of my kind. *This* was my kind, I realized. I was a
human being first, a Letter Writer second.

I'd had that backward for far too long.

I gave Edson a bowdlerized version of my recent
past, letting him know that I'd been in a coma, that
everything was now fine and I'd been given a clean
bill of health, but that I'd been out for so long that
my life had been pulled out from under me. I'd lost
my job, my house had been sold, the proceeds had
been used to pay off the bills that had accumulated in
my absence, and I had no idea where my wife and
son were. Last I'd heard, they were at her parents'
house in Arizona, but that number was no longer
working, and I couldn't find any trace of them.

"No shit?" he said.

"God's honest truth."

"You're living out a TV movie. Jesus Christ, I didn't
know those kinds of things really happened. It's almost like hearing you got hit on the head with a coco
nut and got amnesia.

"Sorry," he said quickly. "Didn't mean to offend
you or anything."

"It's cool," I told him.

He shook his head. "So . . . what? You're, like, looking for them?"

"Yeah. With my used Volkswagen that I bought with what was left of my savings. From my headquarters at the beautiful no-tell motel."

"You gotta get out of there," Edson said. "Hey, I have a rental. In Costa Mesa. It's not much, but I'm between tenants right now, and if you'd like to stay there for a while, you're welcome to it."

"I couldn't—"

"You'll take it and you'll like it. It's yours until you get back on your feet. I mean, shit, a coma? And you can't find your family? You need a village, dude."

I looked away. I felt like crying. I didn't deserve such kind treatment. I thought of all that I'd done in my life, all the damage I'd caused, how far I'd strayed from the person Edson had known as a child, the person I'd wanted to grow up to be.

"Thanks," I said sincerely. "I really appreciate it."

"No sweat, bro."

He asked a million questions about the coma, and I answered them as honestly as I could without telling the truth. He tactfully stayed away from asking about our breakup, but he completely understood why I needed to get in touch with Vicki and, especially, Eric. He couldn't understand why her lawyers weren't willing to let her know that I'd been in a coma or, if they *had* let her know, why she hadn't immediately come to visit.

I professed ignorance, too.

We got to reminiscing about the past. "Remember when you used to write those complaint letters and get us free food and tickets to amusement parks and everything?" He laughed. "That was outrageous!"

The strongest memory he had from our youth was of me writing letters.

I was tempted to tell him everything. I wanted to

be able to spill my guts to *someone*, and it was all I
could do not to blurt out what I was and where I'd
really been for the past year and a half. *Maybe, eventually, I'll tell him,* I thought.

But I'd do it through a letter.

It was nearly ten o'clock when Edson went into his
study and returned with a photo of his rental house.
"There's a map on the back," he said, "so you should
have no trouble finding it. It's right off Harbor, close
to the fairgrounds. Electricity's on. Water's on.
There's no phone, but I got a cell you can use. Here's
the key. You need me to come with you, help you
pack, show you the place, whatever?"

"No," I said. "I think I can figure it out. Besides, it's
getting late. I'll call you if anything's wrong. Otherwise
expect to hear from me tomorrow."

"You got it."

"And . . . thanks," I said again. I couldn't seem to
say it enough. "I really appreciate this. It means a
lot—"

He grinned. "Get out of here, you weenie."

I'd been thinking I had to go back to the hotel, but
I realized now that I didn't. I still had the key to my
room, but there was nothing in it other than my old
clothes, which I was planning to ditch anyway. I had
no luggage, no belongings. Everything was in the car.
I could just throw away the key and disappear, and
since I'd paid in cash, there was no credit card tying
anything to me.

So I drove to Edson's rental house.

Located in the middle of a block lined with similar
homes, it was not unlike the houses in Acacia in which
we'd grown up. This one had a living room, a family
room, two bedrooms, two bathrooms and a fairly large
kitchen. It was fully furnished, and if the furniture
wasn't new, at least it was usable. The electricity was
indeed on, and I immediately flipped on some lights

and turned on the television. I'd grown suspicious of
silence and wary of the dark.

Once more, I was nearly overcome with emotion.
Yesterday, I'd been practically homeless. Three days
before that, I'd been living in a bleak synthetic world
and had been so despondent I'd wanted to kill myself.
Now I was safely ensconced in a suburban house in
which I could live for free as long as I needed while
I looked for my wife and son.

I should have written fewer complaint letters, I
thought. More letters of encouragement.

Which reminded me . . .

I looked around for the mail slot. There was none.
This was obviously one of those houses with an outside box. I opened the front door and peeked out.
Sure enough, a black rectangle with two curved under-
arms for magazines and oversized flyers was mounted
on the stucco wall next to the door. Out of habit, I
opened the top, felt inside.

My fingers touched paper.

I pulled out an envelope.

It was addressed to me.

I shivered as a rash of goose bumps passed over my
arms. Closing and locking the door behind me, I
brought the envelope inside and looked at the return
address. It was from Kyoko.

I tore open the envelope, read the letter inside:

Dear Jason,

 *How can I ever thank you? You released me
from bondage and returned me to my life, and
for that I will be eternally grateful. Do not
worry. I have no intention of seeing you again
or writing to you (unless* you *initiate the contact). I do not know what came over me in that
place. I do not know what made me act so
crazy. The truth is that I am* not *obsessed with*

you but am happy with my own life here in
Tokyo. I wish you well. You deserve *it. Once*
again, thank you very much.

> *Yours truly,*
> *Kyoko Yoshizumi*

I read the letter again. So was Kyoko real or not?
Had Stan been wrong?

Or was this letter fake?

I examined it more closely. It was impossible to tell
for sure, but I thought I recognized a little of Ellen's
style in the use of underscoring.

Besides, how could Kyoko, in Japan, have known
several days ago, when she would have had to mail
this letter, that I would look up my old friend Edson
and that he would offer to let me stay in his rental
house?

A Letter Writer had written it.

What was the point, though? The letter told me
nothing. Perhaps it was just a practice run, an attempt
by the Ultimate to see if he could find me and get
through to me even though I had no fixed address.
Perhaps it was bait. Maybe he wanted to see if I would
answer Kyoko, if she could elicit a response from me.
Or maybe, just maybe, Ellen or whoever had really
written the letter was attempting to get word to me,
was relaying a secret message.

If so, that message was beyond my ability to decipher. I spent another hour attempting to spot a code
within the words, to detect a hidden pattern in the
arrangement of the letters. I even held the paper next
to a lightbulb to check for the old invisible-ink routine. But finally, I threw it away.

Fuck it, I thought. If the Ultimate wanted to have
his Letter Writers send correspondence to me, let him.
Let them do their worst.

2

The letters started arriving.

This neighborhood had early mail delivery, and at nine o'clock the next morning, the postman dropped six envelopes into the box.

They'd definitely found me. They sent their best and brightest after me, literary heavyweights who knew how to manipulate the language in order to secure their ends, but after reading the first letter, I burned the others unopened, scattering the ashes in the backyard.

That first one had been a doozy. *Dear Jason,* it said. *I am sorry to be the bearer of bad news, but your friend Stan Shapiro is dead. Stan killed himself early yesterday morning by repeatedly stabbing himself in the heart with a kitchen knife—*

The letter had been signed by Beth.

I didn't know if any of that was true or not, but I decided to assume not, until it was proved otherwise.

After burning the other letters and dispersing the ashes across the patchy lawn, I went back into the house. They couldn't do anything to me, I realized. At least nothing physical. They might be able to write letters that destroyed my credit or froze my bank account or caused the Secret Service to think I was a threat to the president or convinced others to harass and intimidate me, but they could not attack me directly.

And I had the skills to fight back on their level, should they decide to take it there.

Assuming they would write to Edson and try to get me kicked out of the house, I sped over to a local Sav-on drugstore, where I bought a Mead five-subject notebook, a box of envelopes and a double pack of Bic pens. There was a stamp machine next to the door, and I used my change to buy ten first-class stamps.

I didn't even wait until I got back. I sat in that cramped Volkswagen and wrote a letter to Edson on the notebook paper, telling him not to believe any letters he might receive that disparaged me; they were all lies. I tore out the sheet of paper, folded it, put it in the envelope, sealed the envelope, put a stamp on it and drove to a nearby post office, where I dropped it in the mailbox.

A letter of protection, I called it in my mind, and I wondered if this was where the concept of witchcraft had started, if some outside observer had put two and two together and figured out that some people could write letters that had power, that could predict the future or cause things to happen. The idea appealed to me, somehow.

After returning to the house, I called Edson at work and asked if I could use his cell phone to make long-distance calls, promising I would pay him back once the bill came. He said fine, go ahead, don't worry about it, and I dialed Information to get the number of the Mesa Police Department. I then called the station and said that I was worried about my wife and her parents. She'd gone over there for a visit, but I hadn't heard from her for over a week, and when I tried to call her parents' house, I was told that the line had been disconnected. Could they send someone out to check and make sure everyone was all right?

I gave the police the names and address and phone number, and the sergeant I spoke with promised to call back as soon as he had some news.

He did call back about a half hour later—and he was mad. "What kind of trick are you trying to play?" he demanded. "I don't know who you think you are, but you can't be wasting our time with this frivolous nonsense. We have work to do here. Are you aware that it's a crime to call in a false report?"

"What false report? I'm telling you the truth. I can't find my wife and son."

"Look, I don't know what you're trying to pull, but according to the neighbors, Mr. and Mrs. Reed sold their house and moved to Missouri six months ago. No one knows anything about their daughter or grandson. But no one's disappeared. No one's been kidnapped. There's been no crime."

"Do you have a phone number for their new house?" I begged. "Or an address?"

"You've wasted our time enough."

"It's not a joke! I'm serious! Just give me the neighbors' names! Let me call them!"

A dial tone hummed in my ear as the sergeant hung up.

I wanted to slam that fucking phone into the wall. I was as helpless and powerless here as I had been *there*. My only option seemed to be to drive all the way to Arizona and talk to the neighbors myself. But what if the neighbors knew nothing? What if none of them had a forwarding address? Or what if they had been warned—

by letter

—to stay away from me and not answer any questions I might ask because I was dangerously unstable?

Maybe a private investigator *was* the best idea. I could take more money out of my bank account and pay for someone to track Vicki and Eric down— although there was no guarantee that *he* wouldn't start receiving a shitload of letters with contradictory suggestions.

I had never felt so frustrated in my life. There seemed to be nothing I could do. I was stymied at every turn. If this was a game of chess, I was the player with one piece left, surrounded by my opponent's full contingent, ready to attack me no matter which direction I moved.

In the kitchen, the phone rang.

I jumped, startled. Instinctively, I headed toward the kitchen to answer it, but halfway there I remembered

that Edson had said the telephone wasn't hooked up.
Sure enough, when I grabbed the handset and listened, I heard no dial tone, no sound at all. I jiggled
the catch. Nothing.

It was some sort of fluke, I told myself, a quirk that
occurred periodically whether the phone was hooked
up or not. One time, I remembered, my smoke detector had beeped even though there'd been no battery
in it.

But I knew this wasn't something like that.

I spent the rest of the day running around, buying
enough clothes to last me a week, picking up a few
meager groceries, searching on the Internet at a public
library for Vicki and getting sidetracked trying to look
up information about Letter Writers, although I found
nothing about either. Edson stopped by that evening
with pizza and beer, we shot the breeze for a while,
and I told him I was thinking of hiring a private investigator. He thought it was a good idea and offered to
ask around tomorrow, find a good one for me. I
thanked him. He also offered to pay, but I told him
no. Some things a person had to do himself.

After he left, the house seemed . . . strange. There
were no more dead phones ringing, I heard no noises,
I saw no shadows or eerie lights, but something
seemed wrong, and I realized that it was because the
house did not feel empty. No matter how much I tried
to ignore it, I could not shake the feeling that there
was someone else in here with me. I tried to rationalize it, tried to think about it objectively. Perhaps, I
thought, belief in witchcraft and ghosts had *both*
begun with Letter Writers. The other presence I
sensed might be nothing more than my subliminal acknowledgment of a person living in a doppelgänger
house in the Land of the Letter Writers. For all I
knew, that world and this coexisted in the same physical space, and on some molecular level there was

crossover. Perhaps the family who now lived in my old house had even sensed my presence when I'd been trapped over there and pacing through the rooms.

Perhaps not.

For the impression I had was that this was not something that could be explained scientifically or even pseudoscientifically. Whatever was happening in this house defied easy logic.

Letter writing is an art, not a science, I thought, and that explained the difference perfectly.

I finally fell asleep, long, long after midnight, monitoring a tapping noise that sounded like water dripping in an empty bathtub but was coming from the center of the hallway.

In the morning, a used cereal bowl was on the breakfast table next to a half-finished glass of orange juice. The sports section of the *Los Angeles Times* was spread out nearby, though I knew no paper was being delivered to this address.

I flipped on the television for company, cranked it up so I could hear it in every room of the house and, after checking both the front and back doors to make sure they were locked, went through the entire place, opening every closet, every cupboard, looking for an intruder. Nothing. That did not make me feel any better, and I cleared off the breakfast table, drank a quick glass of orange juice myself and tried to think of what I should do next.

Get out, I decided.

I wasn't tied to this house, I had Edson's cell phone, so I drove to the beach, walked along the pier. Vicki and I used to do that sometimes when we were in college and too poor to go on a real date. We'd grab some junk food, then go out on the pier and sit with the fishermen, watching them cast, watching the sunset, watching the surfers, watching the waves. It had been fun in those happy early days, but it was a profoundly melancholy experience now, walking over the thick boards, smelling the salty air, hearing the cries of the gulls, thinking of times past. I felt old and lonely, and I wondered how I could have let my marriage go, how I could have been so stupid as to choose letter writing over Vicki.

But I hadn't chosen, I realized. It was something over which I had no control.

Edson called just before noon with the name of a private investigator. "He specializes in missing persons," Edson told me. "I had him checked out. He even did some work for a colleague of mine who was trying to track down a lost love. He's good."

Conveniently, the man's office was located in Newport Beach, on one of the top floors of a high-rise that flanked Fashion Island. I called to make an appointment and was told to come right in. I had the feeling strings had been pulled, and although I refused to let Edson pay for anything, I was happy for his intervention. Each second that passed by without my knowing where Vicki and Eric were was like an hour in hell to me.

The detective's name was Patrick Scholder, and he interviewed me for more than an hour about my wife and son, friends and relatives, work and play, trying to glean as much information as he could. At the end of the session I felt drained but vaguely optimistic. I was impressed by Scholder's thoroughness, and I prayed that he would not start receiving letters that would convince him to disassociate from me.

I'd have to write him a letter of protection as soon as I got back.

I paid him an advance, signed a contract and then hurried down to the parking lot. Returning to the rental house, I tossed my keys on the coffee table, walked into the kitchen to get a drink of water—

And the phone rang.

The dead phone.

Filled with an almost overwhelming sense of dread, I picked it up. "Hello?" I said tentatively.

"*Jason.*" The voice was weak, whispery, and I hadn't heard it for nearly two decades, but I recognized it instantly.

It was my mom.

"*Jason.*" She said my name again, and the way she said it gave me a chill. It was like something out of a horror movie, and the fact that she was talking to me over an unplugged phone only accentuated the macabre aspect of it.

"*Jason.*"

There was a click. Then silence.

I put the handset back in its cradle. What did this mean? Was she dead? That was clearly the implication; it was obviously what I was supposed to think. And that *had* been her voice.

There was only one way to find out.

I drove to my mom's house in Acacia, back to the old neighborhood. It had been several years since I'd even passed down this street, but it felt a lot longer than that. Then, I had only been speeding by, spying on my mom, checking to see if she still lived there, if she'd moved or died. This time, I was actually going back to the house, and it felt as though I hadn't been on this street for twenty years. I saw the corner where I used to turn around on my bike before I'd been allowed to peddle out of sight of the house. I recognized the thin section of Mrs. Baumgarten's oleander bush that we'd used as a secret tunnel, even though we knew oleanders were supposed to be poisonous.

I parked next to the fire hydrant in front of our house.

I sat there for a moment in the car, hoping that my mom would come out. It seemed like it would be easier to talk if we met on neutral ground, if we were outside rather than inside. But the door didn't open, the curtains didn't part, and finally I forced myself to get out of the car and walk up the path to the front door.

I had a bad feeling about this.

I knocked, stood there, rang the doorbell, waited.

Rang the doorbell again.

Waited.

Maybe she wasn't home.

I felt sure she was, though, and I stood on my tiptoes and felt around the edge of the porch light until I found the extra key that we'd always hidden there. I used it to open the door. "Hello?" I called. "Mom?" The word felt strange coming out of my mouth. I couldn't remember the last time I'd said it.

"It's me! Jason! Mom?"

The house was quiet. Too quiet. I moved forward slowly, past a new couch I didn't recognize, past a table I did. I could go either into the kitchen or into the hallway and the bedrooms beyond. Since I could see part of the kitchen and there didn't appear to be anyone in it, I chose the hallway.

It was the right choice.

Or the wrong one.

For my mom lay crumpled on the floor. It was the middle of the afternoon, but she was still in her nightgown, which told me that she'd been killed either last night or early this morning. She'd been shot in the head. Around her awkwardly positioned body was a tremendous amount of blood that had puddled and congealed in rivulets that had run together to form a single pool, like a moat, about her. On the wall was more blood, spread out in starbursts like modern art. There were even splatters on the ceiling. I could see only one cheek and one eye; the rest of her face was covered with red. The one eye was open.

On the floor in front of her, soaked in blood, was

a white sheet of paper that had at one time been folded in thirds but was now lying open.

A letter.

I crouched down, trying to read what it said, but the blood had saturated the paper, obscuring all of the words.

Was the Ultimate playing with me, pulling some sort of *Frankenstein* stunt where my circle of family and friends would be knocked off one by one until finally I was the only one standing? I didn't know, but I was determined not to return to the rental house, just in case. Whoever—

whatever

—had knocked off my mom might be waiting there for me right now with a loaded silencer or an unsheathed knife. I'd have to call Edson, tell him that I was going away for a few days, tell him—

He might be next.

Oh, shit. I pulled out the cell phone and immediately dialed his number, but he didn't answer; I got his voice mail instead. *Please be in a meeting,* I thought. *Please be alive.*

I left a message explaining that my mom had been murdered and that the killer was most likely after me. There was the distinct possibility that he himself could wind up as collateral damage. "Do *not* go to the rental house," I warned him. "Stay away. And stay alert. Any weird phone calls, any strange people hanging around, call the cops. Don't answer the door for anyone you don't know. Keep your car doors locked. Keep your cell phone with you at all times. For God's sake, be careful. I'll be in touch when I can."

I tried to imagine his reaction when he listened to that message. He was probably through with me for good. He'd no doubt remember my dad's killing, and of course he'd probably receive letter after letter indicting me for both crimes.

If he wasn't murdered in his sleep.

"Fuck!" I screamed aloud, banging my fist on the wall in frustration. Blood that had half dried broke free of its hardening shell and began to drip down the wall again, jostled loose by the vibration.

I looked down at my mom's still body. I didn't love her. I didn't even like her. Hell, I'd hated her damn near all my life. But she still didn't deserve to die this way, and I felt guilty for the fact that she had been killed because of me. I was turning soft in my old age, and in a way that made me feel better, alleviated the pain. I was becoming human, and probably, if enough time passed, I'd even be able to forgive her for having been the bitch she'd been.

I moved out of the hall, unable to look at the gruesome sight or smell the horrible stench any longer.

Somewhere in Southern California, I assumed, Tom had met an equally horrendous death.

Or was about to.

I got in my crappy Volkswagen and drove aimlessly for a while. It would be dark in a couple of hours. Where was I going to spend the night? Like an animal, my instinctive impulse was to flee, to get as far away from here as possible, but there was no way this POS car would get me out of Southern California. Besides, physical distance was no barrier. The Ultimate had already proved he could track me and keep tabs on me no matter where I went. In college, when I'd driven up the coast, letters had been left for me at motels where I would randomly stop. There'd even been that bizarre incident of the one-night stand where the entire episode had been predicted in a letter.

Did he know what I was going to do before I did it?

If so, I was screwed. There was nothing I could do to escape my fate.

But I had the feeling that that instance was a rarity

if not completely unique. I didn't know what it was about that journey that had invited such outside intrusions into my thoughts or what had happened afterward to stop it, but he had never again been able to get into my head in such a thorough, subtle and intimate manner.

Vicki had happened.

Yes, that was true. I'd been a free man in Paris when I'd set off on my little trip, not a care or encumbrance in the world, cut off from my family, loyal only to myself and my writing and, to a lesser extent, my school and studies. After that had been a period of abstinence . . . and then I'd met Vicki.

Love doesn't make the world go round, Henry said. *Letters do*.

But maybe he was wrong.

I *hoped* he was wrong.

The question was, where should I go now? My mom had been murdered, and the phone call had been a way to let me know about it. What exactly did that mean? Was it a threat of some sort? Was I supposed to get back in line, write a letter asking to be let back in?

Write a letter . . .

I could write a letter to the Ultimate not asking for forgiveness but telling him to fuck himself. I could write threatening letters to him, hate letters, letters predicting his death and disembowelment. I'd written to him before, in *there,* when I was with the company, but my work in that world had always seemed muted, unsuccessful, not as powerful as it had been out here in the real world. I'd been out here when my letters had interfered with theirs, when my words had crossed paths with those of Charles Dickens and rendered his impotent. Out here I was at my best.

Perhaps I could weaken the Ultimate, inflict some damage, do some harm.

I was getting low on gas, and I stopped at an ARCO station to fill up. It was the first time I'd had to stop for gas since getting the Volkswagen, and while the car was noisy and far too small, I was impressed with the mileage it got. I paid the attendant, stuck the nozzle in the tank and looked west toward the setting sun. Newcomers to Orange County always got their directions screwed up, always thought the ocean was to the west because that's what it said on the maps of California. But the shoreline was at a slant here, and most of the beaches in Orange County faced the south.

That's what I needed to do, come at this thing at a slant, throw the fucker off.

I drove down Harbor Boulevard to where I knew there was a Kinkos copy shop. They had PCs and printers that could be rented by the hour, and I paid my ten bucks and quickly wrote an anonymous letter to the chief of police: *The murderer of Kathleen Hanford lives at Apartment 3, 114 Dukenfield Avenue, Los Angeles. The Shangri-La apartments.* I would remember to my dying day the address to which the Ultimate had originally lured me—it was burned into my memory—and I was willing to gamble that if that address still existed, no normal human lived there. The only person able to travel in and out, between both worlds, would be *him*.

I had no illusions that the police would be able to catch or incarcerate the Ultimate or that they would be allowed even to get close. But this would show that I meant business. The stakes, as they say, had been raised.

I bought an envelope and a stamp, mailed the letter to the Acacia Police Department.

I'd have to keep my eyes open from now on, protect myself.

And keep moving.

3

I migrated from motel to motel, using my rooms only for sleeping, and staying for only one night at each. During the day, I went to different copy shops and computer cafés and various businesses that offered office services for rent.

I wrote complaint letters and death threats to the big boss. I had no idea who the Ultimate really was or where to address my messages, but I figured if I sent them to old apartment number 3 in the Shangri-La, my words would find their way to him.

The company building and the adjacent gated community in Brea were gone. If they had ever been there at all.

I wrote other letters as well. To the president and the pope, governors and congressmen, assorted newspapers and newsmagazines and television newscasts.

I was spending all day every day writing, penning letters that for once in my miserable life were completely true and stated the opinions I really held. I still had no idea what the Ultimate's agenda was, to what principles or philosophy he and the Letter Writers who followed him maintained allegiance, but knowing that I disagreed with many of the positions I had been told to take, I figured that by stating my mind, I might neutralize some of the damage they were causing and head off some of the worst effects of their evil words.

I did not like the direction in which the world seemed to be headed, and I could not help but think that the disastrous events occurring around the globe were the result of letters that had been written and sent, read and heeded, and that this was what the Ultimate truly desired.

I was afraid to contact Edson, and each time he tried to reach me on the cell phone, I did not answer, though I was grateful to see his number on the display screen. It meant that he was still alive.

What if Vicki and Eric had been killed?

I didn't want to think about that, *refused* to think about that.

I'd been bopping around Orange and L.A. Counties for a week, staying in low-profile motels in nondescript cities: Garden Grove, La Habra, Downey, Santa Fe Springs, Montebello, Midway City, Buena Park. I had just spent the day at a Copy Shoppe in Pomona and was checking into a run-down motor court by the side of the seedy street that had once been part of Route 66, when the desk clerk said, "That's weird."

"What's weird?" I asked him.

He turned around the log I'd signed so he could read it better. "Your name's Jason Hanford?"

"Yes." I suddenly wished I'd used a fake name.

"I got some mail for you this morning. I thought it was weird because there was no one staying here under that name, so I remembered it." He reached under the counter and pulled out an envelope, looking from it to the key in his other hand. "Whoa! It says here, 'Jason Hanford, Room 112,' and I was just about to give you the keys to room 112!"

I was covered in gooseflesh, but I managed to smile. I took the envelope from him, looked at the writing.

It was from *him*.

Somehow I was able to get through the ritual of paying for my room, listening to the rules and regulations, looking at the map of where the ice machine and the vending machines were located. Walking slowly, pretending to be casual and disinterested, I took the envelope into my dark little room and opened it immediately after closing the door behind me.

Go back to the house, the letter stated. *You will no be harmed. We need to talk.*

That was all it said, no greeting, no signature. I was not sure whether to believe it or not, but considering the fact that the letter had been left for me hours before I had by chance pulled into this place, and its author could have lain in wait for me and killed me before I knew what was happening, I tended to believe it was legit.

He wanted to talk.

The thought was intimidating, although in a way it was also very flattering. My letters had obviously gotten through to him, and while I didn't think he'd allowed me to live because he feared my awesome powers—most likely, he wanted to harness my abilities, have me working for his side again—the fact remained that my letters had saved me or at the very least granted me a reprieve.

It was getting dark. Obviously, I wasn't going to be spending the night here. I needed to get back to Edson's rental house in Costa Mesa. With the rush hour traffic, that was probably a ninety-minute commute. I closed the door to my room and returned the key to the lobby. "I won't be staying," I said.

"I'm sorry," the desk clerk said. "We don't give refunds."

Even as frugal as I'd been, I'd spent a lot this week and didn't want to waste the thirty dollars. "I work for a law enforcement agency," I lied. "Undercover. Our stakeout's been moved. That's what the letter was about."

"Cool."

"So I'll need my thirty dollars back." I tried to make my voice as serious as possible, hoping there'd be an implied threat that if he didn't comply, the cops would be all over this place, looking into every minor infraction.

"Don't worry," the clerk said. "It's not your money. They'll reimburse you for the room."

I didn't want to stay here and argue, but I fixed him with what I hoped was a hard look. "I'll remember that," I said.

"All right, all right," he grumbled. He opened a drawer beneath the counter, gave me my money.

"Come again!" he called as I walked out the door. I couldn't tell if he was being sarcastic or not.

I was on the freeway five minutes later. As I'd known, it was crowded, the traffic barely moving, and I had plenty of time to think. I turned on the overhead lamp, read the short letter once again. Three declarative sentences: *Go back to the house. You will not be harmed. We need to talk.* An order, a promise, a reason. It was masterful. Short, to the point, giving out only necessary information, giving nothing away.

The Ultimate Letter Writer.

Stan had called him that and the name had stuck. Stan had thought of the nickname, too: the Ultimate. Were they accurate? I believed they were. He *was* the Ultimate Letter Writer; he *was* the Ultimate. Which led to the question, why had he written "*We* need to talk" rather than "I need to talk to you?" Why was he pretending that we were on the same level? Why was he kissing my ass? To catch me off guard? To lull me into a false sense of security? I couldn't figure it out.

I drove back to Costa Mesa, to the house. It was night by now and the windows were dark. The drapes were open, but I couldn't see inside, could see only a reflection of the streetlamp and the house across the road.

I got out of the car, walking slowly forward. I wished I had a flashlight.

Suddenly a floodlight above the garage door switched on, illuminating the driveway and half the front yard, and I jumped a mile. The motion detector. I'd forgotten about that.

It provided me with light at least, and I felt a little

less afraid as I hurried up the walk to the front door. I fumbled quickly for my keys before the floodlight went off, since I was now out of range of its motion detector. Opening the door, I reached around the corner, flipping on the living room light before stepping inside.

The room was empty.

I went through the entire house, through the yard and the garage. No sign of the Ultimate. The place was empty.

Go back to the house. You will not be harmed. We need to talk.

Was that some kind of joke? Or had the letter meant a different house? *My* old house? My *parents'* house? It hadn't been specific. I was worried that I'd misinterpreted the meaning. Three declarative sentences. How could there be room for interpretation?

That was the genius of it.

I sat down on a chair, my neck and back knotted with tension.

I didn't like the silence, and I reached for the remote control on the coffee table, turning on the TV so I'd have some noise. I reread the letter, tried to remember what my first thought had been upon reading it. This was what he'd meant, I decided, looking around the room. This was the place. I'd just beaten him here, that's all. He hadn't mentioned a timetable; maybe he wasn't even planning to meet until tomorrow and would be by in the morning.

Meet.

I was going to meet the Ultimate Letter Writer.

Just the idea gave my stomach butterflies. No one, to my knowledge, had ever met him or knew what he looked like.

I admitted to myself that I was afraid to see him. In my mind, he was bigger than life, eight to ten feet tall, more monster than man. But that couldn't be true, could it? I looked again at the precise, almost delicate script on the page. No big clawed hands could hold a pen and write in such a way.

Still, the image persisted.

I glanced around. Would he knock or ring the doorbell? Would he come through the door at all or would he just . . . appear?

Maybe I *was* supposed to go to a different house, I thought hopefully.

It didn't matter. Even if this wasn't what he'd planned, the Ultimate would be able to find me. All I had to do was wait. I fell asleep on the couch sometime in the middle of the night, listening to the inane chatter of an infomercial.

It arrived in a black envelope with a stamp from hell.

I don't know who delivered it or how it got into the house, but in the morning when I awoke, there was a letter waiting in the center of the coffee table, directly in front of me. I reached out, picked it up. The paper was rough to the touch and strange, as though it had been made from a combination of dirt and animal hair. There was no name on the front, or if there was I couldn't read it, but in the upper right-hand corner of the black rectangle was a reddish orange stamp that depicted what appeared to be a pile of mutilated bodies burning in an underground chamber. There was no monetary value listed and no writing on the stamp.

Ignoring the repulsion that was being transmitted through my fingers, I opened the envelope. Inside was paper that I recognized, a sheet identical to those that I had made with my kit all those years ago to falsify my Paul Newman recommendation. The typestyle was the same as the one I'd used, too, only centered at the top was not Paul Newman's name but two words: *YOUR GOD*.

Beneath that was an invitation.

I had been granted an audience.

4

The address, of course, was apartment number 3 in the Shangri-La complex, and the time was tomorrow at noon.

YOUR GOD.

That piece of self-identification was baffling to me. Did he actually think I worshipped him as a god? It was possible other Letter Writers worshipped him, but I sure as hell didn't. Maybe he thought he *was* a god. He certainly seemed self-important enough to have such delusions of grandeur.

Maybe he *was* a god.

No. That, I refused to believe. To do so would mean that I'd given up all hope, and that I would not do. I reflected on how far I'd come since my return. In *there,* I'd been so filled with hopelessness and abject despair that I'd tried to kill myself. Perhaps I'd even succeeded; that part was still fuzzy. But now I was in full fighting mode, mad and ready to take on all comers. I wasn't about to roll over for anyone.

One day hence, was when the Ultimate wrote that I should come, and I was not sure if the archaic terminology was meant to be mocking or intimidating. It was both, actually, and I suppose that was why I did not drive to the appointed meeting spot early, though I was indeed tempted to do so. I didn't want him to see me, didn't want him to know that I was nervous or anxious, didn't want to show any hint of weakness. I needed to be strong for this confrontation. I would be hopelessly outmatched, and I'd need every possible advantage I could get.

The next day was when we were supposed to meet, when I was supposed to appear before him. For though the letter I'd received at the motel had hinted at a meeting of equals, had been designed to make me think the two of us were going to speak on an even footing, the message in the black envelope had made it clear that he was *allowing* me the rare and privileged honor of addressing him with my concerns. He was granting me a favor.

The second invitation was by far the more accurate, and I woke up that morning filled with dread. The meeting was not until noon, so I had plenty of time to think about it, worry about it, obsess over it—which I'm sure was his exact intent. Like a young girl going on her first date, I went through my wardrobe, trying to decide what to wear. I wanted clothes that would make me appear as powerful and independent as possible. But I had only a few shirts and pairs of pants and they all kind of looked the same.

I spent the morning pacing around the house, practicing potential conversations, trying out various approaches. Should I leave early in case of traffic? I wondered. Would he be there ahead of time, waiting for me? Was he there now? What if I was late? Would he punish me somehow?

I thought up best-case and worst-case scenarios. I tried to anticipate what might go wrong. I planned how I would defend myself if he came after me, how I would attack him if I found out he'd had Vicki and Eric killed, how I'd escape if things were going south.

And in the end I didn't show.

It hadn't been a conscious decision on my part, but if my intent had been to enrage the Ultimate, the strategy worked like a charm. I was deluged with letters by nightfall. They were not merely delivered by a postal worker and dropped into the mailbox, although that happened, too. Many of them simply appeared. I found them lying on floors or furniture, stacked five-deep on the center shelf of the refrigerator, peeking out from behind pillows, leaning against the windows on the sills. From the hall closet, I heard a peculiar shuffling noise, and when I opened the closet door, I saw a veritable cascade of letters falling from the open square in the ceiling that led to the crawl space attic above.

I ignored them all.

I was happy that my absence had infuriated the Ultimate so, had stuck in his craw to such an extent that he was churning out letters by the bucket load. But it was a welcome if unexpected side effect. The truth was that, just like in my confrontation in grammar school with Brick Hayward, I hadn't shown up because I was afraid and knew I would get beaten. Basically, I'd pussied out.

As stupid as that accidental strategy had been, however, it had worked. I'd never had to fight Brick and had successfully avoided what could have been a disastrous encounter.

Would it work again?

I decided to play this out the same way.

Dear Sir, I wrote the next morning after waking up and finding crumpled envelopes all over my pillow,

> *You appear to be very upset, but I fail to understand why. I showed in the appointed place at the appointed time, but you were nowhere to be found. I don't know if you were too frightened to meet with me as promised or too busy, but either way, your behavior was rude and ill considered. I assume your intent was to show me that your time is more valuable and important than mine, but I do not believe that. My time is equally important, and I can't just sit around waiting on your every whim. So rather than stick around until you showed, I left. If you ever decide that you seriously want a meeting, please feel free to contact me again.*

I liked the letter. I thought it critical but suitably polite, and it served to put him on the defensive for something he had not done. As I had with Brick, I was blaming the Ultimate for my own failings.

I walked to the post office, dropped the letter in the slot.

By the time I returned, there was an answer waiting for me.

I left it there until the next morning. Between those times, nothing happened. I received no more letters; no one came to visit me. As I'd thought, as I'd hoped, there was nothing he could actually do to me other than write. It gave me confidence. *Sticks and stones may break my bones,* I thought, *but words can never hurt me.*

When I finally opened the envelope, it contained one deceptively simple question: *When do you want to meet?*

I kept my reply as short as his and sent it to the Shangri-La address. *Tomorrow,* I wrote. *9:00.*

At nine o'clock the next morning I was at the beach, on the pier, looking out at the ocean. I was antsy, anxious. I had a hard time keeping still and not fidgeting. But I also felt good, like I was getting away with something I wasn't supposed to. There was an adrenaline rush along with the fear and anxiety, and for the very first time, I thought that I might have a chance against him. In my imagination, he was an angry ten-feet-tall geek, raging impotently in the open doorway of that apartment. I still thought he was some type of monster—he had to be—but he was not a monster who drank blood or tore people's arms off or ravaged cities. He wrote letters. He couldn't be *that* scary.

The thought made me feel good, gave me courage.

I spent the day near the beach, walking aimlessly past the surf shops and boutiques, eating lunch at a hole-in-the-wall place that specialized in fish tacos. I was tempted to call Edson, make sure he was all right, but for all I knew my every action was being closely monitored, and I didn't want to get him into even worse trouble than he was already in.

Sometime in the late afternoon, I walked into the bathroom of a Burger King restaurant to take a leak—

—and found a letter addressed to me sitting on the edge of the sink where I was about to wash my hands.

I looked quickly around, but the restroom was empty except for me. Gingerly, as though afraid it might explode, I picked up the envelope, opened it. Inside was not customized stationery or white typing paper or lined notebook paper. Inside was toilet paper, two-ply, and on it somehow had been written a message in ballpoint pen.

I am coming. Expect me at noon.

It didn't say where, but I had the feeling that at this point it didn't matter. He would show up wherever I happened to be. I'd gotten good at reading between the lines, and I could tell that this was it; he was through playing games with me. It was go time.

Where should I wait for him? I wondered. I was tempted to pick some public spot, force him to show his face in the middle of a mall crowd or on the beach among the sunbathers and surfers. But I wasn't sure that would make me any safer. The Ultimate was not a man who would be embarrassed in public and more subdued or circumspect because others were around. Shit, he probably wasn't a man at all.

That was one more reason not to meet him alone.

But as corny as it sounded, this was between him and me, and it would be wrong to drag anyone else into it.

I decided to confront him at the rental house. That was the closest thing to home turf that I had, and while it wouldn't necessarily give me an advantage, at least I would feel a little more comfortable there; at least I would know how the place was laid out and where everything was, and might be able to manuever around better if called upon to do so.

The question was, what was I going to say to him? I'd been granted the opportunity for which I'd been begging in letter after letter, the chance to speak to him face-to-face, to tell him exactly what I wanted to say.

But what did I want to say?

On a personal level, I wanted him to leave me alone, to let me live my life without any intrusions and to stay away from my friends and family. I wanted him to free the Letter Writers who wanted out, let Ellen and Fischer return to their real families, let my other friends go home. On a broader, more general level, I guess I wanted him to . . . stop. That was impossible, I knew. I had a tough enough time going cold turkey myself, and I was only in my thirties. He'd been doing this for hundreds, perhaps thousands, of years, had been recruiting Letter Writers to follow his lead and do his bidding and had created an entire world for them to live in. For all I knew, he'd been manipulating the course of human events for as long as there'd been written language. He certainly wasn't going to stop just because I asked him to. But maybe I could convince him to confine his letters to others of our kind, persuade him that it would be better if Letter Writers wrote only to other Letter Writers and stayed out of the affairs of ordinary men.

Who the fuck was I kidding?

I should have some sort of weapon, I thought. Just in case.

What kind, though? I didn't know how to shoot a gun beyond what I'd seen in movies, and I would have no idea where to buy one illegally by tonight or tomorrow morning—which was what I'd need to do if were going to use it. So besides guns, what else was there? Knives? Baseball bats? Would anything work on a being that had been around for millennia, that was behind the letters that made up the Bible, for Christ's sake?

I passed by a trio of grammar school children playing rock-paper-scissors. "Scissors cut paper!" one little boy said triumphantly.

Scissors cut paper.

Why not? I thought. Scissors would certainly be a good symbolic choice. And if I played my cards right, they wouldn't necessarily seem like a weapon. They did, after all, have numerous nonlethal functions. While they might be awkward to use in case of a fight, they would be effective if wielded properly and might retain an element of surprise.

Yeah, right.

I couldn't kill the Ultimate with a pair of scissors.

Still, I'd feel better if I brought them, and I vowed to find a pair tonight, to hit a local drugstore if there weren't any around the house.

There *were* scissors in a drawer in the kitchen, and they were even better than the ones I'd been imagining. Old and pointed, with sharpened blades, the scissors looked antique but worked much better and more effectively than newer pairs I'd tried. I used them on paper, on cloth. I shoved them hard into a sack of garbage.

Yes, they'd do.

I'd need all my wits about me tomorrow, I'd need to be at the top of my game, so I went to sleep early, adhering to the Ben Franklin philosophy. Any thoughts of arising early were dashed, however, when I opened my eyes and checked out the clock next to my bed: ten thirty.

Only an hour and a half until noon!

I jumped out of bed, took a very quick shower. I

could not remember when I'd *ever* slept so long. I
hurried into the kitchen, made some coffee, ate some
cereal and toast, looked at the clock. Jesus Christ! It
was nearly eleven!

I was starting to panic. I found my scissors, put them
in my belt as though I were some movie hero with a
dagger sheath. I needed to be ready, just in case he
arrived early.

The doorbell rang.

This was it.

My breath was coming in short sharp gasps, my
heart was pounding a mile a minute, and my palms
were drenched with sweat. I wiped my hands on my
pants, unlocked and opened the front door.

A mailman stood there. At least he looked like a
mailman. Sort of. His uniform was blue and of a similar style to that worn by post office employees, but
the cut was slightly more militaristic, as though he
were a mail carrier from some twentieth-century fascist nation. With a barely concealed smirk, he handed
me a single envelope. I took it from him, looked into
his eyes. He was one of us.

Slamming the door in his face, I turned my attention
to the envelope he'd handed me. It was ordinary
paper, a security tinted envelope of the sort people
used to send checks or money orders. There was no
stamp, no writing on it whatsoever. I took the scissors
from my belt, used them to cut off one end of the
rectangle. I placed the scissors back in their makeshift
sheath and took out the folded letter inside, opening
it.

There were characters on the page, but they were
not part of the English alphabet and did not look
like any letters I had ever seen. Neither Cyrillic nor
Asian, they appeared almost alien, although they
were written in horizontal rows that nevertheless ap-
proximated human writing. This was the Ultimate

original language, I thought; this was what he'd brought to us.

I found myself staring at the note, unable to look away, hypnotized by the strange unfamiliar shapes that suddenly seemed to be moving on the paper, reconfiguring themselves before my very eyes. I could *almost* understand what had been written here, I thought, and if I just stared at it a little longer, if I just gave my eyes and brain the time to adjust . . .

The house faded around me, the world I knew disappearing into gray featurelessness. I stared fixedly at the letter, certain that if I just concentrated a little harder, I would understand the message that had been sent to me. It suddenly seemed all-important that I knew what these words meant.

And then that intense focus dissipated. As though retreating from my sight in a rearview mirror, the letter seemed to shrink in my hands, the movement of the characters stopping, the sense that understanding was close at hand dissolving as quickly as my need, my desire, to know what the letter said.

I looked up.

I was back in the land of nightmare.

My nightmare.

5

The first thing I saw was the circus tent.

I was walking down a dusty road, just as in my dream, and before me was the circus tent. I turned around, hoping to see some indication of reality behind me, but there was only the road winding through the desert, its origin lost in the shimmery heat waves that blurred the distance into an impressionistic smudge. Since last experiencing the nightmare, I had forgotten none of the details, and the overwhelming sense of dread that the dream had produced in me reappeared instantly, causing my jaw to clench, my muscles to tighten.

There was no movement of the hot still air, not even a breeze, but the dirty white-and-red-striped tent flap flipped open as though propelled by a sentient wind. Within the exposed triangular breach lay a darkness that seemed uncomfortably like the one in apartment number 3.

Shangri-La.

Where exactly was I? Had an entire world been created out of the contents of my dream, the Ultimate breathing life into my nightmare images? Had I dreamed of a real place, somehow glimpsing with my sleeping brain this alternate world? Or was I imagining it all as I lay on the floor of the rental house, hypnotized?

I had no idea. All I knew was that I was scared and didn't want to be here and would give anything to be somewhere else.

The canvas flap fluttered in that unfelt wind, slapping against the side of the tent, beckoning me.

I pressed forward, through the still hot air, sweat dripping down the sides of my face. Reaching the tent, I did not even pause. I walked straight inside.

There were no old children with white hair, no prehistoric skeleton, no crucified Christ, his body dead and stinking on the cross. Instead, in the center of the ring was a mirror, a mirror at least fifteen feet tall. In it, I saw a distorted reflection of myself. From somewhere unseen came the tinny sound of Victrola music. Fats Waller or Jelly Roll Morton. Someone playing stride piano. Two men were in the empty bleachers on opposite sides of the tent, both scribbling furiously on paper attached to clipboards. One was Mark Twain. The other was Truman Capote.

Neither of them looked up; neither of them spoke

"Hello?" I called. My voice sounded hesitant and uncertain, tinnier than the Victrola music and far fainter. Already the tune being played was starting to grate on me, the relentless parade of notes becoming ever more dissonant in my head as my brain failed to focus on the melody.

I glanced over at the mirror and realized that it did not reflect the writers, the bleachers or anything else within the tent. There was only me, elongated and hideously misshapen, suspended in a black universe.

On their opposing bleachers, surrounded by sawdust and popcorn boxes and crumpled paper cups, Mark Twain and Truman Capote continued to write on clipboards.

The feeling of dread had not lifted, had not even abated. I was not claustrophobic, but I felt trapped and stifled. I was still sweating from the heat, the music was driving me crazy, and underneath the scent of sawdust was a faint foul stench that made me want to vomit. Trying to hold my breath and inhale as little as possible, I approached Truman Capote, the writer closest to me. I circled the concrete edge of the center ring—

And he hissed at me. Like a feral animal. I jumped back, startled. He giggled in a smug effeminate way, and for a second I thought I had an opening. But then he was writing again, head down, scribbling on the clipboard. I was glaring at myself from the mirror, all twisted body and misshapen head, and I knew that if I did not get out of the tent at that instant I was going to either pass out or be sick.

I ran back out through the opening, past the still-flapping canvas, stopping by one of the pegs anchoring the tent to the ground. Looking around at the desert, I tried to figure out what I should do next. From inside came that maddening old-time music, and I thought of the mirror and the writers and that faint sick smell and knew I could not go back. But where should I go from here? Down the road? Which way? I was stranded here in this haunted nowhere land and didn't know how to get out or what I should do.

I decided to continue forward the way I'd been traveling. Logic dictated that the Ultimate Letter Writer was ahead somewhere and that if I wanted to find him, confront him and figure out how to escape this nightmare world, I would have to press on.

The desert was not as barren and empty as it seemed. I had walked for a little more than ten minutes when I saw a low small building ahead and off to the right. Heat waves distorted its appearance, and I couldn't tell whether it was a store or an outhouse or a bunker or a home. The only thing I could see was that it was dark and vaguely rectangular. Sweat was dripping into my eyes, making them sting, and I untucked my shirt and used the tails to wipe my face. I had never felt heat this intense, and although I wasn't even remotely religious, the thought occurred to me that I was someplace close to hell.

I picked up the pace, hoping that whatever the building was, it had running water or something I could drink. I was dying of thirst.

Dying.

Gradually, the road beneath my feet changed from dirt to asphalt, the shift so subtle that by the time I finally noticed it and looked behind me, I could not see the line of demarcation. Likewise, the desert was no longer exactly a desert. It was still open ground, but in place of rippled sand and spiny cactus, there were now scrubby faded bushes and dried brown grass.

I stopped in front of the building. It was my house. Not the house I lived in now but my parents' house the house of my childhood—

the house where my mom was murdered

—only it was not in a subdivision among a tract of similar homes. It stood by itself on a weedy patch of land, its windows broken, its paint peeling, its front door open.

Inside, of course, was blackness.

A white figure passed by the open door, a faint wisp of misty cloud stuff that could have been nothing, could have been my mom.

The only thing I knew for certain was that I wanted to be away from here; I didn't want to be anywhere near this house. I sure as hell didn't want to go inside, but that was where I seemed to be heading. It was just like the apartment, just like the circus tent, and I felt as though I were Maxwell Smart, going through that endless series of secret doors.

I walked up to the porch, passed through the entryway.

And stopped.

From outside, the interior of the house had appeared to be dark. It *was* dimmer than the harsh glare of the midday sun, but inside, the house was by no means dark. In fact, I could see quite clearly. And what I saw was an entryway and living room devoid of furniture, with every square inch of wall, floor and ceiling covered with rectangles of yellow legal paper, white typing paper and imprinted stationery. I knew what they were, but I moved closer to the wall to check, to make sure. Paper rustled and tore beneath my feet as I stepped to the left. They were letters. My letters. Someone had found or copied or reproduced seemingly every piece of correspondence I had ever mailed, and had meticulously pasted each missive into a continuous mosaic that resembled a madman's wallpaper.

Dear Sirs, I read, *I am a longtime customer, and I am very unhappy with your new style of french fries. . . .*

I turned quickly around, catching movement out of the corner of my eye, but I saw nothing, only the empty living room and the entrance to the kitchen at the far end. I thought of that misty white shape that had reminded me of my mom, and suddenly I didn't want to go in the kitchen. I wasn't too keen on exploring the bedrooms, either.

I backed up, feeling the papered wall on my side as I made my way toward the front door the way I'd come in. Had this whole world been built for me, designed around my dreams and thoughts and letters and life? I didn't know how that was possible, but I could not seem to come up with an alternate explanation.

I reached the door, turned and found myself looking out at that weedy patch of land. Only across from me was not unbroken plain beneath a hot unforgiving sky but something else, a . . . building of some sort.

The place where the Ultimate lived.

It was not a house per se. There was a door in the windowless structure, and it did bear some slight resemblance to a Navajo hogan, albeit a much, much larger one. But more than anything else, the building looked like a giant overturned wasp's nest. It appeared to be made from the same type of gray papery material, and it seemed equally flimsy. I walked forward slowly, unable to stop myself. When I got closer, I could see sections of the wall that looked darker than the others, and small strange patterns of squiggles and dots and curves and lines that reminded me of that alien writing.

It had been made from pulped and recycled letters. Pages and envelopes that had been eaten and extruded by whatever monster lived within.

Monster.

I was no longer imagining some effete geeky creature with perfect penmanship. Whatever lived in this house was stranger and far more terrible. I thought of that stamp from hell, the picture of burning mutilated bodies. I'd been wrong, I decided. He *could* do more than write letters. He could tear me apart and kill me. He could torture me beyond reason. He could do anything to me he damn well pleased.

So why hadn't he done so yet?

I was about to find out.

As terrified as I was, I continued to walk forward, reassuring myself with the thought that the walls of the structure looked thin enough for me to slice through with my scissors should I need to escape.

More frightened than I had ever been in my life, I passed through the open doorway.

Inside it was dark, although not so dark that I couldn't see. Light from the sky outside and from some unknown source up ahead showed that I was in a sort of hallway, although it was narrow enough that I could barely pass through it without turning to the side, and so high that the ceiling was lost in dimness. I reached out my fingers, touched a wall. It was indeed made from paper but was much stronger than I'd expected, as though by some alchemy it had been turned back into wood.

I walked through the hallway and into the open doorway at the far end.

And there he was.

The Ultimate Letter Writer.

He was big, as I'd thought. As tall as two men but extraordinarily thin, not scrawny but lean, hard. He had multiple arms, like one of those Hindu gods, and over his chest he wore a vest made of severed tongues. I remembered those Letter Writers in that hellish secretarial pool, the world leaders who had had their tongues cut out and were spending their eternities cranking out letter after letter.

His pants or skirt or whatever it was that he wore over the bottom half of his body was stitched together with detached human hands, the writing hands or typing hands of his conquered enemies, I assumed. His body itself was hideous, the outline of bones visible in the wrong places, the skin that was stretched over his rail-thin form jaundice yellow and wrinkled beyond belief, like the skin of a well-preserved unwrapped mummy. He had cloven hooves.

But it was his face that, if I lived through this, would forever after give me nightmares. Beneath a mop of black rag doll hair, his eyes were wild, crazy, one wide open and much too big, the other little more than a suspicious slit, as though a brain-damaged child had made his own Mr. Potato Head with parts stolen from a witch's workshop. There was no nose, but the mouth was huge and fixed in a gigantic permanent grin. His teeth were not really teeth but long, thin, sharp-pointed objects that it took me a moment to place.

Quills.

His teeth were quills.

I didn't know what he was or how he'd been made, whether he was a creature that had always existed, whether he'd been put together like Frankenstein's monster or whether he had somehow arisen from the collective id of generation after generation of Letter Writers. *God did not create man,* more than one philosopher had theorized; *man created God.* Perhaps we had created *him.*

Whatever his origin, however, he was real, he was in front of me, and I was going to have to deal with him right now.

We were in what looked like a cross between a throne room, an office and . . . I don't know what. The only real piece of furniture in the huge chamber was an oversized chair upon a small dais. Made from stone and decorated with elaborate carvings, it faced the doorway through which I'd entered and it was where he sat. Next to the chair, on both sides, were pile after pile of various forms of paper, stationery, cards and envelopes. The floor was covered knee-deep with shredded newspapers and magazines, giving the whole place the appearance of some giant animal cage. On a shelf that circled the entire room were hundreds of televisions and radios, all simultaneously blasting their programs at top volume from countries around the globe.

I didn't know what to say, didn't know what to do, was not even sure I could be heard above the cacophonous din. I'd planned out many introductory statements, but all of my preparation went by the wayside in the face of this overwhelming horror.

It was as though the Ultimate had read my thoughts and decided to make the first move himself. With that one huge eye trained crazily on me, the small slitty one shifting back and forth at the same time, he expertly picked up a sheet of lined notebook paper from one of the piles next to him, then bit into it. And a message appeared, fully formed. Like a magician's hands or those of a juggler, his multiple arms were moving, twisting, fingers folding the paper, placing it in an envelope, stamping it and throwing it my way. It landed directly in my open hands. A split second later, a small stack of bound paper landed on top of that, a box of envelopes on top of that, a package of ballpoint pens on top of that.

We weren't going to speak, I realized. We were going to write letters to each other.

It was the way both of us communicated best anyway.

I put the paper, the envelopes and the pens between my knees, pressing my legs tightly together to hold them there. I was about to open the letter he'd thrown at me, when I paused, stopped. I thought of those strange swirling characters that had hypnotized me and brought me to this place, and decided that I would not, could not, look at anything else he wrote. There was no telling what might happen if I allowed myself to become lost in another letter. As scared as I was, I met his gaze and shook my head. I let his envelope fall to the floor, where it disappeared among the strips of shredded newsprint.

Noise like the hiss of a cat, amplified so loud that for a few seconds it drowned out all of the radios and televisions, issued from between the quills that were his teeth. The floor beneath me rumbled like a hungry stomach. The wasp nest walls shuddered, rustled. Both of his lunatic eyes were focused on me. He was angry, and I winced, waiting for the blow that would end my life.

Only it didn't come.

Instead, he bit another sheet of paper, made another message, folded it, sealed it, sent it to me.

I moved backward, let it fall into the shredded newsprint. The paper, envelopes and pens I'd been holding between my knees dropped, as well.

This would be it; this was the end.

I was testing him, I realized, and I suddenly understood something else: I was pretty sure I was going to survive. He wasn't going to kill me.

He *couldn't* kill me.

That's what I really thought, and I remembered what I'd been told by other Letter Writers.

You were public enemy number one around here, Hemingway had said. *They were having their toadies try to outflank you, sending reams of letters to combat your correspondence.*

But they couldn't do it, Virginia had added.

You are very powerful. James Baldwin.

Writers like you come along once in a generation. Stan. *And whether the Ultimate realizes it or not, you're the real deal.*

As ludicrous as it sounded, as ridiculous as it might

be, there really was something different about me. I didn't know what it was, I didn't know why I had it, but I believed that it was there.

That hissing sound came again, and the Ultimate stood to his full height. There was a sudden flurry of movement from all those arms, his gigantic grinning mouth was biting into page after page of paper, and I was deluged by a storm of letters that came at me straight on, from above, from down below.

On impulse, I withdrew the scissors from my waistband and started cutting the letters up without reading them. Soon I was slicing through envelopes like some martial arts master as they flew through the air. It was an instinctive reaction, and one that was as surprising to me as it must have been to him. I was possessed of a dexterity and coordination that had never been mine before, and I had no idea where it came from.

At first the Ultimate didn't seem to notice what I was doing, or didn't care. But then a funny thing started to happen. Lacerations began to appear on his arms, on his face, on exposed sections of wrinkled skin all over his body. Small at first, barely noticeable, they quickly assumed the character of whip slashes, and for each slice of my scissors there was an accompanying flinch and rending of flesh.

He's put himself into these letters, I realized. Not just figuratively, but literally.

It was absurd but true, and somehow the damage I did to the letters was transmitted instantly to him.

Either he did not believe that or did not understand it, though, because he kept on biting and folding and sealing and throwing, creating dozens of new letters every second. I clipped them; I cut them; I rent them. What did they say? I wondered. Were they pleas for me to stop? Were they threats against me and my loved ones? Were they rational arguments for maintaining the status quo?

I had to know. I couldn't help myself. I paused, and as the envelopes fluttered around me, falling to the ground, I caught one in the air and opened it.

Dear Jason, I read—

—and then screamed in agony as white-hot pain seared across my face. I dropped the paper, my hand automatically reaching for my cheek. There was another burst of almost unbearable agony as my fingers touched blood and an open wound. My eyes were tearing, but through the blur, I could see that the two of us were no longer alone in the oversized chamber. An army was gathering. *His* army. Row after row of bureaucratic-looking men dressed in those half-suit, half-uniform deals had suddenly appeared as if from nowhere, and though I couldn't be positive through my teary eyes and in the chaos of the falling letters and blaring electronic equipment, they seemed to be multiplying.

I took up my scissors again and, screaming in rage and pain, began cutting the envelopes as they came after me, that mysterious talent reasserting itself, allowing me to slice up the letters in the air before they reached me, destroying his handiwork almost as fast as he could create it.

I expected at any moment to be tackled by that growing rank of bureaucrats, to be rushed and taken down, the scissors ripped from my hands as I was forced to read letter after letter.

But though they watched, they made no effort to intervene, made no effort to help him.

Though my arm was getting tired, I refused to stop, determined to do as much damage as possible in the time I had left. Envelopes came at me, I sliced them in two, and I was gratified to see slashes appear on his hideous flesh.

The envelopes changed, became bigger, gaudier, more ostentatious. Once again, I was tempted to pause and just take a quick peek at one of the messages, but I knew that would be a foolish and dangerous thing to do. I could afford curiosity no more than I could afford mercy, and I thought of Vicki and Eric, thought of Stan and Shamus, even thought of my mom, and I kept my scissors moving, kept cutting the letters as they came.

And he started to bleed.

I saw it instantly. From a huge deep slash on his upper right arm, thick blue liquid seeped out.

It was not blood that flowed in his veins but ink.

More and more cuts started oozing, and in what seemed like a matter of seconds, he began bleeding all over. Ink was spurting as though from a thousand broken fountain pens, and the creation of letters first slowed, then finally stopped. He staggered, stumbled, growing weak. One wild arm knocked over a pile of papers, and ink gushed all over the falling sheets.

No one came to help him.

He fell backward, slumping into his seat, and one by one the radios and televisions winked off, the chaos of noise abating one increment at a time until the massive room was nearly silent, filled only with a horrible wheezing that came from deep within his body, the metallic snap of scissors as I continued to cut through the envelopes that had fallen all around me, and the subtle sickening liquid sound of ink pumping from his body.

There was more ink in him than seemed physically possible, and it was flowing from the dais in a near continuous sheet. The scraps of torn and shredded newspaper that covered the floor soaked up the ink and immediately grew soggy, flattening out. The light in here was dim now, almost nonexistent, but in the midst of the mess on the floor I could see body parts—heads and feet, hearts and brains—that had been hidden by the tangled strips of newsprint.

I didn't look too closely. I didn't want to see people I knew.

The bureaucrats remained in formation, unmoving, staring, waiting. There must have been a hundred of them by now.

What were they doing? What were they waiting for? What did they want?

My hands hurting, my fingers numb, I stopped cutting up letters. On his stone throne, the Ultimate wheezed and breathed laboriously. One cloven hoof kicked uselessly at the ground. I could smell the ink, a lovely clean chemical odor that I'd always enjoyed, that all of us enjoyed. But beneath that was another smell, that faint stench that I'd encountered in the circus tent. I recognized it now. It was the foul stink of Christ's rotting body from my dream.

Maybe he was a god.

I didn't know what to do. I walked slowly forward. To my right, the shelf holding the TVs collapsed, taking part of the wall with it, and beyond was the library Stan had shown me, the immense chamber filled with letters and notes all alphabetized by writer.

In front of me, the Ultimate bit into a sheet of paper with what appeared to be his last remaining strength, only he didn't fold it or put it in an envelope. He held it up, forced me to look at it.

This is all yours, it said.

One hand reached out, tried to hand me a quill. It had been yanked from his mouth and both ends had blue ink dripping from them.

I did not accept the offering. For one thing, I was afraid that at the moment I reached out to take it another hand would grab me and strangle me and tear me apart. For another, it just seemed too gross, too gruesome. That thick blue liquid was both ink and blood, and the blood part made me queasy.

I'd beaten the Ultimate at his own game, but it had been too easy to do. It occurred to me that maybe this had been the plan all along. Maybe I'd been groomed for exactly this purpose, to take over as the head Letter Writer. Maybe everything that had happened to me had been designed to shape me, mold me, make me into a leader. Maybe the Ultimate had been dying anyway, near the end of his run, and he'd picked me out as his successor.

I glanced over at the collapsed wall and the letter library. Aside from writing them, there was nothing I enjoyed more than reading letters. If I was to be honest with myself, I had to admit that I could spend days in there perusing correspondence at random, not just looking at the letters written to and by myself and my friends and family, but dropping in on people I didn't know, reading up on their lives and loves, their hopes, dreams and disappointments.

That library was a repository of every letter that had ever been written by anyone anywhere.

And it was all at my disposal.

It could be mine.

He wanted me to take over. Was it what *I* wanted? I didn't think so, but when I considered the fact that I could become the new Ultimate Letter Writer, a kinder, gentler version, that I could reshape our role in the world, make sure that we used our power for good, I was tempted.

More than tempted.

Maybe this was meant to be.

Who was I kidding? Use our power for good? That was where it would start, but that was not where it would stop. The road to hell, as they said, was paved with good intentions, and I knew better than anyone the seductive power of letter writing, the slippery slope to which that led.

I looked over at the library. It would be better to light a match and burn the whole thing, torch the fucking place so it could never be accessed by anyone.

Only I couldn't do that, either. Too much history

was here. There was a lot of worthless shit, yes, and
a lot of dangerous ideas, but these were historical doc-
uments, letters going back to the dawn of civilization,
and I couldn't just destroy that.

I could seal it, though.

By writing a letter.

What kind? A cease-and-desist letter? A letter of
reprimand? A letter of marque?

I turned my gaze toward the Ultimate. He was gone.
In the last few seconds, while I'd been looking at the
library, the life had left his body and now he was dead.
At least I thought he was. I moved next to him, took
from his hand the quill he had offered me.

He moved. His big eye blinked, rolled insanely; then
one of his hands reached out and took hold of mine,
squeezing tight. Even half dead, he had a grip like
iron, and as I struggled to get away, his head flopped
forward and that gigantic grinning mouth closed
around my arm, shoulder and upper back. What felt
like a thousand needles stabbed me as he bit down,
quill teeth sinking into my flesh. I wanted to scream,
but I couldn't . . . and then I didn't need to anymore.
A current of power passed from him to me, transferred by those quills.

His hand let go of mine, his head flopped back,
both eyes closed, and his body slumped, sliding off the
throne. This time he really *was* dead. I looked over
at my arm and shoulder but could see no sign of the
bite, nothing but smooth ordinary flesh.

I could feel the power in my right side, though, a
electric tingling.

I stood tall, holding the quill that he had given m
in my hand.

The bureaucrats had finally moved. Row after ro
of them sank to their knees, bowing before me in
display of choreographed fealty that reminded me o
nothing so much as the Nuremberg rally. The pow

coursed through me, no longer just on my right side but on my left, as well, settling comfortably throughout my body and giving me a confidence and feeling of well-being that was unlike anything I had ever experienced.

I was still holding the quill, the bureaucrats bowed low before me.

This was the test. I had the power to do whatever I wanted. It was all up to me.

I hesitated.

I *could* do a lot of good.

No!

Power corrupts, I told myself, *and absolute power corrupts absolutely.*

I paused, looking around, then found a piece of paper that had not been soaked with ink, and used the quill to write a letter. *To Whom It May Concern,* I wrote.

> *I have sealed the letter library. It cannot be entered or accessed and none of its contents may be viewed by anyone. All Letter Writers are now free to do as they wish and are no longer employed by the company, which has been dissolved. They may return to their previous lives. I wish them well.*

I signed it with my name.

I had no idea what would happen. Many of the Letter Writers I'd met had been from other places, other times. Would they resume their lives precisely where and when they'd left off, or would people from the past suddenly find themselves in contemporary New York or Chicago or Los Angeles? I didn't know, but it was not up to me and was no longer any of my concern. This was it. I was done; I was finished. I would never write another letter as long as I lived.

My letter-writing days were over for good. I threw down the quill and . . .

The world wavered.

The bureaucrats were gone as suddenly as they'd appeared, the scores of men bowing before me no longer visible. From somewhere far off, I thought I heard screams, and I told myself they were screams of joy, though I was not quite sure that that was the case. They were the screams of Letter Writers who had been released from bondage, I tried to convince myself, who were now free to return to their normal lives in the real world and use their skills to attract lovers and complain about entertainment and do whatever they damn well pleased.

Maybe they were the screams of those bureaucrats being consigned to whatever hell they had originally come from.

That was acceptable, too.

The hole in the wall and the library beyond disappeared. The throne with the crumpled monster body at its foot faded away. The ink-soaked newsprint hardened into floor and metamorphosed into carpet.

I was back in Edson's rental house.

On the counter in the kitchen, the cell phone was ringing, and I picked it up, no longer afraid of what might be on the other end, no longer hiding from anyone or anything. It was Edson, and he expressed relief at being able to find me, told me how worried he'd been. Reading between the lines, I realized he seemed to have been worried not for my safety or hi but for my sanity. I asked if there'd been anything i the newspapers or on TV about my mom's murde and he said no. He gently hinted that I might hav been mistaken about that, that there might be som alternate explanation. I didn't tell him about th blood-soaked floor and walls, but let him think that h might be right, that I might have just misinterprete something. I'd contact the police later, find out what had really happened.

I talked to Edson for quite a while, and it calmed me down, helped me readjust, made me realize on a real, tangible level that it was all over. I was reminded of our teenage selves, who used to chat on the phone trashing teachers we hated and talking about girls we were interested in. It felt good to be in contact with other people again, and for the first time in memory, I felt free, free from unseen pursuers, free even from the nagging belief that I needed to be writing, that I was not doing what I was supposed to be doing if I was not penning letters.

After hanging up, I opened the front door and checked the mailbox.

Habit.

There was no letter inside, but there was a small box on the ground directly beneath it, addressed to me from Patrick Scholder, the private investigator I'd hired to find Vicki and Eric. I took the box into the house and opened it up. Within was a report and a videocassette. In a cover letter, Scholder stated that he was mailing me his findings since after numerous tries, he'd been unable to reach me on the phone.

I wanted to watch the videotape, but I restrained myself and read the report first. According to Scholder, Vicki was living in Brea again, working at her old job. She was not seeing anyone, was not dating and spent the time when she was not at work taking care of Eric, who now went to a Montessori school because they offered afternoon day care.

Taking a deep breath, I picked up the videocassette. My hands were shaking as I took it over to the VCR and slid it in. I turned on the television, pressed PLAY.

It was a videotape of the two of them. They were at a park, and Vicki was sitting on a bench, watching

Eric as he played with another little boy. She was wearing clothes I didn't recognize—shorts and a simple sleeveless top—and she looked absolutely beautiful to me. Her hair was longer than I remembered, and she'd done something to make it wavier. The result was stunning.

Eric had grown nearly a foot, and his face was thinner. He was still a little boy, but I could see in his features the teenager he would become, and I hated myself for missing over a year and a half of his life. It wasn't my fault, at least not directly, but I was angry at myself for being who I was, for being what I was, for not being strong enough to fight my addiction.

At least that was all over now.

Eric ran up to Vicki, gave her a hug, said something in her ear that made her laugh.

I started crying. The tears felt good in a way, but they were horrible, too, and rather than try and stifle them, I let them come, let my feelings have their way with me. I was not used to experiencing emotion so straight and unfettered. Hope had been in such short supply for me that I'd grown accustomed to tamping down any feeling that would make me think about what I'd had and lost, what I'd probably never find again. But now I sobbed like a baby, and my heart ached with the love I felt for both of them. Time had passed, a lot had happened, and my mind minimized the messiness surrounding our breakup. I wondered if hers would do the same or if the negative emotions she felt for me had been strengthened and amplified over the past year and a half. From her point of view I was a deadbeat dad, and she'd no doubt received anonymous letters confirming that fact.

My eyes hurt, my jaw ached, but finally I cried myself out, and exhausted, I lay down on the couch and slept.

Hours later, I awoke. I sat up groggily, went int

the kitchen to get myself a drink of water, went into the bathroom to take a piss, then with blurred eyes reread the report until I found Vicki's new phone number.

I picked up the cell phone. Dialed.

"Hello?" Vicki answered.

I recognized her voice immediately, though I hadn't heard it for a long, long time. That cadence and timbre had been seared into my memory, and I would be able to recognize her speech even if I were stricken with Alzheimer's. A flood of memories accompanied that one word, all of them good, and once again the tears threatened to return.

"Hello?" she said again.

I switched off the phone.

I couldn't do it. After all this time, I was afraid to speak to her, didn't know what to say to her.

I stared at the small phone in my hand. Maybe I should work out ahead of time what I wanted to say, practice it. Even better, maybe she had an answering machine. I could keep calling until she wasn't there, until the machine answered, and then I could leave a message. She could call *me* back after that, which would make it a hell of a lot easier.

No. This was too important to be left to the vagaries of phone tag. It was too easy to avoid people that way, too easy to opt out of that sort of indirect attempt at personal connection. Besides, speaking was not my strong suit. And after all this time, after all the lies they'd probably been told, I needed Vicki and Eric to hear my words straight, uncensored, unfiltered, from the heart. If I was ever going to win them back, I needed to make my case in the strongest way possible. I needed to be at my absolute best.

I thought for a moment, then went into the kitchen and sat down.

There was only a moment's hesitation. Then my left

hand was holding down the side of the paper and my right hand was holding the pen.

I took a deep breath.

Dear Vicki, I began. . . .

About the Author

Born in Arizona shortly after his mother attended the world premiere of *Psycho,* **Bentley Little** is the Bram Stoker Award–winning author of fifteen previous novels and *The Collection,* a book of short stories. He has worked as a technical writer, reporter/photographer, library assistant, sales clerk, phonebook deliveryman, video arcade attendant, newspaper deliveryman, furniture mover, and rodeo gatekeeper. The son of a Russian artist and an American educator, he and his Chinese wife were married by the justice of the peace in Tombstone, Arizona.

"A master of the macabre!" —Stephen King

Bentley Little

"If there's a better horror novelist than Little...I don't know who it is." —Los Angeles Times

The Resort   212800

At the exclusive Reata spa and resort, enjoy your stay and relax. Oh, and lock your doors at night.

The Policy   209540

Hunt Jackson has finally found an insurance company to give him a policy. But with minor provisions: No backing out. And no running away.

The Return   206878

There's only one thing that can follow the success of Bentley Little's acclaimed *The Walking* and *The Revelation*. And that's Bentley Little's return...

The Bram Stoker Award-winning novel:
The Revelation   192257

Strange things are happening in the small town of Randall, Arizona. As darkness falls, an itinerant preacher has arrived to spread a gospel of cataclysmic fury...And stranger things are yet to come.

Also Available:

THE WALKING	201744
THE TOWN	200152
THE HOUSE	192249
THE COLLECTION	206096
THE STORE	192192
THE MAILMAN	402375
THE UNIVERSITY	183908
THE DOMINION	187482
THE ASSOCIATION	204123

Penguin Group (USA)
is proud to present
GREAT READS—GUARANTEED!

**We are so confident that you will love
this book that we are offering a
100% money-back guarantee!**

If you are not 100% satisfied with
this publication, Penguin Group (USA)
will refund your money!
Simply return the book before
December 1, 2005 for a full refund.

**With a guarantee like this one,
you have nothing to lose!**